THE FREQUENC

T0096157

ANTHONY JOSEPH

THE FREQUENCY OF MAGIC

PEEPAL TREE

First published in Great Britain in 2019
Peepal Tree Press Ltd
17 King's Avenue
Leeds LS6 1QS
England

ISBN13: 9781845234553

Supported using public funding by
ARTS COUNCIL
ENGLAND

1

Raphael had been writing a novel for forty-one years. On a cedar table in his house of water and his house of chairs, amongst ornaments, trinkets and books, lay his papers. But distractions were plentiful. The bull cow would ramble, the sour cherry tree would bear fruit, the madman would jump, the ravine would need to be cleaned. So he wrote in the latrine, away from the dissonance of the Million Hills, secluded in the stink of shit, amidst the deep hurling scent of ammonia and the banks of dank moss where women stooped to leggo water. Moan Papa, moan, and write your book. But bugs, bees and red ants want to bite the man ankle, the drake duck grunts, the Deacon rings the bell in the church hid in the bush, a phone keeps ringing in the falling down house, the mongoose chases the hairy snake, the Baptist mother delays her thanksgiving service to cuss somebody upside down. So even in the shit-house things came to inveigle and addle the old man's brain, to distract him from the seriousness of his craft. After forty-one years, the novel's characters were understandably restless. Some were elderly, others were dead. Some, like Vince and Giveway, who as boys would pitch marbles in the riverbeds of the imagined city, had simply faded into spaces between words. Ramdass went to shoplift, got caught and heart attacked right there in the shop when police hold him. Tom Denny, a turnkey, got fired for pushing weed, and Luke, who Raphael put in a surreal, Caribbean western, get damn vex one day and ride out like a thief, with his nemesis, the Great Bandit riding close behind.

Raphael was a butcher. He lived alone, high in the Million Hills, past the wooden nursing home and the Credit Union. From there the island spread out below. There was a boy, a relative from a village on the flat lands beneath the hill, who was learning to blow a flute he had carved himself from grief and bamboo. He wore short khaki pants, had a copper-scented head, was awkward and reticent, but he would sit with Raphael on the veranda, silently overlooking the jungles of the rainforest and the deep well of hours. Beyond lay the still, dark sea, and beyond this, the edge of the known world. The maps of their world had been drawn by eminent cartographers who had underestimated the island's size. At the fireside by night, Raphael and the boy roasted cashew beans, then they sat in silence. Soon this boy too would grow and spin from the old man's hand, to leave the hill, to blow and to write his own life. Ella even, Deacon's daughter, whom Raphael had known as a girl among the lilies and rills which ran from the higher parts of the hill, sought her ambition elsewhere – the book, like the island, was too small for her dreams. So between the page and the turning, she too left the book at the foot of the Million Hills. Raphael remained in his room, rubbing bay rum on his knees, writing and rewriting the same movements, then, months later, the concluding sentences of some great chapter.

Raphael told the boy tales of hunting in the hills, of working on cargo ships as a young sailor, and how, every morning, he would rise and fire a rum to start the day, how then he was handsome like a bitch. His working papers were tattered palimpsests, they had been written on over and over again, the original text hidden within the ink and flutter. Sometimes, Raphael would read to the boy from his novel, though the boy could not understand how its multiple stories could occur simultaneously. But the characters, in their impatience, broke needles under Raphael's fingernails, they penetrated his brain with complaints. Then his wife died. Cancer tore into the sponges of her lungs; tumorous polyps filled them, bursting like grapes in a supermarket, where, as a young man, Raphael once had a summer job and deliberately broke grapes as he packed customer's bags. In his white shirt and soft pants, this was his protest against the engines of commerce. One day, when hunger held him, he stole a tin of Viennese sausages. His crime was witnessed by a cashier who told, and the manager, Mr Gary, called Raphael up to his office and fired him by saying: 'Raf boy, you know what have to happen now, right?'

Raphael built himself a tough chapel to write in. He built the soakaway first and then the latrine, where the galvanise stuck like roots into the bug-ridden mud. His notebook was held open on his knees while flies buzzed around his heels and head like constellations. But the rain beat him to print: a vehicle skidded and overturned on a rugged Tobago road; the minister was caught masturbating on a rock behind the school; the Pie Man was strangled with a shoelace till candle wax drip out his nose; a parrot cussed and was arrested and charged; the lizard hid in the malomay bush; in his neighbour's house black instruments for breaking hymens were found; the mad woman turned into a blackbird and fell burning from the power line; the one-eyed fish went totally deaf. The book would overwhelm him at times. It wouldn't listen. The characters had became unruly, ungrateful, deceitful; bottle break, table turn over. Then fragmentation of the text and his leaking eye; at night by paraffin lamplight, people fighting, cussing, some grinning like crapaud when the man trying to write; is like the damn book was writing him. But when he spoke about the book, even Mr Crapaud would come and sit down on big stone to hear him talk. It was to be an important book. Raphael had put all his belly and his stones into it. It would be – *sui generis* – his legacy. It was called *The Frequency of Magic,* each chapter was precisely one thousand words long.

2

Luke had been sent to buy a tin of sardines and six hops bread in the Chinese snackette on Henry Street, and there to meet the printer, Carlos Wong, whose role was to point Luke further north into the plot's trajectory. But instead, and contrary to Raphael's design, Luke took a Red Band Maxi Taxi in town with the man money and headed east and once there he walked among the backroads of the mythic and found himself in The House of Smoke. The House of Smoke stood on the low bank of the Tacarigua River, among fields of rabbit grass and bamboo. The river bank slippery. Tadpoles swam in the water's oily blackness, and toiled like warriors to scale the steep incline. The river itself was still brisk and earnest as an old woman hurrying from hill to town to sell starch mangoes in Tunapuna market, water in her knee, basket on her head. The water was the same water that had run down from memory string, long seated in the land since it divide from mainland, and it running still.

The House of Smoke was home to seven spirits. Each spoke a different language, though in fact such soundings could hardly be called languages. They were vernaculars, basilects, aspects of meaning, fragments of speech. And yet each spirit understood the other. Luke was seated at the kitchen table in The House of Smoke. He had left Raphael half asleep in that corrugated shit-house high up in Million Hills, writing them both into ambition. But Raphael refused to read the one thousand words he wrote each day – not till the big book had come to an end, and so he could never know what was going on behind his back, in previous pages, or that Luke had gone quite Tacarigua. In the next scene, Luke was supposed to ride his bicycle through the city with a bale of cloth on his shoulder, and having again met the mentor/printer Wong, would pedal north into danger, for a confrontation between fish and bread, or big stone and head. But Luke refused to be led, or to be written into yet another scene in which he was to cross a river on a horse or make love to the sheriff's hirsute daughter. Instead, he waited until the old man bent his head in supplication to sleep, and then, skidding off his bicycle, he flung an arm upon the sky-hook and leapt. And where he land? He land on Henry Street, with four dollars in coins wrapped in a copy-book page in his pocket, on which was written: 'One tin of sardine, buy six hops bread.'

The House of Smoke had once been an orphanage, and in this shadowless kingdom of grief milk and brackish water, in which he was seeking a story to act his life in, Luke felt exposed and vulnerable, alone in these charred rooms, where dirty light bled through the cobwebbed window above the kitchen sink. But here, beyond Raphael's pen, Luke could finally begin to see past the fictive eye. He found a chamber hid under the cold rooms of the House of Smoke, a chamber which the children had built to hide or suffocate tears in. They imagined that one day this tunnel would pass from orphanage to paradise, that they would leap through to the other side, away from the cold pigtail and split-pea soup, and the lash, and the house of bondage the orphanage truly was. It was in this pursuit that many became stuck and suffered asphyxia, gasp and beating up for breath under the earth. Once the mark bust, and the tunnel was revealed, several orphans were bitten and killed by the coral snakes the staff sent in there to discourage escape. And whoever they catch in there get beat bad, not nice like last time, but cruel, unusual. Who died? Harry died, Nap died, then Pharoah, the big red-skinned boy with the lisp and the size twelve feet, who used to sing bass in the orphanage choir. Pharoah had resisted being bent, he would not grind spectacular in the corner after being punished for jocking his prick. He was wild and impetuous, but dumb like a bobolee. Fellas used to take turns to fight him like bear.

Eventually the day arrived when Pharoah outgrew his small room and, desperate for freedom, he broke the windows of the dorm while the children jumped on the their beds and cheered as he threw himself out of the suffering house to the hard ground beside the dasheen stream. But he did not run. Pharoah could not bear to be torn away from that prison, even as the doors were flung open. His chest got hot with fear. But let them try to carry him back, let them only put their nasty hands on him and he will box in their breastbones. They stabbed him with needles and he roared, then wept like a mother with cancer, waiting fearful in an airport interrogation room to be deported, in her wig and soft clothes; she know medical care better in metropolis, as opposed to jungle. Pharoah beat upon their jaws with his fists. He kneed them in their sediments. The children watched from the windows to see how Pharoah would die. He turned like a bull to the fighter's cape, bent his head and blew out blood. They killed Pharaoh, touched with madness and etheric sight, and they killed him for nothing. When the children saw this they set fire to the dormitory and many died, burnt to ash and black bone in that stuttering death of smoke. So this was The House of Smoke, this smoke of children burning into air. Luke had been seeking solace here, but felt the engines of the house, its agonies, its desultory conspiracy of despair. Pharoah was dead and buried in the well behind The House of Smoke, which now stood deserted, as a map of the city of glass.

3

Ella, an actor, is trying on shoes in a store in an arcade on Fulton Street. She is careful not to disturb her past, or to twist her heel. She moves beyond the perimeters of the page on which she is written to a side-street cafe with sandalwood burning, dark wooden plates, red aprons, mussel husks, red wine and kemetic ornaments on the wall. Her memory is a canopy of gospel above marvellous trees. She remembers her beloved father in that house of ploughs in the country; barebacked in the green guava field; in Mt Garnett with a can of kerosene, setting traps of fire; in Enterprise Village, depending on his misfortunes for self-respect; in cold New York building a black Baptist ministry, flinging wood and beast like sorrow self. She remembers her mother the dancer, whose eyes she stole. Her sister who married a merman.

That night she moves above the escarpments, apartments and elevations of the city, beyond verandas, vestibules and routes on the outskirts of narrative demands, away from the page and its cages of text. The streets are heavy with human vibration. She moves, pinioned by the throbbing rim of a drum, following its wavering gait upstairs to a crowded room in a downtown club where a quartet from London are playing. Not secret but black. Blacker. Shuffle, new time shuffle. She is drawn towards the sound as a moth to light, to the rim shot, to the bell of the horn. She might have told it differently. She might have said, 'Night is a secret, a promise to keep.' She might have said that the musician was waiting for her at the bar, in his narrow black trousers, dashiki and beads, that he recognised her when she touched him. She might have said he reminded her of a sailor, or that his sound reminded her of the bell ringing at a funeral, flung from a chapel high on a hill, where the cortege has gathered to throw spices and sacrifices into the sea below. His horn was a breathing thing; air hissed out of it. She watches him blow, and following the tapering trail of the melody he probes, falls into the pool of its destination and deepest note. The floor creaks like a ship's deck when the rhythm kicks, and Ella throws her head back and sways to the propulsive ostinato of the bass. She imagines sea salt in the musician's kiss, imagines his eyes as ancient and vast, his gaze as a healing spell, his tongue as a serpent creeping beneath a bench where hogs are slaughtered. He has fought the demon in a room full of spiders. His band swings hard, releasing sound in chambers of excess. They live for applause, crescendos; they get high and fall. The saxophonist stands at the front, swinging his horn like a pendulum, he blows as if tied to a mast in a hurricane. After the band has descended, it is written that Ella and the musician engage in their initial encounter.

She has spent the night in his room on Broadway but will not stay; she leaves in the small hours. The street seems tilted. Burnt oil scent. Sulphur, black water runs in the culverts. A few streets away, a body swings in a basement, dead from exile from the neck down. Somebody Caribbean, somebody so weak they want pillars of nostalgia to brace on, or a bridge to return to regions where water rolls under islands. In the lilt of light, she notices her shoes; they are stained with ashes and fruit. A man is standing in the shadowed doorway of a Chinese takeaway. He wears a long black gown, sultan slippers tapered to a point; the anvil of his beard curls back. He is restless in his skin, speaks to himself then answers. Each gesture of his wrist, beneath the cuffs of his sleeves, occurs in a dark cave of bone. His hot teeth boil in his head. His whisper is a prayer of seduction. His mouth unfolds with the sound of a market, deep east in an island, where fishermen hoist their catch with pulleys, hand over hand. The market is noisy. It is Saturday, a child rides between the stalls; his bicycle bell rings like the knell of certain death. An Indian woman is killing a rooster. Another has laid white sweets on a table. The jewellers' arcade displays ferocious silver, rings and pendants carved from fetish to poison wounds. A boy with a barrel on his back is selling rose water.

At times, one landscape veers into another; familiar locations inhabit alternate spaces, as her world is written into colour and form. Along alleys, the great boulevards – electric air and the sky above – walking west along roads where the rain has been, Ella sees lovers in alcoves, leaning against walls. She needs to rest. Her body relinquishes the will to carry her. A streetlight flickers, perforates the dim morning. A middle-aged black woman is leaning through smoke, fingering the cool air. Another cleans her teeth with the nail of her finger, abandoned from another scene or chapter. She spits and closes her window. The swings are motionless in the park, the playground quiet; the benches are wet with rain. Each bead of water reflects the light of the moon. The sea rolls and roars against the sides of the foundry on the corner of some half-remembered nation. A tree covers the bench; the iron fence is scented with brass and the resonance of children; the playing field is drenched in moonlight and mystery, darkness hovering above the earth like an ethereal shawl. There, in the full span of night, on the bench that is as cold as an abandoned altar where a goblet has spilled, Ella sits and counts the stars, relives the encounter with the saxophonist, sings wordlessly, like an apparition, like a plea. His mouth is still upon her. She listens, but will not wait to be written.

4

Raphael had been writing each night into morning, and still the book wouldn't done. It keep circling, swerving; the plot won't drive straight; it insist on tacking back and sideways and, meanwhile, people inside the book getting damn vex and restless. One by one they start going about their own business. These people have lives. Fellas want to ride; women want to make money. They wait out their volition and getting old; they want action before they die in some glad man plot, or let them fling grip upon the skyhook and jump free to roam into desert, or immigrantly into metropolises with tourist camera around their necks to deceive, because they not coming back, once they done say goodbye to everybody in the village. Raphael, writing forward and never reading back, remain unaware of what happening behind him in pages past. He want them to wait until he finish the whole text, like if everything he write is elegant, fine and permanent. But not so. Things he write into existence disappear when he bend back in the book to ameliorate or elaborate. Fellas leave bobolee in bed with cigarette in their mouth to fool him; some just disappear and others change name or how they appear – mirror front posing in dashiki or leather underwear. The book want to right itself vertical, simultaneous and liminal, perpetually becoming something else. But is too late to stop now.

One morning, peeping from his bedroom window, Raphael sees his cousin Belinda bathing with bucket and cup in the galvanised bathroom in the yard further down the hill, and he has to turn away, to blink and change the scene, to be blind to that madness or the world would end. Belinda wraps herself in a white towel and goes up to her bedroom to masturbate, thinking how she should have done that before, not after bathing, and get sweat up again, but a vibration was passing and she catch it. She remember some old man back she break when she mount him upon that spring bed and her blood get hot. Afterwards, she drinks black coffee, leaning on the swinging kitchen door, gazing upon the hill, pondering such things as why the little gully between the yards have just soap froth and white rice and yet smelling so bad, but how some brown water going down between plum and pommecythere trees, and yet the mammy apple so full and sweet. She raises her cup to Raphael. 'Morning,' she smiles. Raphael raises his hand. She shuffles to her housework, hurrying to wash her white clothes in a bucket, to throw the water downhill to meet the narrow drain that runs alongside the road, the road where later she waits for a taxi to take her to work. She has been a cleaner in the Credit Union for sixteen years. That morning, sweeping between the queue, she hears two women talking:

> : I wake up and one headache, just so, I don't know…
> : Umm hmm, you must been thinking too much.
> : But is sleep I was sleeping, I wasn't thinking.
> : What good for sleep?
> : A lil' rosemary, a slice of aloes; ginger good for sleep.
> : I sell the house. Is $14,000 I have in this bag.

There are rooms in his house that Raphael has not opened, doors which must remain shut. When he returns from working in the butchering pen late that afternoon, he sees cars parked on the leaning lawn, against the hibiscus fence between his and his cousin Moses' yard. Creole food steams in huge iron pots, liquor on plastic tables. The yard is heavy with distant cousins and uncles. DJ Champ has one turntable and one speaker-box to boom dub-wax and roots rockers to the hills. Raphael goes to his room to write, to remember his own mother who lived in the house across the valley, the house his brother Bain lives in now. He recalls how one day, as a young man, he climbed over rooftops and could not find a way down. Down was a drop and sudden death into yards guarded by Creole Dobermen. It was Sunday, overcast and melancholic; the light lay old and yellow upon the grass. He knew each route would lead away from the village and further into corridors, into white-walled spaces, chrome balustrades around cane fields, until he became lost on the edge of oil

15

refineries. He spent that evening in the thorn bush of an elegant spinster who had been torn out from the machines of academia. Below them, a narrow path led to the sea. Acrophobic since the age of nine, he climbed down along the side of a wall, blinking hard into fear, until he was among others transversing similar routes, a congregation crisscrossing the road and the field, away from the hurting house he would no longer suffer in.

He is still writing. The book of hours and of days, the book of memory and of forgetting, the book of salt and of water, the book of the Baptist moan, the book of Luke and the Great Bandit, of the actor and the saxophonist. To tell it further: after his madam died, Raphael was arrested up the islands for smoking hard weed in church. He escaped from jail in St Vincent, and bribed a fisherman to skank and carry him among the Grenadines, past seamount and sea volcano, to arrive again in the land where his navel string bury. There he built his home up the Million Hills, where his kin all settled, where after their roam and reach, beyond their shorthand ambition and dictation lessons, they all found their way back to the squatters shacks, to primitive living, the bush cut back for the new road, a promise still coming. Even Belinda had ambition once, though it was just to wear pencil skirt and work in some air-conditioned office in town, but that could never happen – once man start climbing into her life.

5

Luke had now left Tacarigua, the orphanage and the village on the edge of the city of glass. He had withstood the razor-bladed kiss of death, the math of allometry, the deceit of the scarecrow's tongue. He had dodged spear tips carved from lizard heads, and the efforts of Raphael to portray him as possessing the basic causality of a glad man, or worse, as some tragic imp or protagonist who had lost his way home. He had braced himself against a pillar for invisibility, then, while Raphael slept, he had leapt from the house of stilts into a barrel of water to escape, when he had been given clear paths and requirements. But this page was not turned back to face the past, but turned forward into trackless narrative bush. Poor Luke rambled and ambled across the elbows of the land. He travelled long by the riverside into dark woods and sepulchres of bone, he heard bodiless blues chanted down like rain from hilltop spiritualist temples, but saw no evidence of physical presence there, and he moved on, until the forest gave way to the grassland and the grasses to salt and the salt to dried quagmires of mud and caliche rock, until he arrived at the gates of the Great Bandit's lair, many miles into the heart of the desert.[1] Luke had cried out like Elijah in the desert, but no ravens brought him bread; only the vultures heard his cry; they had seen the splayed flesh on his arms where the sun's blade had gashed deep wounds, where his perspiration dried to piss funk ammonia in the viscose lining of his coat. Carrion crow, too, had heard the bellow of his breath, had heard his sinner's prayer, but they at least were

---

1. The reader may ask, 'Why should Luke be arriving at the bungalow of his nemesis?' The answer is that Raphael had drafted plans for him before he escaped the pages of the text, but now Luke want to plot his own arc and archeology. Luke feel he put himself there, but you can't follow people if it only have one place to go. It have nowhere else for Luke to reach; is only desert there.

compassionate and would not jook out his eyes; they let him live, to suffer. Luke stood at the gates, at least twenty-feet high, with wire stretched taut from corrugated steel to fence around the Bandit's estate, with stone pillars, ancient like those upon entering Wallerfield, remnants of war, deep in wild island countryside. Luke have to tiptoe and stretch high, high-high to reach up to shake the bell, and when it strung, it *bong*, and rung far into the distance. Eventually, after five days, the sound reach the bell on the veranda of the Great Bandit's lair, where sun lash the big man smoking his uncut sinsemilla in a crocus hammock swung across his porch. The big man naked; his drawers are drying on a line. Those who had seen him said he sometimes wore a waistcoat emblazoned with the iconography of Western movies, that the brim of his ten gallon hat was made from stingray skin. Though wide, the hat could not hope to overlap the bulk of him. The Bandit hears the bell and rides his horse out for four casual days before he reaches the estate gates. He finds Luke lying there, sandblast and dreaming that the bead-black of his etheric sight could see through big books and feminine girdles. He had faded behind a pillar for shade when the villain rode up. He tried to rise but collapsed at the foot of the great man who must linger now awhile, till the sun rests, till the path back is shaded somewhat by clouds, and he can ride back across the sand with the young man folded across the back of his horse.

There are beasts that live in holes of the desert, like gaps in language, like holes in the plot, beasts with smoke for eyes. But who black enough to surround this fortress, the Great Bandit's bungalow, and steal his ornaments, his gold-plated Italian pens, his leather and his silk, his solid-state dream recording equipment, his Blue Note 45s? The Bandit has drawn down thunder, he has broken paving stones, he has lifted up lifetimes of suffering and strain – and he has carried wounded men before. But this Luke must be seduced with manicou and cocorico soup, until he reveals all that he knows, all the secrets he holds of the old butcher who carved them both upon that hill, between the salt lick and the whipping blade, writing them each day into existence. The Bandit finds only one copybook page in Luke's pocket. But he knows that Luke would remember Raphael washing his stones in the river, laughing, slaughtering cattle and sheep by day, and writing by paraffin night into morning, drinking cedar wine and easing the plot out like a drifting, abandoned boat. The Bandit know that sometimes even before writer write it, star boy know it already.

They arrive at the Bandit's house in mid-December, twilight leaning on the bungalow roof. The bandit lays Luke down on burlap, in a corner of his kitchen, while he makes him a bed between the buckets and pans, between his stove and his ice box filled with slivers of flesh – fish and dried liver. He will wait for the protagonist to wake from his painted sleep. In the meantime, he will walk into the desert, perch in a guava tree like a parrot and smoke his weed. Sudden images tear at the Bandit's brain, the image of the butcher's writing hand, the desk facing east, the daggers of verbs and conjunctions, the impasto processes of Raphael's prose. He study the page he found in Luke's pocket, but he could not decipher the old man's hand besides hops bread and sardine. He could not know how he himself would come to be written, or whether and how he would die. He was as hopelessly helpless as the engineer they sent the band from Paris who could not mix sound. Grapple and bleep, and the band grumble; the bass man come down from the stage and rap hard in the sound boy ear: 'Turn that damn noise down or I'll unplug every socket it have in here.' The sound boy start turning one set of knob but the music still feeding back.

6

When he allowed himself to be photographed by his grand nephews and nieces, who had only known those metropolises of the North, Raphael would wear bright blue sunglasses and pose against a derelict Cortina and the vegetation on the slow slope beside the ravine that ran down from ruins of cocoa empires, among blushing rivers and riversides. The sun would sink into the channels of his face; his grin would slack, his skin would pinch and clinch and crevice would form like pitch-pine grain. He would pose his smile until his jaw went rigid and locked, then he would have to fix his face again. He was old; he could not endure airplane rides or gamble with his pension. He would not peel back his wood skin too far, and was content now, at his age, to blaze and butcher swine in his backyard slaughtery, to carry go market with a van back full of meat, and at night to write in the spidery gait of a madman.

The boy with the bone flute, though, was seeking a passage away from the island. He sat and plotted escape at Raphael's knee. But escape from the island was fraught and improbable; the queue for visas wept around Marli Street corner. Them fellas in shirt and lie held people ransom in those early mornings of nationhood, and grown men suffered humiliating defeats at those portals to materialism. Reason for visit? Holiday? *Doh lie*. Family in Miami? *Damn lie*. Your father dying in Queens? *You lie*. How much money in your bank account? *Lie*. Them fellas was smart; they know black people catching arse and want to kiss America on both cheeks. Fellas want to see skyscraper and snow, some want to run go Jersey or Atlanta or anywhere they could hide. Plenty of our best skull get bus' up on them desks. Full women who plan their attack for weeks. Who buy big suitcase on Henry Street, fire their work and telling everybody in the village they leaving. Men who know how visa does get, didn't get, not even single entry, much less for multiple. You laugh? Some didn't even make it past the gate. It was not easy, unless you came with house or child, or you old, like Clary, and have business and property. Clary so could go. And you want to ride on him now, append yourself to his passport, because he could go America. And they give Clary visa but he never went. Come with a glint of ambition, your eye long, and they will jam you. You catching your arse, you working as a domestic, they stamp the date of rejection red in your passport and tell you how your ties too frail. They feel thief head would hold you when you reach in New York, seduce you from coming back, like how hard it is to leave for home from some sweet fuck at four in the morning.

The musician was not born of the bourgeois, he was not born in a house of books, or revolutionist doctrine. He did not come from long money, neither jazz, nor pipe-smoke nor professorial folk, but from dirt-poor country people who had made it on to flat land, and who carried the resonance of the earth within them, who knew herbs by name and spoke to spirits that hovered over their houses and gardens. His people were elegant. They were poor but they were clean; they were bucolic – they were invested in the land, tied to it like trees. They could not abandon their ways and they continued to cultivate manioc and barbadine in middle-class suburbs. They held wild hog feasts and danced unashamedly in urbane neighbourhoods. Their mountain ways remained and kept them whole and holy. They were wise but they did not know Merleau-Ponty or Césaire, they had not read Wynter, Carew, Lamming, Lovelace, Mackey, Glissant, Brathwaite, Linton Kwesi or C.L.R. James. They knew politician as crook, trouble man, eat up all the meat, so they vote for the same man for twenty years, a small jumbie-eye man who had cunning and guile, who grasped them in his hand like pan-stick or hard prick. They read big bibles propped upon their knees, and the Brother Mandus prayer pamphlets that came each month from England. They read *Our Daily Bread*, but never read Achebe or Nicolás Guillén. They read words fused to transcendent purposes, and they tied the jaws of their dead to prevent speech or the evaporation of secrets.

The old man knew the boy desired another life, away from the island, so he arranged for him to meet a long-stones and upright bass man who lived upstairs a rum shop, west of the city of citrus and copra. The boy brought his little clarinet and together they improvised wild island jazz in the old bass man's apartment. It was a Sunday afternoon. The boy watched the city from the old bass man's window, saw leaves, calm and drifting upon the cool breeze, then scattering in the gully below. The bassist had played in dance bands, he knew Glenn Miller and Oscar Pettiford music; he could recall a few Count Basie tunes, a few standards, but bring calypso and he playing that bass like a beast. Mighty Spoiler or Duke? He will rattle the wood and spin the bass on its heel. He had some dog-eared sheets of music, good music stored on the shelves above his bachelor bed, like letters from a long-dead friend. The bass man watched the boy with one eye fey and veined and trembling, the other marble-wide and burning. The boy could not play the horn particularly well, but he possessed that naivety and narrow mindedness that were essential in the musical life. The boy, in time of course, would improve upon his ability, he would learn the levers of his engine and, eventually, it was possible that he would climb bandstands in those far and unreal cities of sky and glass.

7

An airport in the early afternoon. Each musician carries luggage and a flight case, and they are driven to the venue to search for their sound. Backstage, they break bread and eat Gruyère, saucisson, and drink cans of iced tea. Testing his line, the saxophonist blows against all sorrow embedded in his lungs – the memory ghost of his grandfather who stripped him naked and forced him to bathe in cold water. If he resisted, was belt all round his back. Once he almost drowned. As a young man, just before he left the island, he was fired from a Chinese restaurant for stealing meat; he run home and tell his grandmother he don't like the work. All these things get blown when he chunk out sound; notes without precedent, substance deeper than surface, notes that vibrate through the plywood chest where his stepfather, Herbert, kept his black and white swingers' porn, in the bottom drawer, along with the Berec batteries for his silver flashlight and the passport he never used.

He pauses to break a piece of bread, to find the frequency of magic. May blackness increase. He wrings his hand. He straightens his reed. Who will find the passway, the trace and track lines up the hill to Raphael's slaughtery? Who will he find at the end of the stave, alone in a corner of the blues dance, feet slipping and sliding? Tanty, trembling from stroke and paralysis, who still can't lift her left hand? No charts were written, no score was recorded, no document was fixed or pinned upon his back like a bill of sale regarding such things. He wakes one morning and his hands are cut up like an unfinished wood carving, hands of cedar and splinters, hung down coy-like, despondent, tree hands, cut up like prose into poetry. Rose Hill. Million Hills. The shady groves, the vines, the parakeets among the river trees, the bamboo creaking along the perimeters of the pasture. His shadow lies flat against the wall. One Saturday, bitter with salt and sweat, he is captured on 110 film gazing out at oil ships, as if waiting for a storm to pass, for the grass to fold back upright.

One turntable was all DJ Champ had, and two big speaker engine drone for the sub, and tweeters like bees strung to sting the ear on vines above the door. Sacred-hearted Jesus, look! Mister Clarence dancing to Lord Nelson's 'Disco Daddy' was the only glimpse we had of him in that elegant rotation as he flit his good foot out, with his head up, dancing, holding out his glass of Whiteways of Whimple, steady, so it don't spill. The older women are smoking jazz cigarettes, drinking gin, gossip in the corners of their mouths.

Aunty Ingrid was young then, had plenty verve. She would stand and sing, unsolicited, with her tremulous voice, wavering between keys but driving upwards into the sweet arc of her highest note in the middle of the living room. Is Aunty Ingrid still alive, still barren, with the soft candle heart? She never had children, she lived alone in the bush. She put leg flesh stench all up in that room with the brittle rags under her bed. Who is still alive in these backroads of the mythic? Ingrid left and turned around, went back a few. Who will bury her when she finally dies, when the coast loses its battle against the suspense of the hurricane and the stinging rain? Who could remain in the hut where fishermen keep their nets and oars, their hooks and fears of drowning? One man say, 'Sea have no branch, I eh going in.' Another one, a Grenadian, bawl, 'You go perish away in the riling surf. It too deep to drown in, too shallow for swimming.'

Aunty Ingrid's house sways in the hurricane, and that night torrential rain bores a hole in the roof, and the gathering pool keeps pressing upon the ceiling, leaking. Ingrid blink to change the scene or the roof will fall in and the world will end. Ingrid say, 'Soon every room will smell of lavender.' But didn't it rain? It rained across the race tracks and back, it rained upon rivers. Didn't it rain? It rained that night but the quartet was deceptive. They played low octaves that groaned in the cavernous space beneath a railway station in the Ardèche. They blow the mournful joy of this blessed bulk, blow showers of sound and the light so heavy.

A woman at the front of the stage is holding a child, burning skin in the air, crying hot tears against the horror of a burning house. The child, not more than three, glances over the woman's right shoulder. Ash. If not the sky, is embers glowing, sparks that blind the tractor driver's eyes. Driven against a mud bank, the tractor overturns and dies upon the man riding it. On the wharf, the tusks of a forklift gut a stevedore, piercing him beneath his waist. His deep croon ricochets against the tax offices and ware-houses, the lighthouse in shanty town and the old KH Recording studios in Sea Lots, and the Chinese rice shop, and the abattoir in Central Market. They take the stevedore to the hospital but he bleed out and was buried in Mafeking Junction. Rain, not fire quench. Rain, bucket a drop.

The musician passes through Lyon that night like a ghost with the horn on his back. He knows liberation is the essence of soul. The woman's house is high upon a rainswept hill. She teaches ballet in the community centre. She makes tea, they exchange alibis, saliva, serums of desire. On his way back from her house that morning, he takes several photos of the landscape, of an arborists' van, a bridge, bleak in this light, vintage cars with paint as dull as old cymbals. She watches him from her window; the motion in her body is like muscle of the endless sea.

8

Wind in the bush like the names of saints. Houses on stilts where the river runs, irascibly brown, where dirt is the fine grain of insect bone and mollusc shucks. A woman is washing her hair beneath a hibiscus tree, a candle burning for sixteen years in the ground, a navel string hidden in the roots of the orange tree. Upwards, is the house on the hill where Raphael lives and writes. His second cousin, Belinda, lives lower down. Belinda, with the broken teeth, the black-ringed eyes and breasts like long loaves of bread. She moves through the yard ebulliently.

Along the soft verge where a river once ran are the stout wooden houses of Mano the labourer and Bobot the thief. The wind flings its net of dust and porous stone, and the scent of cumin remains on the air in the morning after a wedding. The water truck comes down into the valley of silt, poised teetering on that brink and bound to tumble down the bank one day. The driver, leaning with one hand onto a calabash tree, pisses vinegar with legs bent like callipers. The villagers wait with the buckets and barrels they have brought down the slippery steps.

Raphael, whiskered like a tomcat, smiles for photographs. Bone dry, age becomes him. He moves from room to room, with skin as taut as liquorice root, and his shinbone hardened smooth. He has long dedicated himself to the big book which writes him. But Raphael was once a saga boy, too. He would bend over the engines of government buses in hi-soled mechanic boots with black oil on his hands. In those days, women wanted to mount him. But he never satisfy. He cry blood till the blood hole full up. Cuss, but the oil in his breath dry up.

In his room there is an upright bass, heaving like a fat woman who has run up several stairs. She sang, soulfully, but we never heard a thing. Not even from the next yard where a policeman stalks with tall boots, or from the house that Raphael brother Bain renovate further up the river. They say Bain mad, that Raphael writing book, but he biased, that Melchior the fisherman is who living among the people, so let him tell us what happen.

Melchior say, 'Bain pounce the area like a flying frog and blaze up the chalwa, he rush fire, he like a scimitar blade rub with garlic, he have a one-inch punch and a length of iron, and he beating down grown men when he leggo Satan on them in Fifth Avenue junction. The iron warm and sweet where he hold it, and when he jump, the block get hot, uptight and distressed. Full men like Mikey and Caruth was liming cool, but when Bain light spark on the block, they get frighten and leap from the gully bank like ten Tarzan. Then they cuss like fire how Bain come just so and mash up the lime, how he put he nasty hand in the wappie game, how he flam his gambage, how the money men put down to gamble with get scatter in the drain. That mothercunt, Bain. Sweat on him, chew corn, people fraid him. Bain say: "I just had to bat a man in the brewery. I bat him in he face with this iron, till blood and teeth spin out. I fire the work." Telling this gore, Bain laughing. How the foreman glasses break in his face and how the man buck and shiver. How he scramble and scrape the rancid brewery floor, where workers wearing Wellington boots whole day, for his teeth. How Pattison pick up teeth to put them back in his mouth. Bain laugh, "He spring he own water, like chicken in a Dutch pot. Go back for what? To bottle beer? To spit them lump in sugar? To hear some jackass bray and tell me I can't smoke weed in the boiler room? How I can't work bareback? How I late again and he docking my pay? Brother, hear my cry, I could smoke my tampi in any motherarse place I want."

'People say the overseer tack back; he know trouble reach. He afraid but he in front big men and he have to fight. But he not ready, he wasn't expecting to fight that Monday morning. He need more time to think, to analyse the angle, to fix himself. All them karate move he plan to launch in situations like this – turn, break elbow, kick, twist neck, unmask and rip from the nose hole with two fingers – all these get delay. Instead he and Bain start to wrestle like dog on the dirty floor. Bain catch him with a blow and Pattison fall. He get cut beneath his navel deep, and sea cockroach and halibut fall out. Bain know how to survive on plankton and ash, how to tilt his head to swallow crack corn, how to fish with waterproof glue and how to light pitch pine in hideous rain. He know to burst carbide, to chop so it don't heal, how to ectoplast and awe. But after he bat Pattison, somebody put *aedes aegypti* in his water tank and things turn ol'mas. Bain, who so tall he was a whipping blade, succumb to blues now, ground down by the real-time trajectory of life. Now only women and children fear him. He have to fish in muddy drain. Even Sugars in the weed field have no work for him, even the rabbit won't die when he kill it – it buckle and kick till Bain hand get simple and fail. He moan, living alone in the suffering house he patch from wood and bone, jocking his prick three-four times a day, counting crapaud bleat when night come, his vibration twist, evil in his teeth like wire to burst. His brother uphill say he writing big book, and Bain wondering now if he could get a star boy role.'

9

When Luke came upon the Great Bandit that morning, he found the big man crouched over a sky-blue enamel basin in his bedroom, washing his black arse. The blue of the basin was the blue of orphanage walls, the blue of abandoned machinery on country mornings in Wallerfield, the blue of slat-roofed huts for the bull-workers in the far east of the island, the blue of the glimpses of sea between the fishermen's huts on the way to Carenage. The Great Bandit was whistling 'Stardust' as he scooped the tepid water with his wash rag to splash his scounx, shaft and gun sack. Wash it out and rinse that. Wash to have bliss of it. Water sprinkling his ankles and toes. The Great Bandit was tired. He had been hunting black-tongued caribou and land snails all night in the merciless heat of the desert. He had been bitten by hairy snakes and cut by cow-itch bush. He had burst his big toe and skidded on the rims of long-buried steel drums that glinted in the moon, like light cracking into messages from the rebellious history of the land that was buried beneath the sand. It had been nine days since he had answered his bell, and saved Luke from the carrion crows, and rode him back to this ranch on horseback to let the star boy rest and reconstitute. The Bandit feel he is a cowboy now, he pinned the 'sheriff' badge to his breast and rode the red dust billowing like a woman's skirt on a windswept bridge. He did not know for sure if Luke held any secrets regarding the great book. Had the old country butcher imparted its secrets to his protagonist, or were they both locked within the mysteries and metaphysics of the text?

Luke had sat many nights peering up into the space between the text and the physical plane, seeing the words as they were being carved onto the white pages around him. He had picked locks in the old man's brain and, written down to move, he would obey unless driven by some insolent power and compunction.

Then he resisted Raphael's instruction. At times like these, the butcher would pause, drink a whisky, and give Luke the freedom to rock and groove. He would wait a few pages for him to arrive at the same door, in the same house, in the same desert where the Great Bandit had kept him tied to a chair in the dark abyss of his basement for further questioning. Down there, soft dirt and waterlogged wood jutted out from ancestral homes. But Luke feel he slip through a ruse, and now he stood watching from the bedroom doorway as the big man soaped his crotch and underslung areas, and hummed his little tune, with his back turned.

Luke entered the room quietly, with the intention to grandcharge and pierce the Bandit's craw, and then to thief his horse. But the Bandit rose from his muddy squat, spun and flung the basin of arse water towards Luke – dash funk and spray it out like grief milk. The Bandit was deceptive. He approached Luke while the wash water was still floating through air, and he collar the star boy by his throat and press him up against the wardrobe. It rock back and it creak. He have the power to kill Luke, and Luke buck because he had never felt such power before; he never get to feel his own fallibility; he never knew until then that he, too, could die, within or without any system of plot or narrative theory; that he, too, was subject to limit and limb and that he was not some undying creation or superman. But how could he not have known that even the hero can die in the last reel? He had never run around the area like a fugitive from the cut arse belt of justice, with his gum-grinding father following patiently behind, calling him gently, imploring, not shouting, but with cool forbearance, with a cigarette clipped between the fingers of his right hand, and a belt folded in two in the other. He had never been caught between Gordon and Grant and the Bermudez biscuit factory in Mt Lambert, like an imps, against a wire fence with the hot grip and wrist of a father from whom he could never escape, who would drag him back like a dog on a leash, to blaze him strict and spinning in the hot shed with the galvanise roof, where even snakes would hide when the sun was too hot in the afternoon. So when the Great Bandit held him by the throat, Luke was weakened by the audacity and power of the big man, and his sphincter clenched and unclenched. He was afraid. He could not truckle bitter or bile or battle; he was drawn dumb for mercy, thrown out, lonesome, into a dark map of stars. The Bandit hit him two slap and let him drop. Luke cough up phlegm and sandy-nose cheese, and is then the arse water finally lash him, and what a water it was, wow, Mammy, by now it brown, yet still tepid and funky, the wash of arse and grainy stones, scum dumplings scraped off moist with fingernail and rag. Rinse the rag and wring it, and lumps of gutty balm fall in the water, to be taken back up to mend the skin where the hard soap rip it and sting it. The water wet up Luke and he back-back. He thought he could flex but he could not face the big man wet. The bandit hold him down and put him to skin up on a rock out in the yard, tie him down naked and let that water dry on him like sea salt. Then he hit him two slap again and burst his toe corns with pliers. All these things was to make Luke know who the arse was really in charge.

Men had tried to mount her since she was twelve. Young men doing office work in the city, with white shirt and tie, tried plying her with promises. Men who sat grinning on corners scratching the inside of their thighs, tried her with slackness. Peremptory men, who could not wait, waited like crocodiles. They set her in their minds and watched her like fruit to ripen and pick. They lay before sleep and etched her body into the files of their minds, and would draw on these images, which were mostly mere stolen glimpses: Ella, as a young woman, washing her hair over the basin in the yard; Ella walking to school, focused over rockstone on the ridge and into the valley. Their eyes held heavy lids, but they were reckless in their eyeballing, and their mouths held horse teeth, and their hands were always reaching over the wire fence she tried to build between them, their rods prodding against the barrier of her broughtupsy, hoping the doors might be flung open in the brittle heat of some sudden afternoon. But Ella was smart. That never happen. They waylaid her, followed her when she walked past the rum shop, where they threw arrows of seduction, fuck talk, sweet talk: 'Family, family, how you moving so? Come nah, you not seeing me here or what? How you passing straight so? Come let me tell you something.' But she would smile and pass. Old, long-stones men, who should have known better, did not notice that when Ella became a young woman their words could no longer penetrate her ear. They could not seduce her with umbrellas in rain, with coconut ice cream, colour TV, English toffee or jaw-grind pornography. In village discotheques, they would lean like shadows against walls, and when she passed they would reach for her hand to slow dance, and when she refused, their hands remained there, exposed. But these men were not embarrassed. Some rooms had higher ceilings. They would wait for her at noon, at the bottom of the school playing field, leaning on their cars, with palm cupping cock, but they could have been deseeding weed and whistling, or promising her whatever she dreamed of, but still she would not come. She would, once she got older, shit talk with them on the block or in front of the Chinese restaurant, but she would not lift her skirt or sit revealingly, or cuss and carry on in the street. She would make sure the latrine doors were shut to peeping. She would not meet them in that forgotten bush that had grown so bad-minded and brusque behind the Credit Union. She might accept an invitation to drive down to the foreshore. Luther Vandross might be singing on the cassette and incense could be burning for sunset romance, but she would not let a boy put his hands between her legs. Some even take her for Chinese food on Cipriani Boulevard, spend big money on Char siu kai fan and shark fin soup, and tell her, 'Order the lobster if your want, the big shrimp.' But not even a squeeze prick they getting when they reach back to Mt Garnett. She would not go, she would not come. She could not be hoodwinked and skulled into picking up pencils without bending her knees. She would duck. She was choosy.

Then she left the island for acting school in New York, living in Crown Heights, downstairs from a one-armed tailor who stitched rubber masks and tunics. She would pass him on the stairway, she would smile. One day, he invited her to see the complex machinery he kept in his kitchen, his box of smoke, his needles. He was from the north of Montreal; the arm was a stump, he was bearded, the tattoo of a serpent up the side of his neck. He pumped his presser foot, muscle in the gap; she rode him on her knees. This was long before the old folks passed on to the higher temple, before the animals perished in the flood, before corbeau retire from flight, when snake used to walk upright like man. Kisses of the mouth, the ear drum full of blood. This was before she met the Jamaican landlord who lived downstairs, whose basement was a chiaroscuric cave which hid black hash and bubbling broth, the shebeen, the immigrant yard. Go down there any night and hear Vincentians slapping harsh cards down. Ella went for hash and they welcomed her; they knew she too had slept under the stars of the Southern Caribbean. These men told her of stevedores who had fallen over the brutal edge of

33

America still clutching boxes of yam and mountain dew, green plantain and tins of fried chicken. She was told legends of strong men who had died feverish deaths from work-related injuries on this jetty. Men like Norman Holly and humble Hubert Bramble, who a docker's hook punctured on the wharf, whose twin daughters were beautiful. Hubert had lain there waiting to die on a hot bed in Canarsie, Brooklyn for two days, his eyesight fading, relinquishing his hold, the memory of islands. Ella had heard these tales before, but she was not afraid to walk along the water's edge. She memorised Chekhov's monologue from *The Seagull*; she recited Miller. She appeared in plays. She had been to hurricane school. She had seen what the sea could do to islands, she knew the imminent danger of the storm. She knew the origin of floods, how the sweet river could be overcome and drive down from hill to sea, how it would move through parks and synagogues, and push south until the shack-wood crate box houses of fishermen along the peninsula would be rocked and swept away on the tide, leaving the rotten fish scent and husks of shrimp, the black eggs of sea horses, blue crabs, diaphanous ferns, lungs of the island in the black and white image of the deepest water.

Fruit is the song of trees. Each shrub in this garden is anointed with dew, and when the old woman comes down from her wooden house, she feeds the hummingbirds rice from her palm. Long dead from earth and gone into that forever place, nevertheless each morning she is at the hibiscus root, among the lilies, the aloe fronds, the yellow allamanda, among the vervain where the woodslaves roost. With living power in her fingers, she wields a wild hose. Then piously she tends her herbal fetishes – the jump-up-and-kiss-me, the malomay, wonder-of-the-world, the cocoa onion, *eleuthera bulbosa*, which whistles at night, and which she brought from the country mountain of her original kin, down from whence she came through Caura Valley and Susconusco, all the while humming hymns like 'Nearer my God to Thee' – when really it is Oduduwa she serenading, coming down the golden chain from heaven. Day is breathing deep across the land, and the sun beats down with a vexation, hard-hard on the side of the hill. The spirit print of the white horse that get kill and skin still lying rotten as myth in the vinegar tree root, blue fly buzzing there since sixteen years. The land there like it wouldn't heal.

Yvette Cooper is watching from the black-tongued witches house down the hill, with the blackened windows and the wrought-iron chairs and the manchineel tree flowering in her yard. She is waiting for a chance to bust the old woman's throat. Each morning she whispers spells of sin and sudden death into her pillow, flinging hex, dark as her well is deep and odorous, wishing bad mind to fall on everybody head, and especially on the rotund panyol grandmother who she sees wetting her garden and calling each plant by name, who folds the heliconia for a cross on Palm Sunday, so humbly benign that her sweetbread and pone never burn. This is Sister Syl, who sits in the root of the African Tulip Tree, shelling her pigeon peas in peace, who dead yet still breathing incense smoke in that house, bright with the sky-blue jalousie window half open.

Miss Cooper steups, 'I go do for she. Yes, crush must overlap method this time.' She say, 'This woman, this sweet bitch, Sister Syl, she must dead and die again.' But when they clashed in the wild Indian farmland that night, the older woman of the hills was more ferocious and powerful with prayer. Sister Syl do something in the river that put a tremor in the stiff breeze, and her rubric start to flutter and batter Miss Cooper chest. The vibration rip through her like she was wet gazette paper folded in three against tootoo in a latrine where blue flies buzz and heat punctures the brain. Nothing Yvette Cooper did was black enough to wound Sister Syl's piety. Mammy nice. Poor thing. Mammy never do nobody nothing. But ask Clary, Mammy will leggo a lion in your cane-field if you get she hot. Yvette had was to backback and ponder on Satan's plough. What to do, father, what to do now? Throw urine? Burn garlic? Turn into a ball of fire when night come and bite she on she back? Mix cat piss with asafoetida and give she that to drink? Irrigate she rice with cunny-hole oil? Jook out she eye with picker from the tonka-bean tree? Miss Cooper vex, fret and her big leg roll when she walk. Sudden so she start to throw hand, and is so they wrestle, upright in the 'bandon land, going down in the ground like cow foot in muddy pasture, till blood let out the Baptist bell that ring upon the hill, and Raphael come down with camera eye for book and he write everything down.

When the police came in their machine, the lies Cooper wept were as sorrowful as amputacious children. She say look, her dead husband Pattison drawers still hanging parched and brittle on the barbwire fence. Since that day he went to work in the brewery, he never come back to himself. They church him in the red brick cathedral, leaning between immortelles from the architects' dream, razor grass cutting the ankles of mourners. Cooper moan – *uummmh* – how them old woman does moan – how her son sends no mail from Boston. How every seed she sow in Papa God earth does dead before it root. How so? Even bitter bush, much less the sweet Julie mango tree, or aloe to rub against her second skin. So, captured by the anguish of all this, she had no option but to turn to necromancy. She say her shinbone hiding a blister about to burst in hideous rain.[2] And all this time, Sister Syl, pure and narrow like meditation, slip through a gap in language, turn into a hummingbird and escape into jungle.

Ships are returning empty, like diseased lungs from chapters of sorrow. Soon a fire will wash them all away, all the sallow faces pressed against the rim of time, in restaurants, hat shops, dancehalls and museums of culture. Still her son sends no message, no note; he takes weeks to answer when she writes. This is true. When Yvette tries to call, the telephone's ring burns an abscess in her ear, with its thrill of wire and glass, electric water of the ear drum bursting into litmus and absence and distance. She imagines the city where he lives exploding into frivolous life each morning, glitter burst, how sunlight sparkles in leaves there, but with a different light. In Yvette's dream she is with her mother in Port of Spain, buying a seven-inch record with green labels, her wedding song long forgotten. Then it was December; it was red as a butcher's apron on a wall; it was a new road, an uphill highway. Yvette lives in the shut-up house with the manchineel in the yard. She have that sweet bitch Syl to kill to kill and kill but Sister Syl won't die.

Spit.

---

2. It name *Treponema Pallidum* and is syphilis Miss Cooper have. Is a sepulchre of a sore, a wound of the old world. She fed the ulcer mentholated spirits and Mercurochrome but it never cease weeping oil, so could never heal. Rose have it; Ma Mamin have it too. Even Brother Curtis, far flung from a swinging door, got this, died, and was memoried in blues in A. Joseph's *Bird Head Son*.

1 2

To the villagers, Raphael loomed there on the highest point of the hill, aloof or insane, far gone from reading big books: Lacan's *Ecrits*, Merleau-Ponty's *Signs*, Nathaniel Mackey's *Bedouin Hornbook*, several books by Wilson Harris, Earl Lovelace's *Salt*, Walter Rodney's *Groundings with My Brothers*, Van Sertima, Ginsberg, Baraka, Anthony McNeill, and Anthony Joseph's *The African Origins of UFOs*. Raphael dwelt in the rugged chapel of his own business. He was not to be seen barefoot, carrying water in buckets up from the standpipe at the gamblers' junction on Sixth Avenue, or liming in people house and eating their food. He wrote so hard that people expected him to unmount his head from his body one day, walk further into the arid hills and onto the verandas of transcendence and disappear into the fire-sky above.

He was not bald – not yet – but thinning, and what was left of his hair was grey and brittle, like a painting of cane after canboulay. His face was still handsome, but lined with rivulets of stress, one eye up and one down. His presser foot kept pumping in his dreams, like ocean motion in the body after days within the rigours of the sea. He could be seen with his head in hands scarred from butchering, rocking on the mercy seat. So much was written sitting on the knee-high wooden bench he'd built. He was, perhaps, remembering his own mother, her bosom plump and disputatious, who one morning fell out of bed, and was long buried in the clay. She left white sapphires, rocksteady records, unwashed petticoats and uncut collie herb in a riverside cabin.

Raphael, happy in his house of masks, of apparitions and sudden appearances, the dust of insect bones and snakeskin scent in rain, had first to masturbate – like a monk in the secret chamber of his bed – before he could write. Or he would stroll along the side of the mountain, ankle-deep in tilled earth, his pants waist

38

held up with string, his nylon shirt billowing in the wind. He would come back slow-eyed and grinning with inspiration, leaning on the rugged side of his bachelor's shack, to offer a mumbling word to the ghosts and saints of bushes and bugs, as if they had been witnesses to a killing. But the latrine was overflowing, the mercy throne was overgrown with wildflowers, and the thorn bush was creeping to tangle ankles and trap small birds. Come, only a man with a carbide heart could build a miracle in that blessed bush. No neighbour ventured in, rarely any kin, for fear of soucouyant, for fear of snakes and the poetic terror of the dark. Except the boy with the bone flute, and Alvin, his cousin, the hunter.

In the space he had carved, Raphael wrote through each night into morning, amongst the cracked panes of photo frames, old newspapers, difficult books, and the sentimental station on the radio. His basin, his sink, his kitchen, the table, the bowl of green pawpaw and salted pig-tail, ripe avocados, the enamel pan cup humble down on the grill of his single burner, and his writing hand trembling, piercing the gossamer web of the damn thing self. When he knew he had written pointillist text he would smile and sip his coffee. His chapters were kaleidoscopes of feeling, but who would read them? Prose, written in an invented script, notation of prose for motion of word, a kind of sculpture of sound and temperature. He preferred death by fire, grew weary of the broken line, preferred to write his verse as paragraphs as his thought functioned, not falling, but moving across landscapes in simultaneous narratives. On those dry and sun-drenched afternoons, when the corn birds were making mischief on the branches of the pommecythere tree, Raphael would give Cousin Alvin a few crumpled dollars, and send him to walk down into the valley for more paraffin and cigarettes, hops bread, a tin of sardines. Sometimes, so full of salt pork and tears from slaughtering swine, he would bounce like a simple pimp along the river, composing wordless poems in his head. Sometimes poetry rained down upon him when he should be writing fiction, his book of life. He kept his pencil sharp to capture each gesture, each word that fell. Some poems consisted of just a few lines:

I went walking sideways on the hill track
people tried to shoot me
I shot them back

Other poems filled reams of copybook pages: box-car derbies in the red-dirt quarries stained by sunset; a monkey howling in the trees; the paths through the forest worn smooth by bare feet; Manzanilla, the ocean where he and his brother Bain almost drowned – the callous Atlantic side, where the waves were pulleys to death in the deep, in a whirl of struggle and joy. He wrote of the sun breaking into day, how light sparks on the leaves of the banana trees, the sweet sapodilla with its onyx seeds, the Chinese tamarind, its growth stunted in the sloping yard from grief.

On his veranda, spreading his arms across the back of a corrugated chair, leaning back in the too-hot day, he waited for the wind to shift from the trees, for the sinsemilla man to ring his bicycle bell, rolling down from villages hidden in the haze. Raphael, writing like a bitch on the quality of light on water, writing himself into creation, had gone deep into the well. But no one who had left would return to him. They were lost to him, lost to the forest and the river. Luke had ventured deep into the desert, the Great Bandit had fallen asleep in the guava tree, the Deacon would soon burn his own house down. Things happened. Sometimes Raphael caught them, sometimes Melchior the fish man did – and ran it down real and colloquial for the people. But Raphael wrote. His own death upon these hills, before the great book was writ, was the nightmare that kept him awake.

Luke escaped from the Great Bandit's lair and is walking north across the desert with the assassin in horseback pursuit. And if you ask Luke how he get free, he would quote Lord Kitchener and say, 'Don't ask me what happen, you see me alive.'[3] The Bandit squinting; he seeing Luke in the distance, but the star boy at least two days away. He want to capture the map of secrets that Luke holds; is gold, like the hidden annals of Rome, the desire of ages for black secret textology, the path the plot would unravel down and hold death to ransom by the throat. The Bandit know that Raphael's hand rolls steady on the ink-filled oar, and surely Luke knows what the ink is writing. He must know how the villain would meet his death or how the story would end. This is the hidden heart of the desert. Hard sand and parched earth. There is not a shrub, not a bean, not a dry leaf or a jackass backbone, not even the exoskeletal husk of a batchak or man crab in this Hollywood movie. There is only distance and heat. The horizon is blurring into wave and tremor, heavy air, no phantom water or leftover light to float in. Luke is miles ahead – squint him in the distance – and the Bandit's pursuing foot stepping like they pulling glue and can't run from same old run-can't-run-but-sideways-fastest. But mix no matters, the Great Bandit coming. His left shoulder ligament rip from flinging big stone far at Luke, the same hand he would lean to leggo water with against the latrine wall, till the wood there get smooth.

'What trouble is this?' he say. 'Imagine, Luke was dying by my gate; bone hawk and bees was circling to jook out he eye, and I nurse that ungrateful scamp back to life and now the little fucker

3. See 'No Melda', Lord Kitchener in *Lord Kitchener*, RCA Victor – LPB 3027, 1964, UK.

firing blade? Well, let death groove my brush broom, I go do for him! But first, let we begin with discourse, let we come to some agreement, as two big man.'

Lie. The Bandit riding behind the fugitive, piercing the rim of dune and dust density with one thing in mind. Luke start off hot but he weary now. He should be deeper into the future, hallucinating spirit text and ambition, making love to women, growing dreadlocks, but instead he catching the scents of colours, and roaming contrary through burning sand. He running but he don't know where, not yet. He look back and imagine he see the old bull running with the cut-arse belt in his hand, shotgun up on his shoulder, the silver edge of a cutlass grinning, the whip spinning on the Bandit's hip.

Raphael, arriving home from the market with a chicken roti and a juice, was planning to eat and sit down to write peacefully that night, but now he get caught up in a mess of battle and siege and have to route all this out. If he buy a bottle of rum, he one will have to drink it. If he cook tripe and split pea soup, he alone will have to eat it. So he let Luke run and the Great Bandit run with him. But the Bandit horse foot tie up in a flashback sequence and it can't run fast enough. The sand as deep as meditation narrow, and it have highway here that too steep. The dream of water was a ruse. The dream of drowning was an infallible path. The waters of dreams were endless technicolor prayers. So the Great Bandit grew weary and slept.

In this land there were two moons. One was aloof but the other was closer to the ground and could be ridden up under and gazed upon. It hung, luminous, and hummed its blue song; in its presence, souls were supposedly purified and neophytes given gifts of healing and secret colours, but it hung in a region so deep in the desert that few but the Abobo would arrive at it.

The Great Bandit slept with his eyes open like a madman with vengeance on his mind, with the light sleep of a killer of Jesuit priests. He knew Luke could not be far ahead; a day or two, perhaps less. Distance seemed simple in the desert, but it was a serious thing. It was blue light scattered in the eye socket, a way of mapping narrative time. The Great Bandit kept his rifle drawn and his teeth picked clean. Long into the night, when all eyes were shut, he ventured into the underground caves of the Abobo, of which several remained, though most of them had long perished in the wars of melanin. The Abobo, who were born black from skin to sole, still lived in holes in the desert where they brewed high grade melanin in tunnels.

Luke was asleep on his back, the sleep of a man stopped on a street and told by a turbaned swami that he was lucky. Tender as a child, he slept under the starry canopy of the desert sky, like butter wouldn't melt in his mouth. The Bandit emerged from Abobo land, up from the copper plumbing of a derelict volcano and drew his three-canal Gilpin cutlass high. His intention was war, to crush and overlap method, to mash up guru and mash up saint, to dismiss the jury and throw blackpeople in jail, but mostly it was to cleave Luke from the secrets he held. But try as he try he could not bring down the power, and his hand stick. He opened the windpipe of his pistol to shoot, but the shot would not shoot out. He uncoiled his cat-o-nine, but the fire would not fling out; even his bullpistle whip hung flaccid in his hand like some kinda shrimp thing. Luke heard the Great Bandit moan, from a far distance. The Bandit feel he near upon Luke, but he still six hundred miles or more away.

A van rolls downhill on the steep, sunlit gravel, kicking back stones on an ochre afternoon. Cacti and *eleutherine bulbosa* grow loose in the moist underlung of the land. Woodslaves and beetle meat gather in the nape of the neck of the Bacano tree's vast swathes of foliage. The van, driven by Raphael, hidden in the intermittent haze of sunlight and village bush, bumps down, rugged and wild in the well of hours – white and bruised and rickety, a well-oiled and simple engine machine, the gear-stick slack like an old woman's walking stick. Halfway downhill he begins to smell the swift and salted scent of the sea, to feel humidity on his skin. Raphael knows rain, he knows bull work, he knows the fertility of bees.

A young man is walking down along the same path. They are all cousins in these hills, an aristocracy of pigment. The young man is Alvin. Since dawn he has been hunting manicou to no avail, in the jungles behind the Credit Union. Now he looks in the van's back tray and sees the carcasses of several goats that lie entangled, the red raw of their flesh scentless, unless the watcher draws near to witness the corpuscles of this abattoir scene, and then the flesh is pungently primal. The goats' limbs extend out to brightness, reaching towards the infinite. Animal life: the life of muscle and blood, bone, instinct and brain-stem, the tourniquets of mortality. Strange that these creatures do not seem to imagine their own demise, yet struggle to hold onto life. Alvin's grin is naive and genuine, he grins like an anchor; his hair is muffed up in a tropical quiff.

Raphael's foot pumps easy on the rattling pedals, the engine knocking, the van slowing, but it does not stop when it decide to come down the hill. Cousin Alvin is going down to the village market for meat, since he never catch nothing. 'Selfsame but not so much,' Raphael suggest, 'as I have here. Come, flight one in your sack and jump in.' They drive past wooden houses leaning over deep inclines, under mango trees which bruise the galvanised roofs of 4th and 5th cousins. On the other side of the valley, three Baptist women, their heads and bodies wrapped in white, are passing into an enduring image of myth.

Raphael watches from the wheel as they make their way along the old riverside, though there is no water there, not since Africans ran down from Fort Warwick to the French plantations of the North coast, and followed the river through the forest to the mouth of the sea, to be swept away to Africa once more. Once more, the black carrion crow circles overhead, once more the white-tailed monkey swings from tree to swinging tree, once more the scar burst open. Raphael watches children on the other side of the mountain playing, but the architecture of their game is indeterminate from his distance. They appear as fleeting forms, like the cave paintings of the Western Cape. Their voices shoot and scurry among the bushes and behind a copse of homegrown sugar cane as dirt clouds blow among their bare feet.

Later that afternoon, when it becomes too hot to sell meat, the two men return to sit on Raphael's back step, to drink cocoa tea and speak the language of men. Down those stairs, down the undulation of earth is the slaughtery, the killing floor, the place where swine and cattle are dragged, slit to slaughter, the passion room of hell. The table, the altar where the butcher carves flesh from bone, has a shorn edge of wood, and it dips in the centre. This is where the blade returns again and again, sending chipped wood, bone and the blood of beasts falling to the dirt floor below.

These days, the old man's hand trembles above the parted mouth and body of the grand sow, its teeth grinning in his face, then he cleaves it with a swinging blow, divides the hind from the flank, the feet from the fat, the liver from the light. The old man is dying. He knows he sick but he wouldn't tell nobody. Leave him just so. He and Alvin embrace in farewell in the yard and then Alvin returns to his journey, further into the wild hillside. Each farewell is tentative; there is a surplus of bees in this aviary. Is like when that bitch Mr Clary came into the kitchen where his woman was cooking dog rice and tripe, and say, 'Suggs, ah had a blackout', and his voice tremble, because he knew then that he would die. Raphael knew, because it was he who was called upon to drive Mr Clary and Sister Syl down to Cicaye Village, deep east of the island. While they knelt in the Baptist chamber with candle-wax gripping their praying hands, Raphael waited in the hot leatherette of his beige Cortina, parked in the tall grass of orange fields across the main road, across from the church hid in bush, with the yard of marigolds and vervain, the anthuriums and the red poinsettia, and the snackette on the corner that first day he took them there, with the rancid coconut drops which were spoilt from taking too long to reach up country, or else had died in the glass displays that trapped the morning sun along with the pie beef and stale pastelles. Raphael had waited in the midday heat among the orange trees for the old bull Clary to benefit from prayers, to humble down to the Baptist doctrine, to lose his breath and doubt, to succumb to Ma Mamin's healing hands, her holy oils, fenugreek, her incenses. Now, where the hill breaks at the summit and the sky lid seems even nearer, Raphael stands watching Alvin the hunter going up among the bramble, along the high path to his cabin, with the ram goat meat across his back, and the carrion crows harrowing behind.

15

A blackbird is flying from a willow tree in a park where the rain has fallen. In the unfolding fan of a Friday, Ella is arriving at The Bowery. The red polish on her toes is cracked like paint on the fishing boats docked near the rocks at Icacos Bay, where the sea angers quick and keeps history sealed in secrets beneath the waves. The beach is deserted, but a black bellied grouper lies on the sand, one eye up and blinking; it dies watching life harden to stillness, yet holds no grievance. Who will write its day into existence?

Ella's mind disengages itself from the stepping of foot, the swinging of arms, and the energy of the city. What she remembers is a summer near the river, the red slopes of D'Abadie, cousins and country family in a bungalow, the brass scent of the sunlight, the sun-browned spears of rye grass, her first kiss by the river, the muscle of the young man's tongue, the brackish taste of his mouth and the pulse of water running over her feet and around the rock they perched on. He was from the long-grassed farms on the other side of the river, beyond the citrus fields, where his mother raised cattle and maintained half an acre of sugarcane, where fruit overbore and ruined to rot, and parakeets built their nests in the upper branches of the gru gru bef tree. This slim and grinning brown-eyed shepherd boy, whose arms were strung down as if they each held huge stones, would emerge each day, barebacked and gleaming from the river, walking across the field, leading the cows to pasture. Ella watched him from her aunt's breezy veranda, and tasted saliva thick and electric in her throat, felt the warmth and emotive motion of her body. In the erotic imprint of this young man, Ella grew solid and rendered in oil.

He had been in the fields burning the old cane bush; he had been washing shit from the duck house floor with a hose; he had been sitting on a crooked bench milking the heifers in a disinfected pen; he had cleaned the bull pen, where the unprimed concrete floor was muddy with pools of suds, shit and soggy straw. He had sat under the seashell tree, his grinning teeth white in the heat. When he came to her aunt's house one morning to borrow a hose, Ella smelled his copper-scented sweat, and this too left its fetish sting on the insides of her thighs.

Miss Chambers' big son was known to all as the Christophene Boy, and how he get his name? From his Aunty Zeen who arrived at her sister's house from Dorchester, Massachusetts. It was the week before carnival, when muscle is in the air and the fresh paint scent blows along the avenues from the painting of costumes.

When Zeen arrived, she walked through the house, net curtains billowing in the midday breeze, soft-brushing the tops of varnished chairs, taking in the gramophone, the tidy arrangement of the living room, its ornaments and crochet doilies, the wine glasses in the glass cabinet Miss Chambers saved for soulful days. Zeen's big breasts filled the living room, and her heels overlapped their pedestal points. Her *eau de toilet* was lemon and cinnamon. She took up space as she sighed around the rooms as if inspecting each one, as if she was Erzulie, as if she was overwhelmed by the beauty and suffering of the barrackyard quarters. She put a palm to her breast, then she grinned at her sister, Margaret, a single mother and her one piece of boy child.

Then Aunty Zeen leaned on the bottom half of the Dutch door which led to gardens at the back where Margaret planted yam, vervain, zaboca, pigeon peas, where the soursop tree grew strong tasting fruit – she threw urine in the root – where vines of caraili and vines of barbadine tangled on a wire fence. The boy had been outside that day, cleaning bush from the dasheen stream. When he heard his aunt from America, that high bird way she whistled his name, he ran to pick and bring her an armful of chayote, green and hard, the skin veined like a man's hand, still warm from the vine. From then she called him Christophene Boy, and rubbed the crown of his head as she did, as if by right of blood within the meandering plot of kin and clan, born of hills and cocoa fields, with Taino eyes peeping through dawn, she had authority to name him. This was how the boy grew there, shy and surrounded by women to whom he was precious, and this is how, years later, we find him at the river with Ella, neither knowing exactly what to do with their tongues when they kissed. They sat amid silver fishes, the jungle creeping close, and the call of the brown chachalaca bird echoing in the bamboo. All this came to be written of that afternoon in D'abadie, summer, 1984.

The sun was beginning its arc in the city. There was the churn of engines, the hum of industry, workers crossing between offices. Ella waited for the musician at the ticket hall in the station. They had last met six months before, in February. She was in London, acting – he had held her face with both hands and said, 'This may take more than you are prepared to give.' And when she asked 'What will?' he had answered, 'This, what we are will.' She had been staying at a small hotel on Old Street. He came to her room but they argued and he did not stay.

He arrives from the underground arcades of the station with sleepless eyes and luggage, his horn on his back. He kisses her forehead, she leans her head against his shoulder like a bird that has fallen from the sky to die warm and wet, like feathered fruit, in his hands.

16

Raphael's youth was spent upon the Million Hills where the manicou and agouti roam, where antediluvian rivers left dry ravines and trees put roots in the air. His true ambition had always been to write. But as a young man in too tight shoes he had sought clerical work in the babelous city to the west, in the Government Printery, the Mechanic's Union, in the orange juice distillery, in the Infirmary, in the mas boots factory that burned down on the avenue, even in the bread factory where Anson Lee Wah lost his arm. But Raphael's head was hard with prose and teragatonic poetry[4] and the relentless encounter with death upon those roads. Once, on the highway, returning from warehouse work, he saw a man impaled by his steering wheel in a burning car, burnt black, foam puffing out of the cracked film of the head, the hand clawed tight upon the wheel, the gizzard of ashen meat. The car had skidded and crashed into the central barrier and burst into flames. This image was often reprised in Raphael's work, as mythos and motif. There was always heat, except when the crooked fan was spinning, or the air condition unit was whirring and dripping pellets of cold water – if you lucky to pass when it falling – in the cinema next to the fowl slaughtery, on those Saturdays when Raphael went leaping over ravines and dry rivers, rockstone and culvert for kick-up movies at the matinee.

He had discovered his knife hand as a boy gutting ox and castrating calves as apprentice to Mr Billy, the butcher. He knew, from the time the goat head fly off and he wipe the red blade on his apron, that if what he wrote each night remained unread or unpublished, he could still live among the bull pen shuffle and the steel meat-hook and make a few dollars. He was destined then, and resigned, to never leaving the island. His navel string

4. See A. Joseph, *Teragaton*, (London: poisonenginepress, 1997)

bury right there in the roots of the orange tree in Ma Jessie yard, in that sacred spot where dogs succumbed to weeping deaths and, in dying, left oil upon the dirt. He suffered a knotted umbilicus swollen with pus, so they crumbled Jack Spaniard nest in his navel, which for many years remained embedded there, for cockstand potency.

But you think is one set of ketch arse his mother Jessie ketch? Was plenty. Them days is one snack box sharing in six. He remember Jessie powdering her neck and going down the hill to whore with the retired watchman who lived down the range – maybe not whore but different – more nice, like a service she providing. The man name Adam. Now hear what happen. Adam wife dead and he alone in that unpainted house; he have money and wood like child foot, but he shy. Adam like a bat; he only coming out at night. So when he ask Miss Jessie to come and wash and cook for him, she went down to stew chicken and rice. But she must be heft his thing, and give him leg. She come like Eve, she saw Adam's wood, and the poor man spunk out his soul. Is Adam give she money to buy sweet candle and powdered milk, to bring out she jewels from pawn. Is he who give she money to fix she mouth, and to buy frilly drawers and Johnny Mathis record. Adam foot bend from hopping train and falling off the caboose by the biscuit factory. But all skin-teeth not grin. Watch him, he like big leg woman, he quiet, but he smart; he old, but he could cleave coconut with one blow and skin them naked as they born on Christmas morning, and now he have this sweet red woman bringing him ripe mango and arrowroot porridge. She washing his cataract with little boy piss and kissing his nasty mouth. Adam, that scamp, was sick with sugar and he never tell nobody. Is so old people does stay; they know sickness beget death and get frighten, then they get ashamed. Adam would draw bile, want to pass water and faint while he beating box, wake up in pain, unable to walk. Adam dead with all that big wood he carrying; it stand up like police in the coffin. They church and bury him near Jumbie Bridge. He never leave Jessie nothing.

A few years pass and Raphael see his mother Jessie dead in the colonial hospital, with her eyes pressed hot and shut. That was when, to support himself and his brother Bain, he learn the butcher's trade, and build a pen for moaning swine and goats to buckle when he cut their gullet on that rough wooden table. People would roll jitney inside the village to buy hog leg and goat neck, to buy pig tripe and bull stones for soup; those parts he would rugged and cut, from shank to scalp, from back to belly and back. But he also build a habit within a text, through all of this, and would write like a beast from night until morning, as chickens crouched in the tamarind tree, with one eye open, with the scent of frangipani and burning sage floating around the valley. Inside his house, the radio would be playing Al Green and the paraffin lamp would flicker as he wrote. In the yard there were four genera in eight species of woodslave. Variegated. Ocellated. Nine species in four genera: iguana – hard to kill on common ground – zandolie, matte and foot-shaker lizard. This image is his fulcrum of lung and memory, a vision dense and historic, root strata and infinite, the soul of a people, the core text. It was said that his mother's milk remained upon him into puberty, though one day his own teeth would rattle in his jaw, and the fair and reddish down on his arms, at his temple and hairline, eventually become coarse and turn to black, as all things do.

Luke arrives in the stinging rain at the house on Sixth Street, in a desert town of biscuit factories, wide verandas of architects, rum bars, a match factory, Catholic bridges, a Rastaman bakery, Chinese snackettes like Chex and Merlin, and snakes in black ravines. Passing Second Avenue, he remembered the legend of Gary George, who no one believed had joined the police force, until that yellow-bone dusk when they were liming on the block, Gary pull up and show them his Glock. It was a town where there were once several karatekas. There was the tall, afro-headed, soft spoken one whose *gi* fit like a series of barrels, who lived with his Grenadian mother in a canopied house beside the bus route and drank copious amounts of lime juice and knew all twenty-six katas of Shotokan. There was the one who rode a motorbike with a six *shaku bo* strapped to his back, heading west to bust man chest at the National Stadium. But take this as history: the man name was Pig but they called him Peters. Luke and him was tight. Then up Third Street it had Sensi Pittman, a red man, a cocksman; the muscle print in his *gi*; chivalrous and riding quite D'Abadie to pillion the white-belt young lady; then is romance and *kiba-dachi* stance he putting she in. When Luke was young there was also a fruit stall on First Avenue, where a bald dread used to shell out hemp, clandestine under the ruse of selling sweet navel oranges.

Luke arrived there in pain. The Bandit arse water and the desert wind had bruised his face. The salted prunes he sucked had scowled him. He had come to hide, and also to find the roots of his own ancestry. But his old home, a tall house, an indentured mansion built on stilts so water couldn't reach it in flood or hurricane, was now a coil of thieves, a brothel and a stable for leg where men went for pussy. Luke still knew the region well, knew each house and knew whose garden ran over imaginary tunnels. As a child among the soursop branches and tubers, he had built a tunnel once, from his grandmother's yard to the peanut punch shop on the other side of the avenue – the long avenue where the match factory and the basketball courts were. Another conduit dug under an avocado tree reached the Lopez stables on Eleventh Street, another ran from the garret to the mint and white mosque on Temple Street where a wake was held when Anson, the god of bread, was pulled and kneaded into the machine.

Passing along the avenue, he remembered the bandy amble of Mong, the old Chinese man who hunted grasshoppers in the savannah and how, seeing Mong bent over, he knew that rain was imminent. Then there was Emile Fitzroy who would walk through the field by the stables each dusk, with his bandy knees and his BOAC lunch bag, coming from work as a porter in the hospital. And if Luke was playing there, enticing worms from holes with blades of long grass, if he would smile, Mr Fitzroy would give him a hand of sikiye figs, some governor plums, sometimes even sweet tamarind.

Luke remembered how, one red evening, peeping from the washroom to look over the savannah, he saw American Joe and the girl with polio foot who had just moved into the neighbour-hood enter the moonlit field to make country love against a samaan tree. Luke watched the girl warp her crooked ankles around Joe's waist; he watch how she rock and come on, then how she can't stand straight; she have watery funk in her knee. Luke deduce from such nights how them Indian woman cunny-hole high so the blade going in straight when they standing up. He jerk his wood feverishly until he was called inside. 'It have someone for everyone,' he say to himself, and he watched her differently from then on.

Those samaan trees hid empires of batchaks, back-back turkey and horned beetles; the dense undergrowth was tangled up with ti-marie and picka bush, rugged earth, squirrels hiding from pellet gun and iron-pot. At times, men would gather among these samaan roots with liquor and weed, resting from labouring in the paddy or the aubergine gardens, to sit at noon and contemplate the latest suicide by paraquat poisoning.

Returning to the leaning house on the corner of Ninth Street and First Avenue, Luke finds the tailor in the low window's gaze, in a white vest, bent at his sewing machine with its slick wasp waist, black for all salvation, stitching bespoke waistcoats, hems and button holes, a tattered measuring tape around his neck.

By the time Luke reach the red top step of Miss Cynthia and Miss Arterley house, the rain start to fall, and he recall how when these two women was alive, dogs used to guard their plum tree, and now look how red rat and god horse could come in easy, how the jungle could overcome the fruit, how all they try to grow now gone to grudge and rot. Even cascadura fish swimming in the drain the women had the gardener cut.

Even now, walking through those deserted yards, Luke has the sense of violating someone's rapacious eye. Old suburban spirituals, dead and gone, but still breathing. Where Luke stood was a totem pole, and from there he could see how the flood overflow the land with crapaud and salamander, rain cutting up the Indian farmland. Luke know, but he want to know how he know this place so intimate, like bucket know well, like he living somebody life. Raphael writing about this since story get build. But neither nostalgia nor torrential rain could combust and swirl the Great Bandit away, so, for Luke, anticipation was stronger than arriving. The Bandit want to know how he could be following Luke, if where Luke going was the only way to pass.

18

Walking past the match factory again, detergent distilleries, the brewery grounds, far up First Street, Mount Garnett, a long walk up from the old house on Second Avenue. To the north, was Champs Fleur Hill, the high territory of Hilltop United FC. Lower down Champs Fleur was the carpenter's workshop with sawdust on the ground and the night club above it. It has been written, how calypso perforated the night, how the long-suffering wife arrived at this night club to find the old bull constackling a dame.

There was a football ground behind the brewery, and there the musician once saw a young man climb its wire fence after a football game, and the wire hooked between ring and flesh gripped the rim of skin when he jumped down, and the finger's skin was peeled back to reveal its secret. Darkness was creeping slow, the avenue below was sunset red and led west to the house of hot light and mosquito coils under chairs and the old woman, Ma Sylvie, shuffling day long to wash and wipe, to dust, to stitch, to cook, and Mister Clary, easing the Austin Cambridge into the yard after a day teaching woodwork in the institute. In these middle-class regions, there was the burnt milk scent from Hepburn's house on First Avenue; there was Alan Hackshaw's yard, with the Julie mango tree and its low hanging fruit.

The night shift was beginning at the match factory. Then the leap from the wire that kept the young man's finger. The musician could still remember the buzzing throb of that moment's suspense. The stub was exposed upon the wire, and was seen by the young men gathered round, with muddy football boots hooked by the heels, and long socks rolled down from their shin pads, mud on their breath, perspiration in their underarm sockets. The victim's face was a scowl, a silent scream, his sufferation increasing. He had tried, but he could not blink back time. He held the bloody hand tight, till the fingers were twisted and useless and the bone stayed abrupt and unmoving.

The musician knew such pain. The popping sound of stepping on a rusty nail, from running barefoot around a carpenter's yard and the needle for tetanus in the wound, the sting piercing the heart; or the big toe skin-back and bursting from miss-kicking a football in the hard gravel road, the skin peel back like a red skull cap, pepper in the sun.

He remembers how the plum tree never bore full fruit in that Mount Garnett yard; how its branches hung over the shower. Galvanise there to make it private, a hose hung over for spray, carbolic soap in a jar. But what became of that boy's hand? The ambulance brought painkiller gas. Did the attendant retrieve the fingertip or leave it there? That done dead, no use, it gone.

The Mount Garnett River ran clear behind the brewery, through dark bamboo and razor grass. It had once cut a wider swathe, a deeper gully, a steeper bank, but now it had narrowed somewhat. Once, the musician and his brother had tried to locate the source of the Tacarigua River. They had walked high up through jungle lands, upwards past hemp farms and ajoupas. They had seen the glue of laglee traps set for parakeets. They walked till bush enveloped them, naked as they born up Five Rivers jungle. The source of the river was a stream trickling out from under a rock. They took turns to lie across this rock, to stare into the sky. The river cascaded through fauna and field, the whip of its trajectory through the slant land of banana plantations and, further up, uncharted fruit. The land spread out majestically to the southern plains – then progress: factories were built, and the river's fishes fled downstream to the rice paddies of the wild Indian lands where they died underfoot.

Sun Ra might have conducted his Arkestra on the banks of the Mount Garnett River, or maybe Mingus, mercurially battling the stench of a dead dog and the sound of brewery machinery, could have led his octet there, with John Handy, Dannie Richmond and Dolphy. Even Bud Powell, playing solo on this bandstand at the edge of the field.

When he was still learning to blow, the musician played there at the insurance company's sports day, where race announcements were made by megaphone, and the band played in inter-missions. Though the horn still refused to yield to his hands, when invited to blow, the young musician painted a serpent for a solo in 'Haitian Fight Song'. Mingus grinned, ghost of wood and water, his body bent upon the shoulder of the bass, peeping into the bell the boy blew through.

It was at that sports day when the musician saw the white woman sitting on the warm grass, her head rolling back from exhaustion, her thighs gleaming in the sun. Those were innocent ages, when the heart trembled from the rigours of race and etiquette. She was older, her face fully set. She smiled at him, but he could bring no sound or whisper in that world of hard men that could penetrate her ear.

Years later, the musician would cast a glance back at this road, at this avenue and the city further west. He would remember a blade sinking into flesh and how his hand was eager to lose the knife between the culvert and the sewers of a city street. He would remember that a car had come to the house one Sunday morning while he was in the savannah – a wide sedan, with two plain-clothes policemen investigating a stabbing. They used words that brought the fear of jail, licks from the cat-o-nine, being broken on the wheel, hot oil poured in the ear. But it was not to be. Ma Sylvie had saved her sou-sou. Money that he thought he had 'borrowed' from her, she put back in his hand, and he flew.

19

The morning that the musician met him at Victoria train station, Drayton had just come from Gatwick airport and was on his way to catch a train to Bristol. Drayton enter Britain with passport empty and papers in order; those bookkeepers of her majesty waved him through. But with his dread pinned back neatly, dressed in a just a beige blazer, soft pants and brown church shoes, Drayton groan from the cold of an English December. When he and the musician walk out on the station concourse, Drayton lays his suitcase and trumpet case down to stand with hands on hip, back arched, looking around and inhaling the moment. He never left Trinidad before, never sat on a plane, so excuse him how his heart full up to burst and scatter blessings upon England.

Drayton and the musician once played in the horn section of a school band in Port of Spain. Drayton blew angular, his high notes were ambitious, but it hard to blow hard jazz on the island and Drayton couldn't play smooth. Now is England he reach, but is not music that send him.

He has left the island behind, at least for now, though soon the blue hills of Diego Martin will glow intensely from memory; hills of hunters with flambeaux blinking, the north coast road, the long roads east through dense forest and hidden villages, the image of his mother and sister crying long tears in the people airport. But all that gone, water pass, business fix, he will settle for cold for now, metropolis. In any case, Drayton have a woman waiting for him in a warm apartment on the Albert Road.

The woman met Drayton one Panorama preliminaries night, in the North stand, the big yard stage in Port of Spain. She was a tourist, visting for carnival. Now, she making a home to receive Drayton, white-painting wood for bed and table, watering the pots of mint and small tomatoes she grows on a ledge above the kitchen sink.

Outside, the Bristol Avon flows behind the mastering studio she has told him about, the oven door swings open in the cafe nearby, the florist cuts the thorny stems of roses with shears. A key is required for the room of answers. A dream is a wound in time.

On the day that Drayton left the island he was escaping a woman who had tried to poison his feet against movement and pour singular lust into the corners of his eyes. She had worked in the garden pulling up chive, then bent and sweated crotch-wise onto the rice she fed him, to keep him; she had wept and swept her waters upon him; she had put him with his shirt flung open to lie on the delicate bed of her sex.

The net curtain billowed above him; it was mid afternoon; the woman was washing her great breasts in the sink. In the valley below, the school bell rang out; the voices of children filled the void. Drayton see his way free and left the woman a letter on her dressing table, then he leapt from her window and ran. The road he took leaned at 45°, so slant that Drayton found himself leaning to walk against its angle, touching the asphalt surface of the road for balance, looking down to quarry and bone like he was walking around the narrow rim of a mountain. Further down, near the market, he joined in an easter parade. Someone threw him a bugle, and since he had long memorised the pentatonic scale – which a bugle can blow though it can't blow flat – Drayton found that he could play it like a trumpet, just by putting the horn to his mouth. But poison want to eat his foot and rum want to see him, and his knee won't bend properly, and he is slipping, falling off the edge of the road.

But now the woman coming closer behind him and she crying real tears. She was older than him, a full woman, divorced with grown children. She wore the restrictive garments of a woman much younger. She comes barefoot, straight from the bedroom, her drawers are still twisted in her crotch. She is pushing through the crowd towards Drayton, clutching her nightgown closed. A blade grins in her other hand, a blade dipped so deep in hex and desperate love it would leave marks in water. It would slice through skin to flesh and back. Lord Jesus! Get back upon that cross; that bitch don't eat nice.

Drayton get caught in that same run-can't-run, so he running sideways, deep into the otherwise convivial parade as it passes the banks and shopping arcades in the city. Melchior say how the woman palms and her tongue were both black with sin like soucouyant, how they could bury her jawbone in the desert for seven days and the teeth still wouldn't rattle like charrasca. But Drayton say he love her, and he had even told her so once, as she stooped over her enamel basin, bathing off and rinsing her business with a rag reserved for washing arse. He loved her even though she had tried to cut his throat several times. When he couldn't bear anymore to kiss the mouth of her sex, he vomit up vinegar and run.

When he reach the North stand, Desperadoes was crossing, and is there he meet Alicia from Bristol. When she see Drayton running she think is she he was running to, and she hook him, and he hook she, the band play, they dance. Next thing is plan they planning for him to move to England. Is so things does go sometimes. Melchior say the woman heart was pure, a fair bride, he never know a woman love a man so. And is so Drayton end up in England; the man was trying to change his life. So when he hop the train, the musician embrace him and wish him well.

20

When Ella first came to New York, youth still filled the air she was contained in, and her essence and vibration seemed freshly formed. She had come with a scholarship, from a decent home in the flat lands below the Million Hills, the area before the land becomes paddy field, swampland and, further south, oil and natural gas distilleries. Her goal, carried on the towering surf of her ambition, was not simply to enter acting school in the city, but to immerse herself in the craft and tradition of the thing. She memorised monologues from August Wilson and Harold Pinter; she would recite them to poets in the leatherette corners of downtown cafes. But actors would ply themselves against the restraint of her skin, they would scent her essences and undress the contours of her body with their eyes. There were dramaturges and directors she met who tried to seduce her with intellect and guile, but she would slip free each time, as a hummingbird in an orchard (the orchard, for instance, of Adolphus Henry, Commissioner of Affidavits, who carpeted his backyard garden with lawn-grass stolen from the Aranguez savannah. Adolphus had governor plums, sapodilla, caimet, dudus mango and a sour orange tree in that orchard. Ella was like the hummingbird which flew there, from branch to vine). Her talent of wing and flight was such that no one could hold her still in their arms or upon their lips for long. Her fluttering heart, the slender gestures of her pride, had sheltered her for a while and who would harm her, with her soft face, the brown and tender rigours of her eyes? But the city crouches in wait for the weak, it reclaims bones and derelict buildings; eventually, everything must succumb. This, too, is a part of life.

After a time, each glance of Ella became more fleeting. We saw her in Greenwich village, then we saw her on Flatbush Avenue, going down into the subway. We never saw her emerge. We turned away; the moon disappeared; we had lost patience. We saw her buying olives in the Syrian supermarket in Queens, or having lunch alone in a Cuban-Jamaican restaurant in Harlem, or walking through Prospect Park on Saturday mornings, or crossing the Pulaski Bridge, out from a cold water warehouse, her face as rigid as a routine. If we stared directly into her face at the supermarket checkout, she would not notice us. Maybe she did not mean to be impolite, but the longing for home was etched upon her face in those early months, and her hair would be pulled back tightly. We saw her as a woman who desired order and attainment.

In her Harlem room, she tidied the ornaments arranged on a ledge – a blue and white porcelain windmill from a weekend workshop in Rotterdam, her rings, a framed photo of her mother sitting in her veranda tacking a hem. She folded the clean white of washed cotton sheets, and stacked them, luminous and mint, with the patchouli and vetiver scent of pot pouri. She preferred her kitchen clean.

Soon she began to see a young man called Jonathan who once was stabbed in the waist on a skiff for smuggling fish in Zimbabwe. In New York, his life had been brewed in high tension apartment buildings where cormorants and wild geese blew past the windows. His father was a herbalist who'd passed on his green art to his son. Jonathan was slick as a reed. He rode a black bicycle to the outskirts of Manhattan each day, to deal in grain and leaf and dust and tinctures, his hands trembling at each transaction. He had learnt to penetrate the vulnerable underlung of the city, to respond to confrontation with a growl and hissing teeth. His body was long-limbed and able to straddle wide roads or narrow rivers; his grip held both spliff and bull mastiff. He moved illegally upon New York, with the ruse of parallax.

It was his mouth, its curl, lingering and sweet, like the itch of citrus, that had attracted Ella in the Chinatown market where she walked among its corridors of dried fish and ancient meat, buying aloe vera, coconut water and lemongrass. Jonathan saw that she was soft as a petal rained upon, that she was unsettled in the city. He desired her for her vulnerability, but encountered the rigour and muscle of her mind. They seduced each other with the same swagger – the head that leans, the lips that quiver. Jonathan threw his trope. He was patient, almost indifferent, and her paradigm shook, and for a while Ella forgot the woman she wished to shape herself into.

Her father called her from Million Hills, promised to pray for her, beseeching her away from those rooms. She had been seen running, ruined from backstage to shadow. Her skin had lost its glow, her teeth their whiteness, her study suffered. It was true she had endured levels of despair with Jonathan in New York. She had become used to the shadows of men perched on her balcony, like timber leaning in a moonlit carpenters' yard. She had given Jonathan her love, her earnings, her dreams. He was arrested in an apartment in Queens. The paraphernalia of his trade was strewn across each room; he leapt high but was caught and deported on his way down.

That first year her longing for home was constant. Each night her dreams would return her to drives through lush valleys, past the proud houses that were dotted along the mountains, the ancient cocorite palms which stood at the highest point. But what Ella longed for most was not landscape or seascape. She missed her friends – girls she had been to school with. She longed for the simple hill, the land and its people. Theirs was an advanced science of being. In those hills, each tree was given a name, each plot of land kept its secrets. The land was soaked with ancestral blood.

21

Melchior say Boyson[5] used to go by the standpipe to bathe, and in the red dirt of that plum dusk, in that povertous valley, if Boyson lucky, he might see Maxine Alcantara bathing on the slippery bank of the ravine, see how water pouring down, her bodice wet and tight. Men wanted this Maxine, not just because she was fine and red, with Spanish in her skin, but because her mouth was like a trumpet bell with lips curling back. Maxine man was Benjamin Pittman, a karate man who would crank his motorbike on purpose, so people in the village would hear how the engine nice. Boyson would see Maxine holding on to Benny on the bike; the tightness of her denim shorts frayed around her thighs, like belted loaves of bread, and he wish Maxine fingers could entwine around his belly instead. Men more than Boyson envied Benny; grin with him but scheme and skulk to lyrics his craft when he busy playing Jim Kelly in the dojo. But Maxine was rugged and steep, she wasn't easy. She was the type to confront men fully, eyeball and bold them, talk as she see it and cuss like fire if you get her vex. Her father, Mr Alcantara, was strict like police milk; he had seven daughters and knew cut-arse from slap, knew how to handle the zwill, how to throw his hand. He would break a branch from a zaboca tree and beat you with that if you vex him. So Boyson sorcery had to be different. He shy like ti-marie leaf that will shut on the touch and he watch Maxine from a distance as she bend with a cocoyea broom sweeping the yard, and he peep the musculature of her flanks.

Sam Roberts throw an Old Years Night party. DJ Champ playing there; they have plenty food. Roberts put up coloured bulbs, balloons. The house up on the hillside coming down, with the crown of thorns and the orchids sprouting on the stairs going

---

5. 'Bison' in Bim.

up. Champ throw funky disco upon the dancers until water drip from the ceiling in the drawing room. Boyson was on the veranda when he see Maxine coming, flinging hip in that elegant swing of women coming up a hill – bent to the task, unhurried, working. She wearing tight brown corduroy hot pants, sandals, halter back and big round earrings. She was alone. Benny was in cocoa country beating up fellas at a beach training. Boyson adjust and flex; he watch how men start circling Maxine like crab – greasy-lip men like Geen, holding chicken in plate and beer in hand, men who getting old, playing polite, throwing head back to exaggerate and laugh. Boyson wait for a slow tune, and then he approach – Peabo Bryson's 'Let the Feeling Flow' – but when he almost reach, he collide with the fear of failure, turn back and had to humble himself outside in moonlight, watching another man grind a groove on Maxine and Maxine wining back. Boyson wait till the pelau leave bun-bun in the bottom of the pot, till top men drunk and hawking up their guts in the bush, till who sober get pick to fuck. The DJ hand tired, stay running slows: Debra Laws' 'Very Special', B.B.& Q.'s 'The Things We Do…' and Maxine coming down from the frolic house, bounce up on Boyson, coincidental – he lurking at the bottom of the stairs like crocodile. 'H-h-hello,' and he peel back a smile, 'You-you mind if I walk you home, Maxine? I mean, it late, the road dark and I going s-s-same way anyhow, so…we could walk.' Maxine watch Boyson up and down like is the first time she really see him. Them days Boyson eye big-big from peeping, and he lingay like twine, with knots for elbows and knuckles. Maxine say, '*You* want to walk me home?' But she hook him by the elbow and they go. Boyson tell himself, *She tipsy, I bound to put prick on that tonight!* So they walking by moonlight, bush on both sides, and when they reach the sandbox bridge, Boyson linger – was to see what he could get – he lean up on the guardrail and fold his arms like a star boy. When Maxine back-back on him, he know he win, he feel like a man, he feel he thief Benny Pitman girl, he feel she kiss him in a dream and he fall in love. Is now he know what love is. Maxine reach back and squeeze his prick; he giggle and laugh. Is gum she chewing; the perfume she wearing was rose. Boyson wood want to break in three places. Dog barking from the butcher's yard; Raphael still writing. When they reach Maxine house, all light off inside. Boyson wondering if she will give it to him under the stairs, or maybe in the veranda where one corner dark, or in the back of the house, but the chicken coop there. Maxine pull him close – was to kiss and bite him goodnight – but when Boyson feel the punctuation of her breasts, and taste her breath in his ear, he run amok. Quick-quick he start caressing the electric curvature of her thighs. He hand curve the part where the arse reach the leg, he squeezing arse like he squeezing cushion. He play to palm the front, but Maxine push him back.

She watch him, she smile. 'A-A, Boyson, how you fresh so? What you feel you doing, eh? You want to fuck? You feel you could bull Maxine? I bet you eh even start to burst yet.' And she laugh in the young man face and run him from there.

Melchior say Boyson walk down by Silver Mill, but he can't walk straight, have to stagger the gait, have to walk on all fours, blue balls and tender, pain all in his chest, and the dark fading to light above the trees and the rooster crowing, and the river starting back to run, run, run.

22

Luke had now left Mount Garnett and was on his way to Mad Bull Hill. He hoped that when he was called upon in that decisive moment, when men are tested and astonish themselves in conflict, he too would step up to battle with his fists hot and his big heart open, ready to throw his hand. He knew that when Basil came, he would come suddenly.[6] He was no longer afraid. He watched a young soldier step out of a taxi. The soldier walked upon the earth with a fearless grip, and Luke was empowered by this vision. He knew then that no engine or plot could grind him to blush. He had travelled across rough waters and perilous rock, he had been bitten by sand fly, marabunta, tsetse fly and mites more bitey than the raised welts from the Bandit's cut-arse belt. And if he find himself in the desert, what the arse they put him there for other than to crack some jackass carapace with licks?[7]

Luke could not be sure if his memories were his to have, or someone else's, written into historical prose and verse. But he remembered being taken from a soft bed and dragged down the hill

---

6. Personification of the Big Man Himself. Basil is the Grim Reaper, The King of Terrors, hailstone and sorrow, when I dead bury my clothes. For more info see The Mighty Dictator, 'I Don't Know Why the Devil I Can't Get Fat' (1948) and Destroyer, 'Leave Me Alone Dorothy' (1940) (Winer). And Melchior say, 'When Basil bowl you out you can't put no leg before wicket; you have to walk back to the pavilion, you bound to go.'

7. Please, remember is suffer Luke suffer and suffer when he drift away from the text and cultivate hunger in the desert. He thought he could flex, he feel he could defy what the big man put down in writing, but he almost dead and was ready for corbeau to suck out he eye by the time he ring the bell upon the Bandit's perilous gate. You must be feel the Bandit send for Luke by saying he had bush meat by the gallon, but nobody eh *make* Luke come here; Luke come here for heself.

screaming for love in the hot afternoon, torn from his mother's arms. The telling and the who – he never grew weary of hearing it – was the same for everything and everyone upon that hill, from the weak-hearted Deacon sanding crook sticks, to the fisherman skanking to dub roots rockers, with his trousers rolled up to his knees, in the community hall where two bad DJ would clash and rib would rattle from bass. Never mind overwrite or verbosity, haul your arse with that, every soul cage carries its own sorrow within. It is hard to keep up with a place where everything happening at the same time. And feel this: walking in the street Luke would suddenly forget who he was, he would wonder if his consciousness was his, or if, ultimately, he was alone, that he would leave alone, with both hands swinging – no duty-free chocolate or rum, no sugar cake or toolum, no gift to bring for nobody.

Luke entered Mad Bull Hill sideways, like a crab climbing the side of a muddy precipice behind people house, around stilt post and pillar, walking soft where men piss in passing, where the earth moist and rancid – cool breeze don't heal it. The last house he passed on his way uphill was where his father had lay his head and convalesced, after his car overturned on a hot Tobago highway, where he had a comfort woman sap his brow with bay rum, and feed him chicken-foot soup. This woman had Creole blood, with a rounded Taino face. She was humble but proud; her shoulders were straight, with muscle built from carrying buckets of water and children up hills and rocky ocean sides. Her breasts, too, were filled with muscle from pulling up tubers, cassava and tannia, but one-one cocoa does full up basket and she establish her own furniture business and put the first brick house up on Mad Bull Hill. Luke's father had met her at the Bagatelle Parish Fair, in the field between the bamboo and the river. That country afternoon, when with the luscious balm of gospel the leader of the church went walking through the fair shaking hands, the woman bent nice to dish him turtle prick soup from her pot as he passed. People form a long line. Everybody see her heart. Luke father buy a cup. The reader could negotiate the rest.

There were men sitting around a fire on Mad Bull Hill roasting chenette seeds over flame till black and charred, the nut inside hot like newborn wood. Luke sat with them and saw that each had exactly the same black face which glowed in the rippling blaze.[8] From this hill the entire history of the island was revealed. The lights of the jetty, the hotels, refineries, the marinas, Legion Hall, the colours blazing in the mas camps, the audacity of Baptist churches singing down the hill with hymns to burst the centre post, the holy room where neophytes mourned, mothers humming down Ezekiel jitney. Look, the woman catch the power and roll, so you peep the holy pleat – these were all familiar strophes.

At the airport, the Great Bandit had just stepped off the plane. He carried his suitcase in the old style, by the wrist, not on wheels or hip on his back, but holding hard the grip with its plastic handle. His bulk would grow. His good time waste. He hid his eyes behind dark shades, and he was chewing several sticks of black mint gum, ready to bitch and squall. In times of danger, the Great Bandit could become deceptive and vicious; he carried malice in his heart, and razor blades in his wallet, undetected by X-ray or fast camera. He was on his way to intercept Luke, to decipher his hex, to twist and clip the hero's wings with jealous-possessive love. He walked with the bowed-legged movement of a Mexican film star in those Western movies in which the hero died and the villain was undefeated and left the damn film still malicious and hard to dead – like a Midnight Robber burning down house and caliphate. But every time he bent his arms, the thick skin on his elbows cracked like red rocks of lava. Strip the Bandit naked and he turn wrestler, growl how he want to eat people raw, to suck out the marrow from the bone. He ask for Luke in the Government Printery – in this town each department of civil ceremony had a building – and they show him a map of Mad Bull Hill, and in that map he see Luke sitting down round the fire with the same-face men. But when Luke look up and he see the Bandit watching, he reach up to turn the page and run.

---

8. Luke thought they were dead, the way they hung their heads, but they were sitting in a church, in a hall, in senate, in houses of parliament, in community centres, in universities, in civic auditoriums, in ice factories, in rain-lit rooms, in houses of smoke.

23

Long before she left the island, Ella moved with her mother to a house near Chenet Tree Junction. The red dirt yard there was uneven and always sodden, and at the side of the house there were banana, mango and dasheen trees. A mile to the west was the savannah, and to the north the blues and greys of the Million Hills, the coloured houses and their yards. In their new house there were spiders, woodslaves and rain flies, but her mother hung coloured curtains in the living room, they varnished the floorboards, put camphor balls in the clothes piled high in cupboards, filled mattresses with coconut coir, and made a home of it.

In the innocent years after her father left, her mother sometimes went out at night to catch spume from an old tailor who lived down the range. To buy powdered milk and a little saltfish, she had to kiss this man's slack mouth, with his gold teeth grin. Her mother told Ella, 'Them teeth screw down in his gum bone like white people toilet bowl.' In this still wild region beneath the hills, when the world still felt flat, the promise of life spread out. By day the people had ambition, but by night, when the sky shut its eye, the scamps and dregs and the hustlers would shuffle game in the seedy parts of ravines. Vagrants dragging rags and ca-ca, bags dragging them down, would linger near the steep stream which descended the Million Hills to salvage slivers of beef and swine that had come loose from Raphael's abattoir. For Ella, the beginning of the world still lay beyond. Mythical cities of snow and cloud-piercing workplaces, other worlds, other planets.

Behind the yard there was a small copse of mysterious trees. One day, she and a neighbour's son were pelting stones up at the branches, to bring down the brown pods that looked like lanterns made of the softest spit of bees and cobweb paper, fruit which they thought must be sweet like giant sapodilla, but in fact they were marabunta nests, and marabunta wasp does sting you in the ear-hole, cunny-hole, your whole lip swollen, sting stinging all in the back of the head – one big daymare – hallucination, fever for days. In your panic, you slapping them away till your body get whip. So Ella and the boy run down in the river bed, but it dry, just a stitching ripple; they running, trying to hide from the wasps, and somebody, uphill on the far side of the river, throwing stones at them, and the stones reaching them from all behind the salt biscuit factory and detergent refineries, and threatening to burst their skulls like seeds.

This is the world that Ella eventually left behind: the bamboo stalls, the grass verges of a highway where cattle grazed, the stench and noise of markets, the haberdashery of crochéted doilies and colonial cornices, heat blooming in the room where her father once listened to the 7 o'clock news, his eyes steady like black and white jumbie beads behind his glasses, his cataract ripe. His face was still handsome from younger days, with evidence of his indigenous blood from down the main, when his ancestors came in reed canoes, already fully formed as a nation, people who consecrated the land for epochs long before the conquistadors arrived. They had planted tobacco along the Cano Manamo, irrigated the high ground for cultivation. But this was always only one strand, only one corner of a syncretic story, for then comes black Africa to put more thunder in the heart of it, like the merging and blending of blood, bone meat and chicken-foot in souse, into the Creole Caribbean. But for now, know that this history is divergent and vast, know that all the world existed here, in the villages down from the Million Hills, houses on stilts, protruding out from the angle of the land, and the fire-sky was hot and hard upon them.

But the ground around her mother's house, sheltered in Spiritual Baptist distances from prying colonial eyes, remained damp, perhaps from the spittoon of mouths, the washing of teeth, soapy water from bathing, and the rinsing of rice. Her world was not barricaded – the yard that is – by wire or by corrugated fences, or wrought-iron gates, like those houses further east along the main road, in the civilised regions of more suburban flatlands. These government houses reminded her of funereal places, with red ixora and yellow allamanda blossoming, but regimented in their yards. These were places where no door stayed open, and the children inside could only come to the gate to shake their friends' hands, or run through the jungle of their own backyards, but never outside to play in the road or to roam the hills behind the purple nursing home or the white walls of the Credit Union. These were regions of riverless summers, iron bridges, red stucco, dust.

So her lithe body, suspended in this plane of memory, drifts upon the ocean of the savannah, and travels to those dreaming places where her mother sang as she washed and wrung her underwear in the kitchen sink, the song stinging the ear with its mystery.

The summer evening darkens. She has come to the apartment of a school friend who moved to New York in the same year. Prospect Park – a place of wide avenues, ashen beeches moulded within the paving stones of a quiet street – is a closed world of other lives, respectable, correct and poised shut like those suburban spaces of her memory. Ella finds her friend sitting on the stairs outside her apartment. They embrace, and speak late into the night.

In bed that night, Ella revisits the house east of the Million Hills, when all the world was before her; when each individual island was further out at sea, each rumoured nation and continent, the moving waters and the infinite landscape of history were yet to be sailed to.

24

The stage is arranged, the drum kit is built on a rug, a pillow placed in the kick to temper the boom. Blow. The power you have. With what sound? Sometimes malaise is in the body and its embankments, but you don't know love. In Lyon, after the first set, the musician braces against a cold wall, pissing in the snow, flakes soft like talcum on his face, thunder in his throat from pumping out sound. Then the second set. They play Dolphy's 'Prophet', 'Un Croque Monsieur' – with the volubility of Archie Shepp – solos with the reed squeaking, the eardrum bursting. He blows this dirge, this sinner's moan, to remember his grandfather who died with a stiff arm slung up on a chair back, in the dirty light of the living room, a room with one 40 watt bulb set centre. He had to make do with that, no lamp, no flam.

The old man, Clary, Martiniquan stock, tell him either succumb to the telling or regain his history from Raphael book. Clary was old, but he wasn't stupid. He say, 'Don't take this house for no open sepulchre,' and years later the musician found out what that meant. Clary was caught crying in the toilet when his brother Oban dead. That Oban who? Oban who came with tubs of fried chicken ice cream, Mopsy biscuits and warm, plaited bread on those Friday nights, 1978. This was Oban who drove audaciously through the savannah, who don't need no road. Oban who drive on grass, who make road for motorcar to drive any kiss-me-arse place he like. He rev engine in the field, wake the trees, pot hound barking, make ti marie grass turn in and fold. Night inside that field was always black – besides the wild moon, or the two-beam light of Oban car coming through the field.

Out in the gallery, when Oban and Clary spun their tales, was always about how to hunt with flambeau and lance jungle rat, how to catch bush meat. To hunt right was to lance with spear like Taino and Arawak, not to shoot with colonial buckshot and kick back. Mongoose – that meat not good – but it have manicou – hototo! – in them wild agriculture further up the hills. Go with a torchlight or a flambeau, no dog, nothing, just careful in the bush. Oban say if he catch sight of a mama manicou in the trees, when he flash his light and see she have young, he would leave it, he wouldn't kill. But the male, if they big and have hair in their ears, he would throw lance in their motherarse. Them days two man could hunt and catch plenty beasts; men could cross lance like saltires, not like now when them young boy fraid to go bush and hunt, but they will shoot man and man like is ants they mashing.

The musician rolls his horn to let the spit spill from the valve to the wooden stage. He was known for the low note, placed in the underlung of the song; it was his main sweet thing. Later, there was red wine in the house of a dancer. Lyon below, lights along the Rhone to wash the wish of it, wash away the pain. Antique blades were hung on the walls of the dancer's house. Below her window was stone and sudden death. Imagine: to fall and land there in a French courtyard, with your two leg tense like you straining to leggo spume, and them femur shaft gone straight up inside to crack in many pieces, with a boom sound, a crash. Instead, she dribbled on his cock and tore the foreskin back, violently, till he had to restrain her hand like a policeman restraining a thief, not criminal tight, but tight, even though that plastic tear long time.

It reminds him of his first job, construction work building a school. How the workmen tease him that day his mother make bake and bhagee and bring it onto the site for him, in a greasy brown paper bag, in front of those labourers who chewed twigs and bumped around all day, flitting like butterfly, but who never did a damn thing, yet, somehow, the school get build. A radio was tacked up in the tool shed, the stores clerk smoking hemp whole day on the job, a fish-pot bubbling there on a three stone fireside by the river – same river he used to break biche and go swim with his friends, when they uses to crack each other's heads with stone, and stone have no eye. Days when they cross the big pipe across the river to peep between bush at the rasta princess washing her rass with aloes on the riverbank. One man on the building site –

he wore jeans with ironed seams, resoled gym boots, his afro patted neat to a globe above a face like a grasshopper's with sadly protuberant eyes, the beard tapering to a point – came up and grinned: 'You don't know pim? Your prick still in plastic?' The young man was confused. Was his own mother who laughed, who tell him what pim was. In them days the clip of skin that kept his foreskin firm to the shaft was still intact. Was a full woman, Didi, who tear it first.

In Lyon, the musician senses a dull fever, a chill film of sweat upon him. So he leaves the dancer's house with the sax on his back, the young sun burning up dew, catching him moving through a city he has come to know well. Come now. In a taxi filled with North African musk, the sombre driver hums along to a whirring rai cassette. The musician, in the back seat, with his head rolled back and his eyes closed, feels each swerve of the road.

The dancer, turns off the lamp in her bedroom, the wet parts of her sheet are cold against her skin. Then, for both, that hollow feeling.

25

You come with a book in your back pocket and you want to read.
You wash your black arse in the river, and scrape your tongue
across my plate. You drink water from the wrong side of the cup.
You sit in the sour orange tree when the sun shining brisk in the
middle of the afternoon, after rain just fall and the birds start back
singing. You stand up under the dudus mango tree reciting
Langston Hughes' poems. You using words that you buy from
the white man university to conflagrate black people brain. You
come with high-mind book roll up in your back pocket and you
climbing the hill. You going where they tell you don't go, but you
walk like you don't fraid fire, red ants, snakebite, conch, pepper,
wood lice, woodslave, black police nor gonorrhoea neither. Like
you don't mind see the dead man body decayed upon the earth to
liquid grey, corpus and filament like a conch shell, waxen flux in
the carotid chambers, lizards nesting in the eye socket, ancient
and dark in the low grass, the lips like the cusp of a moon bud,
flowering into pus and stain when you pass with big book in your
back pocket.

   In the drum and pump of air there are mysteries and moments
of death repeated infinitely. Dog and man is one. Old man,
another one. Muse, skid around by Jerningham Avenue in
Belmont, run backyard, and the drama school there, thatched
with palm, where bare feet dance upon the hard packed earth.
Clary brother Oban ghost had eyeglass in top pocket, and a slide-
rule tucked under his arm as he moved from room to room. See
him there, eyelid heavy in the bedroom that infest with the scent
of salted fish and death between the thighs – the flesh of Ma
Mamin, unwashed and dying on a country bed, predicting snow
on sea-swept islands. She have people running down giddy from
she dying room to say she prophesy. Mamin say there are regions
uphill, religious prisons, yards where dogs are tied with endless

rope, far cousins who are blacker and closer to the sun, people who are yet to reinvent themselves, living in some primitive hell, toting water up from stand pipe, green calabash trees and mud. Black milk in their blood.

This is what you see: my two-three cattle, my goat, my chickens, my swine, my axe and slaughtering table. But I does lean back in my easy chair and see when things shift in the sky, upwards in that science of silence. You come with big book in your back pocket, but your spirit dark. Check your navel, is your navel you must check. Once, in Santa Cruz, I saw a circling light high above the tallest ridge of Sambocaud village. Was a space-ship, no doubt. I counted fifty-seven circles it turned until it faded. It have a house full of cousins higher up mountainside, so high you need spaceship to reach. Under the stilt house, a family of six been living there since the big man sore foot implode and burst him down on a hospital bed, to suck air and moan. In this bivouac full of children, black bodies collide in the heat. Rice grains lie in silken bile upon the ground. The young girl have to bathe on a sheet of galvanise. What is life for them? The spring water clean and cold, but they have to pass snake standing upright like man in the track leading to the riverside, defying you to pass your pass.

The agouti is lanced with a spear then shorn of fur over the fire. This house of paraffin and this one of linoleum. This place of spells and fetishes, of sacred heart and goblet and oil of asafoetida, lies up among the slack fronds of the date palm tree and the Jack Spaniard's nest. Things are hard: no bread, no flour to fry, mosquito staggering by the latrine door to kill you with sting. You come with your tank on your back to spray for yellow fever mosquito in dirty drain, stagnant pool, but mosquito still singing in people ears. Come now, Christophene Boy, you running to see the tank on the man back? It shape like a space parachute but is larvicide in there. Cousin Alvin build a house, lay down concrete, he do foundation, but the work very rachifee. Let him build, let him turn his spade, it will never stand. But don't watch Alvin slight, he have the seppy, the family history.

Muse, orchid and octopod. Forever accumbent upon the bottom of the boat to drift to far islands, sybaritic, asleep on the dark sea. Tell them I up here, with good heart and broken teeth, not jealous of the neighbour for the paint on her jalousie, or the ram goat that plough seed through rainy season. Walk up the side, past the burial ground. Past the throne room of the emperor – them latrines there dry and hard below and moulded into earth with shit. Wet them down with urine from the old woman chamber pot. Clary built her a plywood throne with a hole to piss and pass numbers through, but she hardly used it. All that invalid age waiting for you. Sickness. Water. Mumble. Groan. Red lavender and orange peel tea. Let me cut the neck of swine and cattle up here, let me hang them up to drain dry, leave me to mind my business, leave me to write. I done see what coming and I fraid. Alvin house falling, like a box of sticks. Friends leave him to suffer, only family will help him pull it back up. Oban was a ghost who moved from room to room, while grown men flung their heads back and laughed on the veranda, and the night was deep and impenetrably dark, and the sandfly bite, the trees fell asleep, and the moon disappeared in that space between drum

and

beat.

26

The killer in the incense taxi throws a shoelace around the driver's neck near Bingham Drive where Mother Mamin lived, up beside the quarry. The car skids off the road and runs into an abandoned cocoa field; the driver's throat bursts into scowls and snuffling breath; a gnashing of metal and vapour hissing, the car pushing through bush, the driver trying to dig the dull blades of his nails into his neck to prise up the black and tight tourniquet. Something there, tight-tight, make it move, stop it stop! Look how Basil come upon him, sudden and rapacious; he didn't knock. The driver presser foot pumping the X till his shoe peel off; the other foot trembles with fear. The poor fella overweight; piss pools in his crotch, the eyes fling up, the tongue stiff with panic. He grunts down to die in the blackness of the mountains, where the blinking lights of bachelor huts are shut with wire, in these dead man hours, eventually to crash into a bacano tree, the back wheel skidding.

The driver was pragmatic. On Sunday nights he beat his wife, then in grief he would walk out into the village and bring her back a box of fried chicken, and fling that on the bed. On Saturdays he would wash his dread and take his outside children to the kung fu matinees at Gem Cinema. During the week he made beef and potato pies, cheese patties sprinkled with pepper dust, currant rolls and hot mango soup to sup. He would set up his stall outside the steam laundry by the bridge – the same laundry where Madam Bruce does be. His name was Mikey, but people knew him as the Pie Man, and at lunchtime he rode his wicker basket of pies to air-conditioned insurance and accountant offices in the little town of the abattoir, the Chinese bakery and old Ackbarali's haberdashery. At night, Mikey became a stunt and race-car rider, pulling bull – what they call unlicensed taxi – speeding along the empty roads from the Croisee to deepest Santa Cruz, over humps and holes, rising and falling, crossing rickety bridges, pot hole and dead dog in the road, through bamboo plantation, jumbie symposium, while his wife was at home, straining her eyes to study shorthand and bookkeeping by candlelight, plotting to build a better life, cockset coil burning under the table to frighten mosquitos.

The Pie Man in his incense taxi groans, makes agonising moans, the car shaking the tree with such terror in the bush, the engine spinning, the pistons grinding – with parts cannibalised and tender from other broken engines. He worries, in his hour of need, that the fan-belt might burst, that the crank might fall out, the head gasket blow – is big money to fix that, my lord, to skim the rim, and body work so expensive, his livelihood, oh gorm, his exoskeletal and superhero costume for carnival to make, money for paint and glue, and the sweet tonka bean heart of his grandmother weeping, the fish falling out the bucket, all that fading, sweet Jesus, somebody will find his porn. He fight up with the shoelace, but he only cutting his own neck with his fingernails, so in this vibration and knowing what coming, he tries to subtract himself from the scene, to release his grip on life, so his head falls forward to the centre of the steering wheel. Then the horn booming out in this obscure landscape, this curious hinterland, the valley of the shadow of homicide, where his cries take too long to penetrate the darkness, flung far from the homes of poor folk asleep under the gru gru bef trees. Restless in his grief, he feels himself falling through an eternity of flutter and suspense, drowning down in that forever water, weeping for the world above. There is no peace in this drop, no salvation, no bosom for succour. The windpipe flails; cold air on the teeth, the bulbous eyes; the body grows weak. Is meat. His armpits are pits of funk. His breath reeking sulphur, his eyes half closed, still peeping. But the world has ended. He has died many small deaths before, but this one is worries. Release the accelerator and the engine shudder and whine, but it stop. Even death have to stop.

The killer in that incense taxi flees into the night, runs through the tall bush, crosses the river, runs through the pan yard. Raphael hears the splash from far away; he is writing upon his rickety stool. Poised with his pen, at the moment of the Pie Man's last breath and starry gaze, he hears the wailing and the rattle in the throat, the roiling of the body as it collapses, the red cord stretched, snapping, relinquishing its corpus and scent, spiralling out towards the infinite, to darkness. He writes that down. He comes to his window to peep, sees the shifting of wind and the imprint of destruction in the cocoa bush. He imagines the meat losing muscle and the slowed whirring of the brain, imagines the dead somebody face, twisted in disbelief and fear. Someone else will find the body, someone hunting iguanas – maybe Alvin, brushing through the overgrowth with a cutlass. He will smell piss. He will nudge the body but hesitate to lift the head from the steering wheel. Instead, he will look in the corpse pocket for verification that is really the Pie Man who dead. He will see from the driver's licence that the Pie Man lied about his age, that he was born near where the writer carves meat and sits on his veranda, scratching the underside of his knee, while the wind blows up from the ocean below. He will see that the Pie Man never have licence to drive taxi, much less to pick up madman and get strangle with a shoelace, to crash deep in a gully, in abandoned old colonial cocoa bush, the mud down there so black and putrefying.

27

Luke shelters in the awning of the ice shop. He has trained his body to withstand stress and wait for water to pass. Abandoned by his mother – but how come the same mother bawling to keep him close? When woman give away children, they don't bray so, but the further she carry him down Ramkissoon Trace that brittle afternoon, the wider her terror grow, like cancer, or hole for urinary catheter – *that they insert* – though that far June she was not to know how she herself would die – *with no anaesthesia*. Luke appeared fearless, bearded, so primitive in gesture that he ate steak with a spoon and spat the gizzard out. He had long left behind the mundane ambitions of less successful protagonists. It is true that once a country bookie rubbed a wasp nest in his eye and, when the time came to fight, Luke was reticent and shy with the instruments of death, but let us not imagine that Luke, taken on this pilgrimage to the palm-swept shores of the island's oldest copra plantation, was not aware of his own character, of his own arc and driven river, of his own strength in this struggle over his portion of the plot. He had run away from the big book, as he had run away from an orphanage, with no motive besides the urge to run until his free paper burn. No, Luke not stupid.

The rain paused and he moved further east to a village beside the sea. There, in a clearing, in an amphitheatre of grass and bony rock, a stage had been raised and a saxophonist, wearing a white cotton shirt, a black silken tie, and blue wasp-waist trousers, was leading his quartet through a modal version of Ron Berridge's 'Afro Lipso'. Luke sits down on a big stone, watching as water ran from the outcrops, seeing the ibises, in watercolour-red, standing knee deep, foraging in the tender grass. The saxophonist stood boldly upright to blow his horn, and the sound was flung up against the sky. He came now with another tune, 'Weariness of the Blues' – long-worn suffering, as wise as jazz. The saxophonist wept and spoke notes from the bell. Luke sat on the promontory and watched the band. The drummer's kick could be felt in the earth, and the bass man was Daddy Stone. Expect magic. The sun began slowly to reveal its brightness upon the waterlogged land. On the other side of the amphitheatre, high on its *summa cavea*, Luke saw the Great Bandit rise from his seat, and dust off his arse. The Bandit seemed to stare directly across the arena at Luke. Is light years it taking, but when that eye reach, it piercing. The Bandit begin to examine the gap between them, he want to bridge the distance, he want to see his friend. The saxophonist shakes the spit from his horn, then plays Lord Blakie's 'Maria', but angular, dread. By now the Great Bandit's malice was motivated by wickedness – besides his desire to unravel the secrets Luke kept. Though it remained his remit to pursue the protagonist, he was now damn vex and primarily concerned with separating Luke's gizzard from his navel. He felt disrespected; he want to be star boy, too. His leap across the valley was ferocious, the black cape sailing up, the fingers extending into claws, the mouth snarling. Luke brace to fight, but change his mind and tack back uphill along the cliff face and gully drop, high above the shores of a mighty ocean, tumbling and hissing out its lung. The Great Bandit alight hard in Luke's path with a power that shook the mourning ground. The big man laugh, his face half in shadow under the loquacious brim of his ten-gallon hat, which he pinched at the tip in the Cuban style. They both lingered in the gaze awhile, as the surf roared below them. Then the Bandit flung his first callous blow, a balled chain flinging out, determined to tangle and pop, and it hit Luke frankomen on his jaw. Thunder shook again, rain, but the sun remained hard in the sky.[9] To tangle with the younger man, the Bandit must task out his weaponry. So he bring rope, rope with a hook this time. Luke must now be agile. He cannot depend on his skill as a dan in shotokan; the Bandit is more experienced in martial arts, and he ox-strong and bitter in the mouth. He know big stone and kick up, even kick up with cutlass, but he know shotgun too. Luke jump down, like to run off the road to avoid head-on collision, like driving in Tobago one

9. The Devil and his wife, Miss Bruce were fighting for a hambone.

time when he uses to smoke. Better jump than be beat upon by the faster blade. But the Bandit fuffle him up with the rope and tie him in several knots. Then he dragging him behind like a sack of wheat, or a sloth caught on land; he carry him down to a basement shebeen, where the sea seep into stone in the back of Los Iros Bay. He mean to crush Luke to must, to open the great lies and locks of prose and plot, to reveal how a butcher, on such a hill, who matriculate from no college or creed, who read no Carpentier, Brodber or Susanne Césaire, and yet could sculpt a book which pressed against the limits of the infinite, a book which held them both as within prison walls. By torturing secrets from the younger man, the Great Bandit hoped to free himself from his own arc and death within the parameters of the pages the old man wrote and those he was yet to write, a text which kept solid and true to the way things went, as plot and thesis, as villain, or hex or ciphers unseen by western causality, from the perils of good, and the processes of evil, to dash 'way Hemingway and Henry James, and praise Earl Lovelace instead.

28

The orderlies at St Robinson's wear faded white overalls and plastic shoes. They shuffle along the gleaming hallways, where death is the hardness of the waiting-room chair, the cold and dirty light that fills each corridor and room, and the sickening and constant scent of burnt milk and black disinfectant. In one white cubicle, stifling in the heat of the emergency department, is a battered machinist. Someone broke his mouth with an axe handle and left him to pulp and bleed on a brewery floor, the incisors pushed up towards his brain. In the next cubicle, a Barbadian grandmother is leaning to one side to pull down her underwear from where it stick up between her business. Doctor just tell her both legs have to cut. Jeez-an-ages – sugar in her blood, worries in the good morning. She nods in agreement, but when he leaves and pulls closed the curtain, she wrings her hands and weeps. When they come to cut her feet, she begs Jesus, but he never really response. She swallow hard and her chest get hot, making a picture in her head of the stumps. After they cut them, they incinerate the fat of her calves – after all them years of walking hillside and gully drop with a bucket, so much coconut oil and bay rum she sap them foot with, now all that history get burn in this foreign place. The doc who do the cut is from Turkey; he want to take his mind elsewhere, to regenerate his spirit from that dismal space, but he have to climb the stairs to see another patient, sweet Lionel. Hernia is his jail, gallstones in his passageway; he can't cross his leg. In such rooms, the gloom of diagnosis and prognosis, the grinding of teeth and the stiffening of bone is too much for the doctor to bear.

The actor lies on a white bed staring up at the ceiling in a quiet room on the fourteenth floor of the hospital. If she is still she can train her ear to hear the murmurs and tinkling sounds as they rise from floors below. She remembers her mother, how in her last years her right knee was replaced with a box of glass; the liquid in it was black and would tilt like a spirit-level when she bent the bone, but she cracked her shin so often on the blades of concrete stairs – with just a suffocating moan – that it eventually grew brittle and shattered into islands. Ella is trying to construct her own precious history, precarious in the boroughs of her unconscious, away from the determinations of causality. She wants to remember the old man in the corner house burning a guava tree to a stump; how, when she appeared in the yard, peeping among the low-hanging branches and the leaves of the shy barbadine vine, she witnessed the killing of that guava tree – its breath in ash, its branches torn, its heart dug out and burnt. Sudden so, in this yard, between the plum tree bark and the lime, she grew years ahead in that moment. So much was gone.

The hospital's noise is constant – a radio dial tuning, the sharp and wounded cry of an outlaw, the sharp moan as a scalpel nudges a thighbone, a telephone ringing, a door flung open, a bed pan falling and spilling swill and surgical instruments, latex plucked like a string. They have found nothing wrong with her body. The doctor refers her to Paganini's *Third Concerto for Violin*, he refers her to the psychiatric department where they give her citalopram.

From her window, she sees the male public baths across the street, where the cold floors and tiled cubicles are stained with the damp musk of men broken to water by the indifference of the city. But hear what happen once. One night, returning to New York from Chicago, snow thick on the ground, trains had shut down frozen on all lines into Manhattan, passengers fought for taxis at the airport. She shared the backseat of a taxi with a writer who had arrived in the city for a conference at Rutgers, and they drove through Forest Hills in the snowfall, while the driver sang along to his Shirelles cassette. She asked the writer where he was staying. Next tune was his room on the 22nd floor, Broadway, West 23rd, unpacking each other like luggage, while the bagel factory in the street below rolled out more dough and the yellow snow trucks growled away the drifts. She still remembers his touch, how light it was, how tender, but also the heat of his tongue. She remembers his black notebooks, his cheap suit, that

87

he wore cowboy boots and had come from Philadelphia with his new book in his back pocket.

Leaving the hospital, Ella travels to Harlem, where her friend has made matzo ball soup. They sit at the kitchen table to eat. But Ella shivers, her feet are cold. Then her knees are deep in a swamp; in water thick with lichen and the tender polyps of bugs and moss. Night whistles in the trees, the frogs trill and speak their stuttering song. She is walking into a storm, further into the swampland, the water rising around her, snakes wrapped around her thighs, old swamp smell – dead leaves, eel, the terror of the deep, pale glow of the moon. The water gurgles, the cool breeze ripples. She is sinking into an abyss, but she is laughing, her head flung back in defiance. Light does not penetrate water at this depth. Here, there are red lava coves where the skull of the earth was burst to mollusc and germ, the craters of the abyssal zone, the viperfish and loa of turtles and snakes. Her lungs find air pockets and damp seclusions, they find wind in the bucket of her gut, in the filament of sea fish. She surrenders, sinks and contemplates the pleasures of the deep, the apparition of sleep.

29

Melchior gave us the seppy on Bain. He was gutting trevally, then he wipe his hand on his pants and say, 'People say he kill a man, Raphael brother, Bain. You know Bain was the darker brother; he suffer; he never went to school; he was a delinquent fella. Bain get a work with Mr Tom; he working construction on the highway, till he beat a snow-cone vendor and Tom hit him two slap and put him to work as a labourer on the university he was building. Then Bain start to behave a little better. He was young, and making money. He drove a green Opel Kapitän, with a red target mark on the roof – till he ride that car over a precipice near Maracas. He helped to build the university library, but he uses to thief the books them scholars import – books of Eden's apocrypha, bibles of imagination, tall American science and sociology book, with pictures of fair-skinned American children, dogs kicking back mud on them in wheat, but never sugarcane. Bain uses to pack these books in his father's house in Mount Garnett Yard, that same house the old man refuse to mortgage to buy motorcar for Bain, a few years later, to support the insurance salesman con that Bain was scheming to thief his head with. Bain try his hand, but the old man catch that the vehicle Bain begging him to buy was really for him to ride around town like a saga boy, park up in bush to smoke tampi and get woman high enough to give him shine. When the old bull get to find out, he leggo wood in Bain arse. He uses to bat those boys so ridiculous in that muddy pen, the man duck uses to stand up watching.'

'Is so?' a young man ask.

Melchior nod, 'Yes, man, is so. Once, the old bull even pull a gun on Bain. Was to shoot him, hard. But Bain say, "Shoot, then. Shoot!" And the old man back away. Bain was bad like crab; he was like a mango-headed jumbie in the garden, a leaning-on-the-fence-like-a-thief-kinda man with rings on eight fingers. After that, he worked in the sewage waterworks, then in the brewery, until he and the super get away, as you know, and he bat the man bad and get sent home. He pull a blade on a police in south, bust a schoolboy scalp with a river stone, spend six months in jail, but come out badder than scorpion sting. One carnival, he planarse a reveller – he meant to slap the man with the flat side, but he cut him. The man was a well known badjohn from south, but he humble down. Bain start to crack plan, plain as black, to thief brick black people was stacking to build with, but then spirit lash make him lose his zeal and ambition in life, so he shave his head and cut down all the trees in his yard.

'But every Carnival he there. He was there at Memorial Square, that legendary Carnival Tuesday in 1974. He was the one who said, "I like the mas when it pretty, but ah doh like when fellas does fight." I tell you, it was Bain who say that. In those days, carnival was real fire. In them days, things would be simple sequin, red feather, wire and dragon mas; people would be chipping cool to brass, then just so the tension would build, and the air would burn dry and heavy. Long time, carnival was licks like fire, not like now the spirit gone. Hear me. We stand up on the side, fellas from the hill. Sun and dust in the street, the vision hazy, the vibration charge. Sudden so, glass start to rain and crash, was lash/lash/lash/lash/lash. The crowd start to scamper. Men who selling orange get table turn over. I hear Bain say, "Fight…," but the way he say it was, like, casual, like, "I did tell you, see…," and we step back some bit, and we in the park deeper now, further away from where the battle raging. Brother, blood and pepper was bursting on the Tarmac. Men in that gayelle was barebacked and flinging bottle, big stone, rope, cutlass blade. They was moving swift and strange in that chamber of violence and confusion. But the brass band stay blasting from the music truck, hard-hard-hard, and the iron man hand was beating fast-fast-fast, and the drummer never drop the beat. Is blood carnival come from, is muscle and blood and fire, is bad man like Legba who build this vibration, is Ma Erzulie who throw powder, so fight does only sweeten the rhythm and blood does season the road. Is nothing, is no problem, let them fight if they want to.

'Bain was rugged in the pick-up, his head thrown back, a

cigarette buzzing between his lips, sometimes with the fellas, holding on to the splintered truck back on the swaying road to the beach, to walk out cool as dusk, knee-deep in the water at Williams Bay, where even a mile out it was just gradually deep.

'In middle age, Bain lingered east. No seed he plant ever sprout, so eventually he renovate the derelict shack his mother left him before she dead, the one she built beside the river when this hill was new, when the mud was ripe. But Bain head not good. He will play cards with the villagers, he will help his brother butcher swine and billy goat, he will even expose hog throat to slit and hook it up to drain the blood into good black pudding; he will divide the meat while the vision hot, but if you get him mad, he will cook and curry your gut, and get away with it.'

The young boy say, 'Is so?'

'Yes, man, is so.'

And something in the image of the blood-dripping meat make the young boy totee get hard in his pants.

Gristle, green like malachite, on the ground from the motorbike crash. The road smeared with corpuscles and bone. The big truck butt the bike like a bull and the rider was dragged from his seat and flayed like beaten meat on the Saddle Road. Something about that junction was death. Between the kick-up cinema and Sangarali's General Shop was a zone of imminent and senseless death, of silent absences, like a wound in time that is soon resealed and forgotten. Plenty people get shoot in that triangle. Big bandit get bore up like strainer; bad police get slap and, many years after the motorbike rider get grind, a steel beam thrust from a hardware truck, shoot loose and pierce a church woman's skull between her eyes, and her car run off the road and into the pet shop and explode. The steam laundry was in that junction, and the green river running beside it. Moss and lush bamboo growing like fire where people throwing rice and washbasin water, till the dirt there get permanently slippery and bright. Was right there in that junction that the Pie Man used to sell his beef and potato pies until he get strangle in the cocoa bush. Upon this particular stretch of Presbyterian road, poor people would be buying lottery ticket in search of fortune, Melchior, would be cutting grouper neck, and telling story till your ear wax melt and run out. Further inside that region, the lens of fiction does seldom reach. In there, deeper and more extensive than cartographer or nice camera can capture, people have a whole community set up for shop, snackette, rum bar and self-government. The place timeless, and it stay so since, and now same how still. Look. Men still plotting revolution; woman selling hemp on the corner; dreadlocks bumping; a young girl washing wares and bathing with truck-borne water, then she disco leg pumping out in hot pants – leggo fire – ites, green and gold.

Once, the musician was walking through the Croisee, down

from the river, hiding between glances, pretending that nothing happen, so no one would notice the way his trousers stick to his thighs, that it wasn't dark brown cloth but wet the khaki get wet. He running with the rebels from stone that pelting from some distant veranda to crack their skulls and run them from there. He fall in water but keep running. Who get hit? Who head bust? Who put Aming on a rock and rub stinging nettle on his prick? Who name call? Which one gut get big from stew beef, and when he catch himself, he working security and grinding malice for thirty years? Run us down to the riverless bridge, to the cemetery on the hill, to the water that leads to the sea, as all rivers do on this island.

Was Melchior who tell us what really happen with the motorbike rider: 'The blood still on the ground, and true talk, the gristle smell like meat, meat that cut and open red, and the corpse still on the truck bed, and people gathering around like kine around a well – restless, fraught, whispering to the body, but really to themselves, asking what it like, this thing, to dead? The rider's body is twisted in supplication, moaning in the flesh and touching the spirit, whipped by the black pitch road.' This was the musician's childhood, among the Baptist flags, bright yellow and red, bamboo creaking in the sun, the devil asleep in the bush, the ambulance arriving too late.

In San Juan, there were several cinemas, from stall to pit, Saturday matinee. Gem had the poultry slaughtery next door, so when kung fu kick miss, it cutting cock neck. And everyone knew that on Wednesdays at the Ritz, the triple X show used to come sudden, hidden inside some detective film, reveal the cunny and balls, the white flesh. Men came there to masturbate in the wooden regions of pit, cum splashed on camouflage jackets. Those cinemas, the river, Jimmy Cliff, parsad, jalebi and gulab jamun, the cow gut that get wash in that market, all these images, detached from their chronology, found themselves transposed to the squeaking of his reed.

He had awoken from the living dream of the islands and found himself under-dressed, in an unlined gabardine jacket, at some metropolitan airport, to start a second life. In the bitterness of winter, he was part of the migrant's familiar story. The heat in his body would last several days, the lungfuls of breath he had saved in his armpits would sustain him until he broke and wept for the island he had left, wept for his history, for his people, for the uncertainty of his future. He made long-distance phone calls just to hear the wavering sound of Sister Syl's voice. Years before this dream of flight was painted, he had been in Independence Square and overheard a man on a pay phone saying, 'Hello, Mammy? I'm in Port in Spain...in Trinidad.' For years, this memory remained as the seed of something inspiring, till it was him saying the same thing. The beautiful sorrow of exile, the salt on the tongue. Making his way through the metropolis, he bore out winter with a fading palette of tropical gestures. He kept them until the wind warmed and pools in parks trickled with life once more.

He travels with his horn upon his back, the bell bent, etched with scars and scrapes, but its clarion sounds blow as if he stands upon some distant hill. He has raided and devoured the un-guarded barn of Europe, its open junkyard, taking what he could carry, knowing that one day death would find him in one of these bars or dubious halls and basements where jazz was flung upon the city and forgotten. He made his way, finding the tune, his frequency, learning the ways of the city, its rules, the language of bodies and sexual energy, intensities emerging, extending out to brightness.

Arriving at the Grand Hotel in Nice, the musician notices the palm trees along the Avenue Gustave, the familiarity of their whitewashed trunks. He tilts his head back to glance at the white verandas overlooking the boulevard. But entering the lobby, he shivers, suddenly cold, sways, and falls to the red carpet. He falls sideways, and his eyes are flung back upon his brain, and everything fades to white, and it seems that all sound and sentience has been sucked into the oriel of his skull. Who will find him inside there? Who will place their healing hands on his head? Who will open their faith and blush like a ghost?

The band place his unconscious body on a soft chair in the lobby and, fan me saga boy fan me, he returns to them. He speaks, but his words seem to be travelling vast distances to reach his lips. He is able to walk unsteadily to the lift, held up by the bassist. Later, falling awake in a soft chair in his room, he suddenly remembers his horn and the concert he must play that night. If the band catch him dying on this road – wow – crapaud smoke their pipes. These men have rent to pay and wives who want duty-free chocolate; they have children to buy snow globes for. The bassist brings him sparkling water from the mini bar, and he leans forward to drink. He will regain himself, but his arms are heavy, like the arms of a farm boy who has been baling bush and milking cattle all day, like bull-work jumbie, like Dennis, who ran away from the orphanage and, after roaming through the bamboo all over Arima and Sangre Grande, came to rest on the banks of the Valencia River, where Doris and Francis Gray set up their little bovine farm beneath a coppice of turpentine mango trees. It was them who find Den-Den by the river, this sugar-haired manchild with the forehead of a bull cow, whose tongue was made of rubber, and take him in. This was Wallerfield: heat of slate tiles, the salt lick, bent weathered wood.

Heat rising in his body, fever of fear, the musician senses that death is sharpening his toes. He retrieves his gleaming horn from its case and sucks the reed, then he waxes and attaches the mouthpiece to the neck, the neck strap to the clip and hangs it around his neck. Puff, but he only hissing air. Distemper in his mouth to blow, pure pressure needed now to break the cage of this lethargy. Try he try, but the power gone. How long has he been asleep? Hours? But it is only four pm. The sunlit boulevard below is still full of tourists. Across the street the sand still has waves that crash onto it; the beach still claims its sunbathers and swimmers. The pool below his window is a perfect sky blue, though there are no bathers in the pool; they lounge on chairs at the edge of it. Above, he sees the faraway factories and ateliers, the white metal bellies of aircraft circling at the airport on the Côte d'Azur. How long has he been so weary? How long has he been wounded? How long has he been so utterly alone? He falls asleep again and wakes just before the pick-up time. No one has to call him down from his room. He is there in the lobby with his sax on his back, ready to leave at six pm.

The van rolls along the avenue to a steep cliff above the sea where the stage is set, wind billowing the tarpaulin that covers it. The waves below are layers of dull undulating blades. To dive in would be to drown, to die and become lung and splintering sound. But he returns to the band, to test the lines; all is regular once more.

Cold sweat moan and he cannot blow hard. Just check the mic and if the mic sound good, then it good. During their set he plays as if possessed, reeling and wailing, jutting from the hip and gut, throwing his head back, bending his body parallel to the ground, losing his eyes in the sound. He blows leaping tongues of flame, but then collapses near the end of his blues, and falls, and his horn cracks to the floor; it tumbles like any old iron falling, but the horn still blowing out sound, and not just sound but fire, and not just fire but blackness, modulating and modal, and the cry folding into feedback. The audience gasps. Something in that sound is pure suffering. They know the metal in the horn is inanimate, but they feel that through it the soul of a man has burst before them, upon this ragged altar where musicians sacrifice themselves, expose themselves, open their hearts and pour out freedom, like poets reaching back to the heat of some childhood sorrow that bury like a seed and too hard to reach, or leaning forward to drown in sin and pleasure so that the world may know what such things are, but it coming out surreal.

Afterwards, what must they do? What must they eat? Bread, grapes, milk and honey, lemon, olives, saucisson; or rum, good cowfoot soup, hard food, boiled turkey and pineapple? They are weeping at the well. They have been hidden in the chill of European winters. They suffer shoulder pain and ignore it, till their hearts burst like gas-fired geysers and they are found dead in the rooms where they hid. Tomorrow his horn must be mended. This is his narcotic prayer. For now, he will rest in his room and wait for her. She will arrive from the other side of the world to soothe him with her kisses. They will lie together where only the star from the blinking neon H★tel sign outside the window illuminates them. They will lie together and listen to Chet Baker: *Italian Soundtracks.*

32

The land there was parched and obzocky. Amid arid grass, there was the scent of goat shit and the buzz of sandflies and bush bugs. Beyond, among the trees, bamboo jungle and vines, a silver river flashed. A thick riot of bees was circling a wound in the water. The sound led Raphael to the corpse and scented spirit of a wild boar that had staggered with fever for several days through overgrowth and ravine weed with worries on its heel. Its ghostly pursuer, a figment of the boar's brain, not lancing the plane of sight, nor piercing a hole in the knots and vowels of the wild boar's thigh, had waited patiently until the boar fell heavy with a selfless sigh, like a poem with no words, but with density of motion and lung, as it slid down the mud. Wayward roots jutting out of the savage earth snarled the skin, broke the sickly ribs, and opened the wound there to fester and lock, till the boar succumbed to air, and it was left to pulp and rot, for maggot to eat it out at the riverside. And so the boar became blood and gristle, rancid protein in the gut, eventually to marinade the earth with its blood and piss, to fertilise with its flesh, to give bush growth and succour for jungle rat and terrapin to suck. In this way the wild boar lived on, Raphael thought, in some form.

Up among these trees and thick bush, there were no eyes to shame, so Raphael sometimes walked naked upriver, through the eddies and the sudden rush of water pouring over rocks or beside the brackish pool where young men had repeatedly drowned, drunk, at birthday river limes. They would set up a boom box beside a three-stone fireside, and the pot there black with hot pepper and curry. Eventually, a young man would venture where the river bank was slippery, his bare foot slipping at an angle, the ankle in the mud – members don't get weary – then the water filled the liver, the lungs bursting like grapes, the toes pressed out in rage.

This spot is not far from where, as a young man, Raphael had foolishly planned to build an ajoupa from which to cultivate the land, or a bivouac to elope to, a dojo to train in like a Shotokan monk, or an ashram to hide in on the mountainside, to meditate on shrub and spiny forests, and how everything perpetually transforms. He did not choose where the land was tall with rainforest trees – which had been there since there were rainforests, land that was mint and soft green. He chose where the scorpion is seated on its throne, and the man-crab waits in his hole with both eyes swinging, and the silver fish scampers to hide from the sun when it spans its blazing gaze upon the earth. Here, beyond the river's way, there is no saddle of rain, no ease, not even a thighbone from the chair his mother sat on, or an underlung socket from the stool the blessed mourners would collapse upon after transcending their physical forms to walk across the desert and return with secret colours and gifts, and then re-enter the body through the umbilicus with black secret technology.

There is a cool recess between the trees, and there are snakes in the Spanish cedar tree and, further up into the bush, there are the ruins of cocoa plantations, rusty bridges, panyol traditions, skeletons of ox and bull fox, razor grass, laglee holding the feet of corn birds to the bough, their wings fluttering, and old verandas overlooking the sea. When he reach, the chained mansion on the ridge was shut, guarded by dogs.

He begins to write.

It was a Saturday afternoon in July 1985. Two boys sat in the tall caïmite tree. Seen from those branches, the southern plains extended to the heat mirage of oil refineries and, beyond, to the Atlantic ocean. The treetops were cool and dreamy within the vision, but the hog plum and the green mammy apple was sour and not good to eat. The boys filled their bags with caïmite fruit, green mangoes, balata, chenet, tamarind and ripe cocoa. There were white flowers, matapal, quenk, the creaking of timber, and the river rolling past in its own sweet way. The house of doors was open. Night fell. The sky down deep west was a colour that had yet to be named.

In Cane Farm Junction, women were cussing in the rum shop; the maxi taxis were booming dancehall as they passed along the

Eastern Main Road, making the round trip to the mall, or as far east as Arima. Life was good. It was Saturday night, but it could have been the Friday before. The souse woman was selling pickled pigs-feet from a white bucket, as was the black pudding man with blood and plenty pepper.

Night in the village of Macoya: the itch of insect bones and bush bugs, the smell of burnt oil frying fish in terrazzo kitchens; and upwards Five Rivers jungle, salt biscuits and coffee were being passed around at a nine nights wake for a stevedore. A boy sat on the bus-route wall eating black pudding from a brown paper bag. When the first scorpion pepper hit him he buck.

'Tell him come. I will wait for him, my brother, my true-true blood. I rolled herb in brown paper guma-guma, I licked it sweet with a kiss. I rolled from country to town. I was never caught shoplifting. But, once, I stabbed a boy on Frederick Street, with a flick blade, simple so it dip smooth into the swooning flesh of his arm. I ran, but my body was heavy; I could hardly carry it. I carried the knife in a green canvas bag, slung across my shoulder. I flung the blade singing down the drains under the city. True east is up, the hills are burning.

Run.'

33

Luke chewed the wood pigeon wing and two bones came out. The woman in the house of wind and light caressed his shoulders with her one good hand as he sat to eat at her table. Her nightgown parted when the wind blew, to cool the dark flesh of her thighs. Edith. Yes, one hand ended in a stump, tied in a knot at the elbow, but she was gifted with the other hand. Her man was gone for weeks, working on a schooner that put out to sea to ship cotton and yam to the archipelago of islands, so doors could fling open and young men could lay their bodies on hers. They could be brought to her house and be sat upon and quenched, they could drink lime juice and eat fish or wood pigeon wing. But Luke was tired. He leaned back in the chair and rolled his hand around his gut. He belched with a bitter bray. The shimmering heat of day was fully risen; soon, the Great Bandit would find him. After the concert in the amphitheatre in the grassland, and the flight of locusts and the lashing of the Great Bandit's sting, Luke had slipped out of each knot the Bandit had tied him in, so even plot couldn't hold him down. There were secrets Luke had indeed thought to tell the Great Bandit, but first he want to walk down the dark path and leggo water come back. Then he run away and bush cut him up. Fever grass, and all flesh is grass, and the flowers of the field are to be cut and burnt, the vision to be etheric in the burning day. All this had already happened.

Edith was a spiritual woman. One time, while playing slavery games in the seamstress shop, showing Miss Thelma how their ancestors used to rock the lower deck with arms entwined and singing sea hollers, Edith buck and catch power. She bawl and twist like ball of twine and it wasn't no holy trick that hold her; was genetic backslap she get in her motherarse.

Now she cleared the table. She toasted flour for porridge and fed the seven man-spiders in her rafters honey and milk. Stretching, she exposed a weeping sore she was hiding on her shin bone; if you see it, pus bursting like rain, like a wound in wood that never healed since she slipped and gashed it, spiritually, on the edge of the pew one Sunday in Teacher Gizzard's church on Mendez Drive. She returned to the table with the porridge, and watched the saga boy sip, standing beside him in her morning clothes smelling of coal tar soap and perfumed flesh. You laugh? Edith could wine like a genie when she must, and she could pray like a saint when she had to. She smoked her herb wrapped in brown paper, meditated when night came, walked out among the carnal dahlias and the whistling of the ceboletta onion. On this morning she was rubbing Luke's shoulders and looking out towards the road.

Luke had drawn his cards. He had deceived the Great Bandit, but he had not defeated him. Raphael had worked hard to hermetically seal the secrets of his text, the slippage and wound, the *mise en abyme* and multitudinous strands that only a book that taking forty-one years could hold. He built his house on stone, not sandy ground. Remember the chapel, remember the mud-brick room, the dirt-floor salvation, the long trees, snake walking like man. Remember when the Deacon had the grace of a dancer, casting spirits out, and then remember how once, in a burning house, Luke was allowed to come out unscarred by fire or burning brick, to come out alive and black in this kiss-me-arse place. The writing hand is a process of gap, and in this gap the liquid text emanates directly from the lung and neck, but what Raphael want to know is how to locate this gap within the simultaneity of islands?

Luke was sleeping on Edith's sofa, in the leather drawers he had stitched for himself, his shoes kicked off, one calf fling up on the sofa back like some Grenadian uncle, dead now, who drove a jitney and flirted with fancy women. This Uncle, Barry, felt he could flex, but his wife was bulling fellas regularly in the small corridor room they shared, with the peep holes in the plywood partition for neighbours to see through, and the cum-crusted wash rags under the bed.

Luke knew he could be five hundred miles away by tomorrow, if he travelled via tunnels built under the desert. But what if he should perish by wild Indian suicide in the deep heat of day, would his secrets be secure? Luke took a shine, he showered. He saw Edith's husband's slippers sat humble beside the bathroom, the shaving razor and foam, his little Drakkar Noir. Luke laugh. A woman came to Edith's door with *Watchtower* magazines, but watch how the serpent hand she hides have scales and plastic nails. The woman inquisitive, she peeping past Edith to see how the woman house set. She say, 'Maybe the man of the house would like to read these?' She want to know if a man *is* in the house. Could it be the Great Bandit – Luke wonder – in the guise of this woman, with her jungle breath and sudden eyes, the thin film of sweat she wipes with the back of her human hand, that look that means *come hither and dead*. But the woman turn sudden and gone like a bat. Edith fetch a bucket and dash away the doorstep with salt and paraffin; she disinfect that peccable spot, throw urine, witch broom, vinegar.

That night, Luke took his things and left. There were rocks in his passway, but he climbed the steep incline, past the marigolds, the zigar bush, the malomay. He made it to the coast, with coconut water in his knee.

34

The actor, Ella, myopic in the fog of dawn, afloat as a sigh, pale and grim in the dankness, notices that she stands before shop windows, notices that she stares blindly into displays of shining silver pans and coloured colanders, and then remembers that her consciousness is her own. She is in a seaside town. Imagine an iron rail and the bay below. Imagine a seascape where there are cormorants and gulls that swirl and stitch the sky with a fury of wings. She leans against the cold door of heaven, the frame crafted from dark oak, cold as the bench the memory-ghost of her father rests on, cold as the string of soapstone beads around the neck of her poltergeist, poised upon some distant hill, waiting to come down. Imagine the warmth of rooms where winter cannot penetrate. All these things she considers, but remembers them in fragments. She is walking along the ocean road, and the white tide is breaking on the rocks below, the jetty rocking in the splash, the sea grey and sharp like a black and white photograph of a cane field after the devil has chased colour from the earth. There is the sound of glass exploding on a concrete floor, the splatter of ruined fruit from the vinegar tree falling to the ground, the sound of water falling. She knocks on the door of heaven but it will not open. She is trapped in the village of her body, a vessel with its own volition. There are men gathered on the pier. Fog, the mouths of fish, cold wooden beams, stone, the sky pouring forth light in the white morning as if the layers of the infinite were parting.

The men on the pier are rebuilding the jetty. She observes their grey overalls, the barrels of their boots. What will happen to her body when she dies? Who will touch her feet? Will she become sound, sound which is the soul of all things, vibration and hum of earth, murmur and echo. What will become of her memory, of the way she moved through Pigale, perfumed and beautiful, swooning in the arms the musician? What becomes of the past? Is it folded in some quantum chamber in the akashic desert, or does it simply fade? This is the dream that keeps her awake. At the roundabout she crosses on the grass. She sees the looming tower of the cathedral, knows that some day it is bound to fall from the hill. The houses along the sea road are shut, shivering in the cold, dew on their iron gates, water on the ground.

A woman enters this road from a white bungalow. She has a handbag slung under her arm; its handle swings against her hip. She is a full woman in her mid forties who wears faded jeans and a white shirt. She hurries towards her life in the seaside town. Ella follows her, at a discreet distance. She observes the woman buy fruit at the covered market, buy meat from the Lebanese butcher, coffee from the supermarket. Something in the walk of this woman reminds Ella of Miss Daphne, a Grenadian domestic who would cross the savannah each day with a basket balanced on her head, as if she was parting the sea, with her arms keeping time and swinging to keep balance, walking tough to work to clean the rich folk houses on Second Avenue. Which particular house was a mystery for years, until she was seen entering the burglar-proofed house of the Sharpes on 10th Street corner. She work a day for a dollar. Years pass, and is this one piece of job Daphne have and hold on to, until something happen in that bungalow that put her back on the road.

But for now imagine Miss Daphne walking in the sun, walking through the savannah on her way to wash and clean; hear her humming her blues in the brittle heat, the dust whipping in tiny tornados against the bare sin of her skin. Daphne's own family kept pigs in pens behind a tall house in El Socorro. Some nights, when they were killing pigs, Daphne would go back there to drink Scotch and scheme. Round there was plenty mud and molasses, rum to piss, pig liver roasted on embers, delicate and rich in the mouth. Picture Daphne leaning back in the bloody yard with a glass of white rum and coconut water in her hand. She stand up beside the fireside where the men are charring the skin and roasting the gizzard. Hear the wailing of swine in that procession of drag, slit, slaughter.

105

Daphne had a daughter who was fairer than she. So much pride she have in this high yellow girl, red ribbon in her hair. She was all Daphne had in this too hot town, she was her luck. Some days the girl would be seen walking dumb behind her bandy-kneed mother. They never spoke and it was said the daughter was mute. By the time they appeared in the savannah, the two of them had walked from their humble timber home on the outskirts of the city, across the San Juan river – frantic with cascadura and cutlassfish – past the red-bricked governors' offices where rates and living licences were paid. The savannah was alive in those days with samaan trees and scarlet ibises. A white horse roamed there – dead now, shot for old age and jointed into segments right inside the manure pit. Then, later each day, coming back same way, with her money folded in two in her bosom, Daphne and her daughter would disappear into the crimson glare of dusk. This went on until one day Daphne came running down the avenue, with her daughter staggering the distance behind. Let the suffering house be opened, and the vision be cleansed. All things end. But sometimes the end is not an ending but a disappearance, and it is this that makes such things beautiful.

35

In those days the savannah was still a field of dreams. The musician had often walked out in the midday sun to sit under the samaan trees to practice his horn while the cattle grazed and red ants fought in the soft dirt in the undergrowth. He would lie on the same grass that the acrobat had pressed flat, and swing his horn to the sky – a flash of sound, the bell singing out in scales and triplets, clusters of notes. His embouchure was still the slack lip of wind hissing, but sudden so one day the puff would uncoil and start to pester the spirit and pierce the rubric of his own ear with solid sound. The old folks would smile at the boy with the ragged horn, the finger clip missing, the water key bent, though it would still dribble out spit, and he was learning. He took the horn to the parish fair, thought he could blow and was laughed at – the horn taken from his hand, in jest, and passed around above him. He was not tall enough, then, to reach the stilt-walking heights of the arms of men. When it was given back to him, the bow was sunk, the bell was bent and the neck was twisted. In those early years he tried to play Marley's 'Guava Jelly', after he'd heard it on the radio while lying across the leatherette seat of his grandfather's Austin Cambridge, being driven along the southern coast, past the thatched roofs of huts on the moonlit beach, taking his aunt and her husband to their honeymoon. He would forever remember that drive through coconut farms and untamed country, the sound of the waves crashing on the beach, and it seemed that this image, along with that of the sunlit savannah, with the white horse and the manure pit, the wide gasp of green lush and the scarlet ibises standing hip high among dew-wet grass, was the sonic poem he would forever aim to inscribe. The notes had to form the vision, the melody to make a portrait of a place he had long assumed to be precious yet impossible. He had, in his mind, painted these images several times, and yet he had not rendered them sufficiently real or tangible enough to remain etched or correlated in the nostalgic chapels of his generation. But without this wind of spirit and creation, he would unravel; the solid bone of his throat would be burst in a house of thunder and adultery.

He returned to the image of his grandfather dying in his easy chair. This, too, he wished to haunt with sound; to sketch his grandmother's pain, her palms torn from washing flannel with sulphuric soap, the abrasion of the jooking board, but also of those fingers twirling cigarettes at christenings and weddings, when she would drink whisky neat and dance to Ace Cannon. These things must be transformed into air, into vibration, into sound. In concert in Boston he blows to conjure. His American cousins are in the audience. They sit with hands clasped between their thighs, and Uncle Moses – the one they say mad – sits tense in his handmade rawhide leather waistcoat and the ten gallon hat that hides the bald drum pan of his skull. He leans from his chair when the saxophone's high note rings, but the others – the doctor, the teacher and the pentecostal preacher – do not understand this music. They sit silently, even as the musician and his quartet tear gaps in the heavy light. Polymorphic sound. Cosmic sound. Outside sound. Sudden sound. The village market sound, the abattoir sound, the jetty and the fisheries' scent in sound. The blue and vicious vitality of rivers and oceans sound. The sound of engines and the sound of babel-babel-babel. The sound of sex and of ear wax and suffering. The wasp-waist sewing machine sound, deciphering the industrial needle in the thumb, in the thumb, in the thumb. The sound of the highway-side factories his mother worked in, building tubes for televisions and laminated radiograms. The needle was a nail, was a pin, was a needle to stitch with. It entered the thumb and her heart burst open. The cedar sour sound of the speakers and the nylon limit of its veil. The sound of remembering and of forgetting. Who has counted each breath? The sounds of the horn, of the bass, of the drums are the cry of the people. The personal sound is the universal sound, the sound of upstairs houses and downstairs vision and learning. The proud sound of tears, of secrets, of shame and of abandonment, of his cry puncturing the noontime as he is dragged away, ripped from clinging to his mother's hip, to be taken down, down,

down, down the hill to a new home in the plains, where speech came staggering to his lips, and word was sound and that sound was the scent of fresh paint on the midnight robber's collection box, the sound of Anson, the god of bread, bawling like a cow from when his hand get wrap up inside that mixer, pull him down inside it and distort the vision, turn him to bonemeal mince, torn from this life, by the stone teeth of a machine designed for the kneading of bread. Hot tears were shed in that slant house on Temple Street. His mother's eyes, the restless beating of her feet. The fragments in the coffin were not her son. The sweet soul of sound coming from the bachelor's shack, set up down from the big house, where he put up luminous horoscope posters, where he build a system to sound. Even the heel was a drum, the tongue was a drum. The house of water and of dirt under the house, the house of rice and black birds and soursop and papaya, and the hurricane's suspense, and the wild Indian farmlands, all these must be writ, or blown, into some homiletic sermon of sound.

36

In Memoriam || Clementine Henry

He would return, if he could find a way back to Mt Garnett. The plane would fly over green hills at dusk and arrive at an airport that once was a cane field. He would return, if he knew there was still a place where his memory-ghost wandered – the one he left behind to continue that life, in the streets of struggle and grime, in rugged lands to the east of the island, in the cracked earth with the parched wooden hand of the breadfruit tree where the iguana sleeps – he would come back. But longing is the myth of islands. There is no paradise there waiting to be reconstituted, yet he seeks to recreate it in the image of every street where something happened, in every cove and corner, in creases between the floorboards, at the house parties where the DJ with the single turntable flung Joe Gibbs' twelves, where the neighbour hung her washing out, a splinter sticking in her foot sole, where his grandmother's palms reacted to detergent with flakes and peeling, where women returned the yeast tree to the sea, hot oil falling from the skillet, where the slipper slapping, bursting the cockroach to phlegm and insect bone. Each fragment that fell between the boards was lost.

As a child, he would lie flat on the floor and peer into the world beneath the cracks; the light that was stored there shone luminous and clear upon the sheltered dirt. There were voices contained there, and he would lie still, listening to the stories they told. Ma Elsa suffer two stillborn, claim she suicidal but instead she went mad. Dead now, she lived under that house among the lump dirt. It was 1957. Her hair stuck in splinters under the floorboards, blades of pine; she ate dirt, clutched bees to her chest till they exploded. See her between the boards, and then weeping, knee deep in the dasheen stream in the undulating yard. The mango tree there, the lime tree, the parakeets, the breadfruit and two tribes of coconut, the orange tree leaning on the galvanise. Visualise the world from there, all the way down to the pilots' house, the wire-fenced school, the grass-green dome of the catholic church, the long dread bachelor, Winthrop, with his tailoring business on Seventh Street, playing his Ohio Players albums on Sunday morning, measuring clients with pins in his mouth, putting tape around their waists.

He would return if he could climb a rooftop and look down. But vertigo, the swaying of branches, the avocado trees, the breadfruit and the barbadine vine, the dog barking, the putrefying scent of the ravine, all these things would bring him down. He would return if all was the same – and so –perhaps never. And what would he be returning for if it was all still as it had been? Then he would never have left. There is no past. It burns to the root. There is only memory, and memory which is not pinioned to text or film is mist, is dream, forever fading. He would return if the wind stood still. If Miss Henry was still alive. If the man who belted his arm with a tourniquet that rain-lit evening when he punched through glass was still there in that corner house, or leaning into the backseat window getting blown, dark night on the avenue. If Miss Henry was still alive, the dogs would still be barking in her yard. He would return if it was still noon, the sun high in the sky, to make the long walk up the avenue from the Catholic school and Ma Sylvie not home, the house locked, the dogs twisting in their dance, and Miss Henry call him up the castle stairs, high there so he could see, for the first time, his own house from above, how the land was set in the map, the rusting galvanise, the avocado tree, the guava, iguanas. She fed him brown stewed chicken, wing bones, a thigh, the dark flesh leaving the bone; bread, home-made, heavy and sweet; freshly squeezed grapefruit juice, the plastic cup still wet from washing. Her house of ornaments and her house of glass – trinkets, the lilac vase of twisted glass. A house where the back stairway leant down into the orchard. It was a world he had never seen before. Birds lived at this height, in these treetop nests. He saw the savannah, vast, alive, the river that divided the sacred from the physical. Sweet Miss Henry, she had no children of her own. For a while, her

111

nephew Arthur stayed there in a room reserved for suffering. Arthur died, withered away with leukaemia. So perhaps all that waiting was wasted. He remembers Arthur on the veranda, his image staggering in that vision; weak. He smiled and sometimes waved, but he never came down, was never seen on solid ground. He stayed up in that high house until he was taken away to die one rain-lit day of majestic sorrow. They fumigate and change curtain in that room, but it remained unused. If Miss Henry were alive, the air would still be moist with love, the white horse would still be alive to run, the Julie mango tree in the orchard would bear plump fruit, the dogs would be fed, the iguanas would fall asleep on the branches of the soursop tree and have their heads crushed by blows from boom wood or metal beam. If Miss Henry was still alive he would go back home, regardless of whether the hardback woman, black as sin, was living in that house now, the house where he was born. He would go, though Mr Clary was surely the devil. How heavy-hearted had it been to leave that house to that sweet bitch and not to Sister Syl's kin. If Miss Henry were still alive she would run down with smelling salts to revive Sister Syl, in that dry season of menopause, when she heard the news.

37

Boyson had walked over riverless bridges, ridges and contours; he had travelled along the coast and seen the sea in the distance. Beyond the ocean lay the mist of history, the dense cities and harbours of Europe and American fantasy. Leaving the city below, the brightly lit world of wild island jazz and political intrigue, he found the house where the woman said it would be, near the lookout to the horizon. Beside the house, there were chickens asleep in an avocado tree, dogs barking, and the wheel-less and bent skull of a car was propped up on bricks beside barrels of rain water. He called out from the leaning yard, 'Good night!' and a light came on in the house. The woman he was looking for was the daughter of a woman his father had made acquaintance of at Mother Mamin's Spiritual Temple – a mother of the church the elder cocksman had scoped while he knelt on the rugged pew, evangelical, like soft candle and honey, one Sunday afternoon. The older man had peeped at the clasp of her waist, had gasped at the tightness of the cloth around her thighs. The woman was on the edge of old age, but she still possessed her formal structure; her hind and flank were robust; when her lips were parted at rest they blossomed like a trumpet bell, gap-toothed; her hair was pinned back with clips. Boyson's father had seen her before at service, but that Sunday was the first time he had noticed the cunning bulk of her, the power in her hips. Ring the bell. The bell there to ring. Ring the thing. So Boyson's father started tapping Miss Phillip bark for sap. Her job in church was to care for blessed mourners and spiritual candidates as they lay on the earth, eyes shut with seals, vèvè for Olokun, vèvè for Legba, the centrepost in the church as the axis upon which they travelled through the Nile Valley, the Guinea coast, through Manitoba even, and spoke to fish and mollusc, bug and rock since everything had life in the spirit world. This nurse, Miss Phillip, would soothe their physical bodies, while their astral bodies roamed the akashic regions.

And now Boyson, a boy who just reach seventeen, soon after he had escaped the pages of the great book, stood before Miss Phillip's daughter Alicia, a pork-legged woman in her early thirties, blooming with heat, with rounded features and eyes like chocolate seed, skinning up on an unmade bed in a house of pale tungsten light and fluttering curtains. There were citrus distilleries below, and Boyson could hear soul music brewing like a soft wind across the hillside. Down in the valley was suffer and ration, poor room shack-backs and black shack alleys and mud and wood propping up a mountain – true talk – road works and lock neck, and gunshot if not, overlooking the valley road. Is every voter for themself there, in those ex-slavers yard that get pave with concrete, but nice house get build there, too – black people children trying to put down new roots in the ground. Some put up nice veranda with wrought-iron chair and palm tree, and inside have ring-bound photo album under the coffee table going back sepia to the sixties. The big dining table have crochet doily between the mauby glass and the good brown wood. Alicia even had a coconut tree beside her house, idyllic dream of the tropics, though each aesthetic gesture seemed out of sync with her somewhat somnolent eyes. In fact, she was cautious and cunning, deception lurking in her vibration, like rain and sun same time. She would whisper to draw a man in close and flytrap him in slow motion. Each word was fully formed and precise, and her glance was so innocuous that no mischief was detected in it, nor in the cutlass leaning behind her door. All this time Al Jarreau singing like a siren across the hill.

Time pushing; the young pot hound want meat. Boyson sit down polite in the woman place, feet crossed at the ankles, grinning, sipping from a plastic cup of Kool Aid and talking one set of shit. Eventually, the woman had to squeeze his prick and pull him in, otherwise he would still be sitting down there stuttering, while the woman want to fuck. Her bed was soft and moist; she open and turn him loose, but he start jumping wild round the woman bed like a cat. His throw was bogus, his waist too eager, the young boy couldn't bull, poor fella, his wood was still in plastic. When Alicia groan and push him away, his waist was still pumping. The youth man had the itch to bone but no ability; he had her to kill but he couldn't hit. So she put him down there. Then she lay back and watched him while he knelt on the bed with his gorgon hanging down unrequited, his mouth huff up and puckered like a fish. Years hence, Boyson would remember her thighs, how round and soft they were around his head, the cupped palm of her breast, and how afterwards he had walked along the Lady Young Road as it curved into the city, and how the incense taxi he took was playing Earth, Wind & Fire. This happened years back in some rebellious place on a hill where the history of blood was shed from stick fight and the push to revolution. Blood was in the air even then, like the lingering copper in the kiss from the mouth of a menstruating woman, her kiss of blood and lovelorn depression, seagrass and vulva.

Boyson would remember that the valley below was a world of darkness and dogs on chains in slippery yards. There was only one room. Bare wood, the rustle of fabric, the whiff of perfume. One room in which they could lie in the glow of the outside electric light, the moon turning its gaze away.

38

The hotel stood on the lake front. There were porters and chambermaids, but the carpets were nests for roaches and the marble sinks were cracked. Traffic passed along a dirty road below his window. There was no hot water for the bath. It was Monday morning, and he had slept, dreamed about sleeping, dreamed once again of Ma Mamin's chapel. He made apologies to himself for perpetually revisiting its muse, but there it was – hid in holy bush. He returned to the bell of Sundays, to the lash of the spirit, the goblets of anthurium and croton spears around the centre post, and the chalked white vèvè on the earthen floor of the chapel.

The previous night, the quartet had been both brittle and gigantic; they cut across time. Midway through the encore he returned to Honeymoon Park, 1979, coming back along the backs of yards, one long drain-side ravine walk, through razor bush, fever grass, stinging nettle and past fences for dogs to bark from. You chop down the cannonball tree with the beat of the drum, like an axe clapping in the mouth of the machine, sideways intimate. You advance as a lion and two bones come out. Get crowned. Then death grooves your bush broom, and ten jumbie jump out. You play deep like a bitch in the groove, like Jimmy McGriff, and the first note shatters a French woman's temple, and the second sends her body diving onto the ground. Black for all salvation. The wood of the bass resonates in the throat like the vibration of a baobab tree in the Malian desert. The saxophonist's fingers were sliding along the pads like bedsprings squeaking, to moan upon the tone; sweat was wet upon his face, gleaming in the spotlight.

But later that Monday at the airport, they held and stripped him naked. They put the jazz musician, in his patent leather shoes and exotic hat, naked. They squint him up rough till he cough up blood. They look in his armpits and underlung, up under his stones, but nothing there. Shoe-sole, instep and insole and nothing there, not even seeds. The men confer, they sure he have thing. They done visualise him coming back from a weed field high up Five Rivers jungle, and Sugars bringing out a bag full of red-beard collie from under the house, and the jazz man saying, 'Take some back from too much. That nuff; you putting too much weed in that bag.' It must have been two gallons at least; it full up a crocus bag; the man throw away weed! Finally, they turn his foreskin over; empty. The drug dog twisting waist to wine like a genie; the dog want to bite the man wood, but the customs men shoo him from there. They put him naked but they could have given him turtle prick soup and see if he couldn't shit it out. The thing inside and must produce.

…The church was jumping. The leader was lining out the hymn, lining the track for the gospel train to pass and leading on each glorious line. The good sermon that Sunday afternoon was four feet nine inches tall, and black like the back of some blue river, hillside jungle ride in a struggle buggy, six hours deep. The preacher call, 'Who without sin coulda jump right in!'

They put him naked but he was clean. They beat his breath but he was slick like a fipple reed. They coulda force-feed him senna-pod tea, and nothing woulda come out. They coulda put mildew on him from bad eye; he woulda wear red-eye jumbie bead.

…So sing, and how they singing? They singing till the tension build and Leader Jim woulda swing the chant, *I have a sword in my hand.* That 'doption rhythm, like fire broom sweeping in front to cleanse the road, like Aaron's rod, was making way for the spirit to descend. The congregation rocking, but they fearful in the spirit, afraid the walls might burst outwards from the power they generating. But that coulda never happen; is rock stone foundation the little church built on. The glory fill with the rustle of white, the candle wax encasing the candidate's hands, clasped in a sinner's prayer.

They put him naked but he had nothing on him. They ascribe badness to him but he was trying to change. They coulda give him warm salted milk and cheese from China and still, nothing woulda come out. They put him naked and his heart was heavy. They let him free but they mark his name in red and wait to catch him in the rinse, to pull his beard and make him eat star anise seed.

Tuesday morning he is surely back amongst the alum stones and the snails, at the seaside market, watching when the seine net pulls shut, the little dolphin get trapped but the black salmon jump out. The salmon petrified of losing air, afraid to succumb, like a lover who dies in the arms of a loved one, bitter to leave yet somehow content. Flash in the eyes of fish upon the splintering table to be divided into chunk and gill. The head is used for soup.

Grief is an aviary of bees. A poem is the frequency of magic. All that was, still is. Each night like the end of a sentence; he returns to the same black spot in his mind, he ponders complication, props sorrow on his wrists and wishes that he was left alone to unravel into language. This and the buying of kingfish, conch, and sea cockroach. Even Oban ghost, which passed through both rooms, was no metaphor, no tenor nor vehicle. Today there is no market to buy fish from. Passing the second-hand record shop he hears Scrapper Blackwell play 'Kokomo'. They had put him in a hot room with no windows or doors, no ceiling and no floor. But *àse*, concentration upon his solar plexus had rendered him invisible.

39

In the courtyard, the roots of an elm tree are breaking through cracks in the concrete. Further along the street, children are playing in a gravel pit. He is sitting on the edge of the world. When she kneels, he bends to wrap his palms around the tangible heat of her back. He fingers the flute of her spine. They press their tongues desperately against the insides of each other's mouths, till the taste of blood comes. He surveys the room for the first time, notices the reams of photographic paper, the boxes of clothes, her Leica cameras on the kitchen table, pans hanging from a vine above the sink. There are no actual walls here, just the earthen ground and the contents of this room set upon it, set against the open expense of a desert that seems to grow vaster with every breath, on every side, so the viewer must continually reassert the vision. She has hung a sheet between the kitchen and the bedroom. Her daughter sleeps on a small bed beside the kitchen, beneath the unframed Basquiat print pinned to the cloth.[10] They do not live in squalor, but they are poor and cannot afford windows, walls or doors. They measure time by temperature, distance by breath. She travels to medinas in Rabat and Cairo, buys bottles of rose water, brass trinkets, copper dallahs. He suddenly feels he is going blind; there is too much suspense here in the desert for the eye to contain. Especially if that eye is paranoiacally critical; there are shadows which furtively bend away from the veracity of light.

They had arrived in Marseille by train, but he could not remember entering a cabin, except that when he closed his eyes, the train felt as if it was perpetually turning in circles, and his head rolled on the back of the seat. Pull the window down and the cool

10.'Riding With Death' Jean-Michel Basquiat, 1988, acrylic, crayon, canvas, 289.5 x 249 cm.

breeze worsens the plight of his narcotic prayer. He does not remember getting off the train. Which desert, which burnt river? In Prague, there were tunnels beneath the winter streets and the offices of The British Council. There were well-lit rooms of candelabras and black felt and polished pine in restaurants that only served squid and eyeless octopus.

In Mt Garnett, the savannah grass was lucky, manure was moist in the black earth, and the river provided life for fishes. He remembered how the wild youth would come down from the Mitagau Hills in packs, to gather in the roots of the samaan trees, and how free they were with gossip and truth; how he envied the way they spoke – their feet planted so firmly, as if they owned the earth. One girl had stood in the roots of the biggest tree, the one beside the old train tracks, put hands to hip and her skirt was snapping like a whip in the heat that blew across the afternoon. She'd said to another girl, 'I hear Timmy fuck you behind the church an' break inside you.' Incorrigibly fierce, her voice was flung across the green ocean like a razor-bladed kite tail, or linen drapery from a window on a hillside shack, where lovers are fighting like tiger cats and tearing in and out of the heat. That same girl in the savannah was the woman who, many years later, while the musician waited with a ball under his foot for his team to come down from the village, would sit with her man in the roots of the same samaan tree, by the same train tracks, squeezing breast milk into the man's eye, as he lay across her lap, like a child, then let the young man straighten up and say, 'Ah boy, don't laugh, breast milk good for plenty thing.' The musician had imagined that this woman had no true home, that she was domiciled in some mystery room, ablaze in the sun but glowing softer as it faded, dissolving into crepuscular wilderness, into some long hidden Indian garden to sleep when night come.

In Ramkissoon Trace, the old man lay upon his day-bed in the hot, so hot afternoon, beneath the window, steadily dying, after working for forty years in the infirmary and never being late, not once; and this, too, had been written, and so it is real that on that day his old blood was so slack veined that he lingered in life like a forgotten vine on a wire fence stretched between hill and river. Those were the days when the musician lived in the suburban jungle town, in times when raised eyes and curled lips were blades enough to run from. Them days, soul man used to skank to Mikey Dread, wearing stove-mouth trousers with buckles near the hem and hi-soled Pro-Keds, twirling soul-stick and riding long fork bicycle with Happy Riders gang along Santa Cruz Old Road.

He has gone to the sink to wash his cock. The photographer will not put it in her mouth after it has been inside her. The sink is an enamel basin balanced upon a chair; there is a white towel there, which is soft. This is a basin like those his own grandmother would stoop over to wash her business out. A river runs under the desert; there are other rooms here which are equally dishevelled and ancient. His horn lies askew on the kitchen table, dead yet still breathing. Earlier, he had been playing Robert Aaron's 'Maimouna'[11] while she had been making rooibos tea. She travels to medinas in Rabat and Cairo, she buys rugs and incense. He watches her sleep. The floor creaks from the movement of water running under the house and the resonance of wood. When she wakes, she takes his cock in her mouth. When it bursts, she nurses it like a wet pup. Consumes him. She rolls. Funk pools in her moat. Then she moans. Twisting her thighs, she ejaculates on the unmade bed, her hot breath hissing out from her throat.

---

11. Robert Aaron, *Trouble Man*, Heavenly Sweetness, HS 030 LP, 2010.

40

Luke was having dinner in a restaurant near the ocean. He faced the door as he ate two cornmeal dumplings with braised abalone, and avocado on the side. He licked his fingers, and sucked his hand. It had been several days since he left the tidy bargains of the suburbs, since then adventuring further south into September, into the jungle towns and the coast that burst with traumatic history. He was just a few miles from where several Africans once leapt from the cliff side and flew – with corn husks under their armpits and tamarind seed up their nose holes. Throughout the archipelago, this legend returns of flight from bondage, always over oceans and outcrops of rock, flying back to Africa. When a people mission bound to free, you can't stop them – freedom must come. Not even Euclidean posture could suspend them forever on the axis of some shackle and bell. No iron forged in European waters, no immoral bilk or sorcery could hold them here, either physical or spiritual. Those who lost their way in space on their way back to Guinea would eventually become unidentified and alien when they reappeared, as was written in *The African Origins of UFOs.*

Raphael knew that when he wrote such sentences that the big book he was writing was his masterpiece and, ergo, that he could die and, *ibid*, that his pen was so accomplished it could write on the writing hand. He knew that words should be allowed to land where they would, and not be subsumed by fixed meaning, that poetry created meaning in the gaps of language.

It was said that from that sacred cliff, a cult had grown – a people who lived in tapia bungalows and tree houses on the fertile plateau near the deepest plummet to stone. Each September, the sky lid veered a narrow distance towards earth, close enough to touch and, leaning from the cliff edge, those who were chosen could stretch and skim a finger against the sky's powdery face, and this was worship enough to receive the spirit gift of secret colours and poetic sensibility. But the sky hook was also a bridge. It was a portal, a spaceway to the higher regions of liminal space. But if you stretched out from the rim of this cliff and failed to reach the sky lid and fell, in the flight down, your body was bound to be broken on the sharp rockstone below and left to pulp, to gristle and corpuscle. Is so? Yes. Is so. You go crimp and rot right there; nobody go help you.

Luke is on the pilgrimage way to this holy mountain. Cocorico bleating in the trees above the origins of rivers from trickling streams. He see water-rock and mud and manjak bitumen along the hunters' tracks, he see a hotel for crapaud, then two poets, walking riverside, naked as they born, in the grinning heat, tramping around ponds where drunks drowned each Sunday. Luke never stop to ask them what they doing there. The summit took four days to reach. Then, entering through the village gate, he saw the thatched domes, observed men smoking bone pipes around the well, glimpsed gardens where midwives drew balsam from malomay, where they grew *eleuterine bulbosa*, wonder-of-the-world, shandilay, jumbie bead, banga seed, zebafam, rocoo root, ditay payee, soft candle and red lavender.

Luke arrived at the settlement at noon. The villagers welcomed him with robes of yellow and brown, explained that these were sword and shield; they wrap around him like a choir, pass him around the unfinished ruins of temples, then take him to the house of Grand Papa Willie. The big man sitting down right there in his teepee wearing the wooden mask of nommo, perforated at the gills. He never say nothing, never raise a hand, never even offer Luke a cool drink of mauby, though a jug sitting nice with ice between them. Papa Willie sit down in mystery, like a veiled Indian bride at the Ashirvada. Then he just touch Luke head and wave him, 'Go.'

When the hour opened and the neophytes moved to caress the firmament lid, Luke was with them at the edge. He was told that if he leapt to meet it, he would rise through the heavy air to cloud-piercing places. They tell him to raise his right hand as if in supplication to the blast of a horn section, or in praise of the black pudding man in Macoya, lashing pepper on the thing, or like the pentecostal singers across the road, whose raised hands held up that church. The pilgrims watch Luke to see how he will buck when he realise that, from close-up, the sky was not blue or black, but the brightest green. Luke get tender, he reach up to touch the damn thing, but then he hear, 'Fucker, you go dead tonight!' and he turn to see the mask Papa Willie wore get fling down, and the Great Bandit reveal himself, yes, and they begin to wrestle like dog, up on the sudden edge, capsize and spinning, hard lash passing, fall and falling.

   Who

      vex

        loss.

Rockstone burst. Then water carry them down; sea cockroach and zandolie bite them. Drown want to drown them, but merman want a piece first. Sea urchin sting them on their seeds, while they wrestling, flinging out head-butt and kick. They puff out and rise from the water and now they upon land, but the fighting still fierce. Each man have ambition to lance the plane of time. The Great Bandit was sure he catch Luke; he lock Luke neck and drag him up onto the river bank, but when he catch himself and look close, was not Luke but a bearded manatee he hold. Luke? Luke gone. Luke gone Paris to make mischief, Luke gone Barbès to bull woman, Luke gone Strasbourg Saint-Denis to buy roast corn and chestnut, Luke gone Malick to cook manicou. Luke want to go home.

41

For a while Bain worked as a security guard in a supermarket. In the evenings he drove down to the foreshore on his motorbike, barebacked in the wicked sun, a saga boy, bumping like a pimp and grinning. He was a real glad man, and built big, so he feel nobody could tap him on his shoulder and jook him in his waist. He used to come out on the block swaggering with the imprint of myth from the heritage of stick men and badjohns born in the 1800s, men who taste and survive the whip of slavery and fear neither man nor beast. But like Sparrow say, 'Man like to feel.'[12] Bain remain hip till, one Sunday night in '78, somebody hit him with a spanner in his centre part while he was disco dancing deep in the crowd at the Himalaya Club. He fall, then come up to fight, but he two knee weak like elbow macaroni, and he don't even know who hit him, but that blow broke his brain upon the angle, till his skin-teeth go from grin to sombre. Now he walking dread like a big drake in the area. He vex to kill but don't know who to wrestle, so he gone seeking across the alluvial flood-plains for a spiritual baptist high priest to bless him and tend the tender bone in his head, but whether the priest use oil or poultice, the wound hard to heal and it stay soft like fontanelle. Sudden so he get call up on that old wooden hill to see the mother he never knew how to love, until he hear she was lying in that cancer bed. What to do? Dialysis swill, trepan terror in her head? Show me where they cut without anaesthesia, hear how she suffer chloroform and hospital food, worries in her lung, pinioned upon the white afternoon. Jessie, between prayers, would turn her head away from the light. She waited till Bain and his brother had left the room, then blinked hard and was gone. Who can forget the torrential power

12. See The Mighty Sparrow, 'Man Like To Feel', from *Congo Man*, National Record Company, NLP 5050, Trinidad, 1965

of her love, the sweet whip of her hand, those Sundays saying, 'Run from there, you playing the arse while fire hot, rice boiling, beef browning black in the iron pot…'? Who could not remember her bellbottom photo in the studio on Jogie Road, half sat on the corrugated iron chair, the waterfall behind her? In them days her man hid black and white porn among the Berec batteries in his bottom drawer and slunk down in his easy chair drinking warm salted milk and listening to Swamp Dogg and Solomon Burke on Sunday mornings. The house beside the ravine was hot with trinkets, eight-track cassettes, linoleum and fabric-fronted speaker boxes, cut-glass ornaments, crotchet, string art, zodiac felt, and the scent of macaroni pie and chicken baking.

It was Carnival Tuesday night; Bain bent to fix his motorbike chain, when Alvin tap him on his shoulder and say, 'Ai boy, yuh mudder dead.' Bain break to water and collapse to the scummy black earth where motor oil and dog fur mangle up with the dirt. 'Bring her back to me,' he cry. 'Flesh of my flesh, let me stand beneath the pommecythere tree, but bring her back to me. I dreamed I rode back to the old house on j'ouvert morning; Mammy was still alive. The governor plum tree was in bloom. I write a four-line song, easy, like a paperclip shape, hooked and eyed with melody intact. The white sun burned. Dash away nostalgia, memory, and the pain of loss. Sing her back to me, like gospel.'

The ghost of Oban walked between two rooms. He stole coins from old man Clary's shirt pocket. Silver money. He left the brown. He lingered there in that liminal gap between rooms, counting his loot, knowing he could not be caught, knowing that he could slip through, like a ruse, like a mask, like a dream, even when the old man came in from the night, tipsy on bay rum, sap his head and shinbone, and say, 'Some kiss-me-arse fella put he hand in my pocket.' But he never knew who, since by then the ghost of Oban was gone. Dead now. The news caught the old man unexpected, like the cuff boom, or the grinding engine of the brekete drum. The sudden dead, with eyes flung up. Big Oban, who used to cut road wherever he wanted to drive – all that gone. Clary sat pining in the toilet, crying slow, manful tears. He stay there so long the shit dry on his arse so he didn't have to wipe, and his old cock run out of drip to drop. It was his woman who heard him moaning behind the wooden door – that oil paint blue and thick. Clary sat there mourning for Mr Henry too, feeling his own proximity to death; he know Basil coming; his chest get hot. He kept sipping from the lip of the rum jar, knowing that death would soon sharpen his toes. Meantime, the boy he kept tied in the yard – to sweep up dog shit, to lash the coral snake, crack the iguana back, wash the duck pen, cut the barbadine, pick the chataigne, and pulp soursop – could only watch him sly, and plot his escape. The boy made tuneless horns from bamboo, catgut guitars from T-squares; he cannibalise electrics, hot wired into the radiogram so the feedback spilt out onto the street, harshly discordant. It make American Joe, from up the avenue, stop from his tampi-smoking stroll, and bend to look inside the house and see that the old folks had gone to church. And Joe – who claim he served in Vietnam and that when napalm burst he bawl, 'Lord, what I doing here? I from Trinidad – he say the guitar sound remind him of his old friend Jimi, though there were doubts Joe had ever passed through New York, or even left the island.

42

Ella meets her mother for lunch at the brasserie near Hudson Yards. Her mother arrives in the green lamé dress she was buried in, with sequin trim and vetiver scent, with folded receipts and pills in her patent-leather clutch bag. Mama walking strong in her black and too-tight shoes with the leaning heels, as she moves from one scene into another life. We must imagine her mother arriving at the riverside restaurant, yet also – simultaneously – see her in her bellbottom mood, in the splendid time of her life.

Ella orders the grilled salmon. Her mother sighs, criticises the choice, the diners, the weight of light, the coloured bottles behind the bar, the brass hinge of the sky-blue canopy they sit under. She will not eat. She considers her daughter, hears the squawk of cormorants above the silver blades of the sea. They are near the water, beside the offices of port and marine bookkeepers. Imagine how a ship pulls the horizon shut, and consider the anguish intimated in that repeated lash of water against the ancient pillars and cornices of the jetty. Her mother nods, long dead since suffocating from pleurisy in the postcolonial hospital. Her feet had swollen, her kidney failed.[13]

Before she left the island, Ella's mother had lived in the self-sustaining empire of her own dream and ambition. She pinned her thumb within a stitch at the Elite Shirt Factory when she was seventeen, and worked on in hot tears. When she catch a glimpse of free, she fled from the barrackyards of Old St Joseph Road, from bacchanalian bridges, from 'All here was once bush.' She

---

13. From the time old people see your foot swell, they start wringing their hands and moaning. They know is time to buy up grog and put down salt biscuit for wake. They will shake their head and say, 'Oh gorm, what a thing some people does go through.' They will bring you strained pumpkin soup in ward 32.

had wanted to be a dancer. She had lifted her dress above her ankles and danced to impress her friends in the varnished ballrooms of Port of Spain, and they assured her she was gifted. She knew the Spanish steps to tunes by Mano Marcelin and Joey Lewis; she danced at the Hilton ballroom. She knew how to dip and sway to Ed Watson's brass, to the bass of soulful calypso. She also knew the Country Club and the social halls of white folk, that the splash of colour in the erotic print, implicit but bouffant and proud, was an elegy in motion for when swing music played the Castilian or fox trot. Following this path to her fortune, she landed in New York in 1972.

She enrolled in dance at community college and danced hard in Greenwich Village discotheques, in warehouses in Greenpoint, in humble Harlem dancehalls, learned tap on hoofer-sprung floors with pulleys beneath. She lingered past midnight, dancing with a man from Vancouver, whose long arms were raised and twisted in the iron rigging of the room. Did he say, 'That's what they say' when she said he could move with hips of precision? Did she tell him that one night a dog walked into a calypso dance in Woodbrook, and stood in the middle of the floor barking and wagging its tail? Did she confess that, where she came from, that image was both symbol and myth, a motif for therianthropy, that the pot hound was really some moustachioed landlord, civil servant or bad police who possessed the alchemy of spirit duality? Did she say that in those longtime dancehalls in town, men used to run garlic through razor blades so the wound would not sting when they held the zwill at the door as people were rushing in – or out – to see or flee from fellas fighting, and never notice they get cut. Ella's mother knew many such stories of exile and longing. She knew how members of the Schenectady Kaiso band, far and lonesome in diasporic whining, would try to bring back bush meat from their dreams. She also knew how trumpeters tuned their horns, how a saxophonist's ineluctable tongue rattled the reed of the inner ear. She remembered how the dancer from Vancouver, with his delicate fingers grasping hers, would twirl and release her to the sky-rhythm of supernatural choreography. But it was not to be, neither this nor that dance, and one Christmas she quietly left and returned to Trinidad. Then, braving rain to buy fish from Melchior one Saturday, Deacon Simmons bring an umbrella.

Ella runs a finger through the condensation on the water glass. The wind rattles against the menu board. The waiter brings the grilled salmon, the lettuce leafs. The whites of her mother's unseeing eyes are darkening. Ella eats, delicately, like a bird, as the memory-ghost of her mother speaks:

'How long have we been here? I am haunted by the sordid death I endured. Each time I died, I fell backwards over a waterfall and kept falling. It have no fear like this, no terror, no sorrow deeper than seeing into the eyes of those who mourn you. Ella, I saw you moving under the trees, but the street was less patient, and its language was less sure, but ask them and they will tell you that I was no saint when I was young. I was a whip, a wound that never healed, a sound that never fade. You asked me once if I was afraid of death, but no, Mammy didn't frighten to dead. Remember how when I was sick, I held you to my chest and wiped the fear from your eyes. I wrung sweet broom in water and washed you brand new, remember? But all through this, Mammy heart was beating hot in her chest, and when death came for me, I was unprepared.'

In Vienna, there is a small jeweller's shop that sells rings and robes and trinkets from the Afghan valleys – rings with the hurtful blue of lapis lazuli set in dirty silver, the heavy talons of Iranian bracelets, copper with its rich and almost blue patina. Ella is on a tram passing along Alser Strasse, where violins are hanging in the window of the luthier's workshop, the Turkish pension with the sauna and the fever of the narrow attic room.

43

Teacher Gizzard held the Saturday night thanksgivings in that house atop the hill, so steep, with the sour cherry tree laden with green fruit and branches leaning into the veranda. Make a hole built in bread with the leader's appointed finger, pour olive oil in its living wound, *break bread and rejoice*, and the bread was shared among the flock, from that upstairs living room to those downstairs. Sometime is oil in the morsel you get, sometime finger. Look out on the quarry up Mendez Drive, the new village being established, cut from red and upturned dirt.

Teacher Gizzard was a warrior for syncretic faith. Behind the Christian altar she shined shoes for Legba, in secrecy, arranging seals and stools for the big man to kick, while humbly humming hymns from her Sankey Book of Sacred Songs – red, pious and moist in every Sunday hand. Big-boned Teacher Gizzard, ambitious for the little church, she kept the books, administered the takings. A liminal servant, she swept the yard or else jumbie make mischief. Somebody throw obeah and next thing coming is church burning down, but not so when Teacher Gizzard put her big knee on the ground. Since Leader Jim was lining out the hymns – since that time when he alone could read – teacher Gizzard was in her gown, ringing bell and lashing the four corners with kananga water. She was the matriarch of her quarry, had come from deepest black of country, from hominy corn, her ancestry of buffalo soldiers who served in the American Civil War and moved through New Orleans and Florida, down the Caribbean liver stream to build villages in the deep south of the island. At those thanksgiving ceremonies, after Leader Jim had loosened his stole and collar, and Ma Mamin, their spiritual mother, had hummed the healing of the house, when night had begun to climb the hill, after a long day working deep in the elbows of the earth, Teacher would call the children in and serve them curried chataigne, white rice and bodi on banana leaves. Then sweetbread and the red and white sugarcake they say she used to grind the coconut for with her teeth, and Kool-Aid, and reconstituted grapefruit juice in styrofoam cups.

Such women of the church always found a way into Raphael's work, with their arms flung up in spiritual ecstasy, with the wet cotton flowers of glossolalia in their mouths. Teacher had gone down on the ground to mourn three times solid, and each time she had spent fourteen days floating in space. On her second journey, she was given a vision by a merman on the Guinea coast, the same merman that give Deacon Simmons a brown and yellow gown as his shield, and whispered secret words in his ear. Ask him what the words were, or if he ever used them, and Deacon would knock his cigarette, filter first to the pack and grin and answer you sideways and tell you what colour to pin up on your flag, or how to make cassava bread or rice-flour porridge instead. From that one merman vision, Teacher Gizzard knew she had to build her own church.

So she bargained a piece of land down the road from her house, all down where the village was still being carved from the neck of the land, and, perhaps as far back as 1979, Teacher wiped her face in her apron and mixed mortar with the men, to set up a place of worship down there on that low elevation. Her money was not tall, so Teacher could only afford dirt-floor salvations, a simple wooden altar, pine-beam rafters for spirits to pour down from heaven upon, a centre post to hold up the sky, and a room for neophytes engaged in liminal crossings. Pure spiritual business in that chapel she was building. Ma Mamin told her not to build it, but the little church was built, and it rolled and tumbled, and the spirit was joyous when the power came down. Then pepper on top of pepper. Jimmy, the leader since Brazil Village days, who Mother Mamin had put in place, left Mamin's church hid in bush mid sermon and went to Mendez Drive. Now there was no one to lead the faithful in Ma Mamin's Spiritual Temple, where Jimmy himself had consecrated the ground and founded a nation upon a rock, where he had planted a concrete cross in the yard.

How long before the repeal of the ordinance that prohibited worship in this way was his diocese erected? For how long, in defiance of helicopters or colonial armies searching the forest for illegal Baptists, did it survive? Hear them sing, *O, watchman on the mountain height*. Leader Jim was Ma Mamin's protege, her sugar dumpling, an Afro-headed firebrand, staunch and shape-shift and stamping his feet in his gabardine shirt-jack suit. Jimmy upon that bridge, upon that lonesome bridge. You could be home eating your supper, the next day Jim could tell you what colour shirt you was wearing, whether your chicken was roast, curry or in a grainy pelau. And now Ma Gizzard's little church, and all the women it contained, was his.

So Mamin's old church in Brazil Village floundered. Then the festering wound on her shin start back to spring pus.[14] Fever in her engine, sugar in the pump of her heart, her lumber get derelict, and now her church was run down. In her pain she flung gossip on Teacher Gizzard. She tried to break Teacher back with spirit lash, but her congregation receded nevertheless, to other churches in the Southern plains. In her house of unwashed flesh, Mamin wept for heaven, she called for Jim but he never came. Jimmy had another narrative running, simultaneously. Jim was busy.

Then, one Friday morning, Teacher Gizzard was buying pig foot for souse in Tunapuna market, when sudden so the boss man ring his bell for her to come home, and she had to leave everything right there.

---

14. It name *Treponema Pallidum* and is syphilis Mamin have. See note 2.

44

At the Prince Charles in Berlin, the centre of the band was a languid cryptogram of sound that could not be deciphered. A secret air-spring of black mystery notes sprung from the ringing bell, the sacred spaces between the pads, fingers and wrist, the intimate rattle of the reed. Iron Duke in the band! The knee get bend to press out wind, the lip get twist to penetrate the eardrum, the incus, the stapes. Red effort of the swollen eye, the pulse of blood, the muscle in flood waters. Think of the dark constellations of Wilmoth Houdini, and a band like Houdini's was a bad and magical thing. Imagine them powerfully live in the room with proper sub bass and tweeters, and not thin and trebly on shellac at 78rpm.

The musician's father was a pan man who carried both double seconds on his back, who, walking strong along the narrow streets of Pipiol Village in Santa Cruz, would cross over ravines overflowing with uncannily lush vegetation and panty wash, and step like pot hound over oil rotting in the mechanics yard, all broken sump and catalytics, pushing between the old woman petticoat and drawers she died and left, now mango yellow on the line and dried stiff with mildew. The corner shop there in the junction is next to where the pan yard used to be. The shop have fluorescent light burning day and night, and corrugated burglar-proof bars, ornate and thick with white paint to keep out cutlass, though bullet could pass through. It have a man in that shop name Fullerton, but those scamps used to call him Marva. Slick and seductive when you pass for two cold beers and cigarette papers, for salted prunes and dinner mints, he would skin teeth and croon; but the wink mean business, so cash and pass your pass in this paradise town at carnival time, when the Barbergreen have action, or he fouti squeeze your wood through the grill. Young boys fraid him.

And if you don't know Barbergreen,[15] say so, but every Carnival Saturday night, God bless his axe, the musician's father would pass through dark bush into the village, going down to the savannah to play pan on finals' night and, poopa, that was the beginning of sound, the intention and invention of the damn thing self. It don't have music like it uses to do. His father in those days – they call him Silvers – was locks-head grey, but balding at the crown. He wore a green and gold tam, gold teeth and silver rings on each finger. Women desired him without knowing why. He fling his zeal, and simple so they would gravitate towards him, to skylark and throw their heads back laughing. They would smell the tobacco on his breath, the kush-kush oil he set like a trap deep beneath his navel, the sweet soap in his beard. All this to be moulded into melody, to be improvised upon, to be spread open and swallowed whole on the nodulous mattress of his bachelor's bed, to be shiver and moan, to be broken like the shell of a nut, to be unravelled like a knot, and then kissed on the neck and the valley of the spine, to be held through the spasms of their orgasms, but then to be devoured again until the walls of the room fell open and the breath was the wind, and each sigh could shift the clouds.[16]

Silvers would put his son on his shoulder and walk up St Joseph Hill to visit an Indian woman he was dealing with. She lived in a shack with a dirt-floor kitchen, and rooms divided by plywood, high up in the dusk. Picture this: her dark hair lying flat against her back. The burnt sienna of her skin. The way she turns her fine and delicate neck from stirring her pot to speak, steam rising in the cool evening, with the voice of a bird. From upon that hill, the outside world was still a dream. In those days, in those

15. The Barbergreen mythical. Is the strip of drag, a simple pitch at the entry into the Queens Park Savannah where the steel bands linger to pass before they cross the big yard stage. They would run their last roll there, jam two-three chord, play half the song and line out the score, stick sweating in the pannist palm, in Panorama competition.

16. It was dried and ancient but valid hash, not goat pill that cause that, and the sky seemed even further away, and each breath was in synch with clouds which moved, sometimes even back and forth, and some-times swollen and soft with each pump of the heart.

villages on the rim of the city, there was still red dirt and ravine, sloping yards, hot doubles selling on street corners.

The musician had come to know the concentric rings of his father's charisma – the way he would flick a match after lighting his cigarette; how his steel pans were tied and retired under the house like the carapace of crabs, and dust had gathered in the lower notes – until some Sunday, the old man would catch a vaps and swing them out in the yard and play 'Sa Sa Yea' or 'Dougla Woman', for everybody to hear. But the man getting big in the numbers and these pan getting too heavy to pull and play, so he let bush and woodslave overcome them. Then it happen that, walking back home from a christening, his knee give way, and when old man knee give way, they does stop to rest and push back to breathe, or try to walk up the incline with crook stick. They does hold their knee, moan; they does rub it with bay rum, vinegar, rubbing alcohol, soft candle; rub even iodine, breast milk, piss, anything, but when that knee bad, it can't heal, it done. Sometime, oh gorm, it bound to cut. Either that or his left hand can't raise, and he talking from under ocean.

Now, think upon the hot room the musician stood and masturbated in, that year he came home to the salt of the sun. That year he could see shadows of continuities, the narrow strands of his narrative and parallel life in the streets he had left years before. Consider, too, his father as a young man, burning bush upon the hill, barebacked in grinning heat, skinning the manicou. Picture his father's silhouette against the red of dusk and flame, saying, 'Yard fowl for brown stew, manicou for curry.' And the double seconds were fading fast to the time of another life.

45

Melchior say they roast that hog whole day and still under the belly was yellow. Sun and fire beat it whole day, and inside the damn thing stay raw. When they finally gain mechanical advantage and cut it down, sea cockroach, spirit level and mollusc, woodlice and hacksaw blade fall out. They vitiate that poor hog. It was a wild hog Francis Jakey did hold in the bush; bright as pink was the day God send to trap that hog in the wire. Francis kiss the ground when he find it. He say, 'God send rain for the pumpkin to fatten; now he send hog for me to eat it with.'

Francis Jakey god was that same god old men used to call when they find themselves getting up every half hour in the night to leggo water, until where they lean their hand supporting on the latrine wall get indentation and brown from oil. That is when you hear them cry out, 'Oh Lord, don't let me lose my stones. Lord, if I lose the use of these, I might as well dead, so if is that you have waiting for me, you better take me now.'

Melchior say is so he own father dead; dead like cockroach get mash and he never know what kill him. Them days big words like 'prostate' and 'haematuria' would tie up poor people tongue. Instead, Melchior father feel is hooks and eyes some woman send for him, some obeah spell to burn his seed, some black magic she build to dull his bone. He rub bush rum, bay rum, Limacol and kananga water. He even try lamp oil; he boil and steep it in ditay payee, wonder-of-the-world, malomay and cocoa onion. Nothing doing; the pain still humming. Big strong man like that reduce to water. Imagine this, riddle me that: the prognosis bleak, the spirit give way like a bad knee. Poor fella, he stop eat. He lie down on that day-bed like a hairy snake, waiting for Basil to come and measure his grave. Imagine that. Even Clary, a man who work thirty years as a woodwork instructor in the Technical Institute, and was never late once for work, never miss a day, know Basil on his way when he start shitting like duck and straining to rise from toilet seat.

The boys drag, slit and slaughter that hog; they cut the neck and bleed it out to make good black pudding. Alvin say, 'Junk it up in pieces!' Another man laugh, 'Souse up the foot and them!' Was then the butcher writer fellah Raphael, when he hear is wild hog they hold, he leave his rocking chair rocking and he bandy he knee down the hill and say he will buy a case of beers if they let him cook it. He say they have to spit it, and he know about spit roast and fire. So the men say, 'No problem,' He's an odd fella, but they know him as a butcher, and they see it as a way to pass the Sunday. Put the madam in the house to grind cabbage, send the madman Bain down the hill for cigarette and white rum, bring ice in bucket, bring cutters, wire up a system, play music.

Is Sunday afternoon so the church singing in the bush. Deacon Simmons watching out the window while the leader lining out the hymns. He waiting for service to done so he could tear off his stole, crack bottle seal, knock grog and tear up meat with the boys on the hill. The butcher tell them cleave and they cleave it, they shave that hog and sear the soft down, rub it down with coarse sea salt. They construct a spit, a barrel to burst wood in. They stoke and temper the blades of the flame till the wood start to hiss and split, and it burn just right and red. The butcher mount that hog by the head from a guava tree branch. A fella ask, 'Is so you does cook that, you sure?'

Raphael say, 'Yes man, is so to roast it.' The men watch him. Drink rum. Then they step back and laugh when they see it truss up there, how it succumb, how the backside taking licks from fire. Was dead it dead no arse, the eye half close, the mouth to kiss. They step back to admire how the trotters point and how the leg thick like a woman backside. They break a white rum seal, and the more knee bend, the more head rim back. Is drink they drinking, and sooting every woman that pass. People passing getting hungry when they smell that hog roasting, and the butcher turn chef, he rip a kerchief and tie it to a stick and say he basting with vinegar and Kool Aid. Hunger start jumping in the men chest, but the chef wouldn't let them taste even the crackling. Eh heh? Eventually, even the sun get fed up and start to pull for home; night start

138

rushing in, and still the hog roasting. Fellas start to circle the meat, but every time they check inside it, the fetish still pink. What it name? Poison. The beers run out, the liquor done lick, but the boys wouldn't leave; they sweeten with grog and shit talk, steady there upon that hog. Was the scent that hold them, the primal promise of burning meat. Eh heh? Yes, man, when they finally cut that hog down – because they did get fed up, they did weary, they did hungry bad – is whole day they eating nuts and corn curls – they beg and the butcher prise it open: worms, mulch and grist, black bee, millipede, jigger seed, drum skin, pholourie and pembwa fall out. Let it rot where it fall. Let us boil a monkey hand instead. Melchior say he eat monkey hand in Zimbabwe. He say, 'Yesmanitgoodman'. He say he lick it down, skin and all.

46

Bain revelled in people's sufferation. He would hiss and curse them bad and wish them sorrow. He watched and waited for them to tremble and faint from exhaustion, to be broken by spirit lash or sickness, glad to see them put palm to breast when the knock they answer was Basil arriving unexpected to measure their graves. He brew hex and spell, prayed for evil. He wished this even for his own kin and country folk, poor people living all in one hole and climbing over each other on the unforgiving escarpments of the Million Hills. Fellas like Alvin, who never went to school and could barely write their own name, men like Bertram, who stuttering and working as a labourer, but can't get paid because he can't say, 'money'. When the panic spines of fishbone got stuck in people's throats, Bain would feign concern, but silently he wished them skittering suffocation, tremendous poverty, suicidal tabanca, surrender under stress, the windpipe broken by a blow to the neck, the skin flayed and ripping back from the arms in flames, the head flailing in vicious nausea, white blindness, the ear oozing foam in fire, the burst skull of the driver who struggled behind the steering wheel in a burning car on the highway between the landfill and shanty town. Bain want him to suffer in front of people, to struggle, fail and then succumb to the inferno, the feet burning in oil, the devil tearing rabidly with steel teeth till the milk fat come dripping down from the bursting skull. He wanted to smell the stink sweet scent of burning flesh, but see the bones of the hand still gripping the rim of the wheel.

He lived in the crack-house and outhouse for many years, lived in the ghetto below the ghetto, then up on that crooked hill where thick-calved women carried buckets of water up to broken homes for bandy-legged men to bathe with Lifebuoy soap, throwing the last sweet water that collect in the bucket over their heads to simulate showers. These were homes built up over many years, from dirt crumbling red, from wood, mud and mortar, one-one brick, one-one cocoa, then hibiscus, lime and bird pepper blooming in the yard, the veranda open, but the way the hill cut, the stairs steep-steep in the sore-foot mother's yard.

Bain went deeper into the gothic of tropical life. He decide he would stop talking to people for a while. He slept with windows flung open, the wind circulating, the village returning to him as sound. His own mother had blinked hard, though for her he had wished life, not death. He had wished her strength to rise from her bed of sores and catheter and dialysis swill. He had fought hideous lizards and six-legged dogs in the abandoned land, he had hunted mongoose and ocelot, he carried a thin glancing blade, and jumbie beads to be rubbed hot in the palm to give her life, but still Ma Jessie suffered to die in the postcolonial hospital, while Carib Tokyo steelband was passing on the street below.

This was the beginning of literature, and of his estrangement from the brother who castrated goat and bull cow, writing a book for forty-one years which no one would understand or even read; from the aunt whose secret he claimed was hairy and fat; to the cocksman Deacon and the Shepherd of the church, waiting for the pilgrims to catch power and roll so they could peep the black insides of the upper cusp of the women's thighs; from Clary the adulterous carpenter sanding chairs from cedar, white pine or pitch pine; from the living myth of the spinster, Yvette Cooper, who went mad in her tree-lined bungalow, became a black-tongued witch, a ball of fire. Bain reflected on how in older ages, women like Yvette Cooper would have been tied and carried upon a wagon through the old country, to be burnt, then drowned in the river.[17] Something about drowning, something about a

17. Mammy said a cart rolled down one Friday from the valley carrying a soucouyant spread and bound by wrists and ankles to the tray back. There were two riders, with straw hats and whips. The woman had been caught brewing necromancy in her falling-down shack, the shack which had lost its vertical alignment and would almost tumble, but never fall, even in hurricane. When they catch her she had her hand in the pot, big books, vèvès and the tragic dust of jumbie symposia. At night she transformed into a ball of fire. Soucouyant. In the morning there were teeth marks on a boy child's arm, mammy nice child, where she had bitten him, entering through any opening – breeze blocks, rat

road that led to a river, about diving under rocks in pursuit of silver fishes, and then being stuck under those rocks to buck and bloat and float. From the road into Caura, he see the irony of the chest hospital, where the road ventured into deep bush, to the ancient valley where once Bain's own kin once grew cocoa, the sepia track, the road from which there is no way back, where the dew of history was still wet upon the ground. Bain pull his beard and say, 'There was a time when everyone on this earth was the same age, at the same time.' And he done talk. He can swim but he don't show off. They say he bad mind, but poor fella, Bain was in pain; bush bug and silverfish was in his bed; he sleeping with envy. All the existential weight of life was like police boots on his corn. But that was him; is who he was.

Bain went through a phase when he uses to shoplift like a beast. He would brush his hair and put on soft pants and hit all them stores in town. He thief from comic book to mortice gauge. He even utilise smoke-screen camouflage and run away with German stationery from Muir Marshall. He thief pellet gun and bulletproof pyjamas. He went quite France and thief jaw-grind pornography from the long-breast Seychelles woman who does sell in Marseille market. He full up his house with shit. But not for greed or money. Was a balm, poor fella; he had an existential crisis. Sometimes Bain would stop sudden in his falling down latrine and forget who he was. His brother, Raphael, cut a key for him, but he had long ago lost narrative thrust. Fade him and let him go, walk him up as far as the telephone pylon and let him crawl like centipede, make him work security in a bakery and be vex all the time.

hole, the louvres left un-shut. Fire – formless, the long jaw and fine teeth of the manicou, shorn of fur and snarling. They said her palms marked her as evil; they were black, swollen with malice. So the men had trapped her in her house like an animal and dragged her out, screaming and hissing like a cat, secured her, and displayed her through the village, and all the while she frothing, head rolling, cursing and speaking in tongues. In fact, both men had penetrated her forcefully in the back bush. The people came down to see the soucouyant strapped to the mercy bed. They burned her, down by the riverside. The crowd giggled and gasped when the fire took; they saw the mouth open, the teeth prong out, the gums peel back and widen, the tongue dry and mottled with scales; saw the writhing unto death. It twisted like this for

47

On returning from the sea, the musician sat on the cold, hard stone, like a near-righteous priest, like the Christophene boy leaning out of the window, as a jet split the sky in two. He felt the pain of distance. He saw his mother's ghost walking backwards up a hill, whispering the names of poems and books of poems in the corners of sacred places. He was in the house on the river bank where an Indian woman wept. Her breasts were smooth and black, but her sore foot was seeping, and she blew toothless kisses. He was there in the Hindu school by the river when the madman ran amok with a cutlass, dividing the meat from the bone, and when he was done, he held the blade like a spirit level across his throat and rock it hard to one side to burst his wind pipe and cough up smoke and mentholated spirit. He was alone in a field in Bordeaux, in a junkyard in Kennington, in the dust squats of Chicago, in Marina Del Ray wearing a woman's perfume, an apron, her dresses. He was on a hill with blue flies buzzing over carrion in the bush beneath the bacanao tree, flying frogs leaping from the magic hidden in the dim-lit house of sparrows and broken chairs. He was at the house of La Diablesse where light will not penetrate.

She lies face down among the grasses of summer; her mouth is the bamboo creaking, the tuber root. He is with the quartet, playing free, his shirt flung open and his eye rolling round to the back of his skull. The horn screams back at him when he puts it down; it will not mute; he cannot tempt it with fugues or arpeggios. But he is older now, less afraid of the deep well of

---

mostly an hour, its spirit print upon the leaves of trees, the trees of eyes and ears. Her flesh burning down to black, they cried, 'We kill you and you don't die, well die now,' and she rolled her head to the side and cursed them, until to her brain foamed and burst into flame and smoke which rose above them, the body falling behind.

darkness beneath his sleep, of the blood trickling through his arm, of scars that are maps, of photographs in which his eyes are closed. The Reverend Frank Wright had been in Paris, playing 'One for John' and 'China,' with Bobby Few and Noah Howard, 1969. Wright was wounded in prayer, bending at the knees in supplication. Who can be that way again? Who can blow such torrential and intimate fury, vent the rage of ages, the desiring of abstract things in strong material sound and limitless poetry?

He is a boy, fearful of the cut-arse booked with the old man waiting on the other side of the bridge with a leather whip soaked in cat-piss and pepper, waiting to break his back with an axe of sin. So he moved upon the dawn, sick with bad souse and gut rot from the previous night's Steel Band Panorama, peeping through the haze until the old bull left the house to go to market. He would rather stay there and sleep outside, under the stars on that rockstone seat and get eat out by mosquito, than go home and get belt all round his back. Indeed, that morning he'd moved like a ghost so the old man would not catch a glimpse of him. The old man had set out in the rising light from home, but he found the boy asleep in bed when he came back from the market and raided his back with the belt, flinging his hand with the tapering gait of a dancer.

The musician has been with the woman he had followed to the market. Her slack mouth could not keep secrets, but her supple knees, her slender back, her high-hip arse, the rigid density of her character and the blossoms of her breasts seduced him, wove him into her. In the tall bed he had to climb, each rung was a griot's kneecap, each step notated in columns of breath. At the top, the sky opened out like a fan of days unfolding; the peninsula stretched past the lighthouse. She laid her body on his – the bulk of her water, her architecture and the trembling of her sex. He had seen this bay before, the same corridors of distance and light, the same gusts of salt air sweeping up from the horizon, the wishes of ships arriving. But soon the woman was gone. He watched her walking away along the avenues with the wind in her dress and her head flung back with kisses. The hotel was in Brittany. He lay marooned on the empty bed in the blue room with the windows open and the curtains blowing. Below, the shallow pool where he drowned each day was still there. He had no muse, no children, no father in heaven, no sky above, no possession but his horn, no home. Drown. In sound and bone. His ear was a microphone buried deep in the earth and his tongue could only sing the sweet and sorrowful songs of the Southern Caribbean.

In the morning, he left to walk upon the rocks that rim the sea; he climbed the hill to the fish restaurant at Port de Bélon. He ate the same thing each day – the fungus in the shell, the mollusc in the mud, the pink oysters, the husk. He'd seen her that Saturday morning and followed her to the market, her basket on her hip, the land merging into concave and parabolic light. Now he has returned to sit on the cool rockstone like a penitent ghost.

It begins again in the tropics. It begins again by the stagnant pond near the pilot's house, his four daughters and his fighting cocks, the white woman in the yard, the mother of the pilot's children, she who hid from the neighbours, but was seen being taken out, bent double from poison. It begins again with the woman with sorrel flowers in her basket, beneath the hog plum tree, overlooking the abattoir. She was as light as a ghost. So light she did not even cause the shy ti marie leaf to shut when she walked past and touched it.

48

Most of these streets are photographs, places of high contrast and the neon blue of suspense; rain like the night's weeping sore. Remind her. Let her flow past the library and the Port Authority. She is an aspiring actor, new to acting school, sitting on the floor of the drama studio. When it is her turn to act, she stands to play her part. She lifts her arms above her head, she leans her head to the side, she turns to face the narrator's gaze. She has no fear of falling. She has drowned before. She has moved through each episode and knows the seawater's illicit vapour; the way the current pulls, and how sometimes it is surprisingly strong, pulling and tumbling and crashing, hurling the skull and shoulder to the ocean floor. She has heard the sorrowful blues of the southern Caribbean. She has stepped with bare feet upon the wooden floor of the cocoa house, and cold, it was cold. She has walked out onto a verandah overlooking the sea from the green mountains of Maracas; she has lifted her head to gaze upon the lights of the city from high in Cascade. She has knocked, but the door to heaven would not open, and the riveted room of remorse stayed locked shut. She was torn out of momentum, was burst to bone in a house of cormorants, with wings thrashing. She had opened each window and turned each photo of the dead around. She had stood in that liminal gap between her body and her reflection in the mirror of infinity and could not recalibrate herself, or set her arc to a narrative of returning.

She flies to meet the saxophonist that summer, in Stockholm, and is transfixed again by the asphyxiative beauty of his obligatos, though she disregards his dark and penetrative beauty, the elusive maps of his palms. He has seen the naked flesh of her neck, the nacreous pearl of her necklace, the tensile bone of her spine, the reddened skin beneath the straps of her summer dress. He has written a melody for her. 'A song like home' he says, and sits naked in the hotel room with the horn between his thighs, to blow it. The melody is the salt song of a sailor's death by drowning, the sadness of inconsolable longing. She listens, as if this song was the last song sung in heaven, as if it played in the background, on the radio, while driving with her father to the beach.

Once, coming down from the school of blue and dubwise matters, passing by Ackbarali's haberdashery, down past the Presbyterian school near Newallo Ville, she had seen the aftermath of a robbery at Republic Bank. The body of the guard lay twisted on the cool concrete of the glass door's threshold, a hand reaching out and cupping the air, and his eyes flung open for mercy. This guard, a fella name Benson, in those tough times, would have woken from dreaming at five that morning, in the hillside shack where he lived with his wife and six children, would have showered with a bucket of cold water and a pan cup out in the yard, would have pressed sharp seams in his gabardine uniform, to go guard people money. But remember, behind where he living, men like Rawle Singh and 'Pee-Pee' Danclair living too, and hard talk was more like whisper or prayer, when gun talk was near. His woman come quite from where she working in Maraval, hovering above the body with her hands to her mouth, but her tears won't run down yet.

Ella had also seen the drowned body of a boy pulled up from the river bank in Caura, his belly was yellow and domed like a convent. The dead envy the living because they are still among the revellers. They say, 'I walked among you, I was there, I want to come back.' The living envy the dead because the dead know what is there on the other side of the mirror.

The musician kisses her forehead, enfolds her like a bird among the essences of his neck. They drink into dawn and then they make love. After, she cries like a child waking alone in a house where all the lights are lit but where each scream echoes back.

She acts in temples of silence; the director knows her strengths. He snaps his fingers; linger a while, dip me in that well. But she resists the plot, will not memorise the script, yet each word she speaks fits the scene. Drum: a swarm of locust falling through the rain. Rain: the recombination of memory and light. The theatre she acts in is an archive of glimpses. Each window reveals another landscape: the tundra, copra estates, peat bogs, the haze of bugs upon a flax dam, the sharp shadows cut by sin and sorrow. From each wound: the wind. Each street inside this theatre leads to espionage. She takes instructions from the director but dislikes his method and philosophy. At night, she ties knots in her tears and masturbates gratuitously whilst kneeling beside the bed. What can the director tell her that she has not already felt in the part? All these characters are herself; she has internalised them. She will not enter a room as an accomplice who murmurs an improvisation. The class will laugh, and that is not acting. Instead, she will wear sandals and a green cotton dress, zipped and safety-pinned at the back; she will remember villages, brackish water, how once she climbed the Grande Dune du Pilat. She will look up; she is an actor, she will act. But when her mother fell upon that axe of terror and died, she could not cry. Can she come down from the stage? Who will act on her behalf? Her brother-in-law, the fireman? Her sister, the soldier? Her father with his liver tied in a bow? After this, she cannot love again.

49

Melchior tell us how Deacon Simmons end up on the hill. The Deacon was Clary friend; both of them was teaching at the Technical Institute. The old man was teaching joinery part-time, and Deacon teaching electrician work. Those days Deacon could fix anything with wire. Any switch or radio to fix was Deacon to fix it. Deacon would unmount a whole radiogram, run voltage tester along the wiring in the living room, he would stutter, 'This, this wire need change-changing,' and his head would shake from the effort. Deacon drove a green Hillman Hunter, rust all round the chassis, but he always presentable – he use to wear long-sleeve shirt and soft pants, side-part in his hair. He would bow, 'Good e-e-e-evening, Mr Clary, Ma Sylvie, good e-e-evening.' Sister Syl used to say, 'Deacon nice eh? Deacon so quiet.' But wait. Deacon lived with his family in Mount Garnett, a few streets east of the match factory, in a misshapen bungalow made from crate-wood and galvanize. Is outside for fire, sink and latrine and bucket for bathing in the yard. People asking, 'What Deacon doing with his money?' But you couldn't ask him that. Deacon breed his wife with five children; more rooms have to be added as each child was born. The wife was a French Creole woman name Brenda, a dancer, and when you go there, she always coy and haughty; like the corners of her mouth did have hook to hang her smile on.

One evening cool, cool, the dusk now starting to blur the day, when a Hillman screech up outside Clary gate. Deacon Simmons jump out, his shirt pull out from pants, shirt button bust down, and the man puffing and sweating like a hog. Them days the old Clary only working half-day. Deacon so nice, Deacon so cool? But wait. It transpire that Deacon catch a bad feelings in the institute and come home early. Imagine: the man salary running out after two weeks, and he have light bill to pay, more child to mind, and furthermore, he get call in the office that morning and the big boss tell him how they not happy with his work – a student complain, so Deacon bound to feel weak. Then pepper on top pepper, coming into Mount Garnett, he meet Pig on the avenue, and Pig lean in the car and tell him, 'Deacs, boy, a man now go inside by you, about an hour ago,' and Deacon must be say, 'What the fuck you telling me?'

And Pig say, 'Yes Deacs, the fella not from round here. I just telling you because you is my good friend; me and you grow up together, and I don't want you to get hurt, but your wife horning you, boy, and everybody know. Oh gosh, man, when you go to work and them children gone to school, Brenda bringing man inside there!'

Deacon lip start to tremble, 'Oh sh-sh-shit man, what to do?'

Pig laugh, 'You stupid or what? The man in your house and you asking, "What to do?"' Deacon never really response. But sure enough, when he reach home he see a black Humber bicycle lean up against his house like a pimp. Deacon park a little further up, he didn't drive in the yard like he accustom to. He sit in the car for a good twenty minutes, looking in the rearview mirror to see if the horner man emerge, but the fella was still busy. Deacon gone sneaking around his own yard like tom cat now. He peep by the window, and between the curtain he see a black man sit down on the bed lacing up his gym-boots, lord, and Brenda lying down naked as she born, with one knee up and the big leg shaking. Brenda look up, and Deacon retract; he hide, and then he hearing commotion inside, things like they tumbling. When Deacon hear the horner man voice his prick get small. The man voice booming like a bull trap in a cell. Deacon decide to act, but lord, what to do? Same time the horner man run outside. He see Deacon stand up there watching him, and all he could say was, 'Ai pardner, wha' goin' on?' Deacon mouth open and it feel like so much time pass, then he growl and make a rush for the man. But like is in slow motion. The man want to ride away, but Deacon grab the bike handle, and the fella pull and Deacon pull, and they tumble in the dirt, and Brenda run out in a sheet, begging them not to kill each other. Deacon vex till he crying, and he and the man scratching like tiger cat and making them grunt big men does make when they fighting. Most of the blow they throwing missing, but somehow the cocksman gain advantage and pin down the Deacon, and in that clinch the Deacon eye get thumb and swell, and the cocksman shirt tear.

The dogs gang around and jumping. Brenda holding her breast trying to part the men, 'Let him go, Hugh, let him go! And Hugh, the horner man, ride away and almost fall. Deacon go inside and see where the man do his thing. He see the empty glass, drumstick bone, some pelau on a plate. He never say nothing. Brenda pulling him and pleading, but Deacon like a robot, blood in his eyes for suffer, and he throw kerosene around the house and burn it down, down, down. Melchior say when he went up the avenue the following day to buy hops bread, the wood was still smoking.

Brenda run to her mother in the country. She keep Ella, and the two youngest, but the older two scatter through the island. Eventually everybody does end up in Million Hills, and this was how Deacon end up there, to live with his long time mistress, Joan. He start driving Joan motorcar for taxi, and every Sunday he in church.

50

Always this falling motion, a plummet to stone and the promise of dream death by falling. Always this memory of a winding road to a cathedral hid high in hills, around several bends and sudden slopes. Down is the drop and sudden death. Same thing happened to Luke after his encounter with the Great Bandit, while reaching to touch the powdery surface of the sky, and they both capsized into a torrent of river lashing rock in rage and hissing sparks of white spume. They emerge upon some primordial land and Luke stagger out and roll about on stone, quite in Barbès, coughing up blood but his body intact, the back good, the foot good, just the neck raze up with claw lines where the Great Bandit try to snuff him out of creation, to cleave his breath as they fell.

Luke had been in Paris, chasing tail all round the market in Clignancourt. The Bandit, when he realise that Luke escape again, get so vex he forget about plot and narrative arc; instead he want to devastate Luke from the pages of the great novel, to remove him totally, instead of engaging in some pleading mode or ruse to steal or seduce whatever secrets the author might have revealed to the star boy – such as the sequence and method of the Bandit's own death, a death which now seemed as real as the solid earth beneath his feet, his gun belt or cutlass hand. The Bandit wears shrunken heads in a necklace around his neck, and his eyes burn like capsicum with envy. He could not bear to see another man prosper, he could not be appeased by the role he had been given, as villainous creep, adrift as a ship upon the metaphor of the sea, or cast in a hurricane and grasping at the oars, rudderless, with no means to change the progress of his struggle or strophe. That was not his portion. If he knew what was destined he could shift, he could duck. When Luke's wood was still in plastic, when they were both still abiding by the old man's vision, the Great Bandit could have chosen to do good work, but he was own-way and wily. Soon as he graduate from bandit school he start to pillage and plunder, he become the blade or the bullet passing. When the iguana raise its head, he say, 'Is fire for you.' The Great Bandit almost sure now that Raphael have him to dead, that even archetypes have horizontal fates, that the great book would be shut, or worse, unread.

What Luke remembered most was that he could not feel his body as he fell, weightless down the precipice. He understood, then, how his ancestors might have flown back to Africa from there – the mechanics of the thing. It was the same as floating in a dark and bottomless well, by leaving the husk of the body behind, or folding it into the gravitational pull of spatial curvature.

The Great Bandit had collapsed on another river's shore. He had wrestled with a manatee. His mouth is hunger, an open sore. The wide-brimmed fedora he always wore was in his hand, revealing his tonsure gleaming clean, shorn of all hair – the dried glue that fastened the toupee to his skull could be peeped behind his ears.

Luke reach back riverside from Europe in time to touch the big man's heart, but like cardiac done arrest the Bandit; the big man fall, and the army of muscles and veins in his head putsch and crap out. Luke inspect the Bandit hip pocket for coins. He wriggled the Bandit's tattooed fingers for the silver rings the big man stole in Vienna, for his gun sack and pellets. He was searching his wallet for bread when the Bandit gasp and cat-spring upright and chook Luke in his throat with a tiny dagger he kept hid in the heel of his boot. When Luke get pierce he bawl for his mother. He panic, revisiting an image he had long mined as memory: the cane field exorcism – fireflies, the bush fires in the hills above, the malevolent spirit shifting its imprint on the canebrake, the glossolalia and the lash, the pork-legged woman writhing on the table. Such things were real. There were tongues spoken there that he had not heard before; unbelievable things had occurred in that tent. A woman, one of the mothers of the church, was saying with softness and warmth, 'Little boy, move from there, clear the entrance, is the gap and portal to a black hole, mirror of infinity; let the spirit come out and pass.' But Luke could not move. The Great Bandit had punctured him with frightful death. The sky lid had swung back to its regular position, and the cliff dwellers and the holy men, the Orinoco pearl fishers and fishers of men had long gone back to their domed homes and hammocks. They had touched the firmament themselves, and now the sky lid and pulse of the cosmos was inscribed on the roof of their brains. The Great Bandit shook his head, leaning as one would clear the ear after a sea bath. His clothes were drenched, his tunic torn, his trousers stuck to his legs, as if he had fallen in a river on his way back from the pan yard, and he walking through town like nothing happen, but everybody he pass could see that those khakis were wet not brown. The Bandit wiped the tiny dagger on the inside of his wrist, he drew breath, felt his beard was brittle with brackish rust, and he touched his heart where it hurt. Then he truss up Luke with twine. That night he built a three-stone fire and cooked river crabs and curried dumplings. Then he perched himself in a tree like a parrot and smoked his hard weed. Time he wake up next morning, Luke had escaped and run down to South America.

But this grief milk thing: know the suffer Elsie suffer under that house, eating dirt and matted hair and rags that ants bite up, and toilet paper that woodslave or black and white salamander shit on chicken wire. They leave she down there to do her business, they leave Elsie down there to dead. It is July 1965, motorcar still curvy, fellas still wearing flannel peg pants, women still wearing calico dress, Sparrow come with 'Steering Wheel', 'Congo Man',[18] and Elsie down below that house in Barataria for two weeks now, from when her family bring her there after her one child dead at five days old, and poor Elsie milk come in and burst. The milk stay full up in her breast with no baby to feed, so it must water out to irrigate the world, or be squeezed into an elder's eye, to cleanse cataract, or seep out sticky and white. Oh gorm, grief milk they call this milk. When the milk turn to blood, Elsie crawl under that house and wouldn't come out. Down in the dirt she grew a beard, and ate so much dirt her breasts dried to wood. Who would be worried? Who would care? Who would dig Elsie out from under this tragedy? The old man washing his cock in the sink? The civil servant beating his Alsatians with a black police belt? The cousin who was a promising athlete, until big books – like Deleuze's *Rhizome* – drove him mad? The woman upstairs in the calypso ballroom in Champs Fleur grinding malice because her husband still seeing the same hardback bitch that feeding him egg bread and green yam for fourteen years? The barebacked tailor sewing silver masquerade boots opposite the Royal Jail on Frederick Street who could tell you how dense with gallow's cry some mornings does be? The camera man obsessed with taking photos of the old fort, the old port, the cathedral, the market with its fisheries scent? The same one who watching the young boy prick

---

18. Both from Mighty Sparrow, *Congo Man* (1965).

and plum, and pick him out to skin up on a hairy rock in short pants for photograph? The woman who escaped heavy poverty on the hill, who lived in a hole in the ground until she hook up the heart of a German pensioner, as a chambermaid at The Hilton Hotel, and moved to Caracas with the old test – later to glean he was a wanted man with a gun under his bed and a criminal past in Germany? She never tell nobody, expecting long money, but is just thirty-two Fats Domino albums he dead and leave her instead. Or the hundred-year-old aunt still grinding sugar cane with she teeth and shooing blue fly from a scar on her thigh that never heals? No, not even the hard-prick priest in the falling-down church where people passing out from rhythm and heat. Nor even the navel orange vendor at Cantaro junction who selling sideways weed, nor the macomere fish man, Melchior, nor Cousin Alvin, nor the barber in the village who know how to fix up when fellas skull plate showing? Maybe the local opera singer who feel that black people can't tell if she singing in tune? No, nobody go care for poor Elsie, not even the shit snake or the mongoose fleeing fire, or the blackbird waiting for rice, or the boy with the whip that cutting lizards in two – look, their thick back burst/sting. So, left to eat dirt till it pack up her gut, Elsie get mad like a jumbie in a cage; she hissing and biting people ankle when they pass. The butcher Raphael, seeing her plight, and fed up hearing her cry at night, fling some mercy her way. He leggo a hose under there and wash 'way cockroach and scorpion nest and lumps of cement with chicken-wire that remain there from long-ago way of building with mud and bush, from since Mr Tom was a boy learning construction work in Tobago; it wash out worm in old wood from leftover carpentry work. But Elsie refuse to leave and she keeping the man from his work. Every time he sit down to write, he hearing she moan, and she is family, a distant cousin, but still he can't turn his ear away, so he leggo mercy again. He invite Elsie to sing jazz in the lil' Sunday band he blowing trumpet in, but she fail; her singing was bad – must be dirt eat out her throat. He try her in butchery, to cleave goat meat from bone, but she flinging blade like sorrow self and junking up the people meat. So he put her in the book he was writing, he put her under a house to eat dirt. But Elsie wouldn't behave; she vex like crab;

she watching Raphael cut-eye and cussing. She wouldn't bend to the arc; she was too harden, too own way. She see men like Luke and the cocksman sax-boy run out and explore, so Elsie want to venture out too. So when the old man put her to sit down, she skinning up leg and cussing like ol' higue; she tearing up harp, she never wear shoes. Elsie will thief meat out from cane-cutter' teeth, cigarette out from calypsonian' mouth, money out the Reverend hand. It wasn't until Raphael buy her a sailor dress and put her in a Buddy Williams dance that she start to revive and act decent. Now she washing her mouth out with baking soda and bathing daily with rosemary bush. Now she cutting her hair and taking studio pose on long stool; now she become a parable for change in Raphael book. Is she make Raphael realise that women like her could not be contained: they must run amok and cry out; they must stand up in Central Market and drag cutlass across their navel; they must pump engine and drive taxi; they must draw their own pension and capsize lazy men who getting big like robot.

Melchior say, 'Since they cut Christo seeds, he firing wind. Better they did leave them big. Long time when Christo pop, he used to burst caps, like when I fire shot it go pax! pax! But now Christo have nothing there but sack. Christo had big balls since you was a little boy in these hills, running round barefoot. Remember the morning you stand up in the yard with your totee outside, while workmen mixing mortar? The damn dog Rex jump and bite, and you run inside to lie flat on the bed? Christo had wind ball and bag since you was hunting woodslave, and when plane passing, you looking up between the trees. Even when you was chopping white pine to make wooden men, because you never get no figurine for Christmas, Christo had big balls he uses to carrow in a barry. When he sit down he need an extra stool to rest his stones on. He gone for sea bath and have to tie rope to coconut tree; is a line to draw out in the water so he wouldn't float away. You don't remember Christo pulling his stones in from the sea? Some woman love nothing more than man with big stones. They love the balls to bang them, swing down so they feel satisfy when it slap them plap-plap-plap! It make them feel their man love them. But the pain was deep in poor Christo belly. Sometimes he sit down to play all fours and the blood would draw from his face.

'Is a lil' Indian girl from Aranguez that give Christo that. Pulling bull one night, he pick she up in the Croisee; she must be give him slack and say, "Come down in the garden." Her house on stilts where street don't have no name. She take Christo to roam down by the rice paddy, the bamboo and the galvanise. Christo hearing sarood and sitar in the bush, he hearing Lata Mangeshkar and he get bazodee. The Indian girl give him peas-shell wine and tampi pipe to smoke, bend over and show him puss and Christo want to mount, but she make him wait till midnight pass, when her father fall asleep, and then she bring out the rum.

She rub an oil in Christo palm and his chamber load. Her pit was shallow, but he dive in one time. He greedy, he dive in and hit bottom. The damn fool barrel bend and backfire, but he swallow that pain and carry on throwing leather all 'round the Indian waist. And is from then that Christo notice he stones start to swell like breadfruit, and shining like old man skull plate. He try to keep it from people in the village – he wearing long-crotch flannel pants – but it hanging so low he can't sit down properly, can't run from rain or ride bicycle, can't hunt behind the Credit Union no more. It tender. Sit down there each dusk and watch him lay back in that iron chair, say he waiting for the prodigal to return. Another time Christo was eating an iguana. He love the skin, and Sam Roberts cooking one with Congo pepper and black curry. Christo smell that geera and he couldn't wait. He go in the man pot and dish out a piece, hold the skin in his teeth and pulling, pulling. The damn skin recoil and slap him frankomen in his face! Grown men just shake their head and smile; he was rushing the pot, but it now start to cook. Another time, he self corner a 'guana. It fat. He tie the back foot behind with twine, like police handcuff, ready to scorch the skin and bruise it with green seasoning. He call friends, he bring out liquor, glasses, ice and cutters. When he cut the belly he say, "Waaaay, it have big eggs too." Mr Lalsingh was passing; he say, "But Christo, you sure them thing is egg?" Christo say, "Yes man, you can't see is egg?" And he cover the pot. When the 'guana done cook, he eat the egg first but after he only belching piss. He find it funny that he alone eating; nobody else hungry. You know was the 'guana stones the man eat?

Christo claim he use to live on Bradhurst Avenue in Harlem. He say he gone up there to spread the blessed word of gospel, but he lie. He say Church Avenue in Brooklyn was as long as from town to south, you can't even drive it. But Alvin enquire, "Wow, you mean one street so long, Christo?" Now, Alvin is a bushman, he face like a fairytale witch, he never travel, but he was the first man to fire pellet gun in the village; before he was hunting high in these hills in rubber slippers with just a torch and a lance. Is Alvin who learn us how to cut lance from steel pipe with hacksaw blade, how to angle the hook so it slit to snatch when it puncture, rip manicou down from tree top; tell us how cocorico will see a next cocorico get shoot, and sit there still and wait to get bullet in he tail. Or how agouti will hide his head in hole and think his body conceal. "One road? So long?" Alvin ask again. "Yes man, it long from Brooklyn to Jersey; both side is just church, church, church. Church, funeral home and liquor shop." Christo say once a Jamaican woman cook him cow-foot soup in Brooklyn. He say he lay leg and lumber in her cushioned boudoir, drapes astride the bed. Christo say he bawl like a cow when she open up and he see the puss. He get so excite, he burst – pax! pax! But that was back when he did firing solid senders, not wind. Then he turn over, like roast bake, snoring down the woman place.' When they cut Christo big stones bag, Melchior say, was like gizzard inside.

53

Raphael wrote, 'Put me in that water and wash me down –.' And then his hand stick, stick on the first line, like the red rastaman iron-man hand beating for a brass band, coming down through the dust one Carnival Tuesday, knocking the hubcap high with iron stick, grinning, the sweat pouring down. Since nine that morning he shaking his natty and beating iron hard for the masqueraders in the biggest bikini band, and then the man hand stick – stick when it raise and it wouldn't come down to clang. The band start to slack. They watching him. They depend on that pulse like Egypt 80 for shekere and wood block. If the beat gone, they rudderless. Even the drummer start to miss beat and twist up on his stool. He try to pull the beat back with the hi-hat bell, but the rhythm done uncoil and is trouble to reel it back in. So they dash ice-water on the iron man shoulder, they try to lower the hand, but the thing stiff-stiff. Let it take its own time to soften and bend, it will spring its own water. It was the hardness of the iron, repetitive strain, the licking put upon the wrist that stick it.

The red rastaman name was Sweetman; he was from Trou Macaque village – a real-real character. He would ride motorbike like thief, doing wheelie and skidding in the tracks as if he in grand prix. But this is the valley of bush and precipice; is a wonder he never crash. With his gold teeth grin he manage to hustle his way into a government job, doing labourer work on a school down south. He say he taking about three maxi taxi to reach, so everyday he would roll up on the job two hours late. Then he rush around the foundation ditches wearing a helmet with a shovel in his hand. He working the two hours before lunch, then he telling stories for the rest of the day. He say how once he hiding up a mango tree down by the military base, where the officers used to bring women to bull in backseat, and how he peep and almost fall off the tree when he break. He say another time a woman in the village was talking to her neighbour over the kitchen bottom door, and only coughing. Why? Because he was knocking hard-waist behind she. Sweetman invite the men to come up to the hills to smoke hard weed, and the weed was hard in truth. He transform into a wise man; his chalice bubbling sweet. This dread so charismatic, women desired him like fresh fish; they thought he was half white, or at least Hispanic. He sweet-talk the woman selling bake and cheese – she come deep from the southern bush. This woman would skin up on the cement bags and talk raw about abrasive sex – the friction of leg and lumber, burning with each stroke, and Sweetman there grinning, waiting for her guard to slip so he could fling his sword and clinch. The other workers watching as the rastaman bent his back boldly in gregarious laughter to mamaguy the woman, under the avaricious eyes of the foreman, the stores clerk and stone mason. Even the young boy there, who writing poetry, his prick hard in his pants, watching to see what will happen. Well, the rastaman up and fire the work just so. He leave good one day but never came back. It was more than a year later that we heard how the rastaman had cornered the bake and cheese woman outside of duty, and jam she somewhere down in San Souci – and we laugh.

The carnival after that was when Sweetman start beating iron in the brass band. He tell the men in the band he percussive, how he can beat goat skin, drum skin, so iron was easy. He say how he come from a long line of blacksmiths and ironmongers, so he know iron inside and ironside out; how he have natural rhythm, and in truth, he was good. People come to know the band by the red rastaman; they see him and they bawl, 'Iron dread in the land!' And they would follow that band just to see Sweetman bouncing on the iron.

But the day his hand stick, it was more than rhythm get twist, it was a whole mythology. They put him to sit down, but his hand trembling still. The young boy poet was on the road that day, he was in the crowd, and he see when the iron fall. Months after that, the boy was buying shoes – he was on his way to England – and he bounce up on the dread again. The rasta was selling shoes; he laid them out on the sidewalk and say, 'Buy these quick, brother, the Doc say I have six months to live. Cancer.' The young man try them on and they were tight, but he make them fit. He humble down and melancholy for the days of the dread on the building site, so he succumb and open his heart and wallet right there. But Sweetman never recognise him, and the youth man never tell nobody how, two years down, when he come back, he see the red dread still selling woollen belts and espadrilles on the corner of Henry and Independence Square. This is what Raphael should have written, but instead, in that hand-sticking moment, he had lost the will to write. The bull cow was rambling in the hillsides – it had burst its chain; a woman was beating her daughter on the other side of the hill with a broomstick; and the citrus-scented light of dusk threw brief shadows upon the village. He could write no more. So the dread had to wait until Raphael fall asleep on the plough, to make himself flat and narrow, to slide out flat from the vision sideways, until his hand come back good again.

54

Showboy stand up in the tour bus and say, 'That is not irony, that is something else, peculiar to Nigeria. Imagine, the driver going for road, and the musician on the island going for opposite direction, like if you play music that black but not hitting for dance, the traffic police would raise his hand and point in the direction of Afro beat.' They are all on a bus leaving a festival in Nijmegen, looking out on the road out of town, at the night shops and kebab shops, the shut butchers and offices of workers, the dubwise Turkish discotheques. They drive through the red light district and stare at the women in the windows. The musician feels he knows Europe now more than tropical places. He has lived here for a lifetime of suspense and intrigue. He has suffered. He has been picked narrow by carrion crows and – watch how time passing – he getting old, like scarecrow in haiku. He tells the band about Mikey, whose eye was on America. 'Mikey was the Pie Man from Million Hills, near where I was born; he used to drive taxi and sell beef pies; he dead now; somebody kill him.' But the blurred image of Mikey persists, and the musician sees him walking through the savannah, fading to white.

The news reached him in Berlin. Alvin call and say, 'Mikey dead.' It weighed upon the musician like a flock of baritone saxophones. He used to see Mikey step out slick and sweet, at precisely the time when night just fall, to go drive taxi, but in secret and truth, is bull Mikey used to go and bull. What a what? All things must pass, but still… Mikey didn't have no enemies. But everybody does say that. Some people don't open their business just so, especially when their secrets could roll downhill. Uncle Mikey wanted to go America. Sometimes he sit and build dream in his head. He see himself walking down Fifth Avenue and across Broadway, go uptown and eat a soul food at Amy

Ruth's, sit down in Lennox Lounge with the tall greyhounds and drink sour-mash whisky.

Mikey park up on the bridge, right in front the steam laundry, he squeeze his prick and say, 'Y'see me? My vision outsee this island. Money saving up, contacts with the visa link me up, boss. Every time I pass, the man winking to link me up. He say, "Anytime you ready, come with $500 US," and is papers: fix; document: fix; foreign currency: fix; and by August, I in New York. And once I get my business through, I go send for family.' Mikey say how he hear green grape big like apple in New York, how Yankee grapefruit have no seed, how fried chicken selling in tin, how you buying good leather shoes cheap-cheap, sports jacket, merino drawers, hot shirt, aftershave, all kinda thing, cheap-cheap. He say woman to eat, pussy to beat. Mikey hop, he bawl, he must go New York City! But August come, he never reach the airport. September come, he say, 'Delay.' October, November: Mikey still driving taxi through Santa Cruz and people pointing at him with their mouths. Unknown to any, that man Mikey queue up from four outside the embassy to get visa and get blank frankomen in his face. They tell him his ties to Trinidad too weak, papers not good, money not enough. He get the red refused stamp in his passport and never tell nobody except his wife. That thing hurt him, hurt him, hurt him. It take Mikey weeks to get across it, the misery so deep.

The musician watches the first sun of April anoint the fields, the flowers of graffiti on the station walls. They have travelled from Nijmegen to Antwerp. Heavy in his heart he remembers Mikey at Tyrico Bay saying, 'I can't stay here to dead like a nit in this backward place.' Mikey make his plans but Basil make the decisions, and soon aunts in black and Ben Hur perfume were moaning in the graveyard mud, the rayo trees leaning on the hillside, and up from the russet, brown-stone church a hole was dug in fertile land to plant Uncle Mikey, the Pie Man.

In Antwerp, in the cold spring, the bright eye of the sky leans upon the horn, and the musician feels the weight of time bearing down hard on him, a sorrowful blues, the grinning mouth of the fox. He tumbles like a wave crashing against the sides of a pirogue, the bay blanched by the whiteness of fire, the landscape now the savannahs of Belgium, where a farmer wearing overalls toils among his tomatoes and red onions.

That night, he walks out onto the stage after the band has begun playing. He raises his horn and blows ribbons of notes, creaking in the chambers. The lip thrills, the band swings hard, hard like rockstone in pillow, pump the kick. The audience is transfixed, riveted to the ground by daggers of sound. They play Ellington's 'UMMG', as blues, as a slow, stately blues, and suddenly the band turns a sharper corner, lifts the key high in the neck with a gasp, but the line that connects them to the saxophonist is suddenly broken and out of sync, out of any idea Heidegger had about spatial geometry or *Dasein*. He leaves the stage/steps out of their world/to walk across sand to an ocean. Sand sinks into his toes. He is seeking the crayfish from the fishermen's rope, the flesh which tastes like the blood in his woman's mouth. He wants to succumb to the deep, have her fall upon him, turn her head to face him under the sweet yellow streetlights on the main road outside the hotel where traffic passes, where water creaks in the rigs and false foundations of a boat. She stains him with her cum splash, from a palace of thighs, sighs, then everything converges like an erotic portrait.

55

Raphael saw Yvette Cooper coming down from the water tank with full buckets one morning when, sudden so, as if shook from meditation, she saw him standing in his slaughtery, and stopping to wave, her knee give way. Not just give way but bend and pop like shit from Broclax chocolate, collapse, kilkete, fall apart and fold up like twine, her bony knees and legs flung open. She lived, but, soon after this, suffered a stroke when she went to draw money in the Credit Union and get refused. They put her to sit down in the office while they looked into her situation. Then the handsome jacketman come and bend low to her ear and say, 'Mrs Cooper, your money not good.' Yvette beg, but the man look around to see if anyone could hear, then he affirm, 'Believe me, Yvette, them people in here not giving you nothing.' And Yvette feel her jaw want to open but the heaviness couldn't lift.

Then she get a heart attack on the hill. Neighbour, neighbour, come rock and take her, rock of ages, hand to heart, look she falling backwards into the abyss. They bring smelling salts and boil egg to revive her, but is right there they would find her, a few weeks after, in that same one-sided bed, with electric light and radio on, the room funky-funky from the sauce her body expel, fish still seasoned in her fridge, red butter rancid in the dish. They go in there and find framed photographs of her son in Boston, posing back from snow; a Statue of Liberty figurine in plastic brass; thrift-shop clothes. They find Yvette's accruements in trinkets and gold in her laminated chest of drawers, even Stax and Motown 45s. Her river come down. Basil reach her yard and call her come, and when Basil call, you have to go down. She had lived up there upon the hill for many years after her husband Pattison died. Dust to dust, no energy dies. The body transforms into liquid textology, relinquishes the burden of truth. Yvette move through the dark like a leaf upon dark waters. She beg the doctor to save her from falling. But that never happen. The man only had time to catch the goblet before she fall, lest it spill, and the oceans tilt and overflow the brim. Raphael used to speak with her over the barbed wire fence, her face partially hidden by red chaconia blooms, her hands on her hips, her voice almost falsetto. She laugh when he tell her he writing a book. Now look what happen.

This May, the musician has returned, but stays only for a week to shoot a video and draw hard weed. Time too brief to capture, too narrow to pass through. He comes up to the hill and speaks in metaphors. They tell him, 'Talk straight!' Tanty Belinda chastises him for coming with both arms swinging. 'Not even a bottle of duty-free rum or some foreign thing you don't bring for people?' He talking tall and flinging sharp prose like he want to cut people; big words to bewilder and impress the people of Million Hills. But the old women caress his neck, they lay their strong hands upon his skull and shoulders, they watch him at arms length, turn him this way and that, they inspect him lengthways, sideways, then smile solemn smiles. They knew him when he ran barefooted among these vines. He cannot pretend to be hip, bop, mystic or jazz with them; he must be humble, or they fouti put him with plastic fork to dig latrine; or put him to cut iron bamboo under a riverless bridge with a razor blade; put him barefoot among the ti marie bush and let picka jook him; put him to kneel down on a grater and count to a hundred; or make him burst his big toe on the hard tar road – peel back the skin and salt it; send him along a river with a tyre on his back, the red grass tall and wild; send him across the mountains to the wild Caribbean sea; wash him clean with witch-broom and olive oil; anoint him with shandilay and ditay payee; send him back across the sea.

He is looking for the carpenter's shop that used to be down the track, behind the junction. But that gone; the carpenter dead. They found him alone in his workshop, sitting proper on his stool with wood in his hand, except for the head which was bowed, so the nose drip sandy snot. Is so the carpenter dead like a nit to this world. The cedar smell and red sawdust ground – all that has gone.

Walking through the hills, the musician wants to record and preserve each image, to capture each crook and cunny in the rhythm of the thing. He want this whole kiss-me-arse island to be his muse, but it is busy slipping through his hands, and through his eyes, and through his pores, and through his brain; it fading like a hairline, or as colour dims at dusk; it precious and impossible. In the village below, where he was born, the ground is flat. The houses have bright banisters; the rum shop also sells yellow fried fish. Further east, red and yellow Baptist flags are planted in ordered, urbane gardens. The women he knew and loved in these streets, in these houses, in these alleys and grasses, are gone into the momentum of their lives. They cannot be seduced by the past. They have husbands now, and children. And why should anything of this hill be saved? Because he is an empty space without it. He is the draught under the dining table, the garden at night. Make him go to market and look for his grandmother's ghost buying callaloo bush, buying honey, mauby, mace and red lavender, before he too is gone to that riverside hospital, to cry prayers into his hot hands.

56

Clary would get up early on Saturday morning, jump up and pump engine, carry basket to market, shop around for some chive, some dasheen bush, a breadfruit, some blue crab, some tripe, a piece of king fish, but really he gone in the steam laundry to get his prick suck. He had a long-breast woman, a Madam Bruce, working in there in the steam and the whiteness of nursing-home linen. And they romance, with the river running below, they simple and chat, they kiss like fish, then she squeeze up his wood and give him brush right there in the back where the steam machine spinning. Madame Bruce was Clary sometime companion or longtime madam friend for thirty good years. You may watch her slight and laugh, but don't mind she flat like a bake, Clary alone know the engine she have under that bonnet. She never bend to kiss the young boy, Clary grandson, on the front seat, but when Clary crank the motorcar to go, she might suggest a smile and whisper to herself, 'One day, one day, congotay, is me go be sitting inside of there.'

The old man give Madam Bruce money to fix her mouth. She have children; Clary give her money to buy them Christmas clothes. But still she watching and waiting; she see the big house the man building in Mount Garnett and she measuring how long the garden is, contemplating if the rafters could withstand black magic, or if the garret have room for necromancy. She wondering how long before his house madam, Sister Syl, would dead. She set up sorcery. But the old man blood was close to his skin; you couldn't tell him the woman he love have bad-mind. Get him vex and he leggo belt blister to burst like caps on your skin. Sometimes his grandson had to run under a neighbour house, or into swamp land with tall bush leaning over, to hide from licks when Clary fling out his hand.

But hear the history. The house madam come and dead

unexpectedly. Madam Bruce rejoice. She buy barrel, box, she buy twine and put down, she start to pack to move to nice house. But rewrite that history. She was brushing her teeth one morning when, just so, she catch a stroke and her engine break down. Her tongue fall and flap like rubber, her knee gone through, barrow in a carry they carry she go doctor, but she never come back. She was so cantankerous in death they had to bury her standing up. You see how things does be? Then the old man fire the work in the technical institute, like he get stupid, and he gone quite Morne Diablo to live. He rent boat and learn to fish, he hunt grouper and cowfish all in Erin and Cedros – and lose his money gambling like a fool. Clary realise he getting big in the numbers, but he squander, he still exorbitant. When he go restaurant he ordering lobster and roast octopus; he drinking wine by the bowl. Well, eventually, he happen back penniless and slim, back in the Million Hills. The home he abode black with oil – a mechanic used to live there, fixing engine in the dog-itch dirt. This board house had withstood hurricanes and tragedies, early morning phone calls to come down to the morgue, where blue smoke puffing out the chimney, to identify somebody body.

He get to know a woman down the hill with a taxi business. Clary vex every time the woman phone ring; he know is bucket a drop, money like rain she making. He get ambitious in his old age, and board she to hustle him a loan to build up a carpentry business under his house, but she refuse. Next thing coming was glory days done, the big gorgon failing and taking days to recuperate.

Clary watch how Raphael set up his business: salt lick was zwill blade sharpening. Raphael cutting cow neck and slaughtering sheep, little sheep and large; he cutting goat stones. Clary watch how when Raphael pour out liquor he drinking old Demerara rum from ornate glass, and then he humble down to write. Imagine that. Clary envy the man. He pull out Whiteways cider, but he never have ice. He envy how Raphael butchering yard become a place of gossip and lime to bands of hill-born men, to bow-legged grandmothers who know how to tender the neck of lamb, who know how to cut fowl neck while standing on its foot, then bucket it hot in boiling water, and say, 'Beat up how much you want, Mr. Man, you going in that pot.' One night, one cock

171

jump out Miss Eve bucket with his head hanging by a ligament string. He was a big cock in the yard, used to mount the hens, then stand up on the wall and crow like a governor. Eve hold him, she put him back in the hot water and press him down, and is so he dead with foot screeching out like fork, and get pluck and stew brown, and end up in pelau.

Raphael rearing the animals in the front and slaughtering them in the back. When Friday foreday morning come, them cow uses to moan; they know he have one to kill that day. And is so Raphael used to make his money. Clary see that and he jealous, because butchering is how Raphael could afford to eat what he like, drink what he like and write as much as he want when night come. But Raphael hand was heavy, his writing was thick and black like molasses, hard to wade through. Bring us an axe to rip this ground upon which his great thesis is built. The man wouldn't let a bad sentence rest, nor read the work among stupid people. He would hide to write, and his wood would get hard when he corner the right word. A word for instance, like 'craven'.

57

That night, both narrative arc and river were running against the train line, which now seemed so distant from Raphael's window. Although the line ran across the page, trains had long ceased to roll across the tracks where the acrobat had once crossed, on Saturdays, on his way up Ryan Street, towards the Million Hills. The acrobat was patient, pausing between each routine. He tumbled, performed planches. He somersaulted on the sweet earth beneath the samaan tree, then he sat in the breeze to dry his sweat before he took that long walk to Maxine's house in the hills. There he encountered her father, Mr Alcantara, on the veranda, scratching his inner thigh and smoking his red-beard marijuana. Mr Alcantara had seven daughters, so he was familiar with young men coming across the moat from the road to the house to visit them. When they sat out under the stars, courting, the big man would be on his knees watching from the bedroom window. The hills that surround them would be blinking with tweeters of disco. The acrobat would ask for a glass of water and when Maxine brought it, it smelled of flour. Maxine was of Spanish-Tobagonian genealogy, cut tight from Charlotteville top soil. Her blackness was slender and trim, so the fading sun could beam stars between and upwards to the cusp of her thighs. The acrobat assumed that she was attracted to him, because she was still quite polite at sixteen, and smiled beside him on the veranda wall, even sitting close so their thighs colluded. But come now, come now, if you look down you fall. Polite, yes, but Maxine would not open her heart, or anything else, and she gave the acrobat no assured route to pursue her.

Years later, he would return, arrogantly grown; he was now an architect's apprentice; he had leaned with various women into the human sciences, and was no longer as desperate or reticent as he had been those Saturdays when he walked across the savannah to her house. He sits there again, and the father, now suffering with late life adiposity, waves his arm from the living room where he watches *Man From Atlantis* on the same Sylvania TV. Her mother, in the bedroom, like a Baptist folding white sheets, peeps out, silent and grim. The acrobat confesses that in those sentimental days, when they walked along the old train tracks together, or when he sat beside her in the cool muscle of night, how much he had loved her, that he'd written her poems he'd never shared. Maxine watch him in his face and say she never knew he felt that way, and she throw her head back and laugh, 'Kee kee kee.' He say, 'How you mean? Not even when I used to let you wear my jacket in the cold?' She laugh, 'How cold could it have been in this heat anyway? He say, 'You lie. You must have known.'

Once this same Maxine had brought a snake to school in a crocus bag – a young boa. Its head, raised up when the bag was untied, was like the bruised crown of a hanged man's cock. Its eyes were like red jumbie beads. She kept it under her desk, but so much muscle in that bag it bound to come out. She sit down there and it troubling her foot. The teacher want to know why she can't sit still and read. She had to let it go, let it run out, and it run amok and make trouble in the yard. Snake used to stand upright like man in Eden before he fuck about with God, and the Big Man rip out his foot and put him down to crawl.

It was a macajuel boa, a snake tough enough to snuffle and suffercate anybody from dub vendor to cane cutter. A snake so bad it used to ride motorbike and beat people if they give it bad drive. A snake so smart it could write calypso. The thing cussing black people children upside down; it run out round the science lab, get two hard lash and get sent down to the office for soap to wash its mouth out – and take that literally. It run in the music hall with foam in its mouth and bust way the stuffing in the organ stool, till Mr Thomas fling away his spoon and corner it in the woodwork room to wrestle it weak and slit its neck with a scimitar blade. It uncoiled there like a blown tornado, like a burst balloon, like the big hose the neighbour borrowing water with, stretched taut across the room. But every seventh breath the snake heave, it turbulently knocking back the benches and pissing blood upon the walls of the home economics room. It brusque and bad mind, it cussing like fire and it wouldn't dead. What to do? Teacher Thomas vex because the damn snake blood stain his tools, so he turn his back to it, and everything fade to black.

The snake then enter the darkroom where students developing film; it panic and start to wine like a genie. It knock down the acetic acid and the film get exposed. Students had to run out from there. The serpent spitting blood and puffing smoke. The windpipe burst and it gargling, it eating corned beef and rice. The back thick and black like hard prick. Beat they beat it with fever grass and electric cable, but it wouldn't dead. They call police to arrest it and the police beat it with truncheon until they frighten. They try squeeze up the snake head, but it cussing bad still and it wouldn't dead. Teacher Thomas say, 'Come now, come now.' He alone was upright in the neck, and he seal it shut in a tin tomb where it beat up and bleed out and boil in the sun, till it foam pus and mentholated spirit, and then, two bone come out.

58

Ella arrives at a hotel in Rouen where the windows open onto the highway. Smog and dirty feathers, dust to dust and her mother dead and planted like a seed in the earth. Her mother bequeathed her clothes, silver bracelets, perfumes and talcum powders, the thunderstones she brought back from the desert which, tied with thread over a flame, would not fall, nor the thread burn. But her house had burned down. Her mother had swollen with sickness until her heels spilled over the stilettos she still wore to weddings and funerals. Her gaze narrowed, her old bulk get slack and she peg out, coughed up her soul. She left several vials of pork fat she had been saving for eucharist, and bone-dry goat bone on a plate. She would not eat the gefilte fish in Chicago, instead she returned to the cool wooden steps at the back of her father's house. There she stood in the yard with the lizards and the fresh slime of snake scent, her thumb across the mouth of the hose to spread the spray as it watered the hibiscus and anthuriums. At the front was another garden, oriented north; beyond its front wall was the avenue where she was caught in the sepia of her menopause, walking away from the lens as if she was looking back at her own mistakes, at her own life and death upon the island, at the mildewed cocoa tree planted in dark soil, at the lost paths and viaducts uphill, at the sea. She remembered when her dress caught the flowers of the coming rain, and when the rainflies, created out of raindrops, appeared spontaneously. That day when the camera caught her as she walked up the avenue, her bedroom was a bright marigold yellow, like the painted sun of ancient days, when all colours were luminous. It was so hot in the heat haze that even the mongoose hid under the dry brown bush where it was coolest.

Those were soulful days. Ella, though, suffered under her mother's doctrine; she whipped the sweet flesh behind Ella's thighs with a belt marinated in horse piss and honey until the skin burst, to keep her humble and holy and folded into reverence. Yes, those were soulful days, but bubbling under the rain cloud, the hurricane loses its patience; spirit blow and thunder comes rolling through villages, as if stepping tough through toy empires of fabricated timber and unfinished schools.

Years later, Ella would send her mother photos from Europe, photos on trains from Gard De L'est, the Rotonde in Brussels, at the Flutgraben canal in Berlin. In one image, Ella lays her head against her lover's chest as he leans back in the soft chair of a dressing room. His horn lies between his knees, the case flung open on the ground. Its felt lining was still new then, and where the light met the metal it shone. So this was Ella, and the musician; an encounter from common origins. They were knowable mysteries to each other, books they knew without being read.

But for love, they'd lain fallow and, slunk in rooming houses, were pale from genk and hustle, entangled within emotional matters that were as dense as the gun metal his horn was carved from. That summer, she had travelled with the band from Brooklyn to Boston, past the white picket clichés of Connecticut and New England, and the tall rivers of the northern states. *Ces journées ont été pleines d'émotions.* She was in London, she appeared in Oxford, by flight or by river, and if she had to, she would have travelled by both to get from Brighton to Birmingham.

Now she lies on the single bed in the Kyriad Hotel in Rouen, in all her good clothes. In all these years and regions of restless sleep she is still waiting for a sailor who seems to linger forever outside the realm of a sustainable promise.

The musician stands outside in the yard with his hands shut behind him, in the Million Hills. The blistering salt of returning burns his eye as he looks up from an architect's verandah, and pans his vision across the rivers, where the red gully bush merges with refineries, tall buildings, forests of glass and tourist hotel concourses, with the waters of the Orinoco and Casamanche. These rivers of faces are mirrors into which his gaze returns, into which he descends.

Near Barcelona, a woman drew him far away from the campfire and the limits of the festival. The land was moonlit, flat, with just the smog of light blazing between the tents and the parked cars in the field. She was a tall woman. Her lips were like purple figs, her fingers like the fine bone of Castillian calligraphy. She led him out among the ancient fields, searching for her tent. Instead, they found a great house and its stables, its bricks brittle and crumbling. To enter into this chimerical space they had first to make a ceremony of acquaintances with the people gathered there, where the doors are were wide and welcoming. With the farmer was his wife, the dumb but muscular boy who must have been his son, the farmer's sister, her husband, the DJ, laughing, with a map of islands stapled to his back, the neighbour, a community policeman, and the neighbour's wife, sitting with her thick thighs flung open. There was wine, olives, anchovies and good bread on the table, and dark stairs which lead to European mystery rooms and psychosis.

That morning he woke in her tent, with the heat of their bodies and the sun. She smelled of wet grass and rancid milk, and her breath was hot with copper and whisky. It was morning and he was reborn in the dew; the cattle were making holes in the earth and he had to make his way to the highway. He saw himself as in a film, the plot and corpus of his body.

59

The rifle was loaded with one hundred bullets, its black iron barrel was cold and heavy. Raphael sat rocking on the veranda wiping the chamber to a shine, loading it with buck shot for agouti and manicou – even wild boar could get bore with that. He done gather briar twine to tie up quenk and lappe to carry home when he shoot them. This was many years after the space ship crashed in the El Chiquero Valley, long after carbide was burst in biscuit tin, long after Mingus composed 'Jump Monk', and Willie Jones crushed and overlapped both method and speed with the snare when they played it at the Bohemia, two days before Christmas, 1955. The brisk vision was kept real and hot upon the tongue; the bruised engine was set to ramble; the Bajan mother's leg was amputated below the knee, but the wound reopened. Each time the eight bar motif was encountered the players swung free. The clave ambled but eventually straightened up to accompany the melody. The Guinea hog would skid over the abattoir floor and run back down among the lilies and anthuriums of the wild Indian field where grass grew so tall to the body that the elbows would have to be raised when passing through that infinite land with no solid eastern boundary, seeking rose mangoes, hung low and weighing down the bough, like the arms of the mother who art in heaven and the breasts of the mothering church. Didn't they retain that gospel shout, the gutty moan, the Deacon's rod, his balls bag, his greedy stones? The rose mango tree was God. Its leaves were reddened by the sun, but some were purple, some brown. Under the canopy of leaves there were red mangoes as big as a man's head.

There was a wood shack that sprawled there, in the wild Indian farmlands near Mt Garnett, at the foothills of the Million Hills, set back amongst the fibres and ferns, the protuberant bush, the fertile soil, the topmost of which Jah-Jah took to build black people. The deeper he go, the whiter it get. This house was filled with cousins and grand nephews, black Caribs grinning and working the land. They copulated like lizards, brewed sickly children like Vino, with chills and bronchitis. Built-up areas were unknown to them as earth to seahorse. They were poor folk, worshippers of soil and spill, land fall and gully, the whip snake in the roof, the fowl-cock skimming on the wooden floor, crab-back and gundy, baigan chutney.

Each day God send, the black Indian coming, the strong black one, setting laglee for bird, ploughing the hard earth, straining muscle in the hot bright sun, and struggling with aphid infestation. Each day, there beside the savannah, he was watering and moulding his beds. They were narrow and straight, the less able vines tied to knobbly staves like couplets and quavers. In the warm late afternoon, when he had finished his work for the day, he would sit in his ajoupa eating sada roti and contemplating jazz.

Once, when his father wanted to beat him, the musician ran all around these fields playing hide and seek with the big man, peeping from treetops and hiding in stables, in gaps between the pastel-coloured homes of those who had known him since he'd been born among them, in the house on the corner. These were good people who gathered in the living room one morning to seal his navel with ground Jack Spaniard nest, and to bury his umbilical string under the orange tree root, knowing that one day he too would die, with arms reaching up for life like tree bones, the fingers knotted in regret. That morning, as they watched him run, they wished he could elude his father, but he was caught in his father's iron grip, and spun with blows in the whipping shed.

The father was slick as a vicious myth. The boy saw him once a year, usually at Christmas, though that morning he hadn't seen him for several years. In that galvanise shed when his father drew his belt, the boy arched his back to dampen the votive crack of the leather, and on his father's axis, spun spinning with licks. The taste of his father's hand was not the dry and heavy licks he would get from his grandfather, but that son of a bitch black belt stinging sharp as a whip licks that only an absent father could give. Throw

180

fire! Crack that belt! Oh gosh. You could hear it licking all down by the water tank, all round by Bushe Street bakery. Sometimes it good that life too short.

Now Gallstones Grandfather Buckmouth Clarence lies dead in the desert sand. Now his own son, the musician's father has died gasping for air in the chest hospital after smoking fifty cigarettes a day. His arms grew heavy. His engine froze until he could no longer love women or lift the belt that lay on the bed like an uncoiled crown of thorns. Raphael had been writing his book for so long that he had forgotten what the boy had done to deserve such a sweet cut-arse that Sunday morning. Instead he wrote:

> To the desert. To set off walking through the hard sand in infinite air and fire. Walk true. Straight is the stride for as long as the body has water. But the body, limited under lung and ligament, soon swerves and fails, succumbs to cross-examination, suspicion, doubt, deceit, thirst, guilt. It bucks and rolls and insects build nests in the eye sockets, and the spiritual zest is weighed and sent to a hermetically sealed room where the sun cannot penetrate, and the body gives in to madness. After four days, the brain atrophies and the heart explodes from jealousy. So much mucus and mulch where the body rots in the desert. Or let them carry the body for burial in the bush and step on human shit.

60

A mother's perfumed neck, her foot like cow hoof overlapping the heel, pressed into mud at country funerals. A cousin who gave birth on the back seat of a taxi. The talcum and milk of a newborn, wrapped in its mists of rose and jasmine. The humid flesh of Aunt Bunny, who learned bookkeeping and shorthand in hot extramural rooms in the vigorous city, who wore long gabardine skirts and white ironed blouses, with her hair pressed tight, who had serious ambition for secretarial or clerical posts, until Mikey the Pie Man climbed into her life. But these were the days when a woman of a certain age had to be wed, and men had to write letters of application to court them, to sit on the porch on the wrought-iron chair drinking cherry brandy and reasoning with the father. Your intention? Your job? Your trade? Your lifelong plans? Your money tall? You have motorcar? Your family background? You have child already? Outside woman? Your father beat you as a boy? Your father's profession? Your mother's breed, her skin tone? Your gravitas and dignity? Small island? And if these things were not upright and correct, you never get your papers stamp or permit to come in the people house, to sit at the table in the drawing room and eat the stew chicken and callaloo the madam cook on Sundays. Then to be married mere months later in the Anglican church near by Nimtaz grocery, and be brought to this same house in Mount Garnett for reception, with the bride in the long-trail dress that the mother herself stitched, which had to be carried above dirt by page boys and flower girls, where there would be cake eating and drinking hard wine entwined in the arms of the woman you say you love, or loosening your tie and raising toasts, hearing the mother speech, the father speech, and watching Bunny nephew hiding under the wedding table. He is seven years old and already drawn into himself. He will not play with the other children; his head turns sideways for photographs, he hunts lizards, he draws aeroplanes, supermen, roams alone through the savannahs. But your bride loves him as her own, this boy her mother had received from his mother's wild hip, screaming with outstretched arms. Even the old man at work in his carpenter's shed is tender with the boy, and the boy would sit at the old carpenter's feet and pass him chisels and nails. But the old man did not know how to be a father, he kept his love hid.

Bunny, the bride in her sequined dress and pearls, would leave home and learn to live a new life. Maybe she gave up her dreams too easy to accept that man and call it love, but what she go do now? Throw him out? They married; she going down with Mikey. But Bunny's dreams did not die, and they carried her with pride into each new situation, into every falling-down shack fixed with plywood, every roof that leaking. Her dreams survive being left alone at home from dawn till midnight, in the alley road down Goose Lane, where men gambling hard and smoking ganja, and women were to be taken out only among family. She complaining that her nature spoil, that her youth fading. Build your zest. That nest insufficient, and you can't feed this woman's mind, much less her heart with sweet talk or fried chicken. Instead, there was the cold soap of morning, the hard love before work on the lopsided bed, the rising, falling landscape of his back, the crust of the rag kept under the mattress for wiping – all of which Raphael saw, and years later would write into existence. It would also be written how in sweet 1980, a big truck rolled into the lane, and Ruben Benson come with funk and grinning fishhooks in his beard, and his hip talk and style make Bunny run to confess to her mother that he make her feel like a woman, and she leg trembling now 'cause she full upon her prime and falling in love each day the Mack driving in her yard.

Ruben say he used to play organ in Washington, DC, in be bop combos, then after he reach New York and do the disco hustle, how he drift down to Florida to pick navel orange, and is there he learn truck driving, how he follow Creole tail down the islands and end up in sweet Trinidad. Ruben, the Afro, the horner man, the *perro* with cock in hand, stepping down from the Mack truck at noon, funky as he born. Every day he coming to Miss Dolly snackette for hops bread and cheese, same time Miss Bunny sweeping out her yard, and each day that man venturing a bit further in, till eventually he eating baked chicken in Bunny gallery while Mikey selling cheese pies or driving taxi. Further in with lyrics and yankee twang, Ruben end up inside the narrow shotgun house. Everybody know they bulling. But it never last. Once things get tense, Ruben run.

When the same husband she swear to love get his windpipe rip, Bunny end up right where poverty was waiting for she – between her brothers Raphael and Bain, on the rough side of Million Hills, with her one piece of girl child. She catching rain for drinking water and bathing in brutal mud. Sometimes the family bring a little kerosene for Bunny lamp, a bit of crate wood for partition, some peppers from the mountain. Is not one suffer she endure but plenty. Trouble come in hurricane; wind blow her latrine down. The hummingbird leaping from vine to vine, and the pumpkin flowering, the neighbour dog just bear six pups, the ravine overflowing. The ambition Bunny carry so long, to rise out of what was written, fail and fall; her dream was just a vision, a subplot among many she might have taken.

That suppurating sore we saw on Sister Phyllis's neck was a carcinoma ulcerating, not a bruise from spirit lash. We were a congregation peeping between the intermittent scroll of the gospel plough, listening to the bible talk and the Deacon sing, and watching the white-headed sisters swing at Ma Mamin's Spiritual Temple in Brazil Village. In those days, Phyllis lived in a single-roomed tapia hut set up on stilts on Back Street, Tunapuna, near the deserted train line and the highway, and the wild Indian gardens further south.

On that overcast Sunday, Mamin's temple was stifling with heat. Phyllis had made a vow to wear white and she did, though sometimes her head was wrapped with secret colours given to her by a merman on the banks of the Guinea Coast. We had seen her that barefoot Sunday, returning from the mourning room, with her head tied and weeping with tragic prophecy and anguish, holding the candle by the root and marching home through rainforests, torrential rain and tunnels beneath the desert. Each gesture – her arms bent at the elbows in supplication, the swing of her hips, even the broken spire of her voice – was the sex of sound and transcendence, as she flung her head back and sang, rolling round the mercy bed in the coruscating heat of the little church. Her song was truer than any vine of rhythm or blues. Mamin, seeing the gifts Phyllis had been given, had appointed her to teach doctrine, but Phyllis wouldn't bow to Mamin; her magic was blacker than that. She wouldn't lie beneath the Shepherd neither, nor the Deacon, Leader Jimmy, nor Reverend Prince, regardless of how his whip molasses black or how he press upon her like grinning sin.

Mamin sucked her teeth. We were not surprised when we heard that Sister Phyllis's house had fallen down, that her house was made of mud and grass, and that termites held the lower notes. We had already seen how this could happen. Remember walking along the street where Phyllis lived? Walking past the upstairs and downstairs house, the parlour beneath it, the cool rooms reserved for the shopkeeper's cousins and grandnephews, past the gravel merchant's yard, the Chinese takeaway, the high-shut house of the justice of the peace, where the gospel radio played, incessantly, where the coconut tree abraded the galvanise roof, to find Sister Phyllis on her knees inscribing a vèvè for Shango. She did done start to build a spaceship inside that house.

Later that same evening, Leader Jimmy was asking if we had seen her, and why she had not been to church. It was Sunday. We knew how the land had fallen away into neverness at the back of Phyllis's yard, and how, while fowl cock was crowing in her neighbour's cultivated garden, hers remained knee high with vicious and unforgiving bush, dense with foliage from the midden tree. We knew how that story would end. Walking out in the dew, Phyllis might trouble the breeze, she might brew mandrake root and psychic nut as protection from beasts that were chasing her through the cane field, but we would never see Phyllis in church again. Members would ask, 'Where Phyllis gone?' But how could we respond? We had already watched the burning warehouse full of spices and goods impounded for unpaid taxes. In the dusk and flames, the looters appeared like red ants after condensed milk has spilled – they run come as if created by red sugar itself. Inside, waterlogged and black with ash, were gutted suitcases, their contents spewed out on the warehouse floor. There were shirts still pinned with discipline in polythene sleeves, watercolour brushes and books of Eden's apocrypha, roots rockers twelve inchers from Jamaica, tax-barred from lancing village disco-theques with the new Daddy U Roy sound. Looters like mad ants, until the police flashed the area and run everybody from there.

Come down into Monday, and Phyllis living under plywood in the yard, mad like fire and unrepentant. So some bad-minded people build hex to throw her over. They spread a rumour and next thing, she lose her job in the detergent factory in Trincity. On Easter Friday, we even thought we saw Phyllis laid out to gristle on the road, but it was not her, not this brutal corpse, though we had already forgiven her for dying. The church had left

Phyllis to moan and wander, to wait for the myth of a father to return, but never the father himself. Phyllis walk out in the morning and the sky open up. She wring her hands in prayer. Her chant is boom and gust, but nevertheless she is pierced in battle a mile from her house, in what she knows is a holy war. She stands on the new asphalt road but also on the axis mundi of a hurricane hill top, from where the tumble down seems particularly hocus-bound to doom; people are falling over precipices, or diving, windswept, to die upon those rocks.

Leader Jimmy enters the scene, he shelters under galvanise, but the sea is flinging lash like a Bajan police, and the sting of spray reaches him, even from a distance of several miles. The viewer can move, but in the spirit world directions deceive. But let us follow Phyllis for now. In fact she has disappeared, and we were not sure anymore if Phyllis ever walked these streets, with a neck of light as real as the ground. In the Latin section, music spills out into the street; blue shirtjacks and bullfighting shoes are hung up on nails in the slaughter house. The butcher, keeping abreast of politics, is reading a newspaper. Tomorrow, he will wrap it around goat stones. Leader Jimmy is late for church. He puts on his stole in a taxi. Squeezing the tip of his cock through a pocket, he almost ejaculates. Phyllis is at the sea front. She has washed her hands and feet; each day she disappears into the water.

62

In his apartment there were many rooms. Rooms of water in his house of dust. This is where, in a high project in East Flatbush, New York, that Basil finally came to measure Ella's father for his grave. This is the box room of an old man, where barrels of stale clothes congest the hallway, where shelves hold ring-bound albums of sepia-tinted photographs, where drawers hold legal documents and letters from banks. When Ella got the call that her father had died, she was washing her hair.

In the room, Ella finds a self-published pamphlet from a Vincentian poet who, dressed in suit and cravat, upright in the neck, once waltzed into Brooklyn bookshops impressing younger poets, inviting them home to Prospect Park to eat bacon joints and split peas, and then recited terrible, terrible poetry that never was published, not in newsletter, journal or even church news magazine.

In her father's room there are many bold statements. Stoles and long gowns in pious green gabardine, cosmologies embroidered on lapels and sleeves. In late middle age, when it look like his script did done write, just so he get religious visa to preach in New York. Is Christo who set that up. So Deacon fix his teeth and get his passport, and leave the unfinished bachelor house he was squatting in Chaguanas and gone in Uncle Sam tail. But he grooved deep in grief those early wintertimes. The basement where he first stayed was dark, penitential and cold. In summer he cast his immigrant charm like galvanise in the city, peeping through windows like a saint at a killing, flinging blades of gospel from the wild Caribbean. They put him as a leader in a church on Fulton, and his legend grew, how his Hail Mary fell from a wise fortress, how he crossed his chest twice with a palm to hiss a prayer in glossolalic verse, how the spirit moved him to walk away from the pulpit – like Monk who, at times, would leave his piano stool to dance – even though he had long given up on Jesus. O padre pio, O Saint Augustine, I am passing the corner where you passed and will not pass again. He woundeth not. He lost his hair and his girth was awesome, but women in New York still gave him leg. I want your wings, your unwritten texts, your poems with no words. In her father's room there were vinyl albums:

The Mighty Sparrow - *Live at Lagos Shrine*
Lee Morgan - *Brassorama: 1969 Calypso Hits*
Nara Leão - *Pede Passagem*
The Shadow – *Belmont Funk*
The Mighty Zandolie - *Man Family*
Lord Kitchener - *Ah Have it Cork*
Exuma - *Nassau Fire: Live!*
Agent K - *Feed The Cat*
Andre Tanker - *'Bim' The Soundtrack*
WITCO Desperadoes - *Pan in Honey*
Superblue - *Spiritual Soca*

He had kept these and many more, wrapped and hidden at the bottom of a wardrobe among trousers he had long outgrown but, feeling younger than his years, had refused to lose. Them slacks have funk in the crotch from blues dance and trickling piss, even after shake off.

Ella wants to gather evidence of her father's life, but the life done lived and gone into that gone momentum. Bearded, gullible and tough, Deacon daily bread was his cock in his hand. He lived hard on his heart from pumping out hex and verse, a man's life, of little or no apology. She must tell the Syrian shopkeeper, who welcomed her father when he arrived in the city, that he has died. The shopkeeper, whose name was always Zalaf, would hold his head in both hands, cup his jaw in genuine despair and awe, and shed a single tear at the passing of his friend. He would reflect, for the fourth time that day, that his life too would soon pleat and seal from day to night. One morning he grinding black cardamon with his teeth, or rolling wheat for kibbeh, the next day someone throwing dirt upon the box of his bones.

She finds her father's umbrella, balled-up socks, his lonesome shoes, beer bottles filled with tamarind seeds, newspaper clippings, ties, tie-pins and cuff-links, the old fedora he would sling onto a hook when he came home from teaching in the institute – before the faculty get to hear he burn down his house and they fire his arse from there. Ella is uncovering secrets her father can no longer keep. There are photographs of him with women she does not recognise; a black and white couple leaning on a bridge. Some are pornographic, others sentimental: the leg flung up on the chair back, the woman holding a towel to her breast, and this too is a part of life. She finds an unsent letter, folded in a prayer book in a shoe-box under his bed:

Darling I am very sorry for the words I said. Forgive me, Deacon too hasty. Put a blanket down on the damn floor and I will sleep with you anywhere. You is mine and mine alone, forget church; the Reverend lie. Forget the mother of the church; the mother lie. I know how to treat woman. I will hire motorcar and take you for sea bath in Coney Island. But if I bring you hotel is to bull, then bring yourself, put one leg on my shoulder and leave one on the floor. If I take you restaurant, order the lobster if you want. My gland rise from when I first see you leaning over your basket in the laundromat. Lover, my one and only, Sam Cooke have throat, but even he don't love you like my love. Put blanket down and I will make love to you, strong and tender. Is sweetness you like? Lover, is you alone. Shepherd lie. I love when we make love, my whole body does shake up.

– Deacon Simmons

In her father's life there were many keys without doors to open. God bless his axe.

63

The bell kept ringing in the low lying hills. The bell kept ringing in the biscuit factory. The bell kept ringing in the falling-down house, in the devil's fireside, in the bauxite factory, in the firemen's canteen. The bell kept ringing through the green guava plantations, through dirty villages below the hill. The bell kept ringing but the fruit there in the burning field was green and hard like rockstone, brittle and stunted in the sun.

Every eye was tearful as they stood in the ocean. Entire Caribbean nations stood neck-high in depthless water; congregations walked out as far as the eye can't reach. They were a sea of faces – government officials, ombudsmen, wire-benders, queens of carnival and taxi drivers, each stripped of garments and regimes. They spanned the entire seascape and made a timorous murmur; the heat of their proximity caused the engines of the ocean to churn. As the sun sketched its narrative arc, they were joined by thousands more on the beach.

The musician had flown from Lisbon to Montreal. He had not died. He had hovered thirty-seven thousand feet above the earth and had not fallen. It was there that he thought again about Raphael, that sweet cuss, and the progress of *The Frequency of Magic*, a book he too had escaped from. He thought of how he had suffered as a boy in the Million Hills, from cycles of sadness, joy and depression, and he wondered what had become of Raphael and the book he was writing. He knew that one day Raphael would be found poised rigid over his work in rigorous or foetal mortis, and that he would have to be prised open so he could be stretched out and measured. Fire would be lit at his navel and coins placed to cover his eyes.

In Montreal, the musician had walked the Rue Saint Sulpice, heading towards the port. There he found the Angolan corner shop, open like a bazaar and smelling of asafoetida root, of lamp oil, sisal leaves and tinctures of dried fish in bundles; he had found fetish herbs and their power to poison wounds in the bronze plateau of Bié. Stairs led above to a club where an orchestra was playing free jazz and funk to a full house. He stood at the bar, transfixed by the drummer, an Italian, who compelled the band to swing, propulsive and bouncing upon his throne. How long had the musician been standing there? How long had he been lost?

This orchestra would play in Paris, but they would have to be paid for learning to play Alan Shorter's angular blues, Sparrow's 'Slave' and Shadow's 'Charlene'. They would have to be paid for playing the new dirge, designed to lean heavy against their down-presser time of riotous blues. The Antiguan trumpeter could blow, but he could only play a pentatonic scale, and he blows less and less since his hip was replaced and they amputate his big toe, and the rest of the toes get frighten and buck to carry his weight. Was so he step from stroke, to place his foot flat, like platypus beak, leaning back in his tam with his elbows push out. He had a skull plate shining under the tam, but little grey locks to deceive around the rim. Each urge to blow was a struggle – the knee wouldn't bend, though sometimes jump blues uses to make it kick, spontaneous. He beg his knee to mend, but he know they waiting to cut it at the hospital. Each time they met backstage, the trumpeter would grin and say to the saxophonist, 'I never did think I woulda see you again.' Imagine this inviolable old jazz man, sitting backstage at Le Grande Halle in Paris, his instrument shining on a chair, waiting, serious as chrome. It sat there ageless and fearless and cold; it would not fade from gleaming in its defiance; it would not die. The Antiguan has his eye on his horn, but his lip is black and feeble. He lingers to stare at the youth of the thing, the 'once upon' that gone now, how time so vicious. He say, 'The longest rope have an end.' He bow his head and succumb to the sweeter parts of life. He would not allow the bandleader to help him up to the stage. He would be given Freddie Hubbard's part in 'Maiden Voyage', but the second trumpet would shadow and fill in the spots where his regime failed. The players in the orchestra would not speak of his decline. They would not be drawn, discourteously, into shit-talk about it.

The trumpeter's legend was intact. They knew that he had left Antigua as a merchant seaman at eighteen in 1952, that by twenty-one he was in Spanish Harlem, leading the house band at the Limbo Room. They knew that in 1961 he stowed away on a cargo ship to Paris, moving to London the following year, where he played briefly with Lord Kitchener. They knew that his horn could be heard on Blue Beat and Melodisc recordings, on calypso, mento or zouk, on blue funk or Haitian compas. The trumpeter had lost many comrades in battle. Some had caught heart attacks on stage; one fell into the well below it. Some was good-good friend and confidant, though he would not recognise them if they stepped off ships, or down the rubber stairs of buses in the rain wearing beige raincoats or fedoras, hat held to head, stylishly, for people to watch them.

If Raphael's cigarette could lean from his mouth, its ash would blow into a different story. The harvest is Christmas meat: the leg of pork, for instance, is to stuff with carrot and garlic. Alvin is moving through the thorns and thistles, hoping to return from the bush with manicou, an agouti or two. Raphael calls out, 'Save something for me,' and Alvin grins and waves his lance and swings his hip to mount the steep incline.

64

Luke put a poultice there, he rub olive oil and garlic in the neck wound where the Great Bandit had stabbed him. He fear for infection to linger and fester like a bite from a Komodo dragon, which will simply pierce its prey's ankle and follow it through the jungle for several patient days, humbly with grinning teeth, witnessing the deterioration of flesh until fever infests the marrow, and limp become stagger over crag, rock and malicious landscape. The dragon patient to wait and watch until the bull cow, bison or buffalo falls, then it pounce and rile up the meat. Each has an ankle that can succumb to disease. Even poets catch bone disease, lung infection and blood cancer, but they still swinging blades with dark and strident poems with roots deep in Haitian secret technology.

Luke had once known a poet like this, who died young enough to be remembered, a warrior he had met along the way. The poet was accomplished enough to be raised up to glory and promotion, to be esteemed as legend, cult and canon of revolutionist poetry, drum music, word music, fire music. Luke say, 'Give him his glory. Give him his badge, give him his halo, his crown. Bring down the morning from the sky, a black and comely poet has died. Dig a hole in a loaf of bread with a pointed appointed finger, be gracious and give thanks; if you is stickman and the other man *bois* bigger, genuflect and shake his hand.'

Luke was now on the Greyhound into Savannah, Georgia, flat land and endless firmament, fir trees and Dixieland jazz blowing from a distance. The driver, jeri curled, chewed relentless gum with his whip foot pumping, dancing on the gas. Luke thought of his mother then, how once she come home from work with a needle of wood stuck in the sole of her foot, from whichever menial task she had undertaken that day, perhaps panelling fridges in the fibreglass factory, or shucking corn for carnival soup, or skinning bat wings for souse, or trimming sticks in the match factory, or, once, spending a fortnight scrubbing tractor wheels on the dock, or working as a short-skirted sales clerk in a shoe shop. Her father was still alive then, and she and Luke still lived with him on that hill, and in those days her father uses to hang a psychedelic curtain to give colour to black and white, before he cook enough cornmeal soup in the Poor House in Cocorite to afford colour TV. Luke remember how his mother sit down there in the living room and pierce her sole with a candle's blade to release the splinter, and then drip hot wax on the wound to seal it shut. She never moan, Mammy never gargle with pain, is so she was. Luke recall the quality of light in the room that night, the soft glow set by the candle, his grandfather's handsome face, the fractal light from the TV and its mendacious screen, and his mother, with one foot bent across her knee, deep in concentration. They were lit in that same light Luke would see years later in London, in Joseph Wrights' *An Experiment on a Bird in the Air Pump*, and in the blood-red scent of Basquiat's reverential *Riding with Death*. Luke remembered the smell of burning flesh, the whites of his mother's teeth in the flame, grit-strong same way years later when she battle death by turning to face its hideous tremor, same way and saying, 'Take me, I am deep in the well and the well is dark, but I am not afraid.' Then she blink hard, to change the scene.

Luke found the old woman's hut by accident, as he travelled riverside in search of safe harbour in the marshlands of Wassaw Island. He feared he would die there; he had been pierced by the Bandit's blade but knew then that instead of fleeing, he would have to dismantle the Bandit himself, or the fear of death upon this journey would forever ruin his living life. He had left the Great Bandit wounded on the bank of a river whose smaller flows now passed this way, and it was along this river that he came upon the wood shack of the old sage and seer woman, hidden like a memory, within the womb of bush, among a copse of tall cedar trees. This was Ma Mamin, the mother of the church, bidden to pine in a corner of a vast and variegated book. When Luke came upon her she was sitting, elbows on her knees on an overturned bucket, eating a starch mango and picking the fibres from her teeth. Blue flies buzzed around her syphilitic shin bone. She saw Luke's suffering, knew that he had come from far across the desert, but also that soon the engines of sorrow and sickness would taper her own living dream to dust. Having lost her spiritual temple, Mamin had fallen and spun far from Raphael's hand; she had drowned in miraculous sleep, had hovered over the island, had seen the vacuous flesh of her own corpse, its skin suddenly pale and ancient of grain, not to die but to wheel an' come again. Her ornaments and enamel cups, her hand-sewn doilies were all in place in that Georgian wood shack, even her asafoetida burnt in a milk pan. Mamin cried. Was hers the voice of the hummingbird? Was hers the heavy hand pouring brown sugar in the sweet bread? Was hers the cumin-scented morning? Was hers the pot from which the scent of rotting chicken wafted through Brazil Village, stink till sweet like honey from the midden bee? Leaning over the swinging kitchen door, she had offered plates of pelau to her congregation, but her hand wasn't sweet and they would not eat. Mamin could not help Luke now, she had used all her water for tears, and had her own arc to plot.

65

Out in Jericho, in the Million Hills, they still talk of his second heist of Joe Ducaine, how they hold the jazz boy in Piarco airport mystery rooms to be frisked with dogs and rubber gloves, but found nothing on him. Melchior say, 'Hear what really happen. They stalk him since he reach departures, they scope his haste to depart, then they hold him and cold him up; second time this happen to him.'

'Under his exotic hat he was secretly balding, humble in his blackness, weary from the struggles of the music business. They say, "Take off that." He was coming back from a lil' holiday at home, going back to Europe. He walking tall through the people airport in leather boots, and the officer throw his wicked head back and laugh, "Well, look 'pon you, to ras, who you feel you is?"

'The new road still coming to the Million Hills, and the water truck keep breaking down. They say progress reaching the hills since they run pipe. The women proud that now they have toilet to flush, but is still water closet with cesspool beneath. Faucet have basic water to wash face and arse, but really is same ol' latrine that fulling up they shitting in, not sewage system, please. When it full, they throw mortar to seal shit. Same way now for jazz and commercial pressure.

'Look how they put the jazz man naked and search every hole. How he eat humiliate and boil down like bhaji, how they hit him two slap and send him to go his way. But make we avoid that road. Rental car will roll down good, but your engine will burst coming back up. If they did find the thing in a foraging pouch slung deep under his armpit, then when he was ready for their tail, ready to stand up in court and defend himself, why he happen to have so much Joseph Ducaine in his secret underlung, the house of magistrates would have closed the session, and throw a big concert with roti and reggae music to distract the people instead.

197

All through the trial the musician would've noticed inconsistencies. He could make things inconsist at will. Just by watching a number plate on a truck, rust would erode and baffle it, numbers would change, nothing seen could be relied upon. He lucky; even death want to employ long con to catch him out. Even his woman, screwing her wig on in the morning, had to avoid obvious questions: how could he have been there, in those dead man hours, to play calypso music upstairs the Portuguese laundry, and then have time to capture a heft of Joey and hide it in his armpit before he reached the airport? Who was he with, and so late?

It was like when in boy days he stab Sharkos in Golden Doors with a flick blade that pierced skin and slid, and the knife get fling down a culvert on Frederick Street, but nobody see it. This legend so big that Sharkos' mother take the next morning off work in the shoelace factory to come down in the yard, to fret in her calico dress and say, 'Is you who stab my one piece of boychild?' Well, even a roughneck scamp like Sharkos from the back of Never Dirty had mother too. And why the boy stab Sharkos? Because he was sure Sharkos had stolen from him what he had stolen first – fine markers in a row from the architect suppliers. In that push and pull and seduction of war, he was forced to pull for the blade, to finger the nail nick, to snap it open and threaten to chook. And still Sharkos defiant that he never thief nothing, so the blade get rile up, and ride in. When it pop the skin it slip smooth. Run he run to hop bus trembling, while the same pressure group what did break biche to thief, take Sharkos to the postcolonial hospital, where he get his wound six stitch.

Police reach the jazz boy house that Sunday morning. His grandfather had to fetch him from the savannah. This was blackness and blues, the engine skidding, the presser foot hot like a trigger, exhaust gushing out. Eventually the CID men hit him two slap and warn him, then they pump their engine and gone. It was then the jazz boy realise that the dream of the Million Hills was really an alternate universe. Is a place where a woman would be coming down the rough cut slope of red dirt, innards of earth cut rugged from the hillside, carrying a basket of bread in the hook of her left arm, the basket piled high with loaves like a Martiniquan postcard, or a volcano of bread, or a biblical illustration of a bounty of manna, the richness of Eden. Not everything was real.

The court house was vast, like indoor stadia used for heads of government meetings, sepulchres of formality, red bench leatherette. The jazz man was ready to expose them that day, to open their eyes to bogus narratology. He shit, he shut his room with nail and board. Coming up from town he see the old man writing on the hill and wave, but Raphael never really response. He come to court in tracksuit, amid the camera flash of lights, white stripe on blue. Raphael wrote: "The driver get snuff and the car overturn – was a hard working man, selling cheese and meat pie, crack corn and drama. The man had children; he dead with his hand stiff on the steering wheel and skin-teeth grin." But even though the musician had a memory of that night, he was sure that he was never in that airport, or even on that island, that he was on tour in Spain. He come strong to outsmart the judge, but the court shut down. They done start setting up tent and setting up speakers for sound.'

66

On this night the band was moving through the far outskirts of Brest, beat up by the leaning spray, shook by the water and its roar. There was one dull lit route their driver knew, along which the farm houses and the flowers in the gardens were battered; on this route there was no ease, no succour or balm or poultice to suck out the pus. Dark is the road, the vehicle to some darker place within is its tenor. The rainstorm intensifies; hard European rain, bucket a drop, beats the ear to fear, thunder threatening to split the sky open to a dark that would never end.

If it had been hurricane season on the island, the chickens would have been penned high in their wire coop, though some would be lost to the spirit world; the dogs would have been brought grinning and twisting into the house to save them from drowning; the wind would be knocking at the lifting lid of the kitchen window, the window to heaven that the musician's grandmother would stretch to prise open with a stick each morning God send, a rod that had become smooth and dark with use. That was hurricane. The rain of trees howling; the lash of galvanise rattling; the savannah flooding; the loss of anything not stitched down carried away; the banana tree falling in the yard like a human body; the succubus in the attic shape-shifting to a fleeing ball of fire. The waters would rise under the house, murmuring like djin to come inside. Everything coming up in that overcoming wash: mollusc, hairy snake, kite tail, heartbreak turtle, eel and iguana, mongoose, human tissue, terminal ulcers of the gut and tumours of the liver, lamp oil and melancholy, even adulterous khaki trousers, secrets hid under bush and foundation for forty years rising up to float in that brown water.

He is at the abattoir in San Juan, witnessing the scraping of hooves, the scent of blood, the hook-up gut and the splash and the table creaking. Imagine the bull lung bursting on the walls. Across from the slaughterhouse and market, on the main road beside the bus station, the burger bike and the red-roofed post office, scaffolding surrounded a building being built. Each week, his grandfather's Austin Cambridge would occupy the same parking spot, beside the blue and white walls of the killing yard, where blood and piss washed over feathered fronds of moss, tongues of moss like a cat's tongue. Each Saturday, as the building was being built, in the ferocious light of those mornings, the old man took his bag to market and bought honeycomb tripe and yellow split peas by the pound, king fish, salted pigtails and bacalao, lime, lemon thyme, celery, grouper. The building, when built, was not as tall as the young musician had imagined it would be, when he grew tall enough to stand beside it, to pass among the vendors and the darkened decors of Chinese restaurants, or years later, in punk and black, when rockers galore, from Joe Gibbs to Defunkt, used to blow out from barbers saloons and shopfronts. He had stood among a crowd in the furniture and appliances store that unforgettable Friday afternoon when The Iceman played Frankie Smith and Starpoint, broadcasting live from location on Radio Trinidad. He was in the crowded lanes of the market, ablaze on Saturday mornings with luminous fruit and freshly-cut meat, baskets of chive and dravidian fetishes. At the entrance to the market, the doubles men waited on their basket bikes, leg up on the pedal; next to the stall that sold barfi, jalebi and gulab jamun.

The band stop at a service station; they walk around its concrete floor for coffee and chocolates. The cashier, with his worried gaze and uniform, as if gatekeeping some watery hell or a dream to die in, asks, 'Do you know where you are?' The musician does not answer. He stands cold in the hard light, in the wetness of his clothes. Outside, the lights reveal the rain, and bugs in the swathe of water pounding the earth. The band and the driver run to the van. The wind has become operatic, and the howl of it blisters eyes and the thin skin of the face with centrifugal force, but they no longer feel the rain's piercing sting; they have become pulse and knot within it. Heavy European water, the sodden earth around a farm, the narrow road driven through the country. They arrive at a small hotel on the edge of the city, the rain pulling a river across the land into violent splash and spume.

Endless and without mercy, the rain swoops and trembles. Snakes and river eel squirm in the muddy flow; silt gushes in the rolling water; whosoever it passes over shall be washed away, will be cast aside. More songs about rain, more water. Everything changes. What matters in the end is the resonance of things, the mark they made upon thought and memory, the scar the blade leaves in water, a muscle in the air. He has hidden a mask for years, of suffering that gasp in the darkness. He is a child upon that hill, sitting at the old man's feet, while the writer writes and smokes the filterless Broadway cigarettes he buys in Curepe Junction, at the same time purchasing long fisherman's hooks, flies and eyes for stitching verbs and vowels, and malice oil for sharpening stones and sharpening toes. In another life the savannah would become an ocean; gull, stork and chunky cormorant would stand knee deep in the water. After the rain, the winged termites would come down from the trees where they had been hiding, to be singing, to be cult and ritual. In scenic times, the endless rain is still falling somewhere, but the band is sheltered now in their hotel, waiting for the wind to shift, the scene to change, water to break, a bucket to drop, into silence.

67

His grandmother's chamber pot sat under her bed. Each morning she would walk out in her duster, into the dew, and throw the rancid urine which filled it onto the roots of the orange, the barbadine, the vervain and the soursop tree. All these would taste her thick piss. Sweet in her walk around the garden, she would pray, 'Divino Niño, help me make money.' Then she drain the posey on the dasheen bush, the lime tree, the Julie mango. There were parakeets in the garden. She kept one in a cage, until she found it stiff one morning; she held its body in her palm, before she buried it in that paradise of bees and fecundity. There were red flamingos; the savannah was a green ocean they stood in.

Uncle Clary built the old lady a plywood commode she could sit on to shit, like Bacon's Pope Innocent on his throne. There was the lid to lift, a hinge to open at its back to withdraw the pot of stool in the morning. But Mammy never used it. Mostly, the clear varnished plywood throne sat timorously grinning in a corner of the bedroom, beside her altar, upon which lay the sacred heart picture, dried Palm Sunday palms, the candle burning, the brass goblets, her beads, her thunderstones.

This was before the old man grew sick and his strength faded. Even Rampaul, when he sat in the kitchen those Sunday after-noons, with bulging eyes, and his fisherman's tales of seeing the spectrum of a universe in the scales of a grouper, knew that Clary was sick. He had seen Clary stagger, catch blackout, seen him buck and shiver, then spend months in the postcolonial hospital supping strained pumpkin soup, his gut distended, his eyes burning in his head. The old man was sick but his bulk was still proper. Ma Mamin's prayers had prolonged his life and his muscle was still firm from Bajan hard bone – struggle in his eyes, but still clapping blades. His wicked wrists could still pull shut the hatch door above the stove, like a doorway to heaven in hurricane light, to seal the house, the house he had built with his own hands, like clothes sewn onto the body.

When hurricane coming, was high wind from morning, gusts of wind that howl in gradients – danger not ready yet – but wait, soon the sky darkening, and the radio anointing them with delicious fear. This far south in the archipelago, they would be lashed with the tail of the beast, by its sting. Still, it have enough terror in the whip to make galvanise rattle, to lift nails loose and leave their chambers. Rain fill the river to overflowing, and when the river come down, it wash past Febeau village and San Juan, wash till it come like a living thing, moving across the savannah, humming, coming, humming, drowning darkness and every-thing. When rain fall so it does wash out the land, and what little corn or fruit the old people plant – the lil' tomato, the young banana, the dasheen – all that drown, gone. But the three of them sat safe in the kitchen with the concrete floor, and the curtains blooming in vast gusts.

That kitchen was where the musician learnt to bore a flute from bamboo, where he lay across his aunt's thighs and inhaled her flesh, deeply, and in that scent knew even then that it was something illicit, both sweet and pungent, like sweat and mud and heat. He learned that rainflies came down from the moun-tains after the rain had passed, that even rain carrion have its use, even bush bug and centipede have they link in the chain.

The old man died for the second time that November. Look-ing out to the savannah at sunset, he choke – like duck bone or fish bone stick in his craw. Same time the radio say hurricane coming again, and Mammy say that sometimes lightning had a way of coming inside your house uninvited, so all electric light was to switch off in hurricane season.

One Sunday afternoon, when rain was pounding bucket a drop and wind was hitting wicked from the north, two Indian boy get shock up and twist under a samaan tree in the savannah, sheltering from rain while watching Hilltop United play Mitagua FC. The tree bark peel – there was burst pulp, beige beneath – lightning split the trunk to a wound in wood, combust the spot and shoot its bolt in their solar capitals and temples of humming bone. Ambulance arrive in the savannah. Gather round of people;

spectacle watch them from the window, from a living room paved with ague and shingles. Corpse is all they can see.

This spot was also where, between the wide spread of these branches, wearing two rubbers to bone, the long grass itching, bruising the knees of him, the musician saw thighs flashing in the moonlight. The night cool and deep in the Indian gardens on the other side of the world. Bless her hands, her neck, the dark bones of her ethnicity, that girl who was born of hillside villages, who carried water in buckets, who bathed at the standpipe with Lifebuoy soap. He fingered her in the chicken shop with greasy fingers after the matinee at the Ritz cinema; sweat wet, the upper cusp of her, the plums of her sex and trembling breath. Oil.

Years later, when the musician was visiting, he found her serving chicken fried and shy in a shop on Independence Square. She blushed, but he recognised her and called her name. In the hard light, between the white plastic counter and the smell of frying oil, she was still as dark and beautiful as she'd been those Saturdays. She'd had a child; her mother had died. She still lived in the backroads, among hills and streets he knew legends of, in the same house, the one with the parabolic antenna and the water tank in the yard.

68

Silver blades and several thin penknives, splayed open, stainless and taut, fastened the produce to the table. The table leaned against the right side of the door which led out to the street. On the table were assorted products: sun-dried passion fruit, the brown sapodilla stabbed down, stilettoed and veined wings of flying fish, frogs' thighs, marsupial pins. The old man stood waiting at the door for business, half-asleep, leaning on the jamb and nodding, his snackette open to the heat and dust. The table was ragged and ripped, like wood that had been eaten out by the sea, salt in the wound, salt in the eye, salt in the very strategy of morning.

The old man's daughter was standing beside him, born brown and black haired, almost twelve, precocious and metamorphic, her teeth growing too fast for her mouth. Although the day was hot, the shop itself was dark and cool inside. The hessian rice bags, the flour and sugar sacks stacked in the back bloomed no heat through the room. The back door led to brightness, the eye unable at first to fix upon what it revealed, until, beside a brick wall, it came to rest on a hibiscus tree, a small pile of derelict lumber and broken bicycles. This place was just like how Mr Nimtaz grocery in Petit Bourg used to be, where children would be sent to buy two pounds soft flour, bicarbonate of soda, two cubes of Reckitt's Blue ultramarine, mercurochrome, eight ounces of rice, six of sugar and a tin of sardines. Every Friday, you going there with Mammy and Daddy to make weekly grocery, and you could go in the back and lie down on Nimtaz sugar bags and play with his two sons. But it wasn't long before Nimtaz and his boys die in a car crash. Coming back from Manzanilla, night fall and sea blast on the windshield, so the man can't see, and the car sway out of control and slam into a coconut tree. All their sorrows and brain coral, all the living verbs of their thighs, all the rivers and rivets of their jaws, the bones and ribbons of their necks, the grapes of their eyes, all their stones, corpuscles and swill and lymph – all that burst into gristle and slag for the ambulance to carry away. It make news and put picture in newspaper. Was a big scene and tragic, how good, humble people could dead just-so. One day you riding high, next thing Basil in your arse. Nimtaz and his sons had ancestral Creole gold, from Portugal, India and somewhere in Africa, but they bud and bloom from Caribbean roots. This happen just before Christmas. The man business place had to close down.

Now imagine that the shop on the white-hot street, with the needle in the wood and the passage of light, is similar, but not as bright as the one where Ella's father, Deacon Simmons, waiting, anxious to sell his goods. Light fading and too few penny dropping in the pot. Simmons grinning, but he cantankerous; he old, but he muscular. When things not running nice, he ready to rile and wrangle if you jumbie him too much. He same way since he was a boy in Susconusco village, spitting in the sky, leaping across ravines with leg span in baggy pants. He never once fall in the dirty water. When he play sailor mas, he coulda drink rum and fall asleep content at the bottom of a well. He beat people till police beat him till he cuss God. He boil down when he catch religion, but he wasn't easy; he was cunning too. This blood was Ella's lineage, her genealogy and heirloom.

Ella stands in the shop doorway watching her life scroll out like a film. Now that her father is in heaven, dead, she must return to the house in Enterprise Village where he once lived. She must return and yet she cannot move towards it. The streets are rivers of veins and empty as maps; the air is damp and suspicious with unripe fruit in the market stalls, soft avocados and parrot fish rotting, rabbit fish, goat musk, goat pill and bogus paraffin. Let her see clearly what she has done. But Ella is only one fulcrum pulling us between suspense and intrigue. How will she react to instances of terror? What brought her up, what was the stem upon which was she raised, leaning into the wind like this? Baba Oba and Baba Shango in the unsmiling earth, a candle flame in the sacred heart, a womb of bush. All that is beautiful is dying, just as what once was river is now a dry path passing the trodden road that leads from the snow-white airport to the cane field, to the chest hospital, old riverside, hill back and gully, down to the taxi stand in Curepe, and then the drive through brittle heat, past the drive-in cinema to the plains of Chaguanas. There is no direct route, not even for the panyol bushman on the donkey cart he accustom bringing the cocoa home on, in panniers, till one Amerindian Christmas, while painting the outside of his house red, he fall from his ladder and never touch the earth. Look, Poopa Lezama fall and keep falling. His body is left behind to cough up blood and struggle for breath on a hospital bed. His is a long-to-dead time, coming from down the main in Macuro, the landscape of river town and the South American delta; the power keep coming back to physical stricture. Ella has become invisible, like the silence of glass, like the empty spaces between memories. But she will not weep in public. She moves along the cold distance, she bridges the interstice by flight or train or walkway; the asphalt road is hard beneath her feet. Bleak and ancient hunger, the lingering lance in notions of guilt, the sorrow unto death, the gravity of islands.

69

The Great Bandit, wounded in this bitch of a kitchen, defeated by intensity and resting in a rooming house in an abandoned college for retired saints, applies the sap from aloe to his face. His good face done gone now, slashed with leaves from running through the long blades of razor grass in pursuit of the saga boy Luke. He had been almost blinded in battle, cast out of sync. Manatee bite him, then he had found himself exoticised and exposed like pussy in the glossary of a big book, braying like a jackass. His neck was blue-black with scales of muck and cracked skin. He, too, before he lived alone in the desert, had once lived within the rooms of a respectable life. He had worked in the coffin factory beside the graveyard, the same hard ground his mother was buried in; nameless grave and grass making undisciplined bacchanal upon her bones.

This was the same urban graveyard his good friend Arvind was buried in. Arvind had not died for free but by mystery and strangle – and being thrown over some precipice on the foreshore, with fifteen Trinidad dollars and a bag of weed in his pocket. Oil seep out his wood, and now no record or receipt exists of Arvind. Once, he had sat with his shirt blowing open in the rich people insurance office, at his desk each day, assessing the Billboard charts – for which he had algorithms to predict the rise and fall of hit songs and long players. He knew the mechanics of the thing – who might jump into the top ten or to number one. Arvind once took the Great Bandit to the top of the insurance building they both worked in; this was just after the Bandit had graduated from bandit school, and Arvind show him how small the island really was, that the sea was just a leap over the colonial fort, that distance and independence were dreams. Arvind never wore necktie, never buttoned up; he wore his long hair down and was a cool rebel in the rum shop, beers every Friday. Arvind say, 'The same sea I come here on, black as black as you, same how, don't watch my name Ragoonanansingh, watch my chains.' Then he pull up his sleeve to show his silver bracelets. And the Great Bandit throw his head back and laugh, but he knew it was true. The news of Arvind's death that Monday morning was like wild breeze rolling through the carpark. The whole office congregated at the coffee machine. No one was sure how to act or what to say or do or how to cry, since Vin was a rebel and a saint too gentle and high to be hit by homicide.

The Great Bandit has taken two-inch meat and has left the rooming house, he is moving across the land, resuming his pursuit of Luke. He would not rest until they had clashed like tragic beasts in the grasslands, till who dead well damn dead. He had realised by now that knowledge of the plot's trajectory would not save his life, that he would have to sketch and act out his own arc regardless, since he could sink into the ocean and dream deep at anytime, and no one would piss blood or weep for him. But what had carried him this far? It was the faint glimpse of a rumour that perhaps, for once, the villain might not be predetermined to die, but perhaps to win. But he cannot control the writing hand. He cannot write himself into and out of the book. He had been driven to sin and worse than sin; he had been envious of his own kin, envious of every fruit people pick, every gift given to Luke, every heroic gesture the young man made: Luke this, Luke that. Now, pushing deep into jungle, the Great Bandit came upon a bridge, but the bridge was almost vertical. There were bamboo rails to venture up, above the leaning river, but there was a powerful drop. He going up, but turn around to see a black and crab-faced man standing sixty foot or more behind him, with a horsewhip flinging down, clearing a path through the slave market. The dust making fever rise, a fever both hereditary and perpetual. Run. The Great Bandit is looking for Luke in the hideous jungle, stepping over villages like a conquistador. There is a tower in this forest. The tower appears nearer than it is, and it takes the Great Bandit forty and more days to walk to it, thigh high through the pampas grass. There were in fact two towers, one behind the other, joined by a narrow arch of orange-red brick that built this babel of voices. On the promontory of this gap between languages, the Great Bandit pauses. He has a vision of himself as a wire bender smelling his fingers, then as a blackbird among the chicken hawks and lizards of the island, then black and perpendicular as a contrary child, a step-outside child picking his toe corns and eating them, even peeling them with hacksaw blade, and cutting too deep and sometimes bleeding the dermis beneath. In previous iterations he had chanted midnight robber speeches into the mangrove, had slit through bone and gristle, scraping cutlass clean and narrow on the hard plantation road at canboulay. Raphael had sent him down along a street where bombs were exploding, like in some Italian war movie, but the Great Bandit would not skin or ease up in battle; he was ferocious and aiming to kill, maim or strangle.

Luke hid in this jungle beneath those pillars of anthracite. Where the sun met the arch it could split time into stars. He is waiting, with luck and tension, equally determined to clash and flail, to see who could flex. These two big man have to bounce under the towers. Throw your hand, call your money, one man have to dead.

In *The Frequency of Magic*, Raphael tells the story of Prentice, Jack Blake and Jim. This happened many years ago, when bullfrog used to smoke hard weed, and *bois* for gayelle used to cut from black poui or gasparee wood, when Prentice wanted to kill Jim, and Jack Blake wanted to kill Jim too, but Jim was not afraid of either of them. Jim was from Upper Cadogan village, where taxi wouldn't go, where sin and shame living side by side like corrugation vine, where hand feeding hand and gun-mouth narrow-narrow where shin bone meeting ankle, where even rain does fear to fall sometimes, and all matter of animal walking upright, looking for people to bite.

Jim was leaning on a pillar post overlooking the village, spitting banana seeds, then he bump down to the avenue. He was a solid soul stick twirler, dressed all in black with cockroach killer boots. He climbed the rickety stairs at the back of the Black Silk Bar in Chenet Tree Junction, a place they say never sleep, and indeed, far gone midnight, the barber still cutting hair, the chiropodist open, naked bulb bright in calypso snackette, and they shelling out fried chicken and pigeon peas rice. Shortcut does end up in cut-up down there; people does get their neck lock off or chop-up. Is not one suffer these people suffer, is much. But they still ready to ramp; they licking hand like puss, eating roast bake and buljol. When night come they roasting fowl and assuming 'gouti look back position, skinning up on the sweet man bed, jumping window when they hear the husband jitney pull in. They will pull out wood still dripping oil, because oil don't spoil. These days, they say how massa day done, how the village evolve, how the ghetto get gentrify, how Tanty Merle and Uncle Mike dead long time and gone to grave. Now they leggo rock festival and open whisky bar near where Melchior selling tuna and shrimp.

But that couldn't stop Jack Blake and Prentice from jacking

Jim up on the Black Silk Stairs. Prentice and Jack have malice against Jim and it long in the tuber root. They clapping blades for his demise since cunny never have hair nor cunny hole, and they bind in cahoots versus poor Jim. So when Jim flash the spot, all three start to wrestle on the stairs and the stairs start to rock in that muscle of a motion when grown men fighting like android. It hard to watch. Because the eye too slow, the meditation too narrow, and the vision going against eye expectation; you seeing what you don't often see: man at man throat, hard and primitive grip of man hand, big men getting collar-up.

Jim muscle grip Jack Blake wrist, prevent it from piercing. That hand was twisting to puncture Jim liver with a blade. Jack mouth start gargling, he bawl, 'Let I go or die, leggo I!' With his free hand he reaching for Jim throat. Prentice confused. Men from upper rooms at the Black Silk get disrupt from their wappie game, come outside and watch how these three men fighting on the stairs like thief from thief from thief. But they mainly wrestling; blows hard to fire in that limiting clinch of strength and rage, wrist like snake rubber twisting in aluminium bucket. Was worries in the junction, and Swamp Dogg start singing from the barber shop below, *Spirit dust, your head colour red...* No one could part them.

At times like this a simple blow could kill or maim. Sometimes the hit may come unexpected, like an old black Duke with a cane, who if you get him vex, could still place a blow precise enough to burst your head. Don't mind you is villain and you young and fierce, he will hit you. That's why men must be careful when they fighting, because a stray blow can kill, and then you charge for murder; you facing jail. You did just come out the road to buy six hops bread and tin of sardine, and you get in tryst with some reprobate, and next thing you get lock-up, and somebody else minding your children, some other man dealing with your wife.

Prentice rush in stupid. Jim chook him with a shank to the floating rib, but Prentice still fighting. Jim chook him again in the same place and twist it until blood run out, and Prentice bow to mercy and fail. Prentice get licks like a stepchild who, after running wild in the neighbourhood, over ravines and up plum tree, get held by the neck and receive a sweet cut-arse, belt all round his back.

Jack Blake trying now to cut Jim on the wrist; but Jim get the handle and Jack Blake hold the blade. Jimmy bawl, 'Leggo de damn blade!' When he pull, he cut Jack to the bone. Jack moan. Jim was a demon; he bad like cut-tail snake. Jack wrap the bloody hand in his shirt and he run to seek solace upstairs in the Silk. And that was the first time that Jack Blake, known to barry dead man in a carrow, give o'er and cry out. Poor fella, he was in pain. Siren coming up the road, but Jim jump forty feet from that balcony and flee like a lizard. He run up the quarry behind the frolic house, as villain, beast and killer of men. He hard to dead, long to kill, like wild rabbit neck cut, but it keep kicking.

Raphael write it down and he done with that. He close the book for the night. He turn off the radio. He defy Aristotle, Hemingway and Forster. He never say why these men were at war, what who do, or who do what, he never give clue to accord for merit or role, for causality or motive and yet, krik-krak, the action roll; he make the reader read and, somehow, the story get told.

At the reception in Berlin, the Nigerian diplomat looks on as the last of the dancers leave the floor. Then he rises from his Chesterfield chair. He grins as the other diplomats and the women with them mingle and merge in the white and elaborate hall. He shakes the musician's hand, declaims that this was the hall Nigeria built with sweat and blood. Then he spins his wife into the scene, carelessly, as if she were a wheel, and calls to his minion to take a photo of him, his wife and the musician. He says he should be in the middle, since he is tall for his ethnic group. His wife bows her head and smiles. His beige polyester kingpin suit is two sizes too small, so his cock prints out in the crotch, and the sleeves ride up on his wrists. He wears his red cummerbund high up on his chest, and his bald plate glows. Outside, in the courtyard, on the richly embroidered concrete, in the stadia for chariots, he shakes the musician's hand and says, 'My brother, play well.'

The musician genuflects, then turns away, checking his own hand for blood, to be washed with pitch-oil soap and very cold ice.

On the road to the university, the high commission's driver is grinding his jaws with kola nuts, glancing around to praise the musician, who is sitting forward on the firm backseat of the diplomatic taxi. The driver rolls the balls of his feet across the pedals, feet that have travelled many miles along rivers to arrive there. That afternoon, the musician emerges at Aranguez savannah. An old school friend is passing along the track that hangs from the floating rib of a hill – no earth below but wind above – around the field where he used to climb the trees for plums in 1977. Sugar-headed, the friend always had that copper scent of a boy from those slum jungles up Nabiola Trace where the musician's uncle took him once, to measure at a tailor for two gun-mouth pants with stove mouth and sister-boy buckles at the waist, with hook and bar closure and turn-up hem in soulful style, in good green cloth, like gabardine or twill, with jigger button, zipper and all kinda thing. But them pants never get make, and the jungle reclaimed the promise. They never returned to Nabiola Trace in that jitney, with the rickety terrazzo machine jumping in the back. Each time those trousers were spoken of, the uncle shrugged against the manchild's complaint. It was a grown man's promise made with slack intention. Maybe money fail. Maybe the tailor hand break. His woman horn him. He can't press a stitch.

It is one a.m. and the old friend is walking high above the land on the hovering red dirt track, where the branches of fruitless trees make the trail treacherous and hooded as a vale of vines, reaching out over soft ground for children to run upon. This friend has not seen the musician for several years, but passes him same way, not wanting to stop and chat. He appears agonised when asked, 'What's life like?', and seems eager to escape once more from the nostalgic. He says, 'I good. I around, I lingering,' and moves on with his way. It is true that life has not changed much for him, and since he has not lost his history upon these hills, there is not much to reminisce upon.

The savannah is lush again, as it used to be, ocean green and infinitely Eden, with young corn blooming at the far side. The perimeter rim is like a race track that floats. But the house on the corner, where the old spinster would smile from her balcony and say a friendly word as the musician passed, is gone. He would be returning from errands to the shops on Bushe Street, with sardines, hops bread and tins of fried chicken ice cream. Now there are showers high on platforms in a leisure centre where that old house stood. A gym, a cafe, a library, administrative offices. Every room can be seen through the towering glass and chrome, and the raised balconies overlook the savannah with its samaan trees, and the young sugarcane blades still lean away from the scythes of anthropologists, further south, in the old plantation field.

Up Bushe Street, there was a football team, Blackpool United, and at dusk the players would come scraping the uphill road with their football boots and their chattering. Now, where those players used to pass, the musician is surprised to see restaurants, a puja emporium, a Chinese fromagerie with long begging queues each Sunday morning. The light is yellow, bright as 1979. The radio broadcasts from a shed in a deserted yard announcing a list of deaths to organ accompaniment. Then the Ice Man plays 'Love Me' by Yvonne Elliman. Is this the yard in which the old woman kept parakeets? Was this where Ma Sylvie lived and died, a woman with faith the size of a mustard seed, who knew prayers that could move mountains and defeat black-tongued bitches in the spirit world? When the musician came to the yard and felt the grief of its emptiness, he wept. He knows that when he himself has gone into that gone momentum, nothing will be left of this place, apart from what has been written down.

In Berlin, the snow is falling two days before Christmas. The musician is walking in a covered market where he finds palm oil jars of vitriol and egusi, fetish of regret and stockfish, fetish of gari, fetish of bliss, tincture of must-love and potash to cause instant infatuations. He is still the child in the world, the boy child searching for his mother, so soon herself to be wounded with a catheter. At the university that night, the band are most pungent in the closing segments of 'Beat-Out-House Blues'. The diplomat stands and cheers till his cummerbund bursts.

72

They are somewhere between Christmas in Antwerp and New Years Eve in Amsterdam. It is Sunday, it is a haiku with snow on the ground. Eventually their image will fade from every photograph they have ever been shot with. Their voices will decay from ears which have heard them, recordings of their sound will fade from data and wax; no melody or image seized in dreamtime can ever be retained on litmus or gratuitous film. Nothing can survive, not even the strong box of sealed Black Saint and Strata East LPs, neither those by Sun Ra, Billy Harper, Tyrone Washington, Pharoah Sanders or Jeanne Lee, hidden in vaults, pressed with Afrocentrist artwork, but as yet unissued.

Their hotel room is a liminal space in which the musician is perpetually contemplating jazz and suicide. Pull him in, pull him up. He has travelled great distances, from hillside to hilltop, he has walked high along the coast, he has seen the landscape spread open like a scene from a faded tourist reel of island vacations. Ella has fallen asleep with her mouth slightly open, dreaming of rainforest nations. He listens to Clifford Thornton: *The Panther and the Lash* (1970) then *Gardens of Harlem* (1974). He watches her sleep. 'Shango-Aba L'Ogun'. Islands have their songs, they have their beautiful and sorrowful songs, they sing their history.

In Rotterdam, the rain had begun its swirl when they started to play. He blew and was exposed when he took the hot horn from his mouth, and the bass probed the corners of his body. Roots in the sea, branches in the sky. He cannot have everything. Let her go. But who can deny a woman who sleeps, who exudes warmth, invariance, patience, who falls in love and keeps falling. Nevertheless, on this night he has no more secrets to keep from her. In the Italian restaurant in Amsterdam, with the dusty bouquets of dried red peppers hung from nails on the wall, she held his hand

and said, 'I wish you mountains, I wish you life.' She will not disappear gently into the dark eye of night.

In early autumn, in Sicily, they visit the epicurean widow in her white house overlooking the bay in Milazzo. This woman, an Italian, originally from Napoli, was, as a dramaturge in New York, both a benefactor and confidant of the actor. Now retired, she lives alone in a wide house atop a hill with overabundant foliage reaching up, and a less than cared-for garage beneath, an elegant but dusty living room, with a bent broom leaning in a corner and sweet red ants shuffling in deltas of fine silt in the creases beneath the skirting board. The woman, once an actor herself, with her long neck and fine bone structure, is elegant and lithe in her flowing flowered dress, with thin fingers, and toes spread in leatherette sandals. She walks through rooms filled with porcelain ornaments, cut-glass carafes in cabinets, purple and green potpourri, the vulgar crystal chandelier her late husband bought in Brussels, the oil-painted portraits by the less famous, and the soft furnishings, the polished brass feet of the day bed, the Arabic themes of hessian rugs that cover the cold terrazzo floor, the soft, misshapen cushions on the iron rocking chairs. The drawers, casually open, are filled with receipts, old fountain pens, refolded letters and black and white photographs – the accruements of a life of importance.

They are on the verandah looking over the bay. The widow shows her teeth, and her eyes sparkle as she enters with the tray of cranberry juice and lemon madeleines. She places the tray on a white iron coffee table and sits, swinging a slim leg over a knee with rakish flair. The skin on her calves is unblemished, olive, like the skin of a pear.

The musician and the actor are on the run, from train line to junction, from love and its tragic fate, from bright yellow rape fields to green seas, from Europe to the literature of islands. It is late afternoon. They sit in the honey warmth of the light; the melancholic hues of the Tyrrhenian sea islands. The peninsula in the distance looks deserted, and those restaurants along the Palazzo D'amico that haven't yet closed for the season are empty. The retired actor leans forward to break a piece of madeleine, then she hums a false tune, this widowed dame, feigning insouciance, but as she brings the cake to her mouth, her eye is up. Perhaps she prefers musicians with palms open for coins on the pier, but simultaneously she desires the desire of younger men who present themselves to her as perfumed rogues, with open shirts and uncombed beards.

The musician smiles, he meets her eyes, then, as the two women talk, he surveys the living room again: the paintings on the walls, monochrome photographs of Italian street scenes, a child's face, Japanese line drawings of sunflowers. The sea unfurls on the coast, and the sound fills the room, even here, high up on the hill. He searches the teacher's face as she talks. Then his eyes search her body – the fine, slim wrists, the narrow fingers, the still-lean flesh of her thighs, her breasts, the softness of her hips. Her body has retained its secrets; he does not have to imagine that beneath her dress it has also kept its shape and intimate function. When it is time to leave, the older woman kisses him on both cheeks, and the pleasures of her small breasts press against him. She embraces Ella, then holds her at arms length, as if seeing her for the first time. Goodbye to Sicily, goodbye to the verandah overlooking the harbour, to a retired dramaturg with a dozen silver hummingbirds in her hair. She is on the brim and soon it will be too dark to enter that bush with wood or metaphor. They walk to the gate, passing the fern, the orchid's silk, the tulip's slender neck.

73

At the end of the corridor, the goods' lift went up to the second floor, and then there was another corridor, dim all the way down with herbaceous shrubs on either side, lit from overhead by a row of white tungsten bulbs, which glowed yellow by the time their light reached the ground. This was the indoor farm where surrealist rice and rhizomes were grown. By the time we arrived that day for Boyson, he had packed four boxes of cherries and ginger root. Yes, brother, it was 1989, and Boyson was coming to the end of eighteen months incarceration in a Swedish penitential greenhouse. When we entered the greenhouse we saw prisoners wiping each leaf and speaking to each branch, clarifying the earth beneath, tending the mollusc and husks into which these experimental trees had put down roots.

Midway through life, loss becomes nostalgia. It was so with Boyson, that when he looked back at those years of youth, what he chose to remember was walking down slick from Million Hills to Chenet Tree Junction with Kouros cologne all under his navel, or how his Uncle Harry's wife, Marva, would jheri curl his hair, those Saturdays in Morvant, and how his green-eyed uncle himself was never there when he was having his head held over the sink and washed among the sound of chickens, the gossiping in the neighbour's yard, and the wash of traffic on the Lady Young Road.

Those were soulful days. On Friday nights, Boyson would go to the dancehall above the Chinese bakery in Barataria. He would drink and fling his foot. This was a place where young folks from the villages went to learn the motives of the body, to gauge their aromatic power and flex. Another spot was the elaborate discotheque on the island's west coast, the sea right there, the waves blooming up on the foreshore, and people dancing upstairs in air-conditioned rooms – before they built condominiums there.

Boyson would iron a seam in his jeans, button up his shirt, put on bolo tie, line up to go in there and fall in love, over and over again, with every pretty girl that came down from Petit Valley with talcum powder on her face. Boyson shy like crocodile on the dance floor, but when the DJ play 'On the Wings of Love', he would turn gunslinger and extend his hand for slow dance, and in that dance, he bust two lyrics on them, and next he upstairs on the soft chairs plying them with rum and coke and tenderness. If they get catch, he had a beat-out spot waiting for them in the hills. On Saturday, Boyson would wash his one Levis and lay it to dry on the galvanise roof. The savannah was a green ocean in those days, breeze was cool and Indian sweet to the root. In the yard, the orange tree and guava tree were still alive. Boyson would set out in the afternoon, east to Macoya to fall in love all over again. But so many friends had left the suburbs in migrations to London or New York, that Boyson too, began to contemplate a way out.

Now, as he packed boxes of penitentiary fruit, Boyson considered the ability of his memory to preserve the location and specific vibration of places and events, without him knowing at the time that such things were being recorded or becoming sentimentalised. Boyson could remember, for instance, how once a DJ set up illegally within dark and unfinished regions of a high apartment building downtown, pumping out primitive dancehall above the rooftops of the city, and the police vex but can't find the sound to shut it down, so they driving back and forth over the flyover. Boyson remembered how he moved that night like a saga boy, between the beams of scaffolding, with a narrow-eyed girl from the housing projects. In those soulful days he saw beauty in every female face that smiled at him. So, this was Boyson, his eye on love, and then he was working as a stores clerk on a construction site in Carenage, but he never lift a hand to assist the men. Boyson sit down there in the hut smoking tampi whole day and listening to Dear Jenny radio call-in for agony. Eventually he get to know what the real labour of hands meant, when he get work to pump the machines which ground corn, flax – and arms sometimes – in the flour mills, where there was the lifting of heavy sacks, the work of overalls and boots.

When he come out from there, he turn badjohn. Yes, my sister, one time. But nobody know what demon posses Boyson to bore that man's rim in the discotheque, where everybody dancing. Why he grind so much malice when a man bend and whisper something in his girlfriend ears, why he insist she confess, but vex when she tell him and open up the man carapace.

From when he release, Boyson remained vigilant against any threat of fight or route back to jail. The judge promise next time to send him so deep down in hell that he would be trapped as within the pages of a book that was never read. So, when Boyson returned to those hot-up rooms where lovers kept the walls erect, as he sprang back and jumped when the DJ played 'Silent Morning', anybody mash he corn, he'd be prison-polite and smiling, 'Pardon me, brother, one time.' Then he get hold shoplifting from Hi-Lo and get six months for theft by deception. But somehow he escape the island and end up in Sweden. And if you ask Boyson how, he will quote Lord Kitchener, 'Don't ask me what happen, you see me alive.'

Leaving the greenhouse, Boyson is suddenly swollen up with tenderness, nostalgic for the blue of the blue door up from the disco bakery. Things will be alright. We live and die, and what is between is ours to keep.

74

The mouth of his horn, when lifted up gleaming into brightness, was as evangelical and pure as a Sunday morning in Wallerfield, pure even as the honey oil sipped at Ma Mamin's Spiritual Temple, or the coolness of water in the mouth after a day roaming neck high in the fever grass, or among those brittle guava trees that never bore ripe fruit, stone hard like copra or hernia root, spindles of trees that stood sparse in unbirthable soil, the pastures gone to waste there, near the river near the little church hid in bush. If he stares slack-eyed from the back seat while driving through the French countryside, the grass at the side of the highway becomes a murmur, a blur which returns him to the arid fields around Ma Mamin's yard.

When the horn comes down in Marseille that night, each of the accompanying instruments builds to a crescendo, which is dense enough to step inside and balance along a narrow path between the vibrating cascades of sound, waterfall keep falling. The band plays with enough centrifugal power to generate motion, to split wind into light, which is music, which is magic, which is a poem with no words, which is the poet's daemonic presence and the beating of wings, which is beautiful and dying. In fact, its immanent end is what gives the music its strength, a fulgence so fearless in the wild back of night. Open the gate. The bell there to ring, ring it. Let each musician play their play, let them go through, let them ramajay and go down deep into the heart of the thing, let them be thorough in their explorations of instrument and mind. This is the prayer-sound of the jumbie in the dew of dawn, the seppy or the flying frog which sticks to the neck, that can only be lifted with a hot iron or it ripping the skin; it is the woman whose name is Phyllis, spinning her faith in meditation, then leaping from a tower and landing softly. Let each musician pray to their own god or Janus-faced deity. Legba. Let them invent new colours and describe them with new words, new sounds, new notes, new chords; let them bear down and moan, each one, one by one, to play with/inside and with/outside, to split the brain in two, to break the mind, to listen and to play equidistantly, simultaneously, like the rain that circulates to feed the entire island. Let each player hear sound as colour vibrating, hear how each note may connect to another, sound as shadow and flux, wonder and fluttering wasps. Let them listen and be true to the route they choose, let them align the two, if needed, or be free, three or more, four or nine. Yes, let each one come out, one by one, let them play, and eventually all improvisation becomes rhythm, and then hymn. But this rhythm thing we talking 'bout, sometimes you can't hear it tight, but everything have rhythm, right? This rhythm thing we talking 'bout is spirit and pulse and precipice and nation and drum resistance and knots of thick black love. To play is not to think, but to be thought itself.

They are in an amphitheatre, an arena. The audience is seated but will soon be compelled to stand. To bring power down, the musician must draw his spine back, lean from the electric wheel of his brain into the double-stopped snap of the bassist's lowest string, like the waves pulling the ocean from the sand, like breath pulling the clouds back and forth. He must think back to those experiences that have remained as motif and palimpsest: the resonance of loss, of longing, of some salted melancholy in the throat that cannot be dislodged by time or drowning. He lingers at the entrance to magic. Then, swinging up past the mechanic shop on the Saddle Road, and the brief gasp of the cemetery, then going down past the San Juan river where he once walked, thinking he could follow it all the way from Susconusco to Aranguez savannah, where the bamboo plantation and the iron bridge once stood. But he is oppressed by the muscle of the river, its wild truth and difficult vision, its wide angles and forever time. So he turns to walk back up the steep banks of the river, to the ground where his ancestors were buried, and where he knows he, too, will be put down in the sweet mud to rot to bone meal one long, hot singing day.

Years later, passing through San Juan in a rented car, he will see a cock poised and crowing prominent on a tombstone at this very

225

cemetery. He will stop to take a photograph which, developed, has an odd grey blur, as if some density of light hovered above this burial ground, darkening the lens. This is what he blew, when finally the battle between drum and bass revealed a clearing, a green pasture. That is what he ran to. He had seen such pastures beside the railway in Alicante, or from a car window driving through Sines or Gloucestershire, each time wishing he could stop and walk across the motorway, to sit with his back against a tall tree, in the cool shade of noon.

Each musician emerges from the rainforest whole, drenched in their own waters. Each has received messages from the future, and, leaning into applause, they leave the stage to return once more to those Rabelaisian chambers beneath, to lay hold upon liquor and smoke. Each is a part of a part, and a part which is equally whole and singular, not distinct but both, not distant but distantly close and infinitely liminal. Later, when they walk out into night, they find the world still oblivious and cold. Carry him. His back is a small copse of feathers, his neck is a knot of twigs, his tongue is of smoke and the fire thereof.

75

Uncle Martin, the saga boy, who wore tight black trousers, army boots, sunglasses and open-neck hot shirt in the seventies, went for a job in the Catholic Bank, beneath the looming precept of the Church of Immaculate Mendacity, because Adolphus Henry, the civil servant, said he knew people there who could put work under him. When Uncle Martin went, he meet wire grill down the counter, and when he asked for work, the receptionist gave him ease – though she was not callous or spendthrift in her sonnet of dismissal – she simply said that there was nothing there for him, besides a bucket of black disinfectant waiting to throw if he came back. So, after many failures and menial work, this uncle lay himself under a bridge and read Lacan until he went mad, angry at all faiths and signs. *Ecrits*. But he had an old alto saxophone, this uncle, which he kept penned in an inglorious spot beneath the bed where he entertained women.

As a boy, the musician had found this shining something and blew and found it open to his touch and breath. Uncle Martin had *blown* it sometimes on Sundays, in wild island jazz bands, but he could not *play* it. He himself had stolen the horn from his grandfathers' mattress-making shop, where the old man had hung it on a wall, so by the time it reached the musician, this horn had spoken through multiple mouths and was anointed by ancestral breath. This was so many years ago, way before the musician knew the names of trees in the yard, or why his aunt kept a rag under her bed.

In Berlin he lingers along the Spree. There is no sorrow like his, no loneliness as deep as this distance. Ella has come from Vienna, she has walked through Europe to find him. Her tallow soles are torn like cane stalks ground in a threshing machine. They embrace, they share commonalities, original vicinities, and are drawn together by a common hermeneutics of language. But when she visits the temples of his eyes, she knows there are no books about love being written there. Still, they make love upon a white bed until the sun rises over the square. Later that morning she will return to her life of acting and speed. Who will find him sitting alone in a restaurant and offer him the life he desires? Who will pin a broach on him or, in that time forever gone, boldly unfasten a fluorescent badge from his chest and, with that sharp-boned face, walk away slow and defiant through the carnival crowd gathered in the small town a few miles outside of the city, then two years hence get shot down south in some police and bandit scene, in the stink and mottled yard of a poultry farm, with the badge stolen from the musician still pinned, but now an emblem for pullets to pluck?

He had not been able to reach his father by telephone; the day had come and gone. The news had filtered down through the elastic fabric of time. He shivered with night sweats, grew suddenly old and mortal, his lips torn like road-kill at the side of a country road. But that morning in West Berlin, the goshawk still sang its song, whistling like a piccolo pitched up into a canopy of stone. He saw the old land in his mind, but felt he no longer longed for it. He had exhausted its riches and rivers of memory. He had followed along the road and found the well down a gorge and the sea blue and coruscating in flint limits below. He had stood knee deep in a river and knew that nothing was real. He knew that distance created hallucinations of longing, that his grip on tradition was evangelically narrow, as was the idea of leaping into the torrent. But that Sunday, the cattle were heading out to pasture and the air was cool and sweet with manure. He saw his father standing on one of the Million Hills, barebacked, with steel pans on each shoulder. But he could not stay there; the band were diving deep into the old country now, for a baptism where sound tapered into bucolic densities. The master percussionist, a guest who had come from Paris, held the *ka* drum between his knees as around a woman's waist, to beat rhythms from Gabon and Martinique. The master could remember ancient slave moans, swooning and trembling sufferings no one could near imagine. His eyes closed, he beat ferociously and seemed to spasm when the spirit shook. But what must the musician do? Run back to the copra nut field? Dig dirt? Collapse in soft water on the floor of an abandoned school? Feign Caribbean sleep? Carve the butcher's bust from diorite then whistle? Make a bust of Fats Waller?

The musician phones his cousin Alvin, the beloved one in the gully who makes barbells from steel poles and cement, who does not age, but whose face is permanently scarred red from wars fought with bees. Alvin tells him that his father caught his last breath like a train; how he flung his arms up and hooked his gasp on a caboose, blinked hard, and rode it in. His father relinquished his memories: the thick files of women he had rubbed to fever on unmade beds, his sex letters – all that gone. The funeral came and went. The double second steel pans were sold in the San Juan market, near that infamous bridge where the river ran past the steam laundry. The sun bitched hard and cussed the dusk. Alvin caught five ravine fish and several species of land crab. Malick river came down. The bull cow tumbled in the swirl, a mountain chicken was hunted and boiled, and the bush bugs and salamanders would eventually find new trees and memories to climb. His father rotted in the earth. May spirits build nests in his beard.

76

Somewhere between words and verses, between pages and chapters, then in that gap in language between letters and moments, something happens offstage or off-page, at the side of a screen set up for viewing kick-up films starring Big Bolo or Chen Sing in the basketball fields of El Socorro, or at Ritz cinema – across from the fried chicken shop – where a young man tickles his first pim. Blink and you miss the scene: the gunfight in the ice factory, the violent thrashing of a death by drowning. Neither was reserved for Luke; nor for him was a death like Khrisnamurti's fading eye upon the stillness of the vinegar tree outside his hospital window, until a breath that is as tender as the hair on a girl's wrist stirred it. Luke had never lost consciousness – apart from once being outside of his body, spread out like starfish from high grade in a park where a carnival was passing, where sequins were stitched to the glittering breastbones of serpents. Now he leaps from a tower where poets retire to write those grief-giving words that render flight to poems in their final verses, as Eric Roach did in 'Finis', before he stepped into Quinam Bay. Luke has leapt from the tower's great height, but the Great Bandit, as witness to this and much besides, is not impressed. Luke cannot make him blush by spreading out poetry before him.

At present, there are two occupants staying in the first tower: an old St Lucian poet in a wheelchair, whose feet, though, are in the sand, the surf, or the boat floor. The other, though critically paranoid, photographs ghosts in the forest, and rises from his sick bed to write ostentatious verse. Both men have become rivers, and when they are called, they will not move easily towards the door, instead they will burst and unravel over the archipelago, and rills and tributaries will surge seaward from Kick'em Jenny to L'Anse Mitan.

An old Jamaican trombonist lives in the second tower. He

leans back in his festival chair and can no longer blow the glowing horn that is laid out before him. He has no wind to sail his throat, no breath to blow, but help him to the stage and when he sings, the audience applauds. It is ok, he has already aerated entire mountains with the sound of his horn.

Luke is leaping, and the Great Bandit knows that wherever he goes, death sharpens his toes. The Bandit knows that his own death upon this road can only be observed, never experienced. But come now, let us break a piece of bread, let us blow gage, let us anoint the reader's head with oil, let us play the poem like a piano, like Monk's shoulder swung into the swing, enjambed at intervals, swift corners and curvatures, into the ringing, singing, sweep of the thing, tap the heel and toe, bop the head back, once more with feeling. But like the audacity of the moment impress upon the Bandit, and one tear-bead runs down his cheek. Oh wow, his life was much too brief; won't death tide him over, just another year? So he begins his blues, the gospel blush, but everything happens at once: his life in the desert, his killer instinct, his wife's death by fire, his eldest son's suicide, how the soles of his feet felt as he climbed the rough bark of the avocado tree.

As the sheriff of a desert town, he was cruel and rapacious. He would measure for fit and put proud convicts to crouch naked in sealed tin cubicles, and put them out in the desert noon till their skin bubbled and stuck to the rims and sides; then the sides would be unlatched and fall to four parts, and the ripped, ripe skin would burst into combust and pus. Even as a boy, he would catch wasps and beetles, then burn them alive in hideous matchbox discotheques. Even the humble sea cockroach was escovitched in wicked pepper, till its tissue moaned and sank further into mystery, to tantalise and treble his tongue with lime and desire. But let us not drill holes in his skull, let us not air his linen, let us not break the Bandit's back with critique and hurtful words, let us not assume the limits of his own volition, or penetrate his breast bone with a long red bream rib-bone to hear him cry out. The Great Bandit, as a man, as a beast, naked and brave in an adulterous bed, in that time of the morning when he wore waistcoats and nothing else, without malice, without fear and so, without violence, was nevertheless prone to profligacy. Brutality increase, evil came easy to him; his hand was heavy whether making pone or junking ham. But it is Luke who ramp and throw the first blow, which catches the Bandit on his shoulder. O breastbone of ages, a dagger! And the bone there shatters. This should be the climax and quench and how the story ends, here in the forest, beneath the poets' tower. But the Great Bandit trembles, he see himself licking his fingers in a chicken shop, after eating the two inch meat. He chooses to improvise autonomously, not to die but to catch fire, to blaze his *bois* desperately upon Luke, to cry out with rage, till sparks spin out the wood. But Luke won't tap out, not now, and they wrap up in a death dance, till the last slow song play in the community hall, where cocksmen have been waiting to press themselves upon the women who have so far resisted their sweet words. Sometimes you could turn a page, or fall asleep in front of the TV, or leave the cinema to go outside by the fowl coop to piss against the wall and hear them chickens bawling in the slaughtery, spit and come back, only to find them kung fu men still fighting like drake.

77

Raphael decide to write his own death, so that when he did die –
apart from his wood and his papers, and the gun drawer full of
colonial letters embossed with marvellous stamps, and the old
red money, the coppers and the unfinished manuscript of the
book he was writing for forty-one years – they would not discover
that he had been sick and never told anyone, preferring to suffer
alone in the wound of silence, afraid to tell, because to tell might
make it real. Say the word and its potential splendour is imprinted
upon the palimpsest of etheric experience. Say the word, 'telluride'
for instance, and be burst into sores and cracked lips, because that
word record somewhere and will be actualised. Among his
drawers of flannel trousers and jockstraps, they would discover
volumes of Raphael's juvenilia: collections of finely wrought but
self-indulgent and unpublished poetry. They would be impressed by his bibliography: *Blacks of Eden*, *The Desire of Ages*, *The
Phenomenology of Deception*, *The Sickness Unto Death*, *The Book of
Questions, How to Write Black Poetry*. They would find celebrated
texts by Lovelace, Naipaul, Makoha, Brodber and Nichols, collections by Morris and Brathwaite, Eric Roach's *The Flowering
Rock*, transcendent texts by Lennox Raphael, solid collections by
Malika Booker and Roger Robinson, even cult and decidedly
fetish texts such as Anthony Joseph's *Teragaton, Bird Head Son,
Rubber Orchestras* and *The African Origins of UFOs*. They would
find books by Paul Keens-Douglas and The Mighty Chalkdust,
then Aimé Césaire, Glissant, Benítez-Rojo and Nancy Morejón
come in. Long black books for decolonisation of the mind. And
in the living room, where Raphael kept his vinyl, stacked alpha-
betical and vast, the map would be full with over 500, 000 albums,
all annotated in foolscap folios and collated and separated into
genres and protected against the flash of sunlight on shelves:
Elvin Jones, Hot Lips Page, John Klemmer, to exhale and blow

gage, Roy Brooks and Rahsaan, with arms of Vishnu, on stritch, manzello and nose flute – all the species of sax and reed machines. Hard US card and black inside: *Black Saint and the Sinner Lady*, Sounds of Liberation, Strata East, *Monk plays Ayler*, the lauded Sabu series, Ellington's *Afro Bossa*, Robert Aaron's *Trouble Man,* Woody Shaw, Billy Harper's *Priestess*, Adam Pieronczyk and Alan Shorter, Amina Claudine Myers and endless calypso. People would say, 'Wow, this man have jazz knocking dog', meaning a vast amount. Raphael had collected these from trips to New York, some from local stores overcome by floods and salvaged by hustlers to be sold waterlogged on Frederick Street, now cleaned and immaculately kept. Even his own kin would be cussed to concussions if they touched this grail while he was alive. Re-searchers would also discover multiple pairs of shoes under his bed: grey leatherette brogues with crumpled heels, gravedigger boots with blades for sharpening toes, the slippers he wore when cutting the bull-cow seeds.

In the backyard, the cattle and swine would be reprieved; they would not be slaughtered, but be let out of their muddy pens to go roaming over hill and river. A few, though, would be snared in traps and bled out of oil by hunters. Chickens would leap out of the hot water bucket and skip about and flutter with neck slit and smelling of death with feathers so wet and warm.

Any characters left within the manuscript would be sent down to the shop by prodigal kin to buy cigarettes, condensed milk and margarine, or be cut down in their primes with plans and opin-ions; they would be beaten for stealing avocados, be slit open in other slaughteries, would have their kidneys roasted and served with vintage pepper; would be beaten with a white pine floor-board while washing the duck pen; would be punctured with harpoons and bruised with nunchakus. The house would be cleared of the old man's things – his tools, the guns, unused cartridges. His books would be boxed and forgotten in the derelict room of some cousin or aunt whose house was the only one on flat land. His records would be shared among nephews and old saga boy dancers, entire discographies carried under arms like children taken down the hillside crying. His gun would choose his brother Bain, who escaped from jail with cunning and guile, and wasn't so insane after all, who saved his money to buy bricks and put down foundation since this was the way that folks progressed in this society – by stacking bricks and bags of cement outside their wooden houses, as promise and ambition to be witnessed. *Oh, so this one and that one building brick house now?* But though bricks build up, sometimes they never amount to a whole house or even a latrine. Bags of cement would get hard and have to be busted by barebacked labourers; red brick get thief and have to be hunted down. The butcher's knives would sit silently on a table in the yard. When alive, he would walk down in the morning and draw for the sharpest blade. In death they were left untouched, as if they held the old man's spirit, not to be contaminated by the living. The manuscript he had written, *The Frequency of Magic*, would be flicked through by his less literate cousins, who were better used to hunting manicou and iguana, who smoked hard weed in secret – so as not to offend the matriarchs and elder members of the clan, since such things were still sighed upon and denounced – unless it were sharing. The great book would not be stored in an archive at some metropolitan university, nor would it be studied in academies of literature, nor critiqued by scholars and journalists whose reviews were published in broadsheets or literary journals; it would not be published in hardcover or trade paperback, nor placed on syllabuses or shelves in high houses to be read in times of famine or grief. Raphael decide to write his own death but nothing happen.

78

At times, perhaps on the runway at Schoenefeld, the musician would suddenly remember that he was not European. He felt this in Venice, Helsinki, Avignon and Madrid, but yet he could inhabit each space as presence and particle wave. It was true that in the limits of lung and the limits of gravity, each stood apart and gasping for air. Is not so the big book say? But the more he stayed in those metropolises with their palace yards rimmed with cherubim and satyrs, the more he wondered where the monuments to his people's struggles were erected.

So he arch his back and puff out a lungful of grapes and rage, and sea water and fowl-shit, and he don't give a damn what come out, he know he done mark to perish. Each combination of notes in his solo could be followed to its source in the hills, each figment of melody could be sketched on the balled pulp of his mind, but to follow the melody's trajectory was to become captive within its imprint and coagulating force.

Sonically, the band were superior. Other combos feared them. They could arrive anywhere, unannounced and burn holes in the very fabric of time. In Berlin, each solos simultaneously, transposing the melancholic rainlight upon the city that night. Each man have the gut and agony of life, so when they play they each rebuke spurious faith in bishop, guru or jumbie symposium. They run away from doctrine. They had all heard the legend of the pastor who said he was building his church on currency captured in the collection box, but who was building his own house upon the rocky outcrops of a terrible river with bachelor galvanise against hurricane, boiling green fig and butterbean to build his powerful wood, while the little church was built of rotten wood on bare earth, so sharp stones niggled the knees of members as they knelt in prayer. And for that, the members bind in cahoot and lash him with spirit; they plot on his demise.

When the pastor learned what the members had planned, he delivered the following sermon. He said: 'I am going to tell you the terror of the dark and deep ocean, about the pressure pushing you down to succumb, to release your grip on life, to laugh in turbulence, to be led away into mischief and into laughter, into the absence of fear of drowning by suicide. I am going to pass through Silver Mill. I am going to be three in one, two on either side of the devil in this incense taxi. I listen, I try to catch what passes. When the devil speaks I turn my first gaze, then slip through a gap in language. Now, I am observing the devil, speaking to the self I left in that previous space. And then I am all three. I am the devil, I am myself, and I am the poltergeist. I am both tenor and vehicle riding pillion on this suffering road that leads out of town, past the limits of breath, and now we are pushing towards the rim of something stitched. Oh mother drum, father drum, I stand up on a stool to play you with a stick in the tourist drum shop on Tragarete Road, but nevertheless you are powerfully real and reverberating through the city, and I am not afraid.' But still they push corn husks up the pastor nose and bury him sideways, or the world would end.

The musician has forgotten his name, his fulcrum and axis. He wanders, knocking on the doors of each ancient faith to find it. But he will not find himself resting in the arms of mercy. Instead, he remembers driving a rugged coast, through rain forests, the canopy green and dense, and seeing a snake, standing upright, half its length in the road ahead, its eyes staring, its head up and turning like a turret gunner.

Next morning, they pass supernatural towns, the lake below Cully. The vineyards are frozen. The driver taps the wheel to a song on the radio, the snare drum rattles in the back. The club is cold and its walls are painted black. But minutes before stage time, the musician faints and falls. They put him sitting in a chair in the dressing room, propping up cold nausea. A fever rises, sneaking upon him like a slack-jawed cousin with bulbous eyes for shit talk. But salt to chew, the vinegar tree to climb, the orange root to find where his navel string buried, but to which he cannot return, not now, the river too long. A hummingbird flits from flower to vine; the old woman bends to her chrysanthemums, her ginger root. He revives, washes his face with cold water, the weakness unto trembling, as the DJ shuts down the sound for the band to enter. But the saxophonist is straining to stand, much less to blow, to shatter the drum of the heart. Then the drummer rolls and kicks, the bass grumbles, the sound rises to a flame that consumes the musician, and he rises, hovering in the energy. As he reaches centre stage, his power comes back, like light from blackout, from saint to sinner, from priest to crook. Blow and hold the note, and his hands are trembling. But rise up, you are indelible, you are made of water and stone. Play Mingus's 'Folk Forms', play Sparrow's 'Outcast', play Balake's 'Aminata', play the new song spun upon the bell, play hard blues to lean against darkness and cults of despair. Blow wind in the sail of a black message. All these things must be swung upon.

The musician refuses to visit the white rooms of medicine, he would rather die by fire than know sickness is upon him like a cold that bound to turn yellow. He bound to puncture the sky. He will hide. They will search for his body. They will find oil, floating heavy upon water.

As if she had arrived at that age, done with restless living and ready to settle on flat land, down from galvanise leaning in those muddy barracks up Old St Joseph Road, a hard life suffer in the rich red soil of old slaver's yards, Mammy, also known as Sister Syl, had resigned to menopause and to raising the manchild whose navel string she buried herself beneath the orange tree, since the boy's father – her own son – was gone into the world, not to find but to hide from himself, too self-absorbed to sustain fatherly fruit, a child himself, wayward, taking what life swerve, travelling along any road that appeared along the way. The jamette mother of the boy was not allowed in the yard.

Mammy was dying slow for mercy. Her feet had swollen. A grey ambulance was taking her to Caura hospital. The one dog she have left in the yard start to cry and beg Mammy don't go. Listen, since the foundation stone went down, that black and white pot hound tie right there. And he whirled around the orange tree, where woodslaves ran and woodslaves waited, their heads up abrupt, awaiting the whip of masonry twine. Pepper in that whip would skin them alive.

Each morning, Mammy would go down into the yard to feed her parakeets, in an image that would be repeated in poems until the poet died. There were crocheted doilies in her living room, on which rested black cents, and black thunderstones that fell from the sky. Mammy fingers had by then burned down to the second layer of skin. Sorrow filled, her eyes were tender as dew. It was said that the old man had built that house in Mount Garnett from mud, then lumber, then brick, working day long in the sun, and this too was a story that was passed down through the ages. Mammy taught her grandson how to tie thread to the bobbin so his kite wouldn't fly away over the samaan trees when the reel run out. She taught him to manja and zwill; to fix blades and ground glass to the kite thread and tail, to cut and send other kites over the electric wires, passing over Jogie Road. She taught him how to choose bamboo for flute, how to stitch hems, how to narrow bellbottom to gun mouth, how to burst dry peas with soda and how to cut drake duck neck with the grinning edge of a blade. This was his heritage: the dasheen stream, the jungle and the trees, and she would watch him, knowing that one day he too would leave. She loved him and starched him bright for school. She supplicated herself, going down into the yard where Clary was washing his car every bitter morning, to beseech him for two wrinkled dollars so the young boy could take a bus and eat that day in school. Imagine, this was everyday, and the old bull didn't eat nice in those days; was plenty cussing and snarling. The boy stood stiff in his uniform in the kitchen, waiting out this trauma. Mammy was most times coming back with the bills. But then, grievous with guilt, the boy would walk across the savannah, then a mile upon the old train tracks and into Febeau Village, saving those two dollars for roast bake and cheese. Mammy watched him fade into the distance, in this time of their lives. She knew that her joy was in him.

But what must also be said is this: those days were the sweetest when Auntie Nita came to visit. Nita was middle aged, with full calves and sonorous bulk, her hair tied back: panyol and vintage, black Latin stock, a full woman, walking across the savannah with a burlap market bag swinging at her side. Come now, come. She would bring yam and yellow yamatuta, starch mangoes, plantain, and even a few purple governor plums. Nita would say, 'But like you don't see is big women talking here? Look, boy, go play cowboy in the savannah. Go catch batchack and millipede in matchbox, go build kite with copybook page, go chop sugarcane.' Imagine then these two women sitting on the front porch, with their fat thighs spread across the corrugated chairs. Two women eating cow-heel soup, then tending to a flower garden, chatting among the yellow chrysanthemums, and then Nita was gone with a smile and a wave, her bag refilled with soursop, avocados and ripe papaya from the back yard where the manchild prowled like a lord with his whip among the lizards.

Then the Redifusion radio in the kitchen making noise.

Curtains blowing up and blooming heat through each room. Sometimes these details are what the boy remembers, more than the old man's belted wrist, the welting and the wailing and the gnashing of teeth. He remembers August, the way the trees never lost their sway, and how the land was wild and irreverent, quick to bear fruit of any kind, and alive with character. He remembers how, at midday, coral snakes and scorpions would find cool spots to hide between the roof beams and the galvanise. Mammy would always find them, lick them down and crush their heads with the balls of her feet. The poison sting of the scorpion was roasted to antidote, to cure poison in the bronze plateaus of these yards and estates where poor folks were once tied to ploughs, or beat to brush yards with scythes, and the hook of the blade was bitter, like sin.

He remembers Mammy in the long grass, in the hurricane, the fever bush, in her kitchen shelling pigeon peas, her belly bound tight against all to come. He knows she delayed her own demise for him, absorbed the swollen calves, the heart attack in the bank, the tightness of breath, the sickness unto death, in a hospital beside a river where young men drowned, sometimes two, three Sundays out of four.

Leader Jimmy upon that bridge, upon that lonesome bridge. He hasn't even eaten yet, but already he wants to spew. He has escaped the pages of a great text of marble and rock, rock upon the landscape and shore. He has escaped into the jungle, with nothing but his past, desire of ages, that man dead, o pious padre, o deus maman, dead and like a ghost upon the waters, as upon each splintering rock. In the morning, in the great wash of dawn, the rain bringing down the Baptist boats, the pilgrimage coming, the bus shaking down the winding roads. At the river, the women of the flock pinch up the hems of their dresses to cross over the fording stones, to cross over from blood and rum and bone, rock and stone. Jimmy at that river, upon his knees like a penitent child. Somebody absolve him, somebody free him of his skin, *a-yon-kon wa gbey*, somebody pull his coat for the seppy, for the zeppo, for the secret which can't be got from book or university.

Later, deep in exuberant country, he could be seen catching hell in a pent-up house with a woman whose good foot was turned backwards. And if you asked him, Jimmy would just say he wasn't really looking for a wife, but for someone who could suck the marrow from his bone. Long Jimmy, long since he passed this way, long since he leapt across river and gully sideways, coming up behind the squatters' union and the latrine. Long Jimmy, who once slapped his own father across the face, and left the old man to pine and grind malice. Jimmy, who while sweeping through the grand halls of corn, and the long lanes of cocoa trees, flicked his cigarette into the bush, for its embers to buzz and flare and burn down the whole plantation.

Jimmy had left the church, he had hung up his frock. Now he could be found each Friday at four pm, leaning sly and copasetic like a dealer of rubber for hash against a Ford Falcon, outside some barbering shop on Charlotte Street in Port of Spain, to the soundtrack of Sonny Criss's 'Daughter of Cochise'. Jim knew that Jack Blake and Prentice were wounded deep in the navel, but was sure they would find him; they would be secluding like snake in some awning, rooftop or tenement building, surveying the hill and plotting his destruction. He remembered how, as a boy, he would wonder if all that he imagined was a dream within a dream within a dream, that such things were so because he possessed some precious power that would in time be revealed, as the vision of freedom was revealed to the slave, breaking the chains that tied him to the bondage of dialectic narratology. Ma Mamin knew when she met Jim that he was a conduit and lossless force, still a boy but lining out the hymns for the congregation, his voice ringing clear.

As a young man in the city, Jim had seen a man get split from arse to elbow by a madman's cutlass blade. This was in the dry bed of the river where men gathered to gamble and smoke ferocious weed, their heads turning around like ball-bearing upon socket when the herb held its purchase and put sweet pressure on the flowering litmus of the brain. Jim was bending to throw his dice in a wappie game when he hear a commotion among the men; he looked up and saw the fatal blow coming down on the victim. In the gap between his watching eye and the flesh, Luke experienced the vision as a hook and sling, as if it were he who had fallen from the ledge of a sentence, unto the hardness of the world.

In those days, Jim had been tampering with a red woman from town named Rosalind, a nurse in the Baptist church, until her husband catch them naked. Jim wood was still inside the cunny, and not just the cunny, but the hole. He ran and returned to the hilltop home he shared with the hummingbirds. Is there the Baptist faith call him to worship. Jim had helped Mamin build her church, he had dug dirt to plant the cross in the yard. He had ordained shepherds and washed the feet of mourners. He himself had been on the mourning ground four times solid. He had stood on the Guinea coast and received secret colours and robes. But he had left poor Mamin to rot in Brazil Village when he swept away north to Mendez Drive, to fatten Mama Gizzard and her flock. Mamin never forget Jim for that. When Gizzard fall, Jim abdicate, he lose faith. Since then is struggle all round his back. No matter what he try, the man can't see his way. He turn to pimping but he fail. He try selling ganja, but his hand heavy; he junking up the people weed. He try to hunt rusty dove but he only know town ways. Then he find himself in rab with Prentice and Jack Blake. People start to say, 'A-A, like Mamin protégé lose his way.' But when people boiling like crab in a pan, they bound to bite and crawl over each other's back to get out.

Wounded in that leap from the Black Silk Bar – he had landed on his heel, and the shin bone had pushed its sting into his thigh – he sat by his window and listened to Explainer's first album.[19] Jimmy knows he will be killed, is not so the big book write? But bad man don't lie, bad man confess. So he sit down where he will be found sharpening his axe. Let them come. But who will come now, with arrow or arrowroot, in the last reels and apogee of Raphael's tome? That book bind Jim in like laglee glue. But whoever come will catch a blade, fall again and keep falling.

19. Explainer – *This is Explainer : The Great Young Calypsonian*, Umbala, Trinidad Production – UP 001, Trinidad, 1978.

81

Raphael had written 80,000 words when he bray and kilketay, his engine break, his hand stick, the pen hover dripping ink. But wait a lil' bit and try again, and that hand bound to bend back. It was understandable that Raphael hand would stiffen. Remember, men like Luke gone, Jimmy gone, Jack Blake and Prentice gone and living their own lives. All them people get born right there in that house on the hill. Is plenty work Raphael put on them; he craft them as part of himself. Ask him and he will tell you what Lovelace say: 'Every character is you.' Each night Raphael close the door of his book, he never expect people to escape. He keep writing forward, he never look back; he sure everything and everyone stay where he left them. When eventually he read back and find these people gone, the man bawl like ten Tarzan and tumble down in the sand. 'Lord,' he cry, 'if all that work I put down gone in vain, the whole book go turn a paradox.' Consider who gone: there was Prentice, whose face was somewhat disfigured, the nose protuberant like an owl's because his mother Bernadette had gutted swine in the San Juan abattoir throughout her pregnancy. Prentice, sickly as a child, walked barefoot in the abandoned land that never dry. He uses to tie thread to the slender petioles of Jack Spaniards, after squeezing the needle sting from these wasps, to watch them fly and lift their detritus in trauma like fluttering kites, fly for a minute then fall. Prentice apply for bandit school, but he didn't get through. He walked with a limp since Jim wounded him in battle at the Black Silk Bar, and now, worn weary of living through someone else's language, he was eager to run amok in the world, away from the curse of language, to escape by creeping from mundane sequences. So, late one night, he slip away, unannounced and half formed, from the spine of Raphael's unfinished manuscript.

There were women too, like Bernadette, who were only

mentioned near the novel's end, lifting their dresses over mud and rum at pilgrimages and swine-killing feasts. These women, with cigarettes freshly lit, rolling rum and ice around their glasses and cursing loudly, would embarrass the men, saying things like, 'Next time you touch this pussy you have to pay,' and 'When it rub so much it does get hot, spit on it,' or telling Macfarlane, 'Mac, how you jam like an old man so? Jam better than that, man, take the glasses off.' These were women of Carib, Guinean, cocoa panyol and black Spanish generations, and of them more should be spoken. They had broken the backs of insolent men; they had stood on hilltops before radio was invented and called their children home from far islands or metropolitan archives. These women could not abdicate from their children, and all the cancerous sorrows they endured accumulated in their breasts. Is so Bernadette came to be sitting one Friday morning, on the wooden front step of her home, weeping into the pillow of her own rough hands. Ask her and she say another hurricane coming, another man with a mouth full of hacksaw blades, the gate need fixing, the roof leaking, and the boy child need beating. Next thing coming is chest pain. She was peeling fish and burning garlic. Bernadette rock back and moan; it was just too much, the strain.

Then it have Jack Blake, who as a manchild born dread in these precipitous lands behind God's back; was cutting bush and bulling woman and getting fat off his mother pension. But one day, one day congotay, he come upon his mother naked on her unmade bed with her mouth wide open reciting a wordless poem. Dead. Is then he hold his head and bawl and burst through the page and out of the plans Raphael had laid.

Then there was Anne, who climbed Voacanga trees and tapped them for their milk; Judy who drowned; Miss Eve the carpenter who saw Adam's wood; Alicia Phillip, who had first taken Luke's sex out of plastic, and given him her pim to tickle and kiss. There were women like Maureen and Didi from Ramkisson Trace who were pious and copper-scented. Such women remained hermetically sealed within the pages of Raphael's book, decipher this or not. There were others who hid from his hand and drifted out of his vision and multiverse of textology, out of the architecture and subaltern fabric of his mind. Others had gone but were bound to return, if not hence, then previously, and Raphael was sure to run them down, regardless of bilk or metafiction, because all his belly and stones were wrap up inside the damn thing, wrap up tight like money in black man hand.

Raphael know the life; he know crab back from crab louse; he know pussy from mouth; he know that life have shape and pivot and apothecary, but krik-krak, everything in Million Hills does happen simultaneously. He know that hew as he hack, Mammy wouldn't dead, she wouldn't tremble and dead in some postcolonial hospital, that she ebb and random like the sea, abbadon, abbadon, or the world would end; that even story have story to tell. And when his mother dead for real, Raphael bawl like six bull swine get slaughter that day. Mammy dead crying prayers in the chest hospital; her kidney pus out and fail. It have some things story can't mend.

But Prentice say how we connected to the cosmos by a thin red thread and, when we dream, is with that thread we does space walk. It like a leash that keep you tethered to the physical plane, and if you wake in a rush, or somebody shake you violent, and that hook get unhinge, your brain will addle and glitch and you destined to roam the abandoned land barefoot and shirtless, shamelessly looking for zaboca to thief.

82

Plunge into the dramatic pool and plumage of landslide, earthquake and hurricane darkening the night, but next morning, as usual, the flowers of the garden will be watered between thumb and hose, the sun will trace a line along the sky lid, and below, on the flat ground of the plains, the acrobat will resume his cartwheels on the same spot, as on every day. In those days, the north was blue and mountainous, south was expansive. There were oil fields there, pipelines and gantries, rice paddy swamps and aubergine farms. The boy wore gabardine bells, standing in front of the blue and white Austin Cambridge, among the honey fields and the lilac sky, the orange tree and the lizards, bugs and snails. Even within these vibrant presences, the boy found time to agonise upon life, to ponder its span and architecture, to be curious about evil and melancholia. He rode broken bicycles around the perimeters of village markets, observed abattoirs and the terracotta cruciform of the burnt and derelict cinema where westerns were once shown. He stared into a mirror by a candle's flame in those tenebrous corners of his mother's house, to glimpse the past lives he had lived. Later, when he had outgrown the island, he wrapped his horn in cloth and left, entering into the liminal rituals of diaspora in the foreign north. But this has been writ, ad infinitum.

On this night in Belgrade, he is remembering Raphael. It is the week before Christmas and they are sitting on his veranda high in the Million Hills. Rain beats through the trees to the sodden ground. The calabash gourds, pregnant with necromancy, are weighing heavy on the bough. Hard rain washes bright life upon the wood of squatters shacks. Every December, the rain would flood the valley below, flocks of low-grazing cattle would drown, small children would disappear and later be found bloated and floating in such far waters as Antwerp and Brooklyn. Raphael's house is in the mist and incensed with the scent of cashew nuts roasting. The cicadas whir and the goat kid bleats, not knowing that soon it will become meat. The old man is still strong with tremendous wood; he could bring bison or bull cow to slaughter, pull them screaming up the hill. He was writing his book, and it seemed to the boy that those piles of paper he kept tied with string under his bachelor's bed could contain the entire mountain: the ebb and tug of the river into the sea, and the surrealist fauna – the carpenter bee and its propolis, the woodslave, the picoplat, the firefly, the eels in brown ravines, the sea cockroach, the calabash fruit, the conch. Every doctrine seemed to have pleat. The green guava tree that fire tired try to kill was still alive but hiding in some safer dream. The book contained the milk of religion, the island's topography – those winding and tilted roads driven into mountains, roads like paper corkscrew warp around and old, so the road slant for engines to run straight through. Raphael, in such light, appeared even holy. He would ask the boy for a number, then read that chapter, but then claim it mattered in which order chapters were read. The boy would watch him walk out in his nylon Sunday shirt when he have bull, then swine to slaughter; see him drag them in or pull them out; the throats have to cut.

That same morning, Cousin Alvin is moving through the thorns and thistles with a hunter's plan to scale the heights above the village, to come back with three-four manicou or an agouti or two. Raphael calls out to him, 'Brother, doh take all, leave something in the bush for me. Come, when you finish, I have work for you.' Alvin grins, waves his lance and swings his hips to mount the steep incline like a lizard. At noon he arrives to help with the slaughtering of the bull swine. But the animal screaming like a wolf, pining for life in this muddy hell. Alvin have to pull it in, shit skidding on the concrete floor, pull it onto the hard ground, which no mason trowel take time to smooth, and Raphael hit it two blow with an iron beam to stun it numb, then he cut the throat to hiss and spray. And from this harvest of meat, Alvin will be given a leg to stuff with carrot spears and beads of garlic to roast on Christmas eve.

The boy sees Bain walking down from his ragged shack, dressed as best he can – his old pants rolled up, his holes have a little shirt in them. Nobody know he kill a man. These four build a three-stone fire under the calabash tree to char the sweet meat – the liver burnt to ashen edges, the hog heart and kidney roast and then lashed with copious pepper. Sweetest thing the boy ever taste was this burnt offal, though not in Million Hills, but in El Socorro, in a deep ritual of chant and sacrifice to which his Aunt Bunny had taken him.

In Million Hills, Raphael speaks of his grandfather. How Daddy Muntu, from Talparo, used to reach home drunk and collar him for nothing, pull him up and press him against the wall till all the little buttons bust from his shirt placket and scatter on the floor. Muntu didn't jester. He would break bottle or dining chair across your back. The sound of them buttons falling would stay with Raphael, and be included in an ancillary chapter.

Later that night, leaning back in his rocking chair, Raphael shivers, remembering deceased Daddy Muntu; driving drunk for fifty miles, from one end of the island to the other, the damn fool crash into his own front gate. His body broken, he lingered, for several days to suffer and fade. Imagine that, Muntu had fire above and fire below, but he puncture a lung and couldn't breathe.

83

Sun Ra was on the ark. Prince Nico Mbarga – he was on the ark. So was Art Taylor and Sonny Simmons and Bessie Smith and Superblue, all on the ark, and Joe Tex, Geraldine Connor and Giuseppi Logan, even Robert Aaron; The Roaring Lion and Aunt Bunny were abdominally on the ark. The Original Defosto was also on the ark. Beat rivers of song upon the omele drum, just a cutlass carpenter, no skill with timber; four-eyed fish were on the ark. Who playing war and fraid blood? Who playing mas and fraid powder? Who prevaricate and ruse, throwing holi powder as ritual upon the ark, but don't want ink or water to touch their clothes? Who else was on the ark? Max Roach was on the ark, and Ras Shorty I, Eric Dolphy, Amiri Baraka, Ras Eliebank and Harry Belafonte – them was high up upon the boat. Babatunde! He was on the ark, Olatunji! He was on the bow. Mama drum, you say you coming to come, but you never reach as far as the Leader house, you never hear his sawed-off speaker drum boom dub roots all around the village/bachelor life, and then you hear he bulling three women in the congregation, and the Shepherd raising crook-stick and tapping his foot when the hymn swing, but is suffer he suffering in silence, because he wondering if, while he in church, rocking on his heels, his woman horning him with Leader Jim when night come, and he need a seer man to prophesy, or to tack back and catch them in slackness. But his faith was firm. Every Sunday he in church, he was on the ark, in brogues. Beti was on the ark, Mong, and Vino in pyjamas, the wild moon, fever in his throat, performance poet and stand-up comic, both were on the boat. And the ark was full, but more was to come and coming still. Ethel Waters was on the ark, singing 'Creole Gold'. Octavia Butler, hip good, up upon this boat. The Mighty Sparrow, robed in African wax print and dancing as man. Eric Eustace Williams, dead and living same time, was also wrapped in kente. Larry Lee, masked and southern drawling, played his guitar on the ark; Fats Waller, Courtney Jones and Winifred Atwell, even Gang Gang Sara, blown from Guinea to Les Coteaux, Tobago, who had climbed the great Silk Cotton tree in Culloden, with intention to fly back to Africa, but who fell to stony death because she had eaten salt, she was on the ark. Then The Mighty Spoiler, The Mighty Terror, Mighty Broclax and Mighty Zandolie in proper soft pants, throwing vitamins down his throat. He have a woman to crack in Siparia, he have one to crack in La Romaine, another in D'Abadie; Zando alive but living among the dead, still cracking *bois* around stickman head. Then Pharoah Sanders reach with Yusef Lateef; Earl Lovelace laugh: he see Eric Roach reach on the ark, his book of poems still warm under his arm. Eric did not drown, at least not deeply, so he turned his back to the shore and dove in deeper. When the ark had two days to go before it reach Southampton, here come John La Rose and Charles Mingus, here come Lord Kitchener in 1957 on his way back from New York; here come Paul Robeson and Beryl McBurnie – even Olive Walke rode upon that boat. This was the year the Great Bandit graduate from bandit school and rob 40,000 men in San Fernando, when the river washed down from the Million Hills and cleansed the city, and who eh drown, badly waterlogged, and who eh dead, badly wounded. And the Great Bandit came down with his escort and chariot to survey the land, and found poor black folk had hidden in holes in the earth and in barrels sealed shut with laglee sap from the breadfruit tree, and some drowned, stupid-stupid. But the poets were wise and hid in trees and were never found. The Bandit rode on, and the houses of prime ministers were burnt to the ground, and all around the embassy route, those grand facades of colonial times were volcanically cast to ash and plundered. Then the Bandit moved west, searching for that gold-throated woman who, after making disco love to him one morning, ventured him up to the hills overlooking the city, behind the bridge and quarry and show him where his own navel string bury, and he wonder how he never imagine his own city as a map; its grids and lay lines, the white spume foaming at the lips of the coast. Years hence, the Bandit went knocking at discotheque doors, but the woman was gone; she was upon the ark, anointed with olive oil and sacred colours. Jack Blake was on the ark, and Dominique Gaumont, as was Milton Cardona and Rosetta Tharpe, Odetta, C.L.R. James, John Stubblefield and Yvette Cooper, Jimmy, Bain, but not Kamau Brathwaite, he was not on the ark, instead Baba, the great teacher, had long since evaporated into air, into language, into sound, into the very sex fruit of poetry. Oil does not dry upon his tongue, nor honey on the tips of his fingers. And the ark drove up to Bristol, Brixton, Birmingham, Leeds and Manchester too; it swooned into New York, Boston and Chicago; New Orleans see it too. Then it swing down to Haiti, Cuba, Jamaica, Suriname, Guyana. Remember, this ark respects no boundaries or Archimedes; it moves like a crown on a draughts board, any damn where it choose. Look, it pass through Aruba, Trinidad, Grenada; it move up the Orinoco River, and it never wear necktie yet. St Lucia get it, St Vincent see it too. It come up from the Southern Caribbean, all the way up to Pascagoula Bay, yes, yes, yes, Steven Samuel Gordon, Spaceape, was on the boat with the oar, and Brother Yussef Ahmed was on the bow blowing the big abeng!

84

Sixteen years after they had separated, Brenda arrives in Enterprise Village, west central of the island, on a Sunday afternoon, when men have been drinking Scotch and eating barbecued pig-tails under the shade of an avocado tree. She walks between them, interrupting their All Fours game to ask for Deacon Simmons's house. Her head is reared back and supercilious as she walks, like a woman who patrols the gardens of her estate, hand held in hand behind, inspecting the bull work that has been done. She will call the Deacon out of the shack he has been building with bachelor galvanise and crate wood, since Joan, the woman he was living with in Million Hills, get rid of him. Deacon yard overwhelm by grass that hard to kill; it growing under the floorboards; his outside toilet have a cesspit but no water pumping, so he have to use buckets of water to cash and carry shit down. He comes down into the yard, barebacked and grinning in the government sun, a middle-aged man catching his arse in Enterprise village, with nothing to show for his life, neither loot nor bounty, nor spoils of nothing besides the eight-track machine and the speaker-box cut from white plastic bucket – them same big bucket people does make souse in. Deacon icebox have orange butter growing mould, a jug of water and a slice of shark in a dish, marinating in onions and pimento. From just the sound of his slipper slapping, Brenda could tell that Deacon had nothing left but his name. Once he could charm his way through strife with grin and quiet guile, next thing you know he eating fish broth at your table, and posing for photographs in your father house, the same house Brenda father work so hard to build from tapia, grinding rockstone with his teeth. Daddy never build house for no bird-head boy to take for some open sepulchre, to walk about the yard like saga boy, with toothpick out the side of his mouth, to lick down people girl-child with he hairy cock. But the old man done talk. He watching the news.

When Deacon come in the yard, and the sun hit him in his chest, he put his hands on his hip and he ask, 'How you find me here, where you come from?' Same time the ravine dry. Blue flies buzzing around the swine pens in the neighbour's yard. A dog start to whine and bark at two white-headed Baptists on their way back from church. But after all these years, when he see Brenda, his first love, that wild and vibrant love, this woman who once tore his shirt from his back that red dusk when they were making love beside the sawmill on Jogie Road, he still feel something. So he assess her at arms' length first, he search her face for the limits of her smile, then he embrace her, her beating heart to his, and they are together again, like old fire-stick familiar, like a coil unravelling through time and finding its way back to the centre, like love that seeks again its own source, a love that never dies, but is transformed and reborn. He forgive her. She smells of sandal-wood and talcum powder.

But is divorce papers Brenda bring to serve the man him, and is just so, right there in Enterprise Village, on the gravel road, on that Sunday, in the new settlement, on land the government either forget, don't care about, or abandon to poor people children, that his whole dream turn upside down, and the black and white photographs begin to fade, the cut-glass vase fall and shatter, the iron bed break and reach the floor. So Deacon delaying, asking after their children, if she have man – anything to not take the damn envelope. He know what it is. Deacon Simmons not stupid. 'And your mother, how she knee? I hear she fall out of bed and break it in three places. The farm get road yet? Cars could come in now? The water truck still bringing water or water pipe-borne now? Hurricane pass, who roof get fling off? That road was so bad before, oh gooosh, tyre used to spin, and how Alice, and Ma Quinn? You ever go back Mount Garnett? And your father, he dead yet?' But the letter have to deliver and when she put it in his hand, he bound to take it. So finally he buck and give a bow to mercy – take it, yes – and turn it over, plain envelope, no name, but inside was serious paper to sign. Poor Deacon, his bargain bucket low like a snake's shadow; he have nothing to give but faith, and Brenda not asking for nothing, but if is marry she want marry a next man, and even if that never happen, then is so it go sometimes, like gun-mouth pants that measure but never make.

She agrees to coffee, black and sweet. They are there on his verandah when the night settles in, and the cane fields rustle gently in the distance, and the scent of burning sage and Indian indentureship, the resonance of plantation slavery, all that wrap up tight, warp and wrap up in the dirty light. He tells her how, just last week, a man drank weedicide to die, but didn't, so he ran a blade across his own neck to bone, and did, stretched out stiff in bed. One coffee becomes a reconstitution. They listen to the radio. In this village night, they will talk as old friends in the paraffin glow of his lamp, in the smoke of the mosquito coil, till it is late and he must walk her out the half mile to the main road for a taxi back south, and all the while laughing, remembering, when they were young. Two years later, when she dies from breast cancer, it is Deacon who reads her eulogy, before they put her in the ground.

85

Jimmy lay on the hot floor of his mother's high house in Kandahar Village. The house, which for years had threatened to fall, was now deserted and bent down near enough to touch the earth from the upstairs bedroom. Jim had a vision of paths he might have taken. He could have been a tailor and hung bespoke waistcoats from nails in wooden rafters. He would cut gun-mouth pants from strong cloth. He could have gone to Dorchester, Boston, Massachusetts and blaze crack cocaine and fling his hip at calypso parties. He would pull his wood under restaurant tables, and then touch-up the people cutlery. He would not stay here. He would not wait. He would rather be beaten to a print with a catfish in Benin. He would go. He would not be written out of history, like Joe Sam, Bo Nuggy or Manuel Gogo. He had seen how a cutlass might spark against stone and lose the veracity of its blade. He would steal away to London and shoplift books by Brathwaite and Breton. He would piss and wash one hand. He would stock up rum and salt biscuit tins and prepare for war. He would bully goons for illicit grass in fibreglass alleys. He would play blue devil mas. He would look for fight and throw his hand. He would play in All Fours tournaments, touring each Sunday through wild island countryside and slap harsh cards on the table and cuss like scorpion tail catch a fire, win or lose, same way.

Raphael write his gut to grow from dog rice and butterbean soup, but Jim would run, he would lose weight. The Mighty Conch could pour a cup of rum on his head and ordain him as a master calypsonian. His brother could steal his teeth. His first wife might join a cult. He would live in a basement bedsit in West Kensington and suffer through winter with a one-legged cat and a red-headed woman. Down was the drop but he didn't care; suffer in his stones but Jim tallawah; he could take the blows. He would ride on his knees if his feet grew sore. He would face death with teeth grit and battle, like his mother. His ambition was plotted like a poem composed in the head and never written down. And is not no two line or three, but forty-nine lines in sestets, iambic stanzas, unrhymed. But Jim would not abide. He would spin his way out of plot and causality and twist up the old man's hand. His wood could break in half, but he going back down in Chenet Tree Junction to encounter Prentice at the Black Silk Bar, and when they come upon each other, sudden on the floor, they start to grunt and carray like crab, until Prentice wife, Florence, come from the kitchen, steups and, wiping her hands on her apron, part them and say, 'But Jimmy, what you doing here, ent you ban from here?' Now is Prentice and Florence who running that establishment, and Prentice still have the waist and the wound to show where Jim jook him, and is hard for him to forgive, but he bend a knee and bring peas wine, bring Jim red guava gin, and cutters like tar ham and piccalilli. They sit down to reason, to build a bridge, like man. Since they both jump barbwire and escape from the big book, both men feel they could tackle tiger and win, but sun or rain, both of them wrap up still, like stick in pannist hand. Look, Black Jack Blake just pull up a chair. He now come from London with a brand new toupee on his head; he get this one from Duke Street, St James's, Piccadilly. But his malice dull. Jack Blake getting old, he want to done with villainy, but it not so easy, because the old man holding the deck and table on which their cards were dealt. As night get thick in the Black Silk, these three men, worn out with prison politeness, start back to guff up and cuss again; they so frustrate that every move they make, they have to hide in case is Raphael set them to despise and mutilate, and then they pull right back in.

Jim say, 'Distract him; he like to write sex scene, so give him leg, make him mount, and when he putting down iron, run out from here.' And indeed the nuance burst in Raphael's skull; he hear fuck talk now and he want to bull, so he write it in; then he want to separate the leg from the crotch, press up on wall and render the thigh thick, the meat, the hindquarters, the mouth, with a throat like a valley of gold. He want to know who have throat like goat. Raphael kneel between thighs and gone deaf by leg, and that is when Jack Blake, Prentice and Jimmy reel out the roll and gone again. They was sure they gone this time. By the red iron bridge and the green and white mosque, they pop wood gun to hijack a double-deck bus. Then, after ninety days, walking through a desert for as far as vision bleak, they arrived at the gates of their friend, the Great Bandit's hideaway. They rang the bell and waited, but no answer came, so they walked till their liver string strain, and then gone inside the big man's place.

The Great Bandit was not at home; he was fighting his own holy war somewhere on the left side of darkness, standing beside an uphill highway waiting for Luke to emerge, for the final reel to roll. That night Jim, Jack Blake and Prentice sat on the Bandit's verandah in dark suspense. Wind would swirl around in the brittle heat; it howl and rattle doors, and when these men were silent enough, they could hear music coming from some far distance, in the infinite darkness of the desert night.[20]

---

20. Although not confirmed in the original manuscript, the song they heard was almost certainly 'Fundamental Reggae' by Jimmy Cliff from *Unlimited,* EMI Records, EMA 757 UK, 1973, possibly blowing from Goose Lane, El Socorro, Trinidad, 1978.

86

She wore black tight to the parabolic curve of her thighs and went walking through the city. She walked until she came to the lane of haunted houses, rooms abandoned by ghosts, beside the train tracks, her memory of these places opening like a fan of spells. She smelled the sweet gravel, the gospel manure of country fields, the red stone street, the overgrown yard where her cousins lived. Dash away with them and death will cleanse the land with fire. She wonders how long one bloodline can possess that grievous space. How long before the waters of the storm-flood rise as high as the steeple? How much rain would it take to fill the valley? How much man head would have to burst and blood drain in that hole till it irrigate and pump energy? How soft was the shower of dirt thrown upon her mother's coffin? Would the graveyard be so overgrown that no one could find her mother's grave years later? Neither kin nor green-backed lizard nor faithful hound would know where they plant her headstone. And isn't it ironic that there was a coffin factory beside the graveyard?

When she was new to New York, she found work in a bookshop in Manhattan. There was the boy she met there who bought and shelved books for the history department. He was a poet, they both lived in Greenpoint, Brooklyn, and would walk to work each day together, along the Pulaski Bridge. One day, they were in the broom closet, though there were no brooms there. She was on her knees and he was standing, but then, they reversed polarities. The shop was closing down. Upstairs, the repossessors were pausing to drink tea. They had started dismantling the fittings, removing the unread books from the top shelf first, then the illuminated globes, the brass rivets off the balustrade, and the laminated shelves on which books by Joans and Henry Dumas once stood. These books, upright and devious, were now covered by dust falling from the ceiling, as the steel beams were revealed and the walls were torn out, and the wood-chip counters crushed. In the broom closet beneath, the lovers remained hidden until the final door was broken and the last reel was run.

The agony of her mind was now seeking new routes through language, through the gaps in the rhythms between beats, in beats between spaces, in spaces between teeth. She is strict and stricken, fingers twisting into knots, tight in breath and thought, crying out, 'Let me up, or get up off me.' The stones fall and keep falling.

She is on a train passing along the southern coast of France, from Perpignan to Sète. It is that August time when summer seems most endless, when the ocean flashes blinding white and the sky lid seems furthest away, and opens vast perspectives above cliff faces and bridges. She never became famous, not in this film, though she had starring roles in plays and wove her words like colours, welding them to her lines with precision. Raphael followed her until she disappeared into the glare, the train passing Port Fitou, the forlorn peninsula of Les Sidrieres – though it is possible that he turned away sideways to let her slip past him, intentionally, into another scene. He knew that she would return, and walk across the same idea, that she would be his muse, be sudden bone, be the crack in the carapace, be the socket of the axe, be the girl working in the fried chicken shop, be the mad woman dancing on the roof. But she had been to Marseille; she had walked along the Camibere; she had gone high into the favelas and shebeens; she had walked through the sawdust and paraffin alleys of North African enclaves and hidden markets; she had seen the slanted stalls and walls, the falling streets of Istanbul. She had pinned a jet-black broach against mildew. She had been to Boston, she had been to Rome. She had stood on the fortress hills of several metropolitan cities, but had always seen islands… islands… islands. Each day she would visit the hotel atrium, near the ocean in Sète, waiting as if for a sailor. She would sit in the dappled shade and throw her head back to swallow pills, blend into vine and knotted stems, rest gentle on the waxen leaves of the olive bush, tender like the lizard asleep in the elbows of the lime tree, nervous like birds which seek grain among the fragments of sunlight cast down at her feet. She would order mint tea, place her hands around the heat of the silver pot. There was a cool wind passing, a soft gust that had hidden behind the wall all morning and had now decided, with the atrium deserted, and the sun resting in the late afternoon, to slip past her as she uncrossed her ankles. The chill moved ghostlike upon her like the embrace of a bony child, like the brief panic of a sudden longing, like a photograph she once saw of the musician as a child, dancing, and his dance frozen by Polaroid in his old bedroom, with the eviscerated drawers overflowing with clothes. Those women had raised him. She knew how even in that moment, as they laughed and sealed him shut within the blackness of film, they knew that kidney failure and stroke was waiting for them, that their lives were tapering to a chisel point. Outside the frame of the photograph, the neighbour's pot hound could be heard growling on its chain, along with the symphony of crickets and frogs. In the distance, the rippling sound of a sitar, sarangi, the Indian dusk of the radio. *Geetanjali,* the swamplands and the rice plantations were there. Ella wondered what had become of the dancing child, of those women who had raised him up from stem. When the sun fades she goes to her room. There is no loneliness like hers.

87

Prentice finds a manuscript entitled *The Frequency of Magic* in the Great Bandit's study, and he holds it up to light, as he had once held a cum-crusted wash rag he'd found under his aunt's bed. As a boy he had stood on a gramophone, peeping through the breeze blocks near the roof to catch her undoing her bra, unhinging her girdle, stooping to bathe off over an enamel basin. And when she see him and bawl, 'Ai, boy!' Prentice jump and jump back down.

The manuscript was a thick, ring-bound folio with white stiff card covers on which the title was written in black. It was an annotated draft. It had surely been brought back from a dream, like bush meat to Kunu Supia, and its pages were dense with a relentless text in which the writer, seemingly escaping the critical superego by resisting the vice of concurrent editing or glancing back, had written in a brisk maelstrom of pure liquid textology. The author would not be recolonised by metropolitan publishing houses. But the text was now cold, and it would take a reader several weeks to reveal its craw. Prentice began to read. He found himself reading a scene at the Great Bandit's desert hideaway. The episode was set the morning after he, Jack Blake and Jimmy had encamped there. He read how his consciousness was then reflected in a perpetual mirror, how on finding himself in the book, he had torn open his own shirt and swooned from the feverish nausea of desert sickness. He had then been eviscerated by the angular blades of free jazz, and other examples of quantum harmolodic systems which were equally ferocious. In another scene, he read how he was found weeping in a medina in Rabat, looped into a quandary, in the red pulse of a dream where the heartbeat disappears into infinitely linear time. In another scene he saw God's face and died. He had roamed into a circular world without end, with a tank of rosewater upon his back, not secret, but black. Suddenly afraid, Prentice began to wonder if in reading the book he was becoming his own poltergeist and jumbie.

It was also written, that once in his grandmother's house, where he had stayed while his mother spent a week at the postcolonial hospital, burning inside from her attempted suicide, he had made another discovery. He had found in the old woman's gun drawer an instrument for breaking hymens. It was T-shaped and bakelite black, like a corkscrew. The smooth handle was the width of his palm, with contours for grip and a blunt nib for piercing, and he knew without asking what it was for. The object had ritual purpose and resonance as a fetish of sex. It exuded the power that some plants posses, like *Eleutherine Bulbosa*, with its pim-like stamen and antler. Finding the manuscript was like finding, in some forgotten cabinet or hiding place, fragments of his own autobiography, but written by another hand, and yet deliriously exact to the last pointillist moment and gesture. The sun was now beginning to blister and hiss. The desert had come to life, and the scorpions and wolf spiders, the grasshopper mice and the sandhorse, the four-eyed dirt fish and the kaka roller, the cactus bird, the hairy snake, the marañón cock and the maljo bee all awoke from their homes.

Jack and Jim were asleep on the hard pine floor of the Bandit's living room. They had drunk the big man's good single malt whiskey; they had boiled the dog rice they found in his pantry and eaten that with sardines and chocolate sauce. They had also eaten the stale sweetbread, the fat pork bean, and were now belching in restless sleep. But Prentice was disturbed. The big book jumbie him. He wondered if perhaps he had dreamed all he had known, all the memories of his years on the farm – memory ghost of leaning against the hog plum tree in wild open pasture, of climbing the turpentine mango tree beside the farm house, the salt-lick, the parakeets in the bamboo down by the riverside, poor folk's roads and the simple life of cattle leaving holes in the sodden earth; the orphanage he had run away from; the green river he had swum in; the drum clap of his chest being punched out of wind, suspended there on the corner of Cemetery Street in San Juan; or standing as a child to watch the Happy Riders cycling down Saddle Road, later to learn that some had died along this road, and the pan yard right there on top that hill, from where somebody flinging stones down to the river to bust people head.

He thought about his proclivity for danger and self-destruction, which rose up gradually from youth to manhood in that left-behind land, how he'd gravitated towards bad mind and bitterness, how he'd gone looking for ways to wound and nihilate – and is so he get in cahoots with scamps like Jack Blake and Jim, men whose meditation narrow, fellas who not afraid to throw fire when they catch rage. They were men who would act rather than be acted upon. They were brave, brazen, salt-spitting men, who could cuss hard in public spaces and speak their truth and mind without compunction or artifice. Prentice envied them. Now, as he sat upon the Great Bandit's verandah, the big book lay open across his knees. Poor Prentice read each word upon the next. He turned the page and is like the damn words following him like a ubiquitous gaze. Perhaps all he had known of life was within the book. In which case, was he now reading himself into existence, like the hand that writes the writing hand that writes the writing hand writing? He did not wish to read on; it was like listening to his own heart beating. He closed the book, put it down, and is so that chapter come to done.

88

I paint you, Devil, I paint you upon a mirror, at a festival dense with limit and obstreperous percussion. I paint one eye brown and one eye red. I had helped to build that church, but I would not worship there, not till, not till, not till... But I had laid the foundations and corners, I had cut the razor grass that grew behind the altar; I had swept the mourning room; I had mixed mortar and ground doctrine with my teeth; I had worked like an itinerant labourer who sleeps at night in the fields and hustles by day around suburban neighbourhoods, collecting bottles or do- ing bull work and scything grass with ancient rigour, with the sun cracking my skull, for coins and softly worn dollar bills. So ease me steady on the plough, ply me with rum. Not till the mother of the church passes on to higher numbers will I will play the spiritual game. Then I will fall over precipices and river falls.

I must have uttered some sound. I must have stood high in the cane, or sat tall, grinning in my canoe, because someone saw me and called me by my true name. I ran to the house, which was still a dream, as was the dream of grey metropolitan stone in Inde- pendence Square with its vacuous cathedral, with delphiniums and yellow allamanda growing in the pews, and Legion Hall, gleaming white as in some postcard image of 1971, when carnival was passing. In those days, the wharf was the edge of the world, and you could walk right up to the brim and see the sea below, rolling violently, like a lion pacing a cage. These images were all rendered in the muted reds and greens of costumes in old photographs of stockinged masqueraders in George Bailey's mas band: *Relics of Egypt* (1959), or in those first postcolonial junc- tions, where the developing nation was still policed by policemen in short pants, never mind the seam sharp. This way traffic go, this way that. It was an innocent time, in a dream of island nations. In those days I was young and irascible, harden, a scamp. Even as

I played sailor mas, and threw talcum powder, I schemed, and kicked up dust and was seen dancing in the savannah, while bush fires raged in the hills above and the sun whipped the galvanise, blinking high up in the hills that feed and nourish the city with vibration and zest. I brewed easy evil in straight-jacket mornings, staggered in muddy culverts drunk on joy-juice and red-beard collie herb after skanking all night in the community centre. I had made my Midnight Robber costume that year with silver lapels and crimson epaulets, the long cape emblazoned with vèvès, maps of stars, jumbie and skeleton. My trousers were hewn from hessian sacks, my boots from hirsute leather. I wore a four-foot sombrero. I wore my cilice and rolled my dice. I stood naked in my grandmother's house on Ash Wednesday afternoon and masturbated in the heat of my old bedroom. Then I went looking for the Christophene Boy, the sheriff with the toy gun, the tin badge, the boy I had last seen posing in the quiet colours of 110 film, in khaki pants with one leg out, dancing in his room. I had left him behind, so many years before, and each time I almost clutched his outer garments. He was now a bachelor who rented a narrow apartment on the Eastern Main Road, and still worked in insurance, straight up and down. He wore a striped shirt and tie, was as bony as a whip. He smoked hard weed out of his kitchen window at night and still dreamed of leaving the island. He had even polished his leatherette shoes. He would wear his camera around the neck, as a tourist camouflage, as he strolled into JFK to the theme of 'New Time Shuffle', but with no plans to return. All this came to dust when he was stopped and interrogated in an airport mystery room. He never got through. But he was not there in his apartment when I went looking; he was not there in the discotheque; that was not him in the morgue. That night I slipped through a fissure to pass my hand along the curves of illicit thighs, to glimpse the ankles twisted in supplication, to imagine the suffering unto death, the shinbone breaking into shards, the agonies which, even as a young man, I would seek out simply to know what suffering was awaiting down the numbers. Consumption, pulmonary complications, liver rot, cataract and blindness, cancer, diabetes, senile dementia and rigor mortis were all waiting like words to attach themselves to meaning. Once, my good-good compère, Mr Tom, the long-stones man, the tall playboy in the trilby and cigarette pants, bachelor, cocksman and rake, encountered a heart attack in a blockorama and was embarrassed to shake up and buck in front of people; he shame they see his suffering face. But when the pain take him so, Tom bawl like a cow and humble down in the dirt. That Christmas eve he died, and I shut myself up in a castle of grief, and waited for the sting to fade, the dirt to settle on his grave, knee-high among the tall orchids of St Augustine. They buried my friend standing up and planted rayo trees in the bones of his chest. In those years I would walk miles up the Saddle Road in the burning day, to buy ganja by a green river where children were playing. Blood run among the sandbox root and the bamboo, where I dipped my feet in the hardness of the world and peeped through bush at dreadlocked women bathing, to pull my cock and seed the earth, to fling stones from the hilltop down to crack some boy child's skull. By then I had counted each breath, and kept my mind in hell.

89

They have walked a long mile along the Vltava River to cross the
Charles Bridge, to stand before the statue of John of Nepomuk,
with its halo of five stars and silence upon its lips, leaning, as part
of a mystic spiral, at the arc of the river. John, who endured a
classical death by being flung into the river to drown, was
rendered in oil by Czechowicz, who painted both river and sky as
dark hinterlands, portals of limit and descent, with cherubim and
the white horse that bows its head, perhaps turning away, outside
of the frame, so as not to witness the vicar's death by drowning.
In falling, the vicar's gaze is fixed on the firmament, where light,
like an axe, has cracked the sky above him. *Yemanja Assessu*. The
water beneath the bridge is the same that has forever flowed
through the earth; here it flows away from grey stone and the
cryptic tombs of saints – bohemian sandstone.

She holds his arm as the bridge sways, and they sway together,
under the weight of a feeling that neither can now control, as in
Keats, the 'swoon to death', as in the descending first movement
of Bartok's third string quartet, or in Stephen Watts' 'Praha Poem'
with its cry in the throat. It is autumn in Prague and the tourists
are arriving. It is Saturday afternoon and the bells are ringing from
the stone bell tower in the cobbled Old Town Square. Bells rung
for a wedding and then the bride in her gown and the blue-suited
groom pose for photographs against the bell tower's high bannis-
ter. Their black limousine waits below, and the random eyes of
strangers gaze up at the trellis-patterned train of the bridal gown.

That afternoon, Ella and the musician ride the train from Háje
to Lazarská, and sit like poets contemplating love and death. Later,
they drink in the old town and walk along the crowded streets of
Prague where everyone whispers. The previous night, as he took
the horn from his mouth, laying out to let the bass reverberate its
parabola in their bruised rendition of Rahsaan's 'Sweet Fire', he

had looked around the room and seen she was not there, and had realised then that he had begun to cling to her with the feverish grip of a child.

He had once abandoned her in Geneva; he had left her waiting in the dank shadows of a club in Dassier, and had gone skittering out into the night with the band. The space they inhabited that night in Geneva seemed improvised and permissive, set apart from ethics or expectation. They existed outside of any fabric of anguish or rigorous motion. He had fluctuated that night, between women who knelt between his thighs, and those whose bony shoulders he was moved to trace with his fingers. When he returned to Ella in the morning, he found her in bed, awake.

In Prague, she blends into his embrace, and his arms encircle her, as if they are shipwrecked together and at night are drawn close by fear, as if they are in an airplane that plunges to vertiginous death. Now it is Sunday morning in Prague, and they stand, on the balcony of the Grand Hotel Bohemia, watching the city below. Along Kralodvorska, souvenir store shutters are flung up, a restaurant receives boxes of bearded molluscs and oysters; a young woman calls to a dog. Love in the morning. Ella longs for a home that never was, until the corners of her mind have atrophied into despair and he cannot reach her. She cries, she wrings her hands. Meanwhile, the musician has visions: he is five and having a piano lesson in a room filled with wooden machines. The teacher stands to his right and a window lets in the fading day and everything is dull and dying. He is trying to hold on, to cling to the hem of his grandmother's dress, but the old woman is nearing death, without fear, malice or sorrow, and the dying light is refracted in her eyes. She will not stare too long now, into the sun. The teacher has other students at those machines and they play filigrees of notes, in unison, but the musician cannot punch one sound into his fever, his fingers will not pierce the etheric, until the teacher tells him to play without thought or motive to deceive. He plays a fractured pattern of notes. Then he is standing beneath the sun dial on the promenade of Tarifa beach, looking out to Africa, but still many miles from home.

They leave Prague that night. It is raining; the statues on the Charles Bridge have done all the weeping they will do. What is death? With which chant can it be killed? Such sweetness, powerfully dense and infinite, the layers of your dress, the hummingbird that hovers at the corner of your mouth, the geckos and bugs that dodge the spiral rain, the engines within the brown wooden machines in the piano teacher's room, the antique violins hung up for repair in a shop near Central Park West.

She is not there in the steam laundry by the bridge; she is not there anymore outside the Tati shop in Barbès, Paris. She is not there in the redbrick rooming house. She is not there in the fish house, with a grouper's wing in her trembling hand. She is not there in the abattoir, or the market's covered region. She is not there in her hospital bed. Mammy cancer like it gone. She has gone out into the night, she has evaporated into silence, slipping between the sound of the hi-hat's pulse, out from his enfolding arms, beyond the limits of his aim, into her own particular way above the path of human kindness. But if she is drowning like John of Nepomuk, soon she will eventually float. The musician is already on an airplane, high above the avenue of martyrs.

90

She hears love but he hears music. She is searching but reluctant to find the page she is written on. She avoids eyes, speech, salt. In the early evening, she wanders through the park, sees the trellis in the awnings of the Chinese restaurant, the mural on the pharmacy wall. She is an actor. She mixes perfumes. She is either black or amorphous or disappearing. She heard love but he heard music. Behind the chrome factory she finds a path. Then she is running, as if a spigot burst and harmolodic orchestras were clapping after her heels. When she stops for breath on the wooden bridge, the sky lid seems nearer than where she started. Who has followed into her secrets, behind the mask of her face? Who has held her from falling off the edge of this bridge, onto the rocks below?

Once, her mother loved a fisherman, but his mouth was full of brackish water, and his shoulders were ships. She loved him until one Friday afternoon a propeller punctured his liver and lights. He pedalled himself into town and then lay dying in the poor part of a hospital, waiting for her to reach him from the east so he could close his eyes. But it was Friday afternoon; there was heavy traffic on the Eastern Main Road, delays at junctions, and an accident in St. Augustine. He waited. But when she arrived he had already left. It was then she was sure she knew true loss. Death is to be observed, not to be known. Even the beasts of the air will peer down from heaven to witness. It was not easy, the death of this fisherman. Nine nights the crapaud stayed weeping on the Governor plum tree in the yard. Misshapen fruit ruined to rot. Neighbours gathered in the bright-lit living room, while Ella's mother sat on the floor, etching the fisherman's face out from each photograph with a ballpoint pen.

Ella also knows such sorrow. She wept in a chapel in Vienna, she wept in Perpignan; in Vancouver she sat on Main Street and hooded her head with a woollen poncho; in Paris she remembered him in Barbès; she remembered him in Rome; her heart fell out in Brussels; she wept in Marseille. She used all her water for tears, and it would be months before she could come again. On that night when she first saw the quartet in New York, she had been moved beyond the rim of consciousness, entered other rooms, and discovered that the saxophonist was raised in the same landscape that she was born to. Tonight, there is a new band blowing in the room where she first saw the quartet. They swing in that gap between hard bop and splinters in the rim shot. Each of the quintet wears a black suit and they play hard, but the room is half-empty. The volute scroll of the wood bass is dry like jackass bone that has been buried in the sand of a desert for fourteen days to develop quijada sound. The drummer wears dark sunglasses, keeps his grin of gin beside his stool. Listen. If sound is energy, then energy is motion, then the river of this joyous sound is sculpture for the ear. In the Spanish tinge, oh didn't he ramble, Mamanita, didn't Jelly Roll?

The musicians are oblivious; they still send up tremendous music to the dreaming – long, looping lines, modal blues armed with ball-peen hammers and nails, knocking on the curving rim of spacetime. They navigate through dense forests and return. They seek systems of tradition in primordial waters. Let them call up their gods, let them collapse upon the wheel, let them bear down on the mama drum. Come, sit mama drum, sit down. A drum is a heel. Ella is shaken like a reed in the wilderness of the mouth. Let her tongue be the reed that shapes the sound she hears and the silence between it. Black bees have filled her mouth. She hears love and she hears music, healing vibrations. She will surely recuperate and swim far away from here.

May 4 1981. She arrives at nine am that Monday with her mother at the redbrick estate office where the local people pay taxes and water rates, bills of ownership, probates of inheritance, notices of births, deaths, transfigurations, rates of prostitution determined by weight, notes on Obeah, instructions on which sweet witch to poison with salt. They are waiting in line, the hot inside, the soul of black folk. This red-bricked building still stands solid on the earth, a small fortress of colonialism beside a green river, a remnant of landed mansions and dogs snarling at gates with barbed-wire teeth.

This is the air she hears: the wind through the sandbox tree, the silver fishes gasping upstream, the bovine and bucolic scent of Indian farmland, the faded arc of her own diasporic flight, drifting outwards from the island as islands in archipelagos must, like a kite set free from its line to sail past the sun. On this night she moves beyond her body, to witness the new quintet. Their steam halo is Elvin Jones. Hard bop swinging back to New Orleans, spasm band calypso, so deep in the blues it becomes free jazz, clandestine, like porno between detective movie at Ritz cinema.

Let Ella stand in the empty room while the band plays. She is attracted to its contusion of sound, to the true and precious energy which is both impecunious and ruinous, yet which heals. There is no music like this, no history, no slaver's yard, no barrack room, no sickness, no red step to crack the shin bone on, no prehensile antennae which can pierce the skull like this. What she hears is the impact of her own arc and arrow, the etheric vibration of her tongue in her mouth, her own body vibrating in a field, at the foot of the mountain that she must now climb.

91

If they want to fight, let them fight, mano-a-mano, time to dead; neither man fraid that. Luke want to grapple the Bandit neck, but folds of moss growing there, from bathing in rancid water, from living in the desert where dust blow and stick to sweat; then fester and turn green from bad-mind, from wickedness, and things start growing there, like termite and silverfish. He lock the Bandit neck, but it striated like strata in rockstone; jumbie making nest inside of there, like stinging bees in mud. It tender, it infected, this neck. Luke don't know if to fluff it with talcum, or spray it with mentholated spirit. But when he really start to ply pressure and squeeze, the Great Bandit humble and puff, his neck start pulp and his heart start swell like it gwine burst. He drop to his knee to contemplate his agony, and he bawl: 'If ah dead ah dead, if ah dead ah dead in meh own country!'

It is early morning, dew is still wet on the ground, and all around is jungle, jungle, jungle. The tapir's proboscis twitches, tying the manioc root with its tongue; the manicou and the owl in the picka tree seeing everything. The mountain chicken squat down, waiting to be caught. The parakeet in the guava tree blink one eye to peep, and Mr Iguana, who know death when he see it, decide to stay on the vine; he will not come down until these men finish fight. The Bandit old, but he very deadly. He lift up Luke like a child and dash him to the ground, and the youth man coccyx bend. The body start to beat-up-beat-up-beat-up. The Bandit had planned to reason and debate, but his neck was hurting him, and now he want to know everything Luke know. He know Raphael uses to butcher hog on that hill, throw fire, drink whisky, and write till morning. He feel Luke know what the old man write, even before he write it, so bring the messenger. Luke must know what Raphael intend to happen to them both, out here in this tribal wilderness. He write them to dead or he write them to live? Who else slip out the plot as enemy, and is now perhaps roaming in some mystery, high up in some upstairs and down-stairs house, waiting for the sea to wash the world away, or the crocodile to eat its own head? Like the Bandit forget he was once a youth, just like Luke, among these scenes and episodes; that on Friday nights he drove his Cortina through the city wearing rastaman perfume, and pausing for prostitutes on Sweet Briar Road; that he used to bull like a goat an' agouti-look-back. He even took photos. Then one day he stole his freedom, just like Luke, from under Raphael's writing hand, from a text that meander relentlessly, as if it cut up and often out of sync with anything that had gone before. It was the old man's masterpiece, but he could not expect to hold these people to wait and endure the tapering swerves of his mind without them desiring their freedom.

When Raphael did finally read back and found them gone, he panicked and searched for them, like one might search for a scorpion that has escaped into the corners of a house. Let them go to deserts and jungles, let them stand on the cliffs of Gibraltar, or walk the streets of Prague. He would have to be standing on that street, at the time and precise place when the beautiful black woman was pointing to a dress in a shop window, so he could lean back and peep her flanks, her erotic halo, the pump of her thighs, the firm flesh of her calves.

The text was a living thing, with its own nomenclature of codes and systems. Once, as a boy, he had seen brown sugar slide when scooped into a pile; seen it, too, was alive, with sentience. There seemed to be a power working there in the sugar, like the cane spirit of muscle and back, and the cutting leaves of the cane that had scarred runaway slaves across their faces. Sugar was real, a living thing. Outside of the book there was the desert, the subconscious jungle and its caravanserai, the death to dust, the grape must, and there was no place to hide there, oh carrion crow, oh raptor, out there in the distance. But poor Luke could not know such things. He could not know the true arc of Raphael's design; how the Great Bandit might die in quicksand or water, by poison, or mangled in a mincer in some bakery or meat factory, where the body mangle, but the blade still running, until the lacerated man is cognisant enough to walk to the other side of the refrigerated room to switch off the machine, but by then the thorned worms in the chamber still grinding to a spiral strop strong enough to bead frozen beef, or rip a man's arm off, or to blade him biblically in battle in some jungle clearing, beneath the poets' hotel, the stone tower.

There were many paths Raphael could have chosen. But perhaps it unfolded as he planned. The Great Bandit panicked. What to do now with this Luke; he feel he hot like the knot of a navel string, like he come to terrorise my head, me one alone on the ocean, no brother, no father, no sister, no mother, me one alone? Best to get some bogus calypsonian with a quatro and a shac-shac to come an' measure his grave. So the Bandit throw fire, mano-a-mano. If they want to fight, let them fight. He roar and leggo a lion in Luke tail.

Years later, if the old man vomit and dead, these two men may be still wrestling like grasshopper in the jungle, seeing who will dead first – well, is so these men was fighting.

He had been to Barbès; the streets there were wild with a riot of noise and colour: the pink and blue of the sprawling shop fronts were as gaudy as the cosquelle and ostentatious costumes of the Dame Lorraine in Port of Spain carnivals of the 1930s; the Dame, lifting her dress above the mossy culverts of Tamarind Square while an iron band led the procession from hill to town. He had seen the North African cowboys in the fabrics of the African French. Once they had worked the land or studied economics; now they sow and harvest cheap clothes, bogus brand sunglasses and bootleg cigarettes, they lay their junk immaculately on the sidewalk in the shadow areas beneath the metro, in that dank recess where the trembling heart of Paris beats – Barbès-Rochechouart – like a ravine fish in a schoolboy's palm.

Flung far from the soil of his own homeland, the musician stands in a doorway along the Rue Boissieu, his body twisted in supplication by the uncertainty of each new day. He is waiting for time to pass, for the machine to break; his eyes are closed, his heart swings fast in his chest. It is autumn, a Saturday; bright and meaningless, each breath seems laboured, each glimpse of the passing stream of bodies fills him with sadness. The long roads and early mornings unravel him. Night is his comfort, his bivouac, his harem.

The doors of an unmarked van are suddenly flung open for the gendarmerie to emerge. They are swift and swear they saw him palm something from a hustler; they urge him into an overcast courtyard to search and interrogate him with burning eyes and guns. They search and inspect his saxophone, they lift the padding of its case, they unravel the accoutrements of the saxophonist's art: his cork wax, the neck strap, the spit hole, the container for spare reeds. The tenants of high-ceilinged apartments peer down into the courtyard. This too, the malice and the speed of the city, is an impetus to his sound. As is his memory of Million Hills, as is the book his grandmother read by paraffin light – *The Desire of Ages* – and, later, the bible which lay at the bottom of his grandfather's gun drawer, beneath the long black rifle used for hunting or as a spell against insubordination. There were bullets there too, boxed and some unboxed, blue and golden-topped cartridges as thick as a man's thumb. There were open envelopes with letters left inside them. The plumes of the scarlet ibis on stamps enter into the billowing swirl of sound from his horn. Colonial colour. The falling sounds, the urgent ocean swells which are always metaphors for death and resuscitation; photos of the deceased are turned around. The rocking chair is empty, the bed unmade; the old woman's clothes are packed in a barrel; the blackbirds are weeping on the fence beneath the orange tree. The road is long and leads uphill deeper into bush. The gendarmes find nothing. They leave him there. There is nothing along these boulevards and alleys to soothe his pain, no kiss or fair gesture, no light, only the thigh flesh of a dancer sweeping over him on a rainswept night, in a cold-water hotel near Pigalle. Only the soft mouth and coppery breath of women who arrive at his door in the early hours of morning. He has been to the Southern Carolinas, to Athens, he has been to Oslo. He has ridden on a bus out of Berlin while snow fell on every side. The white storm blew, the airport and stations were shut, and the band was disillusioned and ready to burst into silence. They had suffered hours waiting under the hard light on the cold station floor, while the radio in the cafe played Christmas carols.

Each letter he sent has been returned. She had left Paris. She had gone to Naples. She had ridden rivers and found love of her own. She was now in love with a poet, a demon from The House of Smoke. Maybe she had forgotten him. He had wished upon the fading dream of her kiss, he had waited in doorways, he had hidden in the snow, he had become invisible in stillness. He recalled lying into the hip of her, on a single bed, where she lay upturned and open like a mouth receiving communion. But he had been tarnished by excess and vice, and though he could not lose the buzzing growl of his reed, he had, as Sparrow had sung, run around and lost his zeal. When the quartet played, it opened weeping sores in sweeps and swooning, to dive down into the thrust of blackness. But it was not enough to be kissed on the neck by Europe. It was not enough to be feted in Prague; it was not enough to walk along the coast of Brittany, along the dunescapes there, the cold water clear, the krill, the shells and mollusc husks crunching beneath the feet. He blew gage and was ferocious on stage, but he was not himself in these places. He was consumed by the flutter and wow of fleeing birds, by barren land, by heavy air. He desired the succouring balm of love. Love that renewed itself, love that energised, deceived and destroyed itself. He sought this in every new space, under every sheet, with every lubricious glance, in alcoves and gutters, in the fingers of flautists, along the slender backs of dancers, in the mouths of women from Madrid, in the muscles of their orgasms, in their tears and eyes of universal sorrow, they came weeping unto death, with sudden gasps; the water below, the water above them. He is walking the long white corridor of a hotel, his jaw is locked rigid. He wanders, knocking on each door, but no one answers. Distorted in this mirror between truth and fiction, he contemplates death by fire, death by loss of the self itself.

93

The Great Bandit weary. His heart start to burn like Moruga pepper in his chest. He tired fire shot. Luke belly deep, he resilient. But people want to know. They want to see which man knee will bend first; they want blood. They not satisfy with Raphael's experimental trickery, they already get tie-up in the world of tidalectic narrative, in protagony and antagony, the hero to win, or to dead in tragedy; the villain to froth from the ear and fail; the mentor to sit in a cave with a pipe of sinsemilla and an Edwardian police gun. When people come up the hill to buy the gun, he will lift a banyan leaf gentle to show them, and the riff of the spliff that hangs from his mouth will bob when he drawls, 'Yesmaneetgoodman; is Cuba this come from.' It good. But don't try that, people not stupid, they don't want diversion, they want action, they want trouble to happen. They want to put Raphael in the corner of some rich woman's house, in some broom cupboard, to write till he cough up blood like Jelly Roll Morton, to script out these men's destiny clearly: Luke and the Great Bandit, both men grappling handfuls of each other, by neck and lapel, to jack and collar up, to squeeze into manners and submit, but neither will give over. They roll and tumble in the jungle, they wrangle in the barrack yard, they wrestle, they cat-scratch and bitch, they make commotion, until a woman upstairs opens her window and throws a bucket a black disinfectant between them and say, 'Allyuh move from there. Haul allyuh arse from here with that foolishness.' And they scatter like dog, and carry on fighting in the ravine, right down from where the steelband was practising, beating pan with pencil in secret. But *somebody* have to dead. Who will cough up smoke and dead in their boots, whose back will give way, and break down to shadow and exudate ooze? The truth is that poor Raphael don't know.

Is Melchior who had to wash fish stink off his hands and sit down to tell us what really happen.[21]

'The jungle dense, both man riding antimatic congo pump, steering their cannibalised machines from high above the scene, riding upon the pressure. Is gear stick they pushing to propel through the high bush. Each man trying to run the next man down to the ground. Is thick foliage below, man crab and tiger cat, and both man teeth grit like pilot when engine failing, falling, jaw stiff, the presser foot pumping in panic, but the brakes not working, propeller fail. They land hard on rugged ground, uncanny, lush; they have to pass through deadly spinescent terrain to get to camp; then they have to build a cesspit and a wooden toilet down in the camp, because up on the ridge, in the old camp house and in the gayelle higher up where they have to fight, liana vine tangle and overcome the ruins and it have nowhere up there to shit. So they watching each other cut-eye now, and wondering which one will go down first under the canopy of bush – the incline steep – to dig a cesspit, and get stab in his back with something sharp when he going down. So no man want to move. Darkness meet them there, still upon the ridge, looking down into the camp. They build a fire and crouch down there; it too dark and dangerous now to fight, and to help the night pass faster – since no man will take the chance to sleep, lest he get his trachea punctured – the Great Bandit decides to tell Luke the story of his great love and marriage.

He had graduated with distinction from bandit school, and was on tour – an assassin as apprentice to Bo Nuggy, hired in country regions to cramp and paralyse debtors and scamps – to collect protection money from Turks and Caicos to Martinique; to burn down any hotel that still celebrating slavers' glory – with plantation murals of overseers, the black man in the loin cloth with his treble clef pipe, crouched upon a rock to the side, while the real work of the yard is going on and sugar is loaded upon galleons bound for Marseille.

---

21. Raphael had been arrested and detained at five o'clock that morning by two female constables. They came upon him unexpectedly as he wrote, and all his iron was exposed. For more on this trope see The Mighty Zandolie, 'Iron Man', National Records, Trinidad, 1965.

He had invited his mistress to stay in the same hotel he and his wife were staying in. The woman come down to breakfast; she arrived like a ground dove to the conservatory on the ground floor, bright morning upon her tongue. Dahlias, oleander and orchids lined the sunlit side of the room; Chippendale tables, gold, cut glass, chairs with wooden legs scroll out, elegantly. But upstairs the rooms were decrepit. Was hard carpet that fraying, and doors that creaked; rooms that were airless, beds that were broken. The Bandit had book two rooms; one for he and his wife, and one, which came with a parrot in a cage, for his mistress and him. What happen? The outside woman sit down in a corner in the breakfast area and cry long tears, while the bandit and his wife eating scrambled eggs and roast saltfish. The mistress waiting for her share and watching the man and his wife with a disconcerting smile. When the three of them go upstairs, say-say the Great Bandit split his sex in two; he crack one in the creak bed, crack the other where the parrot peep and jocking his prick, watching. In Raphael's book there were many chapters. He fell in love too easily. It had come to this: the Bandit drift, he start to fall asleep. Luke engage a long blade – was to cut the big man throat – but that can't happen so. The Bandit grab hold of the star boy wrist, he say, "Doh try that." The big man strong; is cow-foot and butterbean he eating raw. Luke feel the power; he twist and resist, but the deeper he twist, the weaker his wrist.'

94

Ella encounters her own face in the pharmacy's glass window; her own dark eyes. Then she remembers the sea almond coast she roamed as a child, her friends who went to work in factories and offices. Sheltering from rain in the doorway of the Ethiopian restaurant on Adam Clayton Boulevard, she stands beside Hilaire, taciturn, with dark skin and hooked nose, one arm grasping the other at the elbow behind him. He wears a glossy black shirt with a Nehru collar, black trousers. They continue to shelter under the awning from showers that seem to increase. This was Hilaire, a Jamaican who would press himself against women in unshifting crowds, pretending to be drunk at the market, or the Saturday dances at the Ebony Inn, but then was seen stalking between the pews of the catholic church for the blessed sacrament on Sunday morning. Hilaire had his strategies, he was a merchant of desire who dialled a line and entangled the unwary within. He would dress in fine fabrics – strict silk, triple wool, robust cotton. He was a man who appeared obsequious, but who listened without looking, who stared concentratedly to the ground as you spoke, nodding his head. But this, too, was fiction. Hilaire was long dead and deep in the ground. He was not there under the awning, not there buying a brisket of beef at the butcher's, he was not there reading big books – Delaney's *Atlantis* – at the Crown Heights Public Library.

In the unforgiving storm the city was washed away; its services were shut down, its midway trains broken on their lines; the rain was washing away businesses, barristers' offices, brick fortifications. Both pyramid schemes and sou-sous were shut. The city seemed to yield to the actor's gaze – changing its shape and architecture as she reimagined it. For her: the sweet earth and all the corn birds in the avocado trees; her father's green garden; the fields of cane burning; shoes with broken heels; the barber cutting the labourer's hair with scissors; sirocco heat and silver-fish; trousers rolled up above the ankles. She is moving along the wet roads after a hurricane, water in her taciturn boots, through worn-down soles. She moves beyond Frederick Douglass Boulevard. Geographies converge: the dirty market, the tennis courts, the postal sorting office. Wandering through the Botanical Gardens, stepping over the roots of huge trees, reminds her of her mother in her yard with a cigarette and a spade, stooping at the crown of a thorn bush, grimacing in the sun. There are orchids here in greenhouses, dahlias and species of ornamental onions with copulating stamens and buds. Her mother sits in the quiet place beside the greenhouse door, lets the water run down. What Ella wishes to find here is the very thing she wishes to hide from – the incredible vision, and the eyes to see it. But blink and the scene will change once more. The sky emerging above the glass roof of the greenhouse is suddenly grey; the kisses of raindrops on her lips are the warm kisses of her lover, the musician's seductive tongue, which probes her mouth for a promise she is unwilling to commit to – and which she suspects he does not truly desire. So she waits, refuses his calls, wraps herself safe, abstracted in the passing of time, in the secrets of her room.

In an exercise during their residency in Paris that summer, the director suggested a game of masks, masks of identical appearance. Each member of the troupe wore the same expressionless and dead face of the mask, the eyes slits with only glimpses through them. No words could be spoken and yet they had to act out each given scene, rich with innuendo and pathos. When her turn came, the director faced Ella at the table, the line of fantasy was drawn, and to mimic the true vine, he kissed her mouth, forcing his tongue through the mask, and then enacted a hurtful parting in which she was left sitting in a darkened room, far away from any place she had wanted to be.

That evening, the troupe drank the house red at a brasserie on Rue des Petites Écuries, where a trio from Burkino Faso were playing, and in the pace of the snare, the hi-hat hissing, she thought again of the musician's wet kisses, of his mouth upon her breast, the hardness of his cock, how he held her thighs like trees in a ferocious wind and devoured her each time, and then the push of his breath blowing against her ear, as he moved away. She forgot the impecunious ruin of him, his reputation as the wandering wind, as a wound in wood. She thought again of how he drowned in her, and how she gave herself to him. Each death was trembling, frail and tender in the softness of morning. They had drowned together, they had both been searching for themselves within what was being written.

She had driven through New England, from Boston to Montreal. He watched from the hotel balcony as she arrived. The streets were white with snow. All was still except the customers entering and leaving the pancake shop on the corner, and the men on the sidewalk blowing heat into their cupped hands. She arrived like a dream from the elevator, leaning so tender against him that he swooned in invisible sleep. Kissing her on her forehead, he held her heat, the essence of her neck, the sacred air sprung between them. Love, deep and mountainous, treacherous with promise, of the atman and mind, of tears and the body's supplication.

She could not sleep; she was walking in a field alone, taking a last glimpse back at the disappearing road. She was sure he did not love her, that she reminded him of what he sought freedom from. But she was a melody he had carved from wind and glue, one that he often returned to at the end of a solo.

95

These men have to dead. So the big book say. These men have to roam out in the stinging bitch of the sun and suffer their merciless fates. They bound to suffer. They must walk out into the desert in search of some denouement in which the hero is vanquished and the villain transcends. Their deaths must be observed. They bad-mind and brusque, like mangrove hound, dada-head hard with knots and terrapin turtle prick-soup. Who build combustion in their ears and tell them they could leave the pages of the great text and undermine Raphael's authority?

It is mid-morning. Prentice, Jack Blake and Jim have now left the Great Bandit's lair. They have decided to walk back to the village where their navel string bury, to the far farm five hundred miles beside the river, where the salt lick is still spinning, and the hog plum tree stay bearing fruit. To lean against this tree on the sloping pasture is to be a child again, is to be nostalgic for the rum shop in Macoya, with the fluorescent zodiac posters on the wall above the pool table, where fellas maudlin with money fantasy; is to be nostalgic for the oyster man at the junction, with a flambeau flame on his table and bottles of hot sauce, coarse salt and limes. The man flung far from India, but he shuck and thriving same time.

Yes, but these men have slipped out of the arc and driven gait of the narrative, and if they escape the rhythm and please, they do themselves a disservice. They will catch their aunt, uncle and nennen to stagger back to the table, like liver which has been cut and fallen to the abattoir floor. They may wait no longer in the house of the Bandit, for he will not come. They may be loyal to the band, but each man carries his own shadow; each sees forms and visions in the sand. They spiral out of sync and things get simultaneous. Look: the old woman belly getting big; the mange dog have pups; the coconut rancid in the sugarcake; the pembwa have worm; Christo waiting in the orange field for the Baptist church bell to ring, to hear the sermon, tremble and be overcome, to spill and overflow into pulp and awesome postulation; for Clary and Sister Syl to hurry up and get blessed; for the match factory to burn down; for the woodslave to grow wings. It does not matter if it is this man or that life; each must plot his own route and suffer the anguish unto death. And so, torn out and threshing, these three men find themselves in the desert, in the fine glass of sand blown to bruise the face and slit the eye. The sky-lid loses its hinge, heaven becomes the same colour as the ground, and the ground unfolds like the ocean, and the only metaphor for limit is the myth of a horizon that promises distance and death. They get licks from blistering heat till their skulls expand, until they can walk no more. They have sung all the belairs and lavways, all the kalindas and drum songs they know. Mix no matters. They have to dead.

Jimmy knee bend first, and he tumble down quite in Japan. His cry hang upon the branches of a pommecythere tree, like a whip and whooping cough, stretched and torn from ligaments of guilt and regret. His knee bend and break; his axe swing his hip and swing him in. He cough up blood, his head turned sideways in the sand. Poor Jimmy dead. Foam bubble out his mouth. They leave him simple so, beat up and bite up by carrion crow.

Jack Blake suffer in the realm of spirits. The garden is barbed with bardos of hell, until he lingers too long upon the vision and his ear drums burst. Old Jack was rode upon by a flock of bees, ravaging his arms, armpit sockets and eyes, whereupon he falters. He sees himself bending wire for wild Indian tiaras on Friday before carnival, hill town track lines and the sea far away. Jack was once a dreadlocks man, the hero on the cusp of some great adventure. Here he loses his hair, then his toupee goes brittle in Ibadan heat, and his false teeth fall out in Port-au-Prince. Until then he had held his age as secret, but now his tonsure was exposed for people to see. Concentration upon the solar capital will not levitate him now. He falls to one knee and sighs, then just so the man start to ululate like a lamb. His gorgon pulses, then like a hanged man he shoots a strenuous arc of funk – ugh – like mandrake root twisted into human form. He moans, not to die yet, but to press up from the knee and to stagger across the page, like the last dragonfly of summer maintaining a crooked path east. Jack Blake and Prentice do not speak. Each is racing for his own shore, against the sea of panic, gross pathology, emphysemic in the struggle. Imagine: the terror of the deep; palpitations of the heart. But grin or laugh till yuh belly bust, these men still have to dead! It was written, dollar in the teeth. These men must perish; blossom of a wound, divide up the meat.

Prentice bends to one knee, he cannot swallow air. He rips at his tunic to tear a gulp for air, but he wheeze and he wheeze and he cannot breathe. He stagger to rise – was to run far from this suffer – but same old running can't run, so he try running sideways fastest.

Jack shout, 'Prento, if you no can do jumping, don't jump.' But Prentice stutter and snarl teeth, he fall down quite in Martinique. He look back in time to hear himself moan, and see himself fall and keep falling, to dust and dust and dust and dust and dust

.Combust

96

His atelier that year was the gushing blur of fields and farms seen from TGV trains through Southern France, trains on tracks upon the high bridges of Aubenas and Montpellier, at Avignon and Marseille. Below, the waters of rivers rolled through the burning light; there were glimpses of the sea on far journeys to stations hidden in the country, passing along the red clay roofs of the Mediterranean, arriving in the afternoon in Toulon, or posing for photographs outside the station at Perpignan.

His eye on her was love, he was sure of it, and he surrendered and confessed it drunk in his room in a creaking hotel one night, up spiral stairways with burnished balustrades. She had followed the band from Lisbon, she had sought him out among nations of inadequate men. But he had become an affliction to her. And as she watched him sharpen his reed and twist the mouthpiece, as he patted the pads and raised the horn to the light to check its alignment, even as the band began and he walked onto the stage, she knew he was incapable of the love he had promised, that his love was only an idea, a panacea against abandonment. An island was all they shared. She grew reticent, distant, distrustful. The band saw him leaning closely towards her when they sat on trains or at station concourses. They vowed to turn away before her body fell. But he was sincere. His aim within him was true, and had she believed him, she would have seen that within the ferocious bliss with which he kissed the insides of her thighs, how hopeless and powerfully disconsolate he was at the thought that he might lose her. But his ambition, built up as a chapel on high ground, was swollen and intransigent.

He was certain, as he kissed her neck, as she leant out the train window with her cigarette, that he could love her, that they could abandon collective faith and escape together to a small apartment in Brittany or Rome. But this, too, was fantasy, as was the dream of a return to the island, to the cool springs up Five Rivers jungle, to the rugged timber of squatters' shacks hidden high up in the Million Hills. They both knew that the dream of return to the coruscating light, to the cumin scent and the water truck, was a lie. There was no gap to enter a place where everything happened at once.

They are in Toulon, at the hotel on the Rue Victor Hugo. He has said too much. He has been too persistent; so deep was his unreachable wound that only her pleading reassurance could soothe him, and that was not forthcoming. He fell and kept falling. She remained on the bridge. He pursued her, as she had once pursued him, until she broke to water in that spinning room and fled with her suitcase along the streets of the festival village.

He saw her two years later, near the Quai des Belges in Marseille. She had grown gaunt and beautiful; her eyes remained deep rivers to drown in. He observed the raised pulse of her lips, her straight and elegant neck, her slender thighs crossed on a stool in a cafe, her long fingers entwined around her knee. She stepped down from the stool to embrace him; it was two in the afternoon, Saturday, in August. There were white yachts in the harbour, street musicians on the boulevards, and the seafood restaurants along the port were restless with tourists. He held the brown warmth of her body once more, inhaled her neck, felt the firmness of her back, the honeyed nicotine of her breath. He felt the soft brush of her cheek against his, and everything they once were was returned to him, intact.

Her companion returned with coffee and water, with the firm handshake of a civilian. They edit the film of their lives.

The musician is in the antique market, walking towards the sunlight glinting on the pier. He knows now that his horn was just a machine. He saw, finally, that, alone, it held no wind, no sound. That he was the instrument the horn was played through, that he was written upon and into motive and complicit suffering by the arc and river of their convergence. But even in that cafe the musician was unable to resist the fleeting glimpse of a possibility. It was possible to perceive her smile as a gap he could bridge, as he had many times before. But in her face there had been a new, polite resilience. He saw in its motion of light and distance, a woman's purposeful detachment, the ability she has to turn away. He knew then that he would always love her, that at moments he would be taken back to their dawn-lit sexual temples, and too, that he could never imagine her with someone else. In his agonising search for her weakness and vulnerability to him, for the veracity and blushing truth of her love, he had found her stronger than he had imagined, and for a moment he grew resentful of her. She had torn down his wood shack on the hill. She had broken the locks to his mansion. She had entered the house of the demon and broken every door. She had ransacked his grandmother's altar and now goblets of croton were strewn upon the bedroom floor. Her words had become blades which cut him diagonally, like fever grass falling in the howling wind, or sugarcane leaning in the new plantation as the possessed woman writhed on the table to be exorcised, to open her thighs, to speak in tongues.

When he returns to his hotel it is late afternoon. Dirty light. He is leaning like a trope from the window, overlooking a street where children are playing. He revisits each corner of their exchange, waiting for her in a place he still hopes she will pass.

97

In Lisbon, the quartet leaves the stage at one fifteen a.m., when all the oil let out from the bell. The band is now a latched valise of mystery and suspense, taut along a tensive field. But on this night, that anxiety, which has always been in the shadow of their sound, will itself lead to the quartet's demystification and demise. The bassist, his broad back and shoulders hung heavy from the effort to bring forth the wood-tone of the earth from the volute scroll and soul of the bass, leans his elbow upon the bar with a wine glass of whisky and surveys the room. Predatory, he knows by the flickering pulse of a woman's glance, the softness of the V where the sternum meets the neck and the throb that trembles there, when he can throw his roll. He works alone in these high-pitched moments after the show, before the club shuts. The pianist retires and walks alone across the street to the hotel. The drummer is on the bar's high verandah, smoking and overlooking the Praça De Alegria and further out, the Rio Tejo. He still feels the sticks in his hand, the kick pedal beneath the ball of his foot, like waves in the body after a day swimming in the wild abyss of the sea. Two women join him, and he entertains them with his travellers' tales, grinning easy, soft and coy to catch them like crocodile. But tonight he packs his cymbals and leaves alone.

The bassist invites a Lisbon woman back to his room for a drink, and the saxophonist, a few steps behind them at the hotel lobby, pulls the bassist's coat before he enters the lift to heaven. He asks him to leave the hotel door slightly ajar, so he can come to listen, please, even to peep the action from the crease. Both men laugh. But the bassist does not imagine the true shape of the other man's hurt. The woman he is with has her own bitch to bear and feels transparent in the bright negative space of the hotel. The bassist shuts his door firmly, hurries to disrobe and then he starts to make one set of love to the woman – a full woman, a woman with a husband and son at home. The saxophonist comes along half an hour later, and puts his ear to the door. He is left to pull his wood in the dim hallway, listening to the sighs, the swooning moans, the animal gasps. He stiffens and bursts, explodes against the door and on the floor. The woman is gone by the light of morning. But after this, everything changes.

The bassist is late down to breakfast and can only sip half a cup of coffee before the van arrives to take them to the airport. He prefers not to speak his secrets. The saxophonist seems disturbed. His grin is insincere, and his eyes shift and hesitate. He sits in silence at the back of the aircraft, staring into cloud mass and sky. The bassist is asleep, his head rolled to one side, his mouth half open. He wears dark sunglasses.

They play in Katowice that night, in the chamber room of the new symphony hall. They release ferocious changes, the drummer crashes militant cracks of the snare in 'Coursil's Stomp'; they play Maestro's 'Savage' as Afro-bop, but their interplay is irregular and there are knots in the rhythm of the thing. But when the bassist takes his solo, it is, however, masterful. The groove bursts and reconstitutes the suggestion of the melody. He plucks deep to the lower frequencies, then grunts with eyes closed, his hands sliding down the neck to pinch and trouble the higher notes which ring like small bells. The audience applauds and stands. But all along the bassist, sheepish and meek, must watch the leader from under his brow. He knows something is wrong, he knows what will happen. He goes to give his leader a hug after the show, and the big man turns and gives him one arm to embrace. The next morning the bassist is fired from the quartet. And is so the whole sound burn down.

He hires a dep for the summer's remaining shows, and then the saxophonist seals himself in a shut-up house in east London, with suffering silence and dried fish and rice, until he can truckle no further. And so, with no sound to become, or kind pasture to rest in, he enters the jungle and climbs one of the two high steeples that Raphael had built to survey his land, fifty-foot high with electric eye. The old man put camera up there, he put up barbwire fence, put rooms there for poets to die in. He would make the mongoose shave off his beard before he come in there, if he could. He build fowl coop, duck pond and hotel for crapaud, but fellas too harden; they wouldn't go there when he send them, wouldn't follow the arc. But time is paper and paper running out, so Raphael put his faith in music. The humble musician was all he had left.

In the next scene, the musician was to tie his heart tight with barrel strap, put away the doubt through which his vision was straining to penetrate to the other side, and then to sadden himself and jump, to die. When the musician look up in the chestnut tree, light shine in his eye like diamond, and he lose faith. But muscle want to twist the air above that spot with causality, so he shut his eyes and leap. He land backstage in Lisbon, waiting to enter the arena, and the pianist pressing his fingers together to stretch them, the drummer tying a bandana around his right wrist, then posing for a photograph. The bassist, laughing to pass around a large conical spliff, and then everything converges | sling your hook up the sky lid | Those were soulful days.

98

But Jack Blake hard to dead. That man manage to cross a desert, the barren delta, plenty river, the burnt sea coast, an upwards bridge, the Devil's boatyard, a small volcano, a guava farm, mangrove swampland, a rainforest and even the ruins of a Taino settlement to reach Sam Boucaud Junction. When he reach there it late. He hungry to kill. He had was to bust open Ignacio Gas Station with a skeleton key for corn curls, cashew nuts and ice cream, anything to put down his craw, because he belly moaning, he mooma dead, and he poopa have big stones, and he so far from home – and he mark to dead – and the big book have pages that turning. He walk out past the village jail, and the church they build on top of that hill where Mammy bury, where they plant rayo on top of her grave. Is only recent, after years, somebody get a tin tombstone and pin that on the white concrete cross that guarding her bones.

Jack was lucky, he catch the last incense taxi that heading into town. He was driven down, past where Cipriani plane crash in El Chiquero in 1934, past Bingham Drive where soon some mad man would fling a shoelace around this same driver's neck, and pull him out of life through the windpipe, until he reach the bone. The driver, Pie Man Mikey, have wife and a baby daughter, and outside children who he bringing butter bread and corned beef, who when he wasn't pulling bull for taxi, selling potato pie and currant roll outside Real Street Steam Laundry. Is so the big book say.

The taxi drive past the blind school, the bamboo amphitheatre where the ground stay moist from the river turning, past that bridge where Jack remember he used to leggo wood on a buck-teeth girl name Selma. She was a lil' coarse but he like to hear she moan, to watch to see she leg tremble, to pump out and gush. She used to cry in a particular way. Scamp, he never work a day in his life, only sit down on street side waiting for hustle to pass or pussy to pimp. Jack Blake have no money, not one black cent, but look, he smoking Broadway cigarette and riding backseat in people motorcar. He lean back and looking out the window as if he is a star boy in some Hollywood movie. The valley breeze cool and the drive through the cocoa bush dark. Crapaud bleating and cicada losing their voice. Jack Blake tender, he reflective. He cogitating how he one survive, how he watch Jim and Prentice suffer and fall down in the desert. The big book must be mark with that, must be so it stay, is so it must be run down like voodoo in the cane. Jack Blake rock back and laugh. Because is not one trouble he face to reach safe, is plenty. Imagine, he walking around a mountain and seeing headlight turning in some distant darkness, and he know that is another mountain he have to climb. Imagine, people with pick-up truck, have space to lend, see a man in tear-up gym boots walking on the black pitch road, but wouldn't stop. Jack Blake feel he walk for about a year. He kiss his own ring.

When the taxi reach Chenet Tree Junction was midnight. Lights still on in the rasta man bakery, but no one there to serve. The hops bread cold, the counter clean, but put in your hand and the rasta man will jump out from behind the oven and bite you. Night life running like nothing happen. Even the Black Silk Bar have excitement: a jazz band playing, the sax man hot, and the market selling crab two for five, but barely alive, and the barber cutting hair and the library still open. The driver parks outside the tyre shop; he expects his fare. He will not work anymore for a box of fried chicken, nor for a bag of Florida oranges, two frizzle-neck hens or first harvest corn. He put up his palm, he must have his coins. But instead is a Creole series of psychedelic prayers that Jack Blake giving the man: 'Oh gorm, the desert pepper hot, bring mercy, Mammy dead, and the arthritis, oh wow, pressure boy, the doctor give me six months to live – and the suffering! I see my two best-best compere, Prentice and Jim, dead like dog in the desert. Lord, they froth from mouth and dead. We was waiting for the Great Bandit, but that mothercunt never tack back. What to do? What it write? I can't read. Is Prentice who read it. If you come see me next Friday, I promise I go give you everything I have, everything! Ah doh lie.'

When the driver sigh and puff out, Jack run out the taxi. The driver run behind his arse and fire two shots with a pellet gun he kept under his seat for this sole purpose – to puncture some runner skull. The first pellet hit Jack Blake in his elbow and crack it. The second one miss. Two more fire, but the darkness dense, and the driver eyesight bad. Jack cut through the bush at the side of the road, through the old cocoa plantation where the driver wouldn't venture – is a brace of leggo beasts living there, men with bone flute and dagger waiting for trouble to find them. The driver watch Jack flee like he slalom-skiing through the bush. The run Jack run to get away without paying was like he kill white woman or priest. Mikey suck his teeth and spit. He stand up on the grinning edge of the abandoned land until Jack Blake fade to black. He done work for the night. He prefer go lie down in a bed and let his woman undress him, heft his wood and gargle his seeds, than to run behind Jack Blake.

99

In the forty-one years he has been writing *The Frequency of Magic*, Raphael has produced seven reams of text typed on unlined paper. Most of these are kept bound with string in a series of lizard-skinned folios he keeps beneath his bed. Several hundred unedited and handwritten copybook pages are collected in a plywood cabinet beside his desk. These are the texts in which Raphael has been perfecting his idiosyncratic interpretation of plot as simultaneous narrative and liminal textology. Raphael does not build this fortress of words to hide in, but to be read, to make what is read real. The man write till his liver strain, he put his belly and stones in it.

He has reached far back in these texts, as far as those faded sepia photos taken in the old Mount Garnett yard, when his grand-mother, Albertina Lezama, was still alive and bending to tend to her hibiscus and her aloe plant, when she kept parakeets and fed blackbirds rice over the wire fence that separated her garden from the green ocean of the savannah. To think of Ma Albertina was to be taken to a place of pure heart and innocent posture, before he knew himself by name, before he took his place in the ditch of knives which was the world of hard men, and the profane ways of deceitful love and flesh.

For this movement, remember that the old man was once a child. Consider that he rode upon the trees in the yard, that Mr Guava tree was his best friend, that Brother Soursop, Sister Avocado, and Cousin Mango tree were humble, benevolent folk, and that he spoke to those trees as comrades and confidants, expressing his anguish upon their leaves. Remember, too, that Raphael was an introverted child. That he stuttered. That he roamed alone through the Indian people farm land. That he often spent Saturdays at the San Juan Public Library reading Walcott and Michael Anthony. That, later, he wrote to cleanse his own dark heart. That even in those early sun-lit days he knew that only poetry approached the realm of truth, that it alone could be tuned to the frequency of magic, that there were things that needed to be stated clearly, but with subterfuge and music. So he poured out his silver. He wrote himself into existence, asserting that he was alive upon that hillside; that whilst he seemed broken as a bull cow in a rainy pasture, he had adventured up the archipelago of islands and across continents, as fisherman, butcher, driver or thief.

Sitting again on this verandah overlooking the Million Hills and, further out, the sea, with the manuscript across his lap, his mind runs again on Ma Albertina, who had raised him up from stem. He remembers how, coming home from a day among the engines of the city, he was told that she had died, how Mammy foot swell, and how goat bone stick in her throat but she never tell nobody, how she became a hummingbird and left the island. They put him to sit with a candle burning in his vision, to marinate in trance upon pain and longing and loss, and then later that night his own mother arrived from the country, busy dying in her own lingering, cancerous hell, but with love enough to light a candle with him for the old lady.

Raphael left and went far away from Million Hills, far from the beginning of the world, and it was years before he returned. But in this rounds, remember that everything that happen busy becoming story, since story is memory, which once written down becomes real. Where the syntax cracks, may the verbiage be dense and lyrical, may it speak its stories and turn tables over. In Raphael's vision of these hills, Nora might be at her wire fence giving her neighbour Janet a handful of freshly picked peppers. These peppers might be hot and bright red. These women might be talking of a wedding or funeral and, at the same time, Tanty Virgin might be walking on the ridge below, on her way back from drawing her pension in the post office, or paying her light bill. Imagine: Virgin walking past her mother's house – Mama Olive Too Tight in her black and white dress – and Virgin might first call out and wave to Nora and Janet. Ma Olive might be sitting on her balcony sucking a soursop or shooing blue flies from her face, as she begins to tell Virgin how that morning Alvin catch two 'guana in a hole and bring them back alive from the bush with their feet tied with twine behind them, before he kill, skin and season them, with intention to curry them down later that night. And as Olive saying it, Virgin standing akimbo in the sloping yard, seeing and hearing everything, even when Janet and Nora talking her bad, because here they measure time by distance.

When Virgin walking home along the mountain, she stop to greet the women at the fence, and they are once again included in the narrative field. Please understand that Virgin want to be a star, too. Virgin want a starring role. And nothing can happen without Tanty Virgin; she is part of the *mise en scene,* so you bound to see her when she pass in the frame, because Virgin have a story to tell. And when Ma Olive drink and slam the ace, she want to be star-girl too. While all these things happening, the wind still troubling the trees, shit snake still eating shit, dung beetle rolling shit too, and a radio blowing soul through the valley. This is a place where everything is happening simultaneously, and everything that happen must be included in any vision captured by flight or landscape data, since, at any point, the details of any process can become unstitched from the larger narrative and take their own routes to reveal their rightful arc and river.

100

Memory ghost of Sister Syl, who rowed the ark to heaven and returned to us as a hummingbird; may spirits build nests in her beard. Memory ghost of black-tongued Yvette Cooper, whose impure heart burst in spiritual war along the second avenue of dreams. Memory ghost of a black woman, with knowledge of shaddock root and obi seed, with sky in the roof of her mouth. Memory ghost of a serpent that ate black lice in the bosom of the governor plum tree. Memory ghost of Felicia, first love at five, with the promise of rain, bone heavy in the sky behind her. That single glimpse of her, then never to be seen again, and yet this image, set back from darkness, defined the moment of rain and mud in the ravine, and of zangee eel twisting in the torrent.

Is plenty thing happen that never get tell. Tongue never speak its own secret. Battymamzelle never show you where it buy it wings. Miss Janet cancer like it come back. Memory ghost of an aunt who caught a stroke and still can't raise her hand, whose phone keeps ringing in her falling-down house. Her wooden bench is cold, and the paraffin lamp, cicadas and the moon, her grip on youth, on life, all that gone – look, even the latrine overflowing. But isn't it an honour – the benediction of life – to witness her fall and fade, to see how life passes, as it must, unravelling from route to root, from bamboo to galvanize, to run amok among poor people children? Has Raphael heard that Deacon Simmons fell in far Harlem? That Prentice swallowed his tongue as he fell to silence in Martinique? That Sister Syl fell at the back of a black taxi and turned into a bag of mussels; that when Alvin fell, heading uphill to hunt, two rolls of film fell out his mouth? That his own brother Bain fell while working security in the gas station? That when they turn him around they find one fat puckering hole in his thigh, hip high, with manjak bitumen inside? And who were soldiers, and who were thieves, false priests and farmers, and who drove the bus, and who baked amazing cakes those Sundays in Wallerfield, and who were carpenters and killers of beasts? One night we pull in the seine and find a fisherman's foot in the net.

The Great Bandit, contrite and all in black, outside of filmic or scenic time, outside of language, in a wordless map, sat at the Black Silk since midnight waiting for Luke. And all this occurs away from Raphael's eye, as he turns to break a piece of bread, to sip a glass of wine. And when Luke appears, the two men embrace; they shed hot tears, their knees bend. The Bandit beg Miss Florence to take leave from her mourning, and she bring them cutters – some slice ham, cashew nuts, some fry channa and a bottle mark 'Corbeau Teeth Rum' with a living green whip snake curl up inside, biting its own tail. They drink, but neither man want to speak, before bamboo stick up in their teeth, and let the other man pull truth from his throat with a skeleton key.

When the Bandit head start to get sweet and sentimental, steam start to seep out his mouth, and the bench creak as he lean forward to Luke: 'I hear you have the seppy, and if you have it, let me know, and let me know if I could capsize the pot… the plot I mean, or if I have to burn the whole plantation down.' Luke take a sip, the grog rough in his gullet, but he playing tough so he don't scowl. Before he could answer, the Bandit continue, 'You have me running behind you like a fool. And now look, both of us get we liver dig out, both of us get fuck. So if you know how the big book conclude, brother, you better tell me the truth.' By now, though, the Bandit get to feel like everything that going to happen happen a'ready, like if the words he speaking coming out his mouth before he have time to think them, and he realise that he, too, is upon this wheel, operating at the frequency of magic. Luke smile, then he lean back and fold his arms. 'Listen,' he say, 'If you want, you could fling up on the sky-hook and re-enter the great book from the side. You could look, but you might not like what you find.'

The Bandit slam his glass on the table, 'The big man have us to kill, Luke! You eh frighten?'

Luke laugh, 'Everybody have to dead, papa.' Then he watch the Bandit, fix in his face, to see what he will do. He know the Bandit

303

is a man who will capsize table, or throw urine in people face. But the Bandit moan and start to bite his bottom lip, he push back his hat and leggo water from his eye. Luke laugh to see the Bandit put his elbows on the table and hold his head to cry.

Sudden so the Bandit raise his head and say, 'Dead you say? Dead what? Dead who? Well, brother, tell them that when fish clap, I swim, but no axe of narrative make by man or woman can bind me in no textology. Ah going in he mother cunt!'

By the time they reach up the hill where the sky-lid swing from, it was late one September night, and pilgrims in white was coming back down the hill, coloured bands still around their heads. From the cliff edge it look like you could reach out and touch it, but that was the ruse. Luke say, 'Take a stick and punch out a hole.'

Inside there was a vision, flying over the island, the house on the hill, the butcher inside, turning away from the page, to break a piece of bread.

for Martina Joseph
August 5 1970 to June 1 2019

Anthony Joseph was born in Trinidad. He holds a PhD in Creative and Life writing from Goldsmiths College, for which he completed a fictional biography of the Calypsonian Lord Kitchener. He lectures in creative writing at De Montford University, Leicester. In 2015 he presented *Kitch*, a documentary for BBC Radio 4, and in 2018 his *Kitch: A Fictional Biography of a Calypso Icon* was published by Peepal Tree Press. *Kitch* was shortlisted for the Republic of Consciousness Prize, the the RSL Encore award and the Bocas prize for Caribbean writing.

He is the author of four previous poetry collections: *Desafinado*, *Teragaton*, *Bird Head Son* and *Rubber Orchestras*, and a novel, *The African Origins of UFOs*. In 2012 he represented Trinidad and Tobago at the Poetry Parnassus Festival on London's South Bank. In 2019 he was awarded a Jerwood Compton Poetry fellowship.

As a musician and bandleader he has released seven critically acclaimed albums.

As a poet, novelist, musician his written work and performance occupies a space between surrealism, jazz and the rhythms of Caribbean speech and music. He is described as "the leader of the black avant-garde in Britain" and his work as "afro-blue to astro-black and what glimmers in between" – *The Times*

Kitch: A Fictional Biography of a Calypso Icon
ISBN: 9781845234195; pp. 272; pub. June 2018, price £10.99

Combining an inventive fictional structure and the novel's investment in language with factual biography, Anthony Joseph engages imaginatively in the recreation of Kitch's world. By presenting a multifaceted view from Kitch's friends, colleagues and rivals, Joseph gets to the heart of the man behind the music and the myth, reaching behind the sobriquet to present a holistic portrait of the calypso icon Lord Kitchener.

Born into colonial Trinidad in 1922 as Aldwyn Roberts, 'Kitch' arrived in England on HMT Empire Windrush in 1948. He emerged in the 1950s at the forefront of multicultural Britain, acting as an intermediary between the growing Caribbean community, the islands they had left behind, and the often hostile conditions they encountered in post-war Britain. In the process, Kitch, as he was affectionately called, almost single-handedly popularised the calypso in Britain, with recordings such as 'London is the Place for Me', 'The Underground Train' and 'Ghana'.

Poet and musician Anthony Joseph met and spoke to Lord Kitchener just once, in 1984, when he found the man standing alone for a moment in the heat of Queen's Park Savannah, one Carnival Monday afternoon. It was a pivotal meeting in which the great calypsonian outlined his musical vision, an event which forms a moving epilogue to *Kitch*, Joseph's unique biography of the Grandmaster.